SUCH KINDNESS

Also by Andre Dubus III

SUCH KINDNESS

A Novel

Andre Dubus III

W. W. NORTON & COMPANY

Celebrating a Century of Independent Publishing

For information about permission to reproduce selections from this book, write to Permissions, W. W. Norton & Company, Inc., 500 Fifth Avenue, New York, NY 10110

For information about special discounts for bulk purchases, please contact W. W. Norton Special Sales at specialsales@wwnorton.com or 800-233-4830

Manufacturing by Lakeside Book Company
Design by Lovedog Studio
Production manager: Julia Druskin

ISBN 978-1-324-00046-4

W. W. Norton & Company, Inc.
500 Fifth Avenue, New York, N.Y. 10110
www.wwnorton.com

W. W. Norton & Company Ltd.
15 Carlisle Street, London W1D 3BS

1 2 3 4 5 6 7 8 9 0

For Philip

Are those the faces of love, those pale irretrievables?

—Sylvia Plath

Some stars went out on me for good; part for me, O sky.

—Wisława Szymborska

PART I

1

OUR GOOD SAMARITAN DRIVES US THROUGH SOFTLY FALLING snow under streetlamps that have come on early. The boy's car is filled with cigarette and pot smoke, and over the rap Jamey plays he's just asked Trina a question. He looks over at her on the passenger side, his wispy beard dark in the dim smokiness of his rusted sedan. Trina shrugs and cracks the window and exhales smoke. Twice their age, I sit in the backseat. It's late in the afternoon but already the lights are on inside the shops and restaurants we drive slowly past, both rear windows streaked with melted snow. Trina takes a deep drag off her cigarette, and she's laughing at something Jamey has just said.

Behind the rapper's plaintive voice is a low percussion beat that sounds to me like bare hands on a joint compound bucket. It's almost three weeks from Thanksgiving but hanging in the window of the bookstore is a Christmas wreath decorated with dozens of tiny paperbacks, and soon we're through the town center and into a neighborhood of big homes going back two hundred years. Many are Greek Revival with gabled pediments and fluted columns painted white to look like marble. Years ago, as I became more committed to the building trade I somehow mastered, I started to read more about architecture and learned that back in the 1800s banks were the first to adopt this look, choosing low gables supported by heavy cornices and wide trim to more closely resemble the temples of ancient Greece.

Banks as *temples*.

And now, like a ripped photo from a trip I never should have gone on, I can still see the glossy raised panel of Mike Andrews' office. It was walnut, Andrews' desk cherry, his tie a full Windsor, his cologne too strong, and he was probably just about my age at the time. Propped on the desk was a framed color photograph of him with his wife, both of them smiling into the sunshine with their ski goggles strapped to their flushed upper foreheads. I'd never gone skiing in my life. It was a sport for rich kids, kids I never knew, and in another time I might have felt put off by that image and this young banker's office. But that warm afternoon in late spring, seven thousand hard-earned dollars in my account, all of my taxes paid and up to date, I felt strangely one with him sitting across from me, just two guys climbing that ladder we're all called to climb, Mike Andrews just steadying its base for me with a generous loan.

But ladders can get kicked over, especially when you're on one. And I had trusted him. That's the funniest part. I had trusted a bank.

Jamey passes the joint back to me, but I shake my head no. I want to tell him to put it out and to be more careful, that nice towns like this are full of cops with nothing to do but look for beat-up cars like his that don't belong, but I don't say anything.

Afternoon has turned to night and we're passing the grounds of Phillips Academy. Under the falling snow the windows of its old brick buildings are warm with lamplight and I think of my son having gone to a school like that, a place dedicated to opening door after door for its students, most of whom come from families for whom doors are rarely closed anyway.

"Look at these fucking houses, you guys." Trina's voice sounds childlike, though she's twenty-seven and has three kids. She's leaning forward in her seat, both hands on Jamey's dash, her cigarette glowing between two fingers. Jamey takes the turn and accelerates down a two-way that is already plowed, salted, and sanded, and the female voice on his phone comes in over the music and tells him to continue on to Jefferson Lane. The young rapper is still slapping the joint compound bucket in time, but now there's the low cry of a synthesizer, the boy singing in a falsetto about his girlfriend or his mother or both. Jamey says something about private property being theft.

I ask him where he heard that Marxist bullshit.

"It's not bullshit. And it wasn't Karl Marx, it's some French anarchist dude. I just took a class."

The female voice says to turn left onto Federal Drive, Mike and Kerry Andrews' street. It's a winding road through a stand of hardwoods that opens into a narrow lane lit every forty to sixty feet by streetlamps, snow falling past their LED bulbs, the sidewalk under them looking as bright and cold as the surface of the moon. But on this moon stately houses are set way back from the street and hundreds of yards from each other. Most have floodlights embedded in the ground, lighting them up from below, and I can see right off that they're of the Federalist period, many of them brick with arched windows and heavy dentil work under their copper gutters. Some even have round living rooms. Jamey's still talking about capitalism and social justice and the redistribution of wealth. I say, "I used to own a nice home too, you know. And I worked hard as hell for it. There's nothing wrong with private property you work hard for."

"But we stole it from the Native Americans."

"Yeah, no shit."

The female voice speaks through the rapper's falsetto, telling us that we have arrived. Jamey's saying something about "boomers" and he pulls over to the curb and shuts off his lights. I'm looking across a snowy lawn at a Federalist painted white, the windows of the first floor lighted, and I'm about to tell the kid that his GPS has it wrong when Jamey says, "Is that it across the street?"

"That's the biggest one, Tommy."

And it is. The entire structure is canted to the east so that I'm seeing it through my water-streaked rear window at a three-quarter angle, but even its side is lit up from the ground by floodlights, and not for security. No, they're the floodlights of a stage, this house the star, and now I recognize from Mike Andrews' Facebook photos the mortared fieldstone that makes up the exterior walls of the first floor, I recognize the bleached cedar shingles above that, their courses tight and narrow all the way up to the fascia and its Grecian key I hadn't noticed on my laptop before. But there are the tall fluted columns on either side of the front door with its round port window matching the round three-season porch that most likely opens to the pool and cabana out back. Under this porch is a three-car garage, each of its doors a raised-panel oak like the front door. I'm shaking my head, have been shaking my head for a while now, my hands squeezing the back of Jamey's seat. "That's it, that's them."

Trina's door opens and the cold rushes in. She's running across the street in her hoodie and pajama bottoms and new white sneakers. I don't feel good seeing her do this. I feel the way I did so many times when I sent my young son Drew out into the cold to buy me a baggie of Os.

Trina runs back to our car, slides in, and slams the door shut behind her. "It has a lock on it. Who locks fucking mailboxes?"

"Bankers, hon," I say. "But we just need to check their trash. I'll do it." It feels so strange to be hurrying across Mike Andrews' street under a lightly falling snow. A car's headlights sweep through the thin stand of hardwoods behind me, and I walk quickly onto Mike's white lawn and into the shadow of a cypress tree. The car slows as it passes Jamey's rusted sedan. It's an SUV, and as it passes the Andrews house I can see through the back window of the car a movie screen hanging from its ceiling playing a cartoon for the kid or kids sitting in the backseat.

Then I'm rushing behind Mike and Kerry Andrews' house. Wet flakes brush my face and it's a relief to see no vanity floodlights back here, but then motion-detecting security lamps come on and shine right on me.

Set into the fieldstone of the first floor is a Palladian window twelve feet wide, and it's hard for me not to think of my own wall of windows overlooking the marsh. It's hard for me not to think of my one lovely acre of land and my homemade home, both taken from me.

From here, standing exposed under bright lights, I can see Mike's daughter sitting at what looks like the kitchen's island. In her ear is a cordless bud and she's eating something while staring at her laptop and then her phone. Soon she'll lift her head and see a man her father's age out in the backyard, his hands in the pockets of his Carhartt jacket, watching her.

So I'm moving again, but now the fires rage along the pins of my broken hips and pelvis and I ignore them and reach over the gate and unlatch the latch.

I'm wheezing and already sweating under my clothes. The bolt sticks to my bare fingers and I have to yank it free, and now the gate is open behind me and I'm standing at the edge of Mike and Kerry Andrews' covered swimming pool. It's dark here. A car passes by out on Federal Drive, and then another. It has to be close to five o'clock, mothers and fathers coming home from work and school. Not the wisest time to be doing what I and my young friends are doing, but it's too late to stop now.

On the south side of the covered pool is the cabana in that Facebook photo where Kerry Andrews sat with a glass of wine in her hand. Next to it is what looks like a pool house and maybe a tool-shed, and I'm about to head in that direction when there comes the muffled groan of a garage door opening. And now light pours from a transom window high up in the wall supporting the round rec room, a light that falls on me and the covered pool, but also on four large trash barrels up against the garage's outside wall.

The squeak of damp brake pads, an engine shutting off, then two voices, both of them male. I hurry out of the light and into the enclosure that holds the barrels. A car door slams, then another, and now the garage door is sliding back down its track.

One of the voices rises in the notes of a question and the other answers. Mike and his son Tyler. And of course Mike would pick him up first, probably from Phillips Academy a half mile away. His wife commutes to the city and back and so has the longer day, coming home each night spent from peddling other people's mortgages. Does that mean that Mike is the cook? Or is he one of those guys who order takeout—they can afford it—or makes everybody pancakes for dinner? Or does he ask his eleven-year-old daughter to cook? Or does he, like Drew and I used to do, prepare a meal with his son, one of them chopping the vegetables while the other pours olive oil in the pan?

Once my wife Ronnie started graduate school, that's what I did. I was never much of a cook, but I looked up recipes online, simple ones made with pasta, and Drew and I learned together. Our favorite was a fast dish made with fettuccine, pistachios, and blue cheese, and my son's favorite part was crumbling up the cheese with his fingers.

On the other side of the garage's wall a door pulls shut and the transom light switches off, and I just stand there a second in the darker darkness. Why's it so much darker here than a few minutes ago? The motion-sensing lights. They've gone off.

Hip flames lick down my legs. I need to lie down soon, but why does *Mike* get to come home and be with his kids?

My hands are cold. I rub them together, blow on them, then feel for the garbage can lids. I unlatch each barrel, then slide their tops down to the ground. I reach inside the first, but it's empty. Inside the second seem to be only plastic milk bottles and empty wine bottles, a lot of them. I picture Kerry coming home in an hour or two and pouring herself a glass, the way Ronnie used to, though Ronnie would stop after one and maybe Kerry just keeps going.

In the third barrel are tied-off plastic bags and I pull out two of them. One feels heavy with decomposing food, but another feels lighter, drier, and I run my fingers along the outside of it and feel envelopes and papers. I'm tempted to check the fourth barrel, but it seems like I've been gone a long time from Jamey's rusted sedan. Mike might even be watching it right now from behind one of his mullioned windows.

I reach for each plastic lid and latch them back into place. I grab the full trash bag and start for the open gate, but no, Mike could be in the kitchen and those lights will go off and then Mike will look out his grand Palladian to see what's what.

The trash bag weighs no more than a gallon of milk, but still my right leg is on fire. Another car passes out front, and it's only a matter of time before someone on Federal Drive calls the cops on the stoner kids parked in this neighborhood they will never be invited to.

Between the sunken garage and the pool house is an eight-foot fence with no opening anywhere. There's the faint sound of rap music and I can only hope that this is coming from Mike's son's bedroom and not Jamey's car.

My heart's beating somewhere above me, and I'm looking at the open pool gate and the snowy backyard, the light from Mike's kitchen casting warmly over it. There's just no other way. I'll have to keep low and close to the house, that's all, and I'll have to move fast.

Carefully, I latch the gate behind me. I turn and the yard has stayed lighted from the kitchen windows only. I lift the bag and clutch it to my chest. My fingers have gone numb. I press my left shoulder to the stone wall of the house, a design flourish that cost thousands of dollars just for the materials, not including the labor, I happen to know. And now I and my flaming hips move one leg after the other so that my shoulder rubs along the cold stones, and as I get closer to the center of the house I hear laughter inside, Mike's laughter, and then my knee bumps a hard metal corner, the bulkhead entrance to the basement.

Muffled but clear comes Mike's daughter's voice, flabbergasted yet amused, "*Dad, stop it.*"

"Oh yeah?" Mike says. "What're you gonna do about it?" Playful, having fun, and I picture him lightly snapping a dish towel in his daughter's direction or mussing her hair and I don't know what I'm going to do about this obstacle at my knees, but there's only one thing I can do, which is to hug the trash more tightly to my chest, sit on the steel bulkhead, its surface dusted with snow, and try to shimmy across it without sliding to the ground. I'm just about to do this when two things happen: Trina whispers my name and a bank of lights snap on her in the middle of the yard.

Her face is an oval of startled flesh under her hoodie, her eyes squinting up at the white glare. Inside the house the playful banter stops and I'm sliding to my feet and running, Trina still standing there gazing up at Mike Andrews' massive kitchen window like what she sees on the other side is a show being put on just for her.

The trash bag is bouncing against my leg and I keep my face pointed to the dark woods at the edge of the yard, grab Trina's bare hand, and now we're running around the corner of Mike's house, me slipping nearly onto my side as we pass the cypress tree, the side security lights flashing on us, Jamey's headlights coming on as Trina jerks her hand from mine and runs across the asphalt lane and around the front of Jamey's car. Mike Andrews yells *Hey!* and I yank the rear door open and toss in the trash bag, falling facefirst and wheezing onto Jamey's backseat, the door still open as the kid pulls away from the granite curb, Mike yelling, "I've called the *police!*"

2

ON THE SUB SHOP'S TV PERCHED IN THE CORNER, THE NIGHTLY news pans its cameras over skyscrapers bearing the president's name in gold letters twenty feet high. There are images of a congressional hearing of some kind, microphones in the face of a white politician from Louisiana, and there are the smells of fried steak and melted cheese, of sautéing peppers and onions, of French fries dripping from a basket.

Trina and Jamey sit hip to hip across from me and they seem suspended in a stoned, edgy radiance. Their faces are turned toward each other and Jamey's wool cap is pulled back on his forehead. He's speaking low and fast, describing to Trina and me, like we weren't there ourselves, what the three of us have just done. And he's so proud that he didn't lose his cool and drove slowly back through all those rich neighborhoods until we hit the highway.

Trina's face is flushed, and while I know that she's high, it's clear that this boy has mesmerized her beyond that somehow. In the flat fluorescent light of this place I take in his dark complexion and the smooth skin of his forehead. His black hair and curly black whiskers. His brown eyes, glazed over by what he's been smoking all afternoon. His narrow shoulders and boyish voice.

"Because there's no way they're gonna find us."

"Why do you say that?" Behind my hip bones are glowing coals. I don't believe that Mike had time to call the police, but what about after? How much of Jamey's car had he seen?

"Because it was dark out and because my plate lights are busted."

"You sure about that?"

"Yeah, it's a shitbox. 'Sides, all you took was some trash. Is that even a crime?"

"I can't believe how big that fuckin' house was, you guys. How much do you think we'll *get*?"

"Maybe nothing."

"That's a shitty attitude, Tommy. I need a cigarette." Trina smiles at Jamey. She has to be eight or nine years older than he is, but her entire face seems to soften and now she glances over at me like I've just caught her in some private act.

Jamey stands for her and she scoots across the bench, and now she's outside leaning against his small rusted car, smoking. The snow has stopped. Her shoulders hunch against the cold.

Without her beside him the boy seems even younger. He picks up our receipt and studies it. "They call 36 yet?"

"Can I trust you, Jamey?"

"Of course." The boy says this before he even looks up. Then he does. "Yeah, man, of course."

"Good."

Behind Jamey two men rise from their booth with their plastic trays and empty ketchup-streaked paper plates. They're both big men, like me, and they're dressed in fleece coats embroidered with the insignia of an HVAC company I hired once.

One of the men nods at me as they pass. It's the tired, brotherly recognition one tradesman gives to another at the end of a long day. I become aware of my old Carhartt jacket over my atrophied shoulders and I can't remember the man's name, but I know that he hung the ductwork for an addition I did in Swampscott not long before Mike's adjustable rate kicked in. The man probably thinks I'm just grabbing a quick dinner with one of the kids on my crew or maybe my own son, and this leaves me feeling both regretful and justified in what we've just done.

Jamey glances out the window at Trina, who lifts her hand in a wave and blows out smoke. He smiles at her, then looks back at me. "You can trust me, dude."

"Tom."

"Right." Jamey studies the receipt between his fingers, then pulls out his phone and studies that. When he paid for our food I told him that I'd pay him back. My disability comes in soon, my

EBT card not long after, though I have to sell it for cash for the liquid pain distracter I need right now.

On the other side of the glass Trina flicks her cigarette butt out into the parking lot, her eyes passing over both of us like we're not here at all. Then Jamey's standing for her so she can scoot over on the bench. There are the smells of damp hair and cold cotton and Marlboro Lights. "You should take it to your place, Tommy, and then I'll come over right after I feed my kids."

"It may just be trash, hon."

"Then we'll go get some more, right?" Jamey looks from me to Trina, then back at me. A teenage girl behind the register calls out, "Thirty-six? Thirty-six, your order's up." Half the girl's head is shaved, a dark tattoo on her scalp. It is the look of the Apocalypse, the look of prisoners of war, and there's the nearly dizzying sense that I have just entered a more lawless world.

3

I HAVE SPENT MANY HOURS CONTEMPLATING PAIN. ITS CONSTANT presence seems like such a dark joke, really. Like the school bully who sits on your chest and spits in your face years after both of you have moved on. My pelvis and hips were fractured years ago. Do they have to keep spitting in my face?

It's close to nine and I lie on plywood over the cushions of my couch in the 8. On the floor near my feet is the Andrews household's unopened trash bag. From here, I can see through the thin plastic the outlines of commercial-size envelopes, a sheaf of papers, and what looks like a pencil. On the other side of the wall there's only quiet: No yelling. No barely muffled video games. No fucking.

All day and night I hear through its concrete walls the muffled sounds of bad behavior. Trina yells at her babies. She calls them names. She swears at them. Sometimes her boyfriend Brian will be there and he yells and swears at them all.

Some got their units here in the 8 by lottery, others because their family names were on the list for generations. I got mine through my former brother-in-law, Gerard, who was a boy when I married his older sister, a man who is now a lawyer and who in an act of pity secured me my own unit here in the 8.

My neighbor Fitz drives a new Mustang. It's red with tinted windows, and when the inspectors come to check in on us, he hides it out behind the dumpsters filled with wet diapers and cigarette butts, with old TV sets and eggshells and used condoms, with plastic toys and empty bottles of wine.

Fitz only pays me seventy-five percent the value of my EBT card. It's what I have to do so that I can buy the liquid pain distracter that keeps me from falling back to the Os. That and toilet paper. Which I'm not allowed to put on my EBT card. After Fitz's cut, I'm left with only $100.38 for the month, and now Drew's birthday is in less than a week, though I have never stopped thinking of my son. Ever.

In the unit across the dirt yard from Trina's lives a young couple. He's black and she's white, and if I add their two ages together, I've still been on this earth ten years longer. The woman's name starts with an *A*, Amber or Ashley, and she must've gotten pregnant in high school, and now they have three brown babies all under the age of six. Those kids are always dressed in clean clothes, their hair and faces washed, two boys and a girl their mother doesn't let play with Trina's kids, who are not clean and who do not wear clean clothes. Trina's little one, Cody, five years old, looked at me one summer afternoon as I rose slowly from my Taurus and he opened his little mouth and yelled, *Fucka*.

In the next unit over lives an old woman. I believe she's close to a hundred. Every afternoon a visiting nurse shows up in her blue Corolla. She spends an hour in there, then leaves. On Sundays, the old woman's son picks her up for church in his sedan, its rear passenger doors covered by white letters in cursive: *Bongiovanni Shoe Repair*. He's a big man like me, though he has twenty years on me and is clean-shaven, his bald head covered with a scally cap he takes off before stepping into his mother's unit.

For the thousandth time I think that I do not belong here. I do not belong here with any of these people.

In just a few days my son will turn twenty, but how am I going to get to his campus a hundred miles west? All because I drove Trina to the lab to sell her plasma to make rent. It's something I do every week, but this time a young cop in his parked cruiser took note of the expired decal on my rear plate, and now, sitting on the plank over two stacks of books I call a coffee table, are the three crumpled fines that may as well be loaded guns pointed at my head. One is for $607 for driving an unregistered vehicle, another is for $530 for driving an uninsured vehicle, and the third—because I left my empty wallet back in my unit—is $500 for driving without a license. The tally pushes hotly through my head: $1,637. And this doesn't even include the cost of towing and storing my Taurus, the only thing that ever gets me away from here.

Usually at sundown I drive out to Cape Ann to see what used to be my home. I leave the 8 and this neighborhood of box houses like the one I grew up in, the vans and pickup trucks in their driveways, the strip plaza across the street with the liquor store and a salon called Dawn's Hair & Nails. I accelerate east for the highway overpass, a McDonald's on the other side, then a NAPA Auto store next to a home for old people, the front lawn just a strip of grass between the sidewalk and a parking lot that was always full. I think of my mother then, of the early dementia that has claimed her, of how I should visit her, but not till I'm back on my feet. A pathetic phrase, really, given how much pain I have to endure when I stand.

Sometimes I turn onto the entrance ramp of the highway. I join the traffic of my fellow human beings and feel, for a few miles anyway, part of them again, a man coming home after a long day's work, a man who had every intention of carrying his own weight.

I glance to my right and left, see women and men behind their wheels, some talking into their phones or driving quiet, their eyes on the road, on the spouses waiting for them at home, maybe, the hot meals, the happy kids.

But other times, I stay on the back roads all the way to Cape Ann. It takes longer that way. I drive east past the gas station and sub shop, the movie theater and franchise restaurant with its Italian name and dimmed sconces. I pass the Lawn and Garden Center, mulch piled in its lot in the summer, cords of split hardwood there in the winter, and how many times had I loaded my van with wood just like that? Then I and Drew—seven? eight?—carried each log up to our rear porch where we'd stack it? And Drew would be in his wool Patriots cap, down coat, and gloves, all of which his dad had been able to buy him.

Soon I'm driving south through the salt marshes, thick stands of pines and birch between it and the grounds of Trevors Academy. Driving by, I look out at its baseball diamond and lacrosse and soccer fields, the brick buildings of its campus built a hundred years before the War Between the States. It's where my Ronnie was raised by her historian father and her mathematician mother, two people I can't deny still loving, but also resenting for while they did not make a materialist out of their daughter, they did raise an elitist, one I could never keep up with.

No, that isn't fair really. She's no elitist, she's an abundist. It's a word I made up, meaning one accustomed to abundance. She spent her girlhood in a brick house filled with books and the savory smells of her father's homemade soups and stews, her mother's ginger cookies and English teas. At night, when she was young, they took turns reading to her until she fell asleep under thick blankets in a room decorated with framed paintings of landscapes and horses and the moon and stars she went on to study at Smith. From when she was a young girl, she and her little brother Gerard had eaten most of their meals in the academy's dining hall with high school students who came from rich families up and down the East Coast, well-dressed teenagers who treated her and her little brother like their brilliant and adorable mascots, so that years later, when I first saw her at a house party off the UMass Amherst campus, there, in the kitchen doorway, stood a young woman with long brown hair spilling out of a cloche hat, an expectant joy in her pretty face that here was yet another room full of people who would like her just for being among them. No arrogance, just a deeply affirming relationship to the world I'd never witnessed or even considered possible, and then I was stepping toward her, a bottle of beer in each hand, her face turning toward mine with a question in her eyes, and I sure as hell hoped I had a good answer.

What used to be our home sat in a grove of pine and cedar trees overlooking a marsh, and it was a miracle that it was ever ours at all. The land was part of a larger acreage I bought from a man who needed some fast cash and less taxable land, and sooner than I could even begin to believe my good luck, I was the owner of one precious acre with an open view of a saltwater marsh and it had only cost me ninety thousand dollars.

That was all I should have borrowed. I had no business asking for any more than that. But when Ronnie first gazed out at that marsh, two-year-old Drew beside us picking up a twig and throwing it, the air warm and smelling like pine needles and the ocean, the view so similar to what she was able to see every morning from the bedroom of her soft and billowy girlhood, that was that. I had to give her the rest of it. I *wanted* to give her the rest of it. And Mike Andrews was only too happy to lend me the kind of money I had no business even thinking of borrowing.

Driving back to our former home, I park just a few yards into my old driveway, then walk through the woods. Sometimes I pick up a long stick and use it as a cane and there are the smells of pine and the sea and I walk as far as the clearing, the very one I cleared, and I lean against a tree and stare at what I made.

It's like watching an ex-lover dining with her new lover on the other side of a crowded room, her hair styled differently, the happiness in her face so apparent. The truth is, the new owners of my home took better care of it than I ever did. Once Ronnie and I and our son moved in, I never stopped working.

The crash hadn't yet happened and I still had more work than I could bid on, but meanwhile there came the winds and snows of winter, the spring rains, the summer heat, then fall with all those leaves and pine needles filling our gutters, one of them bent by an ice dam one bad February. The clapboards needed staining and the corner boards and window trim needed paint and some of the long deck boards at the rear of the house had begun to split, even though I was careful to pre-drill every galvanized nail I drove.

I just needed to take a weekend and start to go at it all. Or get a week between jobs when I could do it. But there was no week between jobs and on weekends, if I wasn't doing paperwork for a current project or calculating numbers for the next, then I was visiting Ronnie's parents, Wyn and Nancy, with Ronnie and Drew, or hosting dinner for some of my wife's new friends from her graduate school or the dance studio where she took classes. Or I took my son with me to tune up my van or get a hamburger somewhere, just the two of us. Father and son.

And then the adjustable rate Mike Andrews had winked at me about kicked in and our monthly mortgage seemed to nearly double itself and all I did was work and worry and work some more and then the wheels fell from the gaming tables coast to coast and I took my three-story fall, and here I am on one of my escapes from the 8, leaning against a tree or stick or both, taking in all the improvements the new owners have made: they painted the corner boards a handsome sage, the clapboards coffee brown; they replaced the bent gutter with one that matched the trim, and not only are there no more dead leaves and pine needles on the roof, it's now thick cedar shingles nailed over my sheathing and my rafters, making everything look not only more aesthetically pleasing but like the true owners of this house had finally moved in.

I place my empty cup on the plank table, then slowly stand. Day after tomorrow my son will turn twenty, and it's highly unlikely that his father will be there, isn't it? Because even if I do open this stolen trash at my feet, and even if I do find something I can cash against the banker's accounts, will this really happen in time for me to get my car registered, then free it from Kelly's Towing and Storage, which is costing me fifty bucks a day, and then drive the two hours west? And I have no idea what Drew is doing right this minute. I don't know what courses he's taking or what his class schedule is. I don't even know how many roommates my son lives with off-campus or if he's living with his girlfriend. I know so very little about this boy who slipped between my fingers like the baggie of Os I seemed to trade him in for.

I set Mike and Kerry Andrews' trash bag on my Formica table and rip it open. Loose papers and envelopes and an empty Starbucks cup spill onto my tabletop and roll to the floor. I put on my readers. I wish I had better light to work under. The first thing I pick up is a greeting card, the cover a sparkling champagne flute. The word *Congratulations!* floats above in a cloud of white streamers. I am about to set it aside, but I open it and see handwritten words by Mike himself:

My One and Only K.A.,
Senior VP! You deserve this, honey. You can see by these
tickets that we'll be celebrating across the pond. So brush
up on your French, mon amour!
Love,
Your Proud Hubby,
Mikey

Mikey? K.A.? *Across the pond?* I study the date in the upper corner. Ten days ago. Did they already *take* that trip? A long weekend maybe? I picture Mike and Kerry strolling along the Seine holding hands, and I toss the card onto the floor.

I reach into the bag for the rest of the trash, but most of it is shredded paper. Mounds of it. I scoop all of the trash out onto the table. Half of what lies in front of me are shredded balls of paper. I pick up a handful and study it, but each strand is no wider than an eighth of an inch and I can make out little. I pick up an unopened letter to *Mrs. Michael Andrews*, junk mail from a car insurance agency in Ohio. There's more mail for *Mrs. Michael Andrews* or *Kerry Andrews* and this bag is clearly from her office, which means they each have their own office and mine was always the kitchen table, Ronnie's the couch where she'd do her homework on a lap desk she'd bought from a catalog.

Kerry gets a lot of catalogs. For kitchenware and clothes, for jewelry and ski equipment, for shoes and spa treatments, and one for lingerie from some designer with a Greek name. There are catalogs for wine and sailing. And there's one from Louis Vuitton with a page marked with a sticky note. I open to that page and see, circled in red ink, a small handbag called a Croisette. It has a shoulder strap and a gold clasp and it costs $1,650. For a fucking *handbag?* And she's *circled* it?

I gather up all the catalogs and dump them onto the floor. The plastic lid of the Starbucks cup pops off, a smudge of lipstick around its tiny hole.

Part of me thinks I should feel guilty about what I'm doing, looking for blank checks sent to the Andrews by their credit card companies, "convenience checks" that can be cashed for the full line of credit. But I don't, because all I'm planning to take is just enough to get my car back, to go see my son, to maybe give Trina a helping hand while I'm at it. Mike should consider himself lucky, though this is not a word I've ever believed in. In this world you make your own luck. And you do it with hard, honest work. *Honest* work.

From my laptop research I found out that Kerry Andrews works in the secondary mortgage market. That she's employed by an office in Boston that bundles up all those precarious loans that men like her husband peddle to working people like me, Tom Lowe Jr. Banks have been doing this for years, I learned, because if they don't sell their mortgages to investors who then collect interest on them, then only the biggest banks would have enough freed-up money to keep lending. But the trouble came when all these sold mortgages began to be pooled together and sold to other investors as securitized bonds. These were then given AAA ratings by the same agencies paid to do just that by the makers of these very bonds and other "securities." It'd be as if I wrote checks to the building inspectors entrusted with making sure that my house frames were built to code. How could I expect these inspectors *not* to approve my work? And yet all those bundled house loans were riddled with debts that could only be defaulted on, and so I, like millions of other fools, got subprimed. I got sub-primed because Mike Andrews, with his affable smile and relaxed athletic demeanor, could see just how hungry I was to build and own my first house. Not just the first for my young family, but *my* first. Ever.

"What do you think you make in a good year, Tom?"

"My best was last year."

"Seventy? Eighty thousand?"

"Sixty-four."

"Let's call it seventy-two, shall we?" Mike smiled and winked. "And that would put your monthly fixed number at . . ." Andrews tapped away at his calculator. I knew there was no such thing as a "fixed" anything in my kind of work, but I remember a calmness opening up inside of me, the rare feeling that someone was actually trying to take care of me.

It was the one thing I couldn't quite get used to with Ronnie, her love for me. A few nights before applying for that loan, I sat at the kitchen table after dinner writing down the price of finish work for a kitchen in Hamilton, and she came up behind me and began to rub my shoulders and neck, her fingers smelling like tomatoes and rosemary. I started to pull away, but she leaned in close and whispered, "You need to let me love you, honey."

Under the mound of shredded paper is an empty Tums dispenser, an Orbit gum wrapper, a bent green paper clip. I pick up the sheaf of papers, but they're nothing but blank sheets of printer paper stuck together from what looks like a large red wine spill along its edges. There are a few other unopened business envelopes, but it's all automatic mail from charities or more insurance companies and a BMW dealership, but none from a credit card company or bank, and what else did I expect? Of course Kerry and her husband would use shredders. Of course they'd never throw out anything that could be used against them.

Still, I pick up the shredded mound and run my fingers through it the way I used to with Drew's hair when I was looking for ticks. In the middle of the mound is something round and plastic and I pull out an empty prescription bottle. Its cap is off. I turn the label toward me. It's written out to Kerry Andrews, *Celexa*, 20 mg once a day.

Celexa?

I make my way back to my plywood couch, open my computer, type in the name of that drug, and soon learn that lovely Kerry Andrews suffers from anxiety or depression or both. I read the list of side effects. Later tonight Kerry Andrews may be lying awake with Celexa-induced insomnia right beside snoring Mike. She might be nauseated or sweating or suffering from a dry mouth or "sexual side effects," which don't get specific, though it can't be good and that's probably the real reason Mike bought them tickets to Europe. He and his K.A. needed a boost of romance.

I shut my computer and stare at Kerry Andrews' trash. I start to feel a rising joy at the thought of some real discomfort—pain even—going on inside the Andrews home, but I can't deny that also rising inside me is a disappointing recognition of their humanity. That even bright, shining lives like theirs cannot evade some kind of trouble.

But I'm seeing again the big glowing houses of Federal Drive and their big private lots. I'm seeing Mike Andrews' massive Palladian window set into fieldstone, Mike's modern kitchen under recessed lights on the other side, his well-dressed, well-fed daughter on her computer and phone, the covered pool and automatic garage doors under a round rec room that probably holds more furniture in it than I've ever owned.

A $1,650 *handbag*?

A trip "across the *pond*"?

No, we are not in this together, and while, yes, it's probably true that Mike and Kerry work hard at what they do five days a week, it's not an honest living.

Honest. My face warms with shame. I have never stolen from anyone before. All my life I've been a man who *works*. But after my car was towed away, Trina and I had to walk home from the lab in the rain. She'd pulled the hoodie of her sweatshirt over her head, but it was soaked. So were her shoulders and the hems of her Jimmy Neutron pajamas. Pierced into her right ear were a silver cross and a blue star, small and dull looking, and as we walked along, my hips flaring, she put her thumb out, then pulled the hoodie off her head, her hair so drenched that her face was all one's eyes were drawn to—her cheekbones, her nearly full lips, her eyeliner running along the sides of her nose.

Almost immediately a car slowed and a bearded kid rose up out of it, our Good Samaritan, Jamey. "You guys need a *ride*?"

The inside of his car was warm and smelled like cannabis. The backseat where I sat was covered with political science and engineering textbooks, and hanging from the rearview mirror was a locket holding a photo of a golden retriever. Jamey told us his name and asked where we were going.

"Amesbury." Trina turned to him then. She tucked a wet strand of hair behind her ear. She smiled and said, "Can you take us there? I gotta get home to my kids."

It was quite masterful how she said this, really. Her tone was almost playful, like she might have had some sort of sweet reward for him if he'd only do what she asked, but the word *kids* canceled the possibility of that sweet reward while also assuring him of her maturity and ability to follow through, all while she stared at him with pale blue eyes in a wet face.

Then we were pulling up to the 8, our identical two-story units covered with vinyl siding the color of a public toilet. Weeds poked through cracks in the asphalt lot, and the concrete steps leading up to my stoop were out of level, their risers also cracked.

Jamey wrote on a slip of paper what looked like his phone number and Trina told him that she didn't own a phone.

"How can you live without a phone?"

She shrugged. "You get used to it."

But she took his number from him anyway and was already at her own door before I moved, the hems of her pajama bottoms sticking to her shoes.

And, yes, it was her idea to steal someone's credit card information.

The screws holding my hips together may as well be heated steel. I rise slowly and take the white plastic bag and then I get down on one knee and push into the bag all the crap from Kerry's office from the past week. All of Kerry's catalogs. Her shredded mounds. Her red wine spill along the edge of a sheath of good paper. Her empty Tums container and prescription bottle.

"*Tommy?*" Trina walks in the way she always does because I never lock my door. Her eyes have cleared and she's in a thin blue robe, her feet in untied sneakers. Her long hair is wet and combed. She jerks her head in the direction of Kerry Andrews' trash bag. "Haven't you opened that yet?"

"I have."

"And?"

"Nothing. It's all shredded."

"*Fuck.*"

"Trina?"

"What?"

"I'm no thief."

"Are you sure there's nothing in there? Let me look."

"Go ahead."

It doesn't take her long, her back to me. But after she sets the catalogs and mounds of shredded paper to the side, Trina opens every envelope of junk mail, rifling through pages she's not taking the time to read, looking for anything, I guess, with dollar signs on it.

"Trina?"

"Who rips up their fucking mail?"

"Trina?"

"What?" She turns toward me. Her robe has opened slightly, the skin of her sternum pale above her cleavage. She pulls it closed. "I need that money, Tom."

I can only nod. Ringing through my head is Mike Andrews' raised and slightly rattled voice. *I called the **police**.* It felt good to rattle Mike. It felt good to know that he might have gotten just a taste of what it's like to be preyed on. Just a little.

"Get a job. I'll watch your kids." Though I don't mean this, and I know it.

"*Right*. If I don't work under the table my fuckin' rent goes up. And how are you gonna watch my kids? You're useless. I'm getting that money, Tommy."

She moves so fast by me that she ruffles the air. There are the scents of hair conditioner and washed cotton, and I think of the dirty laundry, including some of mine, that she carries a half mile to the CVS plaza where there's a Laundromat, its big machines taking quarters earned from her own plasma.

The morning my car was towed, Trina was nervous. Drunk the day before, she had her boyfriend ink a new tattoo halfway between her navel and pubic bone, even though she knew that plasma sellers like her have to wait six months after getting a tattoo before they can go back to the blood-separating machine at Maverne Medical. She stood there in my unit, just feet from where I lay on my plywood couch, and she was wearing the Jimmy Neutron pajama bottoms she lives in, her T-shirt tight against her breasts and waist. She drew deep on her cigarette and blew smoke out the side of her mouth. Then she told how her boyfriend Brian, with his shaved head and tattooed neck, etched into her a heart broken in two, "You know, down low."

I wasn't going to ask her where or how low. But before I could say anything, she hooked her thumb behind the waistband of her pajama bottoms, then pulled them and her underwear down until there it was, a red broken heart on a red patch of skin above a rim of dark pubic hair. It was like glimpsing the bright crack of your own future and you couldn't say whether it was blessed or cursed, only that my breath lay still in my chest, and I said, "Oh Trina, they'll only see that if you show them."

She must've known what she was doing because she kept her thumb hooked in her pajama bottoms and underwear—pink? blue?—a second longer, her eyes on mine in almost a mournful way. Then she let them both snap back into place, and now my hip fires are burning. I need my pain distracter, and I need it now.

4

IN THE NARROW KITCHEN I PULL MY JACKET OFF THE HOOK AND head outside into a softly falling rain. The air is cold and smells like the overflowing garbage cans in my tiny backyard because it's a rare day when I can make the trip to the 8's dumpsters without having to rest and cool the fires, even when I use the kiddie wagon Trina found for me. I wait for a car to pass wetly by in the street and I'm aware that my work boots are untied, and I have no idea of the time, though the lights are still up in Dawn's Hair & Nails. Near the window a young woman is teasing the hair of a much older woman talking into the mirror.

Through the plate-glass window of the liquor store, I can see the owner Larry is not working, which won't be good for me. Instead it's Larry's son-in-law Paul, a gum-chewing thirty-something-year-old in a camo sweatshirt, and as I walk in his eyes are already on me like I came in to shoplift.

"Evening," I say.

Over the stereo's speakers come the warmly combative voices of men talking sports. Larry, a quiet man who has owned this shop, he told me, for over twenty years, plays classical music when he's working the register, its rising violins often making me feel like the world is a mystery and I've left it behind, and then I'm setting onto the worn counter the cheapest bottle of vodka they sell. Paul's eyes are on my whiskers, my old open Carhartt, my T-shirt hanging out under my sweater. I say, "How are you today?"

It's the upbeat tone I use whenever I know I look the way I do. Like I'm a degenerate and not a man with an education and the skills to build this store, the counter between us, the floor Paul stands on.

He rings up the vodka without a word. I hand him a twenty, and Larry's son-in-law drops two pennies into my open palm, which I drop into the plastic cup holding dozens more. It's a minuscule act of generosity even I can afford, but Larry's son-in-law's eyes are on me like I'm an empty fire extinguisher. I grab my vodka bottle by its neck. Then I'm crossing the street under a cold rain, my sockless feet damp and slippery in my old work boots.

WHAT THE VODKA DOES, its liquid burn trickling down my throat, is make my hip fires feel like less of a problem. It's like that story I read in one of my colleges of those British and German soldiers declaring their own truce on the dawn of Christmas morning, 1914. Slowly they emerged from their opposing trenches and drifted into the gray waste between them, and there they traded smokes and plum pudding and even sang carols together before the sun set and they were called back to the violence that was their duty.

I rest my glass on the plank beside my couch. I put on my reading glasses. Sitting on my belly is my open laptop with its screensaver image of Ronnie holding Drew as an infant. This was in our apartment before I built the house. Our baby son had just breastfed, his tiny body swaddled in white, and Ronnie's shirt was unbuttoned, her long hair pulled up in an untamed bun. She wasn't wearing any makeup, which I preferred, and I walked into the room on tiptoe, holding the camera to my eye and saying "Hey" just before I pressed the button to Ronnie raising her face to me, her eyes lit by a dark and deep and nearly secret love.

Off to the left of my ex-wife and baby son are the three blue folder icons of my research: *Big Pharma, Insurance, Banks.* I open my browser and tap my way to Craigslist. I haven't used it since the months of our foreclosure when I sold whatever we owned that I could: our couches and upholstered chairs; our dining room set and guest room bed and bureaus; the oak bench in the foyer; almost everything but my tools, which I still hoped to be able to use again one day. What a time that was. What a lovely time.

I spent most of it on my back, high on whatever my doctors kept prescribing me, my ten-year-old Drew bringing me peanut butter and jelly sandwiches or my urinal bottle or the mail that I didn't even open anymore. Ronnie had set up my rented adjustable bed in the living room so that I could be near the downstairs bathroom and the kitchen and so that I could look through the wall of windows out at the woods and the marsh, the sun setting into it every night like an unrelenting statement of some kind.

For a few months after my accident and the surgeries we lived off the little Ronnie was beginning to earn, and we borrowed from Ronnie's mother and father, two people who'd managed to be comfortable without ever having much. Their home had always belonged to Trevors Academy, and while they owned a camp on a lake in New Hampshire, Ronnie said she would rather lose everything than ask them to sell *that*.

She was standing a few feet from my bed when she said this. She was still dressed in her work clothes, a blouse, light sweater, and black rayon pants. Drew was in the kitchen doing his homework at the small island, its granite top a forest green with deep charcoal veins running through it. I drove a hundred miles into Vermont for that slab and I made it long enough to seat six, the hope being that we might still have more kids to fill our expensive house on the marsh.

Ronnie was sharing a small office in Essex where she saw her clients, a word I found odd for a therapist to use. It made me think of customers for advertising executives, not the women, men, and teenagers my wife met with for fifty minutes at a time, six a day, four days a week. Before she went to graduate school her degree at Smith had been in astronomy with a psychology minor, something she added because her friends kept telling her what a good listener she was. And she found that she enjoyed studying human beings even more than she did the cosmos, that she was ultimately far more curious about people, though throughout our first weeks and months together, I only seemed to notice how curious she was about *me*.

Why do you drive a van?
Because I'm a carpenter.
Why are you a carpenter?
Because I'm good at it.

Do you like doing it?
I like creating things, yes.
Did you always want to do that?
No.
Why are you in college?
Because—I don't know.
What?

We were lying in my bed together. It was in an apartment I rented with two other students, both younger than I was by ten years, like her. It was winter. Maybe morning, maybe afternoon. A hard sunlight shone across the foot of my bed and her bare foot sticking out of the blanket. I lay on my back and she was on her side, her body warm beside me, and now she moved and rested her leg over both of mine. "I mean, do you want to do something else?"

"I must." I laughed. "This is my fifth college." And I told her of having gone to two community colleges and now three state schools, of having enough credits for two bachelor's degrees, though I hadn't earned one yet. No, what I had earned was debt.

"Why do you think you never finished?"

Nobody had ever asked me that before. "I don't know. Work kept getting in the way. And—"

"What?"

"I guess I never really felt like I belonged in those places."

She was quiet a moment. She ran one finger in a light circle over my chest. "Maybe you just want to go farther than your parents went."

This hadn't occurred to me. I didn't think much about my mother and father. Or at least I didn't think I did. What had occurred to me, though, is that I never felt as if I really belonged to the people I came from. I was raised on a dead-end street in a box of a house covered with asphalt siding. From the TV room I could look through a thin stand of pines and see the northbound lanes of the state highway. My mother was fifteen when I was born, seventeen when my little brother Charlie came along, twenty-four when our father, Tom Lowe Sr., died of a heart defect while driving a forklift in the warehouse that swallowed him.

Ronnie. She was so different from all that.

I tap my way to my emails and type in her name, her responses to me appearing in a short stack from the most recent one I sent her to the first written six years ago when I'd been living in the 8 less than a week. I was newly clean and still on the Suboxone, but I spent a lot of time on my couch staring at the sloppily sheet-rocked ceiling of my new subsidized life, some young woman on the other side of the wall swearing at her kids, an idling Mustang outside blasting rap. I kept picturing my wife and son in Edward Joseph Flynn's historic home on Salem Common, my own home sold off to who-knows-who, and I snatched open my computer and wrote to my soon-to-be-ex-wife: *You should have just killed me. I hope you're fucking* **happy**.

Hours later, she wrote back:

Tom,

I'm not proud of how I ended things with us. And you know I tried to save our family. But I couldn't save *you**, Tom. And I had Drew to think of, and when I was given a second chance I suppose I just took it.*

You can't blame me or anyone else for what happened, Tom. And can't you see how privileged you are? You're an educated, white, American male. No one is more free on this planet than someone like you. I know you can't do carpentry work anymore, but stop feeling sorry for yourself, Tom. Do it for Drew.

Veronica

Which is why I need to sell the only valuable things I have left—all the tools in the basement of my unit. They took me years and years to collect, buying one or two at a time but only when I needed them. And I see my former brother-in-law Gerard and his pained expression the last time I saw him when he and his work-out buddy, another corporate lawyer, set aside a Saturday afternoon for a little corporate altruism and hauled my tools to the 8. The truth is, I should have sold them all years ago. But if I had, it would be like selling the last of my once-toned muscles, my genitals, my very bones—broken or not—my brain and hands that, together, still knew how to do so much constructive good.

But instead of selling them, was I really going to be a *thief*?

I tap my way to *Classifieds*, then *For Sale by Owner*, then *Tools*. One image after another comes up. I scroll down to see color photos of compressors and reciprocating saws, circular saws and jigsaws, Japanese pull saws and hand planers and worn-handled chisels, and it's clear that I'm going to have to take pictures of my tools before I do anything else.

Through the walls come the sounds of simulated video-game explosions, one after another. I swing my legs off the arm of the couch and set my laptop on the pine plank beside the tow driver's business card. My car has been locked away for three days already, each minute costing me something, and Drew's birthday is in two damn days.

5

FITZ'S UNIT IS TWO UP FROM CAL AND AMBER'S, JUST BEHIND THE old woman's and across from the dumpsters. The rain has stopped, the dark asphalt glistening under the streetlamp. I stop and take a long swallow from my bottle. I'm cold. Or my body is, though this seems to be information delivered to me from far away. My hip fires have burned down to coals on the screws that hold my bones together. I still owe seventy thousand dollars for that final operation, and it didn't even take.

The shades of the old woman's unit are drawn. On either side of them come the flickering colors of a TV and I think of her son's Italian name—Bongiovanni. I wonder if she's from the old country and not this "new" one that throws away its old and its broken and even those barely getting started.

From the second-floor window of Cal's unit comes a low, warm light behind a gauzy fabric. I'm sure that young Amber hung those curtains herself. I picture her reading books to her children if they're not already asleep. I have spent very little time around Amber—or is it Ashley?—and she's a bit of a mystery to me. Short and stocky with a pretty face, she seems to move through her days like a soldier following strict orders from a commander she trusts completely, that if she simply performs every task put before her, then she and her kids and Cal will all rise out of this place to somewhere far better. The few times she's looked directly at me, usually carrying groceries and kids from their hubcapless Geo, her eyes have the hard light of one who expects help from no one. She's no abundist, but she's not a Trina either, who's been given nothing and so only takes.

I swallow more vodka. I need a word for that. A word for someone who's only known scarcity. I spell the word out in my head. And then I see two words: *Scar City.* Yes, the scars of a scarcitist. I'm certainly one. And so is poor, dear Trina, her scars desiccating her heart in a way that Cal's and Amber's have seemingly gone untouched.

Fitz's Mustang is backed into its parking space like he's prepared to make a quick escape. I screw the cap back onto my pain distracter. I knock twice on the front door of Fitz's unit, the door swinging open before I've even lowered my arm. Standing there is a woman in a peacoat and she's laughing at something Fitz must've just said. She steps past me and smiles at me without a word, her silver hoop earring swaying against her cheek. For the second time today there come the smells of cannabis, and Fitz is standing in his doorway in a polyester robe, black with red piping at the lapels and the sash cinched loosely at his waist. "Thomas." He says this like he's been expecting me for hours.

I hold up my bottle. "I bear gifts."

A small-engined car starts up, its headlights passing over us both as Fitz invites me in and closes the door.

Fitz's unit is identical to mine in its layout, though Fitz's entryway feels bigger to me. I follow him around the corner to his small living room, where Fitz's couch is right where I have my own couch, but Fitz's is red leather. On either side of it are two lamps, their shades covered with red scarves, and facing the couch is an open laptop on a stool. A microphone and some other kind of device are attached to it, and a pink dildo rests on Fitz's coffee table beside a tube of K-Y, its cap on the edge of an ashtray filled with pot seeds and plastic-tipped cigar butts.

"Don't mind the mess, man. Ice?"

I say please and sit in one of two easy chairs. Across from me are some flattened cardboard boxes against the wall, above them a widescreen TV where, in my unit, I have shelves filled with books from all the college courses I ever took.

Fitz emerges from the fluorescent-lit kitchen carrying two glasses filled with ice. I fill Fitz's outstretched glass, then my own. I sit back, my hips screws grinding, and I glance at the dildo and tube of lubricant. So long since I've felt the stirring of my own libido, though what Trina showed me the other morning, that seemed to do something to me. "I didn't mean to intrude on you and your lady."

"No, man, she's my business partner." Fitz closes his laptop and sits down on his red couch. "People pay to watch us fuck. It's just another revenue stream, brother." Fitz crosses his bare leg and pulls his robe closed and drinks. His head is nearly bald and appears perfectly shaped, and in his left earlobe is a tiny diamond stud.

He looks like a man who has just put in a long hard shift at honest work, and I find myself feeling a slow-growing admiration for this. But it's the kind that makes me feel small in two or three ways and I take a deep swallow from my glass, though I'm getting the cement-limbed news that I may be drunk. *Revenue stream.* It is not a phrase I've heard in quite a while. And *just another* too. "What do you *do*, Fitz?"

"Nurse's aide. I told you that. That's where I met Lynn." He nods at the dildo. "She's a nurse." Fitz taps a cigarillo out of a Black & Mild box beside the lamp. "Want one?"

"I need to sell my tools, Fitz."

"You don't need 'em?"

"I need my car back." It's what I want to say, though the sentence itself seems to have come out in one continuous gush of words. "How many've you got?"

"What?"

"Streams." I nod at Fitz's laptop. "Revenue."

"Enough to get out of this fuckin' place."

"You're moving?"

"One more score and I'm gone, brother. Hey, ever notice how they don't *want* you to succeed? I know they got ten million people waiting for one of these shitholes, but if you start to make some real coin you have to hide it. I mean how am I s'posed to save for a place of my own if I can't live here cheap while I'm doing it?"

"You find a place?"

Fitz exhales cigarillo smoke. "I mean I'm a fuckin' foster kid, Tom. I ain't never had a home. But I have to hide my Benjamins from the government before I can live my American fuckin' Dream?"

"I used to own a beautiful home."

Fitz nods like he does know this, though I have no memory of ever telling him about it. "You got subprimed, brother. That won't happen to me." Fitz stands and walks over and pours more vodka into his glass. "Man, this is cheap shit, Tommy. What happened to your whip?"

I just stare at him.

"Your ride, man. Your wheels."

"Got towed."

"Motherfuckers."

"That's why I need to sell my tools, Fitz."

"My last foster dad might buy 'em."

"Last?"

"I had four, brother." Fitz pulls his phone from his robe pocket. It's in a gold case, and he taps the screen a few times with his thumb, holding it out flat between us like proof of something.

"That you, son?"

Fitz's last foster father Sal says something and Fitz asks him about Betty. Then he holds the phone closer to my face. "Tell 'em what you got."

"Hello?" Sal sounds like he's put in a long day and only answered his phone because it was Fitz. I lean forward, my hips screws catching on fire. "Tom Lowe. How are you, sir?"

"How do you know Fitz?"

Fitz says, "He's my neighbor."

"Oh." Sal's tone flattens out and it's clear that he doesn't expect much from any man living in the 8.

"I had a successful business for years, sir, but I got hurt. Fell off a roof."

"Sorry to hear it."

"I always respected my tools. Never left them on a job or out in the rain. Replaced cords whenever I needed to. WD-40'd them. Never worked with a dull blade." There's the feeling I said all of this clearly, though one word may have been joined to another a little too closely.

"That's the way to do it."

"But I got hurt, Sal."

"So you said. I don't need any tools."

Fitz raises the phone closer to his face. "How 'bout one of your guys, Pop?"

"You got any cordless drills?"

"Three at least."

"Send me some pictures, Fitz. I'll see what I can do."

I thank Fitz's last foster dad and sit back, but my heated hip screws sit back too and I need to stand, but now my drink glass hits the floor, spilling ice before rolling to a stop.

I'M EATING BEANS AND RICE off a plate on my lap, Fitz beside me on his red couch. The TV is on, *SportsCenter*, two men and a pretty black woman talking football statistics, but Fitz and I are watching Fitz's laptop. So strange to be sitting beside him while watching him have sex with Lynn a foot or so away. And they're doing this on the very couch I'm sitting on. I did not ask to see this. Or did I? Getting from the easy chair to here is a bit fuzzy, though there's the memory of Fitz scooping up the ice on the floor into my glass, then saying something on his way to the kitchen about food, his black polyester robe rippling softly behind him like a royal cape.

"She's hot, huh bro?"

The beans and rice are going down well and I'm grateful for them. I want some cold water but don't want to ask. When I first moved to the 8 Trina made it clear that Fitz sold pills he stole from his work, and for me, who'd been clean for only a few months then, it was like hearing that a rattlesnake lived under my bed. But now I'm watching that rattlesnake push himself in and out of Lynn. It feels wrong to be watching this. But it looks like Fitz is slightly drunk too, and his expression while he watches himself and Lynn brings me back to Drew at age nine watching tape of himself pitching on the mound. There's an almost wistful quality. A look of wonder that he's actually seeing himself do the one thing he wants to do, and look, he's doing it pretty well.

Now Lynn moans out of sync with the football voices coming from the wall and I say, "Mind if we turn this off?"

"Jealous?"

"Yep, jealous."

Fitz closes the laptop and belches. *"Cerveza?"*

I shake my head. I'm thinking of the word *jealous*. It wasn't an emotion I knew well until Ronnie's betrayal. And with the father of one of her "clients." But could I blame her? What had I become? Ronnie was still young, thirty-four, lovelier than she'd ever been. Hardship had done something good to the abundist. It had put her on some sort of cosmic alert that made her move through her days with an air of dread, clarity, and purpose, her eyes straight ahead, her chin up like she was forever waiting for the next assault. So different from the girl I met in Amherst years earlier, the over-loved child who expected joy and wonder at every turn.

The O I took every day made me constipated and libidoless, but they also made the conflagration that burned in my fused pelvis and hips some absurd show from another country that I didn't have to watch. And so I watched other shows.

For months I tried anything I could to hold off the bank, even writing to my brother Charlie in Germany. It's where he'd been stationed and where he met his wife. On the computer I sometimes see photos of my brother's three kids, all with her blond hair and high cheekbones, but with Charlie's easily caged recklessness. He was always the boy who could start a fight but never get into it himself, the one who'd say that somebody should host a party though it would never be him. He seemed to be a boy born to take orders but not give any of substance himself, and so he seems content to take them from Ulrika, a woman I met only once when Ronnie and I were flush and visited them in their small stucco house behind a community garden and a commuter train station built after the bombings of the last war.

In my letter to Charlie, I asked him for a loan of ten thousand dollars, an amount I knew my younger brother did not remotely have. Charlie wrote back: "I work in a German *factory*, Tom. I'm sorry, but you're on your own."

On your own.

Funny. The exact words Mike Andrews used, too. This was over the phone. I called him from my adjustable bed two to three times a week, though Mike would rarely be "available" and when he did pick up the phone he kept offering the same solution: "The bank is willing to charge you interest only, till you're back on your feet, Tom."

"We can't afford that, Mike."

"I'm sorry, buddy. I wish I could do more for you."

Buddy. I pictured Mike Andrews sitting at his cherry desk. I imagined him staring at that skiing photo of him and his wife.

"Can't you just freeze our mortgage until I have an income again?" But doing *what*?

"Banks don't do that, Tom."

Maybe Mike did not say *You're on your own*, but I was. Those long days when Ronnie was at her office and Drew was at school, the O moving like warm milk through my veins, I lay on my adjustable bed and looked around as best I could at this house I'd built. I stared up at the ridge of the ceiling thirty feet above me, its smooth plastered surface canted at forty-five degrees down to the wall of windows I trimmed with poplar. I remembered being strong and healthy, standing on the interior staging with my cut pieces and finish gun, the sweet smell of poplar dust in the air. I stared up at the loft, its railing hand-milled maple I'd splurged on. I was a man who could see through floors and walls and ceilings because I had cut and fastened each and every joist, stud, and rafter.

Yes, I borrowed more than I should have, and yes, I did not pay enough attention to just what an adjustable rate really meant, but I was always careful when estimating time and materials on all my projects; I was prudent and I tried to be smart and only a few times in the past had I lost money on a job, so I decided to build my family's home mainly myself. I'd sub out only what I couldn't do with my own hands and tools—the excavating and foundation work, the electrical and plumbing, the HVAC, and yes, coats of plaster across the surface of every wall and ceiling. This added another twenty-seven thousand dollars to the budget, but Ronnie insisted on it. It was what the walls of her girlhood home on the grounds of Trevors Academy had looked like. "If we don't, honey," she'd said, "it'd be like putting cheap makeup on a beautiful face."

The nine months it took me to build our house, she used that word a lot—*beautiful*. What I was doing for them was "just so *beautiful*." It felt that way, too. But also miraculous, and every day that I worked on building my home I felt like I was in some temporary state of grace, every traffic light green, the sun on my back; I felt it while clearing my lot with a chain saw and stump puller, hauling off rock dumped in my trailer by the excavator I hired, a quiet kid from Maine with a 35-ton Cat; I felt it surveying and marking the corners of my footings and foundation, driving out to a local farm for hay bales I spread over those newly poured footings to protect them from a late spring frost. I especially felt it, felt bathed in the sustaining warmth of it, that morning when the first of my framing materials were delivered and I began to lay out, cut, and nail the floor and first walls of our house.

There was the hydraulic moan of the compressor, the gas fumes from the purring generator, the sawdust from the kiln-dried two-by-sixes I culled myself one at a time from the lumberyard's stacks. It was April, then May, then June, and Ronnie started bringing me lunch every day. She drove up in the white Subaru she still owned from college, and most days she brought Drew, who was almost three, his hair dark and curly, and our little son would run to where I was working before she could even call to him to wait.

By late May I'd glued and nailed the first floor's sheathing to all the joists. I'd framed the second floor's loft and three of the four exterior walls, though the one facing the marsh, the one that would become the wall of windows, was still wide open to the water and sky, and my family and I sat on the plywood lip of the floor deck, eating tuna fish or chicken salad sandwiches, Drew sitting on one of my thighs while sweat dried under my shirt.

Ronnie hadn't decided yet to go to graduate school then, but as she bit into an apple and stared out at the tall grass of the marsh, I could already sense her restlessness. For a while I thought this was her desire for me to hurry up and finish this house so that we could move in and make it a home. This only added to my own joy about what I was doing and how carefully and methodically I was doing it. But most nights when I got back to our small apartment in Salem, Ronnie told me that my supper was on the stove or in the oven, that Drew already ate and don't let him watch any TV, and then she kissed me and was out the door for a book club meeting or a night class she was taking in art history or child psychology, or maybe she got together with a girlfriend from college who was almost done with medical school, or drove herself to a local dance studio where she took Zumba or African classes, then went out for a drink with a few men and women she'd just been moving and sweating alongside.

For the most part I felt fine about all of this. Let her get out of the house for a while. What was wrong with that? She was a bright and inquisitive person, and like millions of other young mothers, she could find only so much stimulation and sustenance in the hours-long company of a three-year-old. Besides, it gave me uninterrupted time with my boy.

I got down on the floor with him and played with plastic dinosaurs, which Drew loved and knew all the names of, his favorite being a *Micropachycephalosarus*, a word I had a hard time pronouncing though my son didn't. Sometimes we'd draw pictures together, me taking one color and Drew another. My fingers would be scratched and swollen from the day's work, sawdust still in the hairs of my forearms. Lying on my side stretched out on the floor, I could feel my son's narrow back against my chest, and I smelled his hair and I loved listening to Drew talk, his high voice excited at whatever we were making together.

Later, I carried him piggyback up to the bathroom to help him wash up and brush his teeth, then I tucked Drew under his covers and lay on top of the bed and read to him from whatever book Drew picked, though *Cloudy with a Chance of Meatballs* and *Night Cars* were his favorites. So many nights, Ronnie nudged me awake on Drew's bed and I turned out Drew's light and followed her into the bedroom, where usually we made love, and after, she wanted to tell me about the class she attended or the people she had a drink with after dance, and I fell asleep hearing her animated sounds and they followed me into my dreams.

"You want me to take those pictures now, Tom?" Fitz is leaning in the doorway to the kitchen, thumbing through his phone. He drinks from his beer.

"I need eighteen hundred bucks right now, Fitz. Can you lend it to me till I sell my tools?"

"No can do, brother. I never touch my principal."

"I need to see my son." I set my dinner plate on the coffee table next to the pink dildo. "I need my car back, Fitz."

"Then show me your tools, dude."

6

I'S CLOSE TO DAWN ON THE THIRD DAY SINCE FITZ POSTED PHO-
tos of my tools on Craigslist and I've gotten only two emails
about them. The first was from a Yahoo address, a man who'd
signed his name "CJ," wanting to know what I was asking for my
planer. I wrote right back that it was in great condition and *Make
me your best offer. Sincerely, Tom Lowe Jr.* But CJ hasn't written back.
The second was from a woman named Denise Joy Arnold. She
wrote that her sixteen-year-old son was depressed, but that he'd
shown an interest in building things. She went on to say that she
was a single mother and had no money, but could I recommend
which tools she should buy her son and would I mind if she paid
me in installments for "a few months"? I wrote back:

> *Dear Denise, I'm sorry to hear about your boy. I used to own a
> construction company, and if I was still healthy I would have
> hired your son to work for me. I would have been happy to teach
> him many things. But I got hurt, Denise. I got hurt, and I have no
> income and I need money to go see my own son. So, I'm sorry, but
> I can only sell to people who can pay me now. That said, maybe
> you could drive your son to a nearby construction site (make sure
> the builder is licensed), and ask if they'll take him on as a laborer.
> It's how I got started. Sincerely Yours, Tom Lowe Jr.*

It *was* how I got started. And since I was sixteen, I have
always worked.

And I still hope to, even if that means that my disability check
gets canceled. For three weeks about a year after moving to the 8, I
was an Uber driver, mainly for young men and women who'd had
too much to drink. This generation is so much more responsible
than mine was. They left their cars parked in lots behind the bars,
and they filled my Taurus with the smells of cologne or perfume
or beer or puke or those vapes they inhale, most of them staring at

their phones as I drove them wherever they wanted to go. But even with the wooden slats I placed on my driver's seat in my Taurus, I couldn't tolerate sitting for long.

For a while I worked at a standing job. A cashier at the Island of Convenience only two hundred yards from my unit. I worked the night shift because darkness outside my windows feels like me now, the sun an assault, and I enjoyed selling cigarettes and scratch tickets to the good working people of the world. I enjoyed wearing the company smock over my shirt announcing to anyone who entered that I could be trusted to take their money, I could be trusted to give them correct change and to smile even when my broken bones forced me to wince, my right foot on a short stool behind the counter.

I was never one to wear a harness. No roofer did unless it was an OSHA job. But until I fell it'd been a good day. It was early September, the sky as pure and cloudless as if all was forgiven, and from that three-story roof I could see over the tops of oaks and maples, their leaves just starting to turn, the slate-roofed spire of the Methodist church rising above the town's center.

Ronnie and I were only two months behind on our mortgage then, and I was sweating under my clothes, pulling one asphalt tile from its bundle as I was still setting down the one before it, lining it up quickly and nailing it off. The time of nail guns had come and there was a factory-efficient beauty to squeezing that trigger just once in both upper corners, each tile fastened down in seconds before moving on to the next. It would've been better if I could have hired some kid to hump the roofing bundles up and down the ladder for me, or to rent a lift, but the budget was the budget and if I was going to finish that roof on time I'd be able to drive straight to the bank with my check, which would bring me to being only one and a quarter payments behind.

That church spire towering over those trees behind me that afternoon, it felt like some reminder to me that this life of ours is suffused with mystery, and who's to say that I'm not supposed to learn something important from this latest challenge?

I was at the roof's edge. I'd just taken my hook blade to the roofing tile and sliced it in half along the edge of the tin flashing that ran up to the ridge. I glanced up at it to gauge how much farther I had to go, but the sun was on that flashing, a blinding green, and I shouldn't have turned then and reached for the next tile. I shouldn't have gone over three straight hours without water or a break. I shouldn't have been working alone. But *who's to say*? That phrase a feather in my head as my own body seemed to unmoor from its very center, and then the air itself shifted and I was somehow rushing through that air, my hands lurching for the soffit and the blue beyond as if they could possibly save me.

I tap my way back to what I wrote to "CJ" about giving me my best offer. Still nothing. Fitz told me that *I* should set the price, not my future buyers, and so I spend the rest of the morning clicking onto the photos of my own tools, writing down their exact models and trying to remember what year I bought them. If they're still being manufactured, I look up how much they cost now, new, and I cut that price in half. By the time I'm finished, I'm hungry and thirsty and need the bathroom. Outside my window it's raining again. I post all my prices, then add up how much I'd have if I sold every one of my tools: $3,650.

Wouldn't that be something? I haven't seen that kind of money since months before I got hurt over ten years ago, a thought that slices into old cuts still wet: after my fall I should have gotten a check from my insurance company for a cool one hundred thousand. But I hadn't been able to make the last two months' premium payments and so the company that specialized in taking care of self-employed men and women like me owed me nothing. Years of faithful payments and they owed me not one fucking thing. Nor was there any homeowners' insurance to help out because the bank that foreclosed on that house I was roofing was not considered a "mortgagee in possession."

And was there a human being I could have spoken to plead my case? Oh many. But they were usually young, well-meaning kids not long from having tossed their caps and gowns and were now working the front desks for well-dressed men in brick and glass buildings forever protected by the fine print on crooked contracts with suckers like me.

I need the toilet and I've been on this couch too long. If I stay too still for hours, even lying flat, the hip flames flare. But first I write back to CJ: *95$. Good as new—*

I'm about to close my laptop, but the Craigslist link comes up, and there's a new one from "Denise Joy Arnold."

You sound like a very nice man. I'm sorry you got hurt.

Kind Regards,

Denise

I write back: *Thank you.*

I rise slowly from the couch and climb the stairs and use the bathroom. *"Tom?"* Trina's voice rips up the stairwell like a shard of glass. "You haven't got your car back yet?"

"Nope."

"Fuck."

From the street come the low throttle sounds of a truck. I glance out my second-story window and see a U-Haul passing. I go slowly down the stairs, gripping the rails on the walls, pushing up to keep the weight off my hip screws.

Trina's smoking a cigarette. Her hair is wet. "I need to get to the food pantry."

Last night, stepping out onto the stoop for some air, I saw Trina's boyfriend Brian drive off in a Pontiac. It was the first time I'd seen him go anywhere that wasn't on foot.

"What about your boyfriend's car?" I move past Trina for my kitchenette.

"Brian?"

"I might have a can of soup." The light above my stove seems dimmer than usual. I pull open my cabinets: A can of beef broth. A can of creamed corn. A can of lima beans.

"He doesn't have shit. I'm fucking taking care of him now too." Trina leans against the fridge and blows out smoke. Her pajama bottoms are low on her hips and her feet are bare, each toenail painted a different color.

"What about the Pontiac?"

"That's his mother's and she friggin' needed it back." Trina pulls open my fridge and looks inside. Ash falls from the cigarette between her fingers onto my floor. "*One* egg?"

"It's yours if you want it. And these." I take the cans from the cupboard and set them on the counter.

Trina grabs the creamed corn. "Brian's jealous just cuz I have a new friend."

"Jamey?"

"And Shannon's being a little bitch again, Tommy."

"What's she doing?"

"She don't listen to me. She treats me—" Trina stands there, her eyes scanning the kitchenette like she just lost something precious. She lifts her cigarette to her lips and then she lowers it, and now she's trying to shake off the tears that are coming, both eyes squeezed shut as her shoulders heave up and down, and she's crying. "She fuckin' hates me, Tom. She really *hates* me."

I step in and hug her to me. "No, no, she doesn't hate you. Come on now."

"You don't see how she looks at me. She *hates* me. She hates me worse than I hated *my* mom." A wailing in my ear, Trina's wet hair against my nose, her braless breasts against my chest.

"You didn't hate your mom."

"I *did*. I still *do*. *Fuck*." She pulls back, my arm falls, and Trina's eyeliner has begun to run. She's looking straight into my face like she's just revealed some terrible secret. Then she's gone, my storm door slamming behind her. Through its smudged glass I can see that it has stopped raining and across the street the sun has opened up on Larry's Liquors and Dawn's Hair & Nails, the wet asphalt gleaming like fake jewels.

7

HALF AN HOUR LATER I'M SITTING ON THE DAMP CONCRETE OF my top step eating from a pan of lima beans. While they warmed on the stove I checked my email again, but there wasn't anything from Craigslist. I tell myself to be patient. I only just posted all of my prices. I need to—*what?* I can't even drive me and poor loveless Trina up Bridge Road to the food pantry. Never mind surprise my son with a birthday visit.

I jab the spoon into the beans and push some into my mouth, but I'm shaking my head and seeing Mike Andrews and his big house and enclosed pool. Now Trina's daughter Shannon—twelve? thirteen?—is crossing to this side of the street in tight jeans and a tight white sweater. Even from where I sit I can see the red of her lipstick, the dark pools of her eyes. When she reaches the roadway of the 8 she gives me the look she uses on her mother's boyfriends. Like I'm bad news. Like any man in the company of her mother can only be bad news.

A few minutes after Shannon goes inside, Trina's yelling and then her front door slams and she steps out onto her stoop just as a small rusted sedan pulls up front. The driver's door swings open and Jamey's standing there smiling at Trina. She's put on some eye makeup and blown her hair dry and she's wearing her pajama bottoms and hoodie sweatshirt, her feet in black sneakers I've never seen before. And I don't know how Trina could've called Jamey for help again when she doesn't own a phone.

She says something to him and then she's pulling open the passenger door, but just before she gets in she looks over at me on my step with my pan of beans. "Want anything from the pantry?"

"Steak au poivre with a béarnaise sauce?"

"You're weird."

Jamey smiles and nods at me before climbing behind his wheel.

As I watch him turn left and accelerate past the strip plaza, Trina just a profile in the shadows of Jamey's car, a cool ripple passes through my guts that's not quite jealousy but something close to it. Dread, maybe. The darkly dawning sense that something bad might just happen to somebody good. And I hope they're not off to steal more trash again.

It all started when Trina was sitting on my couch, smoking a cigarette and taking "a fucking break" from her kids, which is how she always puts it.

"Tommy?"

"Yeah?"

"Ever think of doing something bad?" Her tone was carefully neutral. "You know, to get someplace good?"

"Like what?"

She reached into the center pocket of her hoodie and snatched out something she slapped down onto my plank table.

"What's this?"

"Read it."

It was a stamped and opened business envelope. I picked it up. Typed on its front center, above her address, was the name: *Mrs. Anthony Bongiovanni.*

"How'd you get this?"

"The trash. When I was throwing mine in the dumpster."

"Trina, honey, you can't take people's mail."

"Read it, Tom."

I opened the letter and saw the words *Congratulations* and *excellent credit score* and *Pre-Approved* and *$10,000 limit* and the name of the bank that sent this to old Mrs. Bongiovanni. I dropped it onto my table, sat back, and looked up at Trina. Her arms were crossed, and she was tapping one foot, her lips in a straight and defiant line, though she looked like she was already waiting to be punished for something she hadn't done yet. "She's a thousand years old, Tom. Nothing will happen to her."

"Trina."

"What? She doesn't need it."

"She lives here with us. That means she has no money."

"Have you seen her, Tom?"

Yes. A tiny woman with a slightly humped back, her arm hooked in her son's as he guided her slowly to his shoe repair sedan for church. I nodded in the direction of the old woman's mail sitting there on my plank. "What're you going to do, sign it as her and wait for the card to come in the mail?"

"She's already approved, Tommy. I just put down my address."

"Trina."

"*What?* She won't even get in trouble, I looked it up. That bank has to pay for it, not her."

"The bank?"

"Yes, Tommy. Look it up. If it's stolen, it's not that old lady's fault."

Stealing from a bank. I thought of driving into the lobby of one, I even thought of driving up to Mike Andrews' high white home on his green, green grass. But not to rob him, just to be *seen* by him.

But not to steal from anyone. I had never thought of *that*.

"Trina, you don't think law enforcement will knock on the door of the address that was used to steal that card?"

"Then I'll put her address on it and watch her mailbox every fuckin' day. It comes like an hour before that nurse ever gets it for her." And then she explained how she could get the most money by buying gift cards with that stolen information and then selling them at a discount. "That's how you do it. I looked it up." Trina unfolded her arms and stared at me. Her lips parted and she looked like Ronnie did in those months when we were both still fighting to keep our home. Like she was counting on me to come up with something but blaming me at the exact same moment for never being able to.

"That's ten thousand dollars, Tommy. I could get a decent car with that, maybe a nice apartment. Pay for day care and get a job."

"Doing what for work?" I tried to keep my voice even, but it came out sounding like I had no faith in her, and I wanted to take it back. She crossed her arms again.

"I can work, Tom. Who do you think does everything over

there?" She jerked her head in the direction of my bookshelves and the wall behind it and the muffled machine-gun fire behind that. "Who do you think cleans and friggin' cooks and makes beds and washes clothes I have to carry in a fucking trash bag down to the Laundromat? Who sweeps the place? And mops? And has to still help Cody brush his teeth cuz he doesn't do it right? Who has to heat Brian something at two in the morning just cuz he's got the munchies because all he does is get high in front of his fucking video games? Who has to fuck just because somebody wants to fuck? And does he care if I'm still dizzy from the lab? What am I gonna do for *work*, Tommy? All I *do* is work." Her arms dropped and she snatched up Mrs. Bongiovanni's mail and was halfway down the hall, her voice like a fallen scarf on the floor. "I thought you were my friend."

After she left I lay on my plywood couch with my old laptop and did my own research on credit card theft. And yes, Trina was right about them being used to buy gift cards that were then sold for cash. There were whole YouTube shows made to protect the consumer against this kind of thing. But I left those videos and started reading articles on predatory behavior by the credit card companies themselves, and that's when I found something called "convenience checks." More and more now credit card companies were sending these to customers to cash right away, usually for the full line of credit. Fast money. But if the cardholder doesn't pay it back, the penalties are huge.

So much better than what Trina had planned. What was she going to do anyway? Walk along the streets with her new gift cards and knock on doors to sell them? She was right, too, about what would happen if someone's account number got stolen. The credit card company has to deal with that loss, not the victimized customer, who at the most might have to come up with a fifty-dollar fee. That would probably be quite a lot for Mrs. Bongiovanni, but what's fifty bucks to Mike and Kerry Andrews? A nickel for Trina? A dime for me?

I rest my pan of beans on the concrete and walk out onto the roadway toward the dumpsters and Fitz's place. My pelvis feels like a bundle of shattered bones. On Cal and Amber's front strip of grass are five plastic tombstones and a big pumpkin hanging from a hooked metal rod. I picture Cal driving that into the ground between his McDonald's and Walmart shifts.

Parked in front of Mrs. Bongiovanni's unit is her visiting nurse's Corolla, and I walk by it just as the nurse walks out of the unit. She's a tall woman in a down coat cinched at the waist, and she's carrying a canvas bag by its handle, her pocketbook hanging off one shoulder. Her eyes are on the phone screen in her hand so she doesn't at first see me standing there in the road, but when she does she stops, and only when I see her startled eyes do I begin to picture what I must look like, this big man who needs a shower and a shave in a loose sweater and wrinkled khakis, standing there sockless in untied work boots.

"How's she doing today?"

The nurse walks around to the back of her car. She opens her trunk, drops her canvas bag into it, and slams the lid. "I'm sorry, you *are* . . . ?"

"I'm her neighbor." I smile and gesture toward my unit in the 8. I want to tell her that I've lived here quite a while, but that I've never had the pleasure of meeting Mrs. Bongiovanni. The nurse pulls open her driver's door and swings her pocketbook onto the passenger seat. She turns to me. "Patient confidentiality. I'm sure you understand." Her tone is patronizing and now it hangs in the air like the smell of something rotten. Before she's fully seated in her clean little car, I say, "Yep, the Hippocratic oath and all that. First written in Ionic Greek, no?"

The nurse gives me a look of fear and pity and then she drives up to the dumpsters, where she turns around before driving past me standing in the middle of the road. At the bottom of the street in front of my unit, the nurse flicks on her right indicator, the small red light blinking like a silent alarm, and I yell, "Have you even fucking *heard* of Ionic *Greek*?!"

Trina's front door opens and Shannon steps out. She's eating from a bag of potato chips, the generic kind that people donate to the pantry where her mother is heading right now, if she's not pulled over in Jamey's car somewhere getting high first. "Why aren't you in school, Shannon? Isn't it a goddamned school day?"

Shannon stops chewing. She looks like she wants to say something, but then she disappears inside and I'm knocking on Fitz's door. It's a futile gesture, I know, because Fitz's Mustang is gone, but maybe Fitz's last foster father wants at least the three cordless drills. There's the shadowed memory of Fitz in my basement as he held his phone over those DeWalts, then snapped a picture. Then Fitz took many other pictures. Somewhere behind me a dog barks. In the air are the smells of fresh garbage and the sadly festive scent of dead leaves. I'm aware that I can see my own breath, a shiver rippling across my chest. Stuck to Fitz's door is a square decal, white with black lettering: *This Residence Is Protected by Smith & Wesson.* In the middle of this pronouncement is the silhouette of a revolver, the kind cops used to carry. I've never owned a gun, but on my lone walk back to my unit, my hip screws beginning to melt, the image of that revolver keeps floating through my head.

8

IT'S JUST AFTER NIGHTFALL AND I SWITCH ON MY STAND-UP LAMP, lie carefully back onto my plywood couch, and check my email again. Nothing. I open my *Sent* folder to make sure that I did, in fact, send CJ that price of $95. I did. I stare at the screen-saver image of my beautiful young wife and son. Then I open my *Banks* folder and scroll through stories of the one and only banker to go to jail for his part in the calamity that was 2008, Kareem Serageldin of the Investment Banking Division of Credit Suisse. His friends say that he was a man who made millions of dollars a year, lived alone, worked long hours, and felt genuinely contrite about inflating the value of his bonds to make them look valuable when they'd actually lost over one hundred million dollars. It was hard to hate a man who felt real remorse for his crimes, but why hadn't one other bank executive been punished? Not one.

I tap my way to the public Facebook photos of Mike Andrews and his family. His boy is blond like mom, while the girl has Mike's slightly darker hair. There are color photos of his house, or at least pictures of him shirtless under the sun on a tractor mower on the green lawn of that house. Rising up behind him, it's a three-story gabled obscenity, its roof spotted with copper-flashed sky-lights and covered with sand-colored architectural shingles, its mullioned windows tall, their sills gleaming with a baked white finish. In other photos there is the swimming pool, Kerry Andrews in a summer dress holding a cocktail in the shade of the cabana.

This one I have returned to many times. Lying back on her chaise lounge, she's smiling into the camera, her sun-bleached hair newly styled and touching her shoulders. Kerry Andrews is clearly a lovely woman, but this isn't why I keep staring at her. No, it's because she has stolen the expression Ronnie used to carry and then didn't anymore. A face of celebratory accomplishment. A face of hard-earned contentment.

Ronnie had never been more beautiful than when she was earning her master's degree, planning to study for her license to hang a shingle and counsel people who had lost their way. We hosted summer dinner parties out on our back deck overlooking the marsh, and Ronnie would be tanned and muscled from her daily kayaking out on the basin, her eyes bright with the kind of self-sustaining joy that came from living a full life. One of our dinner guests had been a classmate of Ronnie's father's, but instead of pursuing a life of the mind like his friend Wyn, he had pursued the making of money. A lot of it. The man's name was Gordon, and he wore a blue silk shirt, his Mercedes sedan parked out in my gravel driveway. Before dinner—steak tips I'd been marinating for two hours—Gordon and I strolled out to the edge of my lawn. It was a patch of grass in a bed of pine needles really, and we both stood there and stared out over the open marsh. This Gordon was an inch or two taller than I was and twenty years older, and he carried himself like someone used to giving soft-spoken commands to underlings in skyscrapers overlooking bustling ports of commerce. Ronnie referred to him as one of her father's "bling-bling friends," but what was so strange about that moment standing with Bling-Bling Gordon and looking out at the July sun setting into the marsh is that he seemed to see me as an equal.

He turned to me and said, "I envy you."

"Me?"

"Yes, you make things."

Soon I was cooking steak tips on the grill, turning each one, and then I squinted at the smoke and when I opened my eyes I was lying on my rented adjustable bed in my living room, no longer able to make things ever again.

Those lost days, I found myself thinking a lot about my parents. Unlike me, my father was a small man with a small face and deep eyes, but what I remember most clearly are his hands because his right was missing two fingers. I was told he lost them in an accident at the warehouse, but my father also put his money down on the dogs and dice and any other game of chance he could find, and when I got older and asked my mother if my dad really lost his fingers at work, she'd change the subject. Once, she may have said something about my father's bad habits, but she had a weakness for men with bad habits.

One could never call my mother a beautiful woman, but there was a kind of practical sensuality to her that seemed to draw men. Norman was the first. He was her customer at Carla's Copy Center, the job she took and kept after our father drove to the warehouse one morning and never came back.

But Norman drank. And Norman smoked. And Norman yelled at me and Charlie and then he slapped our mother and she hit him in the head with a glass casserole dish that shattered and one day Norman was gone. When I was twelve or thirteen along came Frank, a man she'd met on her night out with the copy center's bowling team. He was a round insurance salesman who wore red ties over white shirts, the buttons straining at his gut, and he called me Mick and Charlie Dick and he spent a lot of time eating Kentucky Fried Chicken he'd bring us before dozing on the couch in front of the TV long after we'd all gone to bed. He was on the road a lot, and when he was away for days it was like our mother was a drooping plant who'd suddenly been given water and light.

After Frank came Steve, my favorite because he was kind and had gone to college and taught music at the technical high school. Steve was already losing his hair but kept what he still had pulled into a ponytail, his narrow face covered with blond whiskers, his wire-rimmed glasses holding lenses that magnified his eyes so that he often looked to me like a benevolent animal of some kind, one who got our mother to enjoy pot and acoustic music and even books, or at least the idea of them, because he always had a few in his canvas satchel. When I was fifteen—spending my afternoons drinking stolen beer with my friends under the train trestle, stealing snack food from the grocery store, sticking our heads into unlocked cars looking for whatever we could find, once a pistol we shot in the woods, then threw into the dumpster behind the liquor store—one night Steve handed me a copy of Hermann Hesse's *Siddhartha*.

"In the shade of the house, in the sunshine of the riverbank near the boats, in the shade of the Sal-wood forest, in the shade of the fig tree is where Siddhartha grew up."

Reading that sentence for the first time in the small bedroom I shared with Charlie, it was as if I were reading about myself: *In the shade of the house, in the sunshine of the highway near the droning automobiles, in the shade of the pine trees, in the shade of the dead-end street is where Tom Lowe Jr. grew up.* Siddhartha and his search for who he was meant to be, it was *me* on that river, it was *me* on those banks, and it was *me* who began to see books as doorways to worlds that could only help me rise in this one.

And I did rise. I sure as hell did, though books didn't have much to do with it, and Steve, whom I think about now and then and feel only grateful to, was carrying on with one of his students at the technical high school, a dark-haired girl who drove onto our patch of grass drunk one night in her Ford Pinto, rising out of it in her denim jacket and ripped jeans, screaming, "Steve's fucking me, too, you stupid fucking *bitch*!"

There was a commotion then, one that lasted for days, and then Steve too was gone. The Lowe family was once again living in a period between men who were unworthy of our mother, and it was not so unusual for her to make us saltine and butter sandwiches for dinner, to choose to pay for oil in the burner instead of the rent, many times our landlord knocking loudly at the front door that *he* clearly owned, and not us.

For years I feared the ghost of that man knocking on my own door. Even when I was flush. Even when times were far better than good. And so when he finally did show up, I was like the man living on death row for years who wakes up one morning to the key turning in the lock, almost a relief descending, a certain sort of peace.

That's what the O brought me. It calmed me by cooling the fires, but then after weeks or maybe months there came my feeling that there were forces in the house who weren't friendly.

Three times a day I made myself slide out of my adjustable bed to use my walker. I'd gotten so weak that I had to stop every few feet to catch my breath, my arms shaking, my heart shooting off like a drunk with a nail gun. But I wasn't drunk. I was floating on the Lake of O.

I could not call Ronnie's loss of love for me a sudden thing. She cried next to my bed and she told me to get help and she called my doctors to stop the Os from coming into our house. But there was always a way and I would find it, and now there was Frank sitting at our kitchen table in front of the wall of windows, my mother's former boyfriend Frank. He wore a white shirt and a red tie and he was eating from a plate of Kentucky Fried Chicken. "Hey, Mick."

"What are you doing in my house, Frank?" Maybe I didn't say that, but I thought it. Frank wiped grease from his chin with a napkin. "It's not your house, Mick. It's the bank's. Forget to pay your bills?"

"I got hurt. Can't you see I'm hurt?"

Frank shook his head and bit into a chicken breast, its skin hanging. "You screwed up, Mick. You and Dick, your mother was too soft on you boys. Now look at you."

"Get out of my house."

"*Your* house?"

"Get out of my fuckin' house!"

"Dad?"

It was Drew. He'd just come in from outside. One of his friends stood in the doorway behind him. Ian? Casey? And they were both staring at me leaning on my walker like I'd just strangled a small animal in front of them.

"Are you okay, Dad?"

So sincere, that question. Drew's voice high and scared and wanting only to help. How many times had I heard that sound and those words from my son? And I used this to make him complicit. Anything to help his daddy. Anything to help him get better.

This was late fall, early winter. Outside the wall of windows the hardwoods were bare, their black branches sticking into the evergreens like swords. To the south the long grasses of the marsh were wind-flattened and the color of unwashed hair, the sky gray for days. Except for one white afternoon in October it hadn't yet snowed and I could no more imagine being out there than I could will myself to roll across a field planted with mines.

Though inside wasn't so wonderful either. Frank had refused to leave and soon my father came along, though he rarely said a word, just sat on the lowest step of the staircase sipping from a Dunkin' Donuts coffee cup, his missing fingers barely able to hold it. He was dressed in his warehouse clothes—a sweatshirt and Dickies work pants and steel-toed boots—and sometimes he turned into my brother Charlie and he'd smile over at me sadly with his small face and deep narrow eyes, like we'd all planned something beautiful and look what you did, Tom? *Look.*

Don't tell Mom, okay buddy? We don't want her to worry.

But even with my leaden vision and O-thickened blood, Drew's loving help cut into me, and then my father asked me just what I thought I was doing. He was leaning over the stair railing looking down at his grown son, and it occurred to me, lying there staring up into my dead father's face, that I was twenty years older.

"I'm in pain, Dad. Can't anybody see that? I'm in pain."

My father shrugged. "Who isn't?"

"Tom?" The storm door slams behind Trina and she walks into my kitchenette. I hear her set something heavy onto my countertop, then comes the squeak of my cabinet door hinge and the rustle of paper and the clank of one can after another being stacked onto my cabinet shelves. "I got you creamed *corn.*"

I want to tell her that I actually hate creamed corn but instead I thank her. I tap myself away from Kerry Andrews' favorite book, *The Cider House Rules,* and her favorite musician, Jackson Browne, and her favorite movie, *It's Complicated,* and her favorite sport, which I don't even glance at because my fingertips burn and the fires are raging deep between my hip bones and Trina is standing at the end of my plank table holding my pan of lima beans out to me. "You left this outside, Tom. Can I dump it?" Her tone is more of a tease than a scold, and in the dim light of my lamp Trina's hair seems thicker, her cheeks flushed, her eyes softer somehow.

"I need to get my fucking car back, Trina."

"No shit." She walks into my kitchen and turns on the faucet. She says something over the running water, but I can only hear a few words. *Nice* and *sweet* and *fuckin' Brian*. I open my email and there's a new one from Craigslist: *What will you take for all of these? —Cesar Ramirez*

All of these? There's a tremor in my fingertips and I start to type *$3650*, but then I delete that and write, or try to write because my hands are filled with a throbbing electrical current: *$3500 for the whole inventory. These are very well-maintained tools, and I'm probably selling them cheaper than I should.* Should I write that? Why not? It's the truth. Jesus, $3,500, could this be *possible*?

But they're yours if you can meet this price.

Though I'd probably go as low as $3,000, maybe even $2,750. But don't look desperate. Don't show him your desperation. *Sincerely, Tom Lowe Jr.*

"Tom? Did you hear me?" Trina's calling down to him from his entryway. "They had ice cream. I put some in your fridge." Then comes the slam of the door and almost immediately Cesar Ramirez responds: *Will you take 3200?*

I don't even have to think about this. *They're yours.*

Three *thousand* two hundred dollars. I'll be able to get my car back and still have twelve hundred left over. I picture myself taking Drew and a group of his closest friends out to the nicest place in Amherst. A steakhouse maybe, some low-lit establishment that serves juicy prime ribs on thick platters. I picture myself being able to rent a room for the night in some B&B under pine trees, me and my son sitting on the porch drinking coffee or tea. Drew's turning twenty and it's time that I told him a few things about this life, something that might truly help him.

Can you deliver them to our shop in Lawrence? —C. Ramirez

Mr. Ramirez,

I'm afraid I can't do that. I'm disabled, which is why I have to sell my tools. But I'm just down the road in Amesbury. Can you pick them up? —Tom Lowe Jr.

A flame flares along the shaft of my screw. It's time for some liquid relief. I have just enough EBT cash to buy one more bottle, and why isn't Ramirez writing back?

No problem. Is tomorow night good?

I notice how the word *tomorrow* is misspelled. I ignore this. *Perfect. I'm at 21 Hampton Terrace over in Amesbury. Please bring a cashier's check or cash.* Writing these last four words has made my hands hover over the keyboard like I'm praying.

Ramirez writes back: *Your phone number?*

Should I admit that I don't have a phone? If a man doesn't own a phone, how well maintained can his tools be?

It's being fixed. But you can find me at this email address if you get lost.

On the other side of my wall comes yelling, Brian this time.

I'll send my sons over at six.

I'll be here, Mr. Ramirez. You'll be happy with the quality of these tools. But my hands are still shaking and I have to type that last line three times. *Yours, Tom Lowe Jr.*

I close my laptop and drop my head back against the armrest and I stare at the water-stained ceiling. *Three thousand two hundred dollars.* Jesus *Christ.* And day after tomorrow I'll ask Fitz for a ride to the DMV and then Kelly's Towing, though it's too bad Ramirez can't come tonight and save me another fifty in storage robbery. But this isn't the time for petty greed. This is the time for gratitude and for celebration, and no generic pain distracter tonight, no way.

Trina's screaming. Something hard knocks against the wall, but her screaming goes on without a break so I know that something got thrown and it wasn't her. This probably has to do with the kid who drove us to Mike Andrews' town and then to the food pantry, this Jamey who has somehow made Trina look soft and happy. For a second, as I pull on my old work boots and leave the laces untied, I think about knocking on Trina's door to try to make peace between her and her tattoo artist boyfriend. But what wisdom can *I* give? I stand and reach for my coat and shake my head over and over again: *three thousand two hundred dollars.*

9

LARRY WORKS THE REGISTER TONIGHT AND HE SEEMS HAPPY TO see me and so I'm tempted to tell him my good news. But Larry doesn't look so good. The skin of his face seems to sag a bit and his eyes are rheumy, and Beethoven's *Moonlight* Sonata plays above all those bottles of liquor and wine like some melancholic warning.

"You doing all right, Larry?"

"Never better, Tom. Never better."

On my walk back across the street I can only admire the older man's spitting into the mortal winds, and I remind myself that except for the hip fires that burn inside me daily and nightly, I still have my health and I should be grateful for that. I should be grateful for many things. This sale of my tools, number one. No, my son Drew, number one. That I *have* a son. That despite everything, I still have Drew. And the 8. Walking up my concrete steps with my bottle of good vodka from Poland, I tell myself that even though this is a refuge for rejects like me, every room a square cell in a block of square cells, all of it covered with loose and cracked vinyl siding, its windows cheap and drafty, it's shelter even I can afford and that's no small thing.

In my kitchen I pour the vodka into a clean coffee cup, though my ice tray is empty next to my sink. I'm surprised Trina didn't refill it for me when she washed my pan earlier, because even with the chaos that seems to make up so much of her life, she's bothered by loose ends—dirty pans left outside, Cody's Big Wheels left in the street.

On my way to my plywood couch, I grab one of my neglected books from its shelf. It's a thick hardcover, and once I'm settled under my lamp I open to the middle of the book and read: "Bless you prison, bless you for being in my life. For there, lying upon the rotting prison straw, I came to realize that the object of life is not prosperity as we are made to believe, but the maturity of the human soul." —Aleksandr Solzhenitsyn

The maturity of the human soul. I close the book and read its cover. *The Gulag Archipelago.* There comes the wispy memory of a professor on the Amherst campus, a clean-shaven and sallow Italian who wore suits that were too big for him, his accent heavy, and between his tirades about social injustice he'd stare out the window for long minutes without saying a word. This book had to have come from his class. And it comes to me that I, too, am an *exile.*

But why does someone have to be stripped of prosperity to fully mature? Why is suffering the only way? What about my happy hand-built home in the pines overlooking the marsh? By rising up in the material world, not through swindling and deceit, but from hard, honest work, I'd, yes, matured.

And then it was all taken away from me. It was—nope; I remind myself that I'm celebrating tonight. I sip my vodka and swallow its sweet silver flames. *Three thousand two hundred dollars.*

After getting my car back I'll drive myself someplace I haven't been in years. A mall. I'll take a long shower and shave and I'll wear clean clothes and socks and I'll tie my shoes and then I'll be walking down those wide, shiny corridors to buy my twenty-year-old son something he can really use. But *what*?

That summer day Drew drove up with his girlfriend to the 8. He was between his junior and senior years at Trevors Academy, where his grandparents still taught, but because Ronnie didn't also work there she had to pay the full forty-five thousand a year for Drew, a fact she reminded me of whenever she could, I who couldn't offer much at all. I couldn't even afford lunch with him at Applebee's, a court-ordered social worker sipping her decaf coffee six feet away. I was O-less for quite a while then, but it still wasn't long enough for the judge, who'd found my "history of drug addiction, erratic behavior, and poor judgment" to be a danger to my own child.

There came a knocking on my storm door. "Hello?" It was the voice of a young man and it was like hearing the voice of an ancestor.

"Knock again." A girl's voice this time. Warm and eager. By now I sat up. I rubbed my face and stood. There came three more knocks and I ignored my walker and made my way to my front door, where on the other side of the plexiglass stood my tall, beautiful son, his dark hair—Ronnie's—blown back from his tanned face, his lovely girlfriend standing beside him. It'd been months since I had last seen him in the booth of an Applebee's.

"Look at you." That's what came out of me as I reached for the door handle, the cheerful tone of a man who sees his son all the time, who cares for him consistently, who talks to him every night before going to bed. Not this jobless bum on a plywood couch in the 8 he'd lain on for four days straight.

"Hi."

"Come in, come in." I pushed open the door, but my face warmed at the mess waiting. "Never mind, this place is a dump. Let's go sit outside."

And so the three of us sat on the concrete stoop under the late afternoon sun. Trina's youngest, Cody, was riding his Big Wheels tricycle in the roadway. Then skinny MJ, his older brother, got behind Cody and pushed him so fast toward the dumpsters that Cody couldn't keep his feet on the pedals, and now he was screaming and MJ was laughing and calling his brother a little faggot. Drew's girlfriend watched them with what looked to be horror and fascination and then a compassionate sadness. Her small shoulders were tanned. Sitting close to her, I could smell sun lotion and shampoo. Around her neck was a thin gold chain and I wondered if my son had given it to her.

Drew was standing and talking about how many miles to the gallon his Camry parked across the street got, how it only had thirty thousand miles on it when "we" bought it. And it was hard not to picture who that "we" was, Ronnie's new husband Ed, a man of means chumming it up with my one and only son, who looked to me that afternoon in front of my stoop to be the very vision of love and hope. I couldn't stop staring at his high cheekbones and deep eyes, at his slightly crooked lower teeth, at his broad shoulders and long torso, his big feet in blue flip-flops. And

Drew was clearly nervous. He was talking too fast and he kept glancing from his girlfriend Hanna to his father, then back out at his first car.

I said, "I should've bought you that."

Drew looked like he'd just been slapped. His lips parted and he stared down at Hanna, and it was as if my son had been running happily up a hill and his own father had pushed him back down it. "No, that's a good car. I'm glad you have it."

Drew nodded and looked away from us both. MJ had stolen Cody's Big Wheels and was riding it like a scooter, bending down to hold the handlebars while kicking up speed with his free leg, Cody crying and running after him. Then their sister Shannon, who'd been sitting on the concrete steps, walked into the center of the road. She was wearing denim shorts and a red halter top, and when MJ came speeding by she backhanded him sideways onto the asphalt, the Big Wheels skidding into the dirt.

MJ pushed himself up and pressed one hand to his cheek, his eyes filling. "You cunt!"

Drew looked like he felt he should do something, but then Trina came running barefoot down the steps in her pajama bottoms and an inside-out T-shirt. "Goddamn you kids! Can't I take a fucking nap for once in my *life*?" She rushed out into the road, grabbed MJ by the arm, and jerked him to his feet. "What'd you do, Shannon?"

"She *hit* me."

Cody had already picked up his Big Wheels and was climbing back into its seat. "MJ was being mean again."

"Shannon, I asked you a fucking *question*."

But Shannon, a lip of baby fat pushing over the hem of her shorts, was already walking down to the street.

"Where do you think you're going? Get in the fucking *house*! Shannon!"

But her daughter was soon out of sight and Trina was barefoot on the warm asphalt, Cody already pedaling past her up toward the dumpsters, and now Trina's boyfriend came out on the stoop shirtless. "Everything cool?"

"MJ, get in the goddamn house." Trina pushed her son in the

back and MJ took his time walking up the steps past his mother's new boyfriend Ricky, who'd be gone before the leaves fell.

Drew turned to me. His expression was filled with pity and confusion: *Why are you here? Why?* But then his girlfriend seemed to remember something and she said: "Let me take a picture of you two." She stood and held out her hand for Drew's phone, but after he gave it to her he just stood there, staring over at Trina and her boyfriend sharing a beer on her stoop, and it became clear to me that coming to see me that afternoon was probably Drew's girlfriend's idea and not my son's.

I said, "Come sit next to your old man."

Drew sat.

"Get closer, you guys."

That's when Drew put his arm around my shoulders and leaned in, but it was like my son was holding his breath and just waiting for this to be over with, and why *wouldn't* he feel this way?

That night I emailed Drew's address, which my son had had since his freshman year of high school.

Dear Drew, it was really good to see you again today. I know you're mad at me and I don't blame you. But I couldn't take those supervised visits anymore. I know this past March the judge said we were free and clear of them, but I was tired—really disgusted at myself—for not being able to take you to even a cheap lunch somewhere. I guess I was starting to give up then. I didn't write that I often felt Drew had a better father now anyway, that maybe my son would be better off if I just drifted away, something Ronnie must've agreed with because she'd only sent me one email all those months, "Your son misses you." *I did try to get out of that darkness, though. I got a job at the gas station up the street, but it turns out I can't even work a cash register for half a shift. But seeing you, well, it's given me quite a lift. Can I take you out for an ice cream or something? —Love—Your Dad*

A day later Drew wrote back. *Yeah, okay.*

It was just the two of us. The sun was down, but it was still hot, the sky streaked with rose-colored clouds. My son and I sat at a dirty picnic table eating ice cream cones that were melting too fast. A dozen or so men, women, and kids stood in a line under the fluorescent lights of the takeout windows, and from across the street came the amplified rock and roll of the mini golf course. The halogen lights had come on, and a young family of four were taking turns whacking their balls into the mouth of a blue whale.

Drew was still in his work clothes from the grounds crew of Trevors Academy—cargo shorts and a polo shirt with the academy's insignia embroidered over his heart. When it was time to pay for our cones Drew reached for his wallet, but I touched my son's wrist and pulled out what little EBT cash I had left for the month. Then I gave seven dollars to the pretty teenager who'd served us, seven bucks that could've gotten me three cans of soup.

Now my chocolate walnut ice cream was dripping down my forearm and the screws in my hips were beginning to heat and I wanted to stand but stayed put. Drew hadn't said much. I said, "That Hanna's lovely."

Drew licked his ice cream cone. "I showed her our old house."

"You tell her I built it?"

"Yeah."

"That why you showed it to her? So she'd know I wasn't always a bum?"

Drew shrugged. "You got hurt. It wasn't your fault."

"No?" It was hard to talk then or to swallow my ice cream or to still be looking at my son, who'd grown so much so fast without me. I wanted to tell him that the worst part of it all was not being able to provide for him, my only child. I wanted to tell him that it *was* my fault I had fallen. It was my fault because I got greedy. I bought land and then I wanted a perfect house on that land. It was my fault because I didn't take the time to study the fine print of my loan papers. It was my fault because I didn't take into account that my work, even in the good years, never had a guarantee of being steady.

Tacked to my bathroom wall is that photo of me and Drew that his girlfriend Hanna took. Drew has his arm around his old man, and while I look pale and pasty, my thinning hair matted on one side, my whiskers almost white, Drew is lean and tanned, his dark hair windblown from the beach where he and his girlfriend had been all day.

A week after taking this, she drove up to the 8 and knocked on my unlocked door and handed me a small white bag from CVS. Her curly hair was pulled up and she looked both lovelier to me and younger too. She was smiling almost shyly at me. "Drew really likes this picture of you guys. I made you both a copy."

Then she was driving off in her small Audi before I could even really thank her or ask if she'd like a glass of water or to come inside. Hours later, lying on my plywood couch, I kept thinking of her and I didn't know why. But then Trina walked in to get away from her kids, to smoke a cigarette and complain about the "fucking asshole" boyfriend she had then, and I knew why I couldn't stop thinking of my son's girlfriend; she was an abundist like Ronnie, her young and healthy presence clearly loved, which made her, therefore, so very loving.

In the photo, Drew is smiling, yes, and his arm is around his father's shoulders, but it's the managed smile someone would have in the presence of a stranger. In Drew's eyes is the dark light of some kind of confused hurt, that and an almost defiant resignation.

And how could that not have come from what I made him do when he was only a kid? I'd just sold my van for eleven thousand dollars to Teddy Griffin, my quiet and competent excavator from more joyful times. But I told Ronnie I only got nine thousand for it, which I asked her to give to Wyn and Nancy, who'd lent us more than that. Then I asked Teddy to write me a check for that amount but to give me the extra two thousand in cash.

"Why cash?"

"For my pain pills, Teddy. Know anyone?"

Teddy did, and soon Drew was running out into the cold with the three hundred dollars his father had just slipped him, Teddy's van driving away and Drew rushing back inside, his cheeks reddened, his wool Patriots cap pulled over his ears, a baggie of little white Os in his outstretched hand like a gift he'd been saving up to give his father for years.

"Don't tell Mom, okay buddy? We don't want her to worry."

And Drew nodded with the grateful gravity of a boy who'd been given a man's job, and now I squeeze my eyes shut and try to shake that image out of my head. I take a long pull off my vodka and Trina's yelling again, this time at her two sons, and the gunfire and explosions stop. What I need to do is leave this place. After I get my car back I should take that extra twelve hundred and put it down on a room in someone's house. That's all I need. Just one room with a sink and a toilet in a quiet house owned by some old widow or widower. Someone who doesn't yell at their kids or play loud video games or get tattoos "down low." But I've looked for places before, the same way I've looked for work, and all I've gotten is closed doors.

But I shouldn't be thinking of myself anyway.

Before he turned eighteen, Drew got some of my disability check every month after my rent was deducted, just over two hundred dollars. But now he's no longer eligible and my check is smaller, but on the day it comes in, I buy a money order for a hundred dollars and push it into an envelope with a note: *I wish I could send you more, son.* Or *For a six-pack or a meal.* Or *Work hard, buddy. And have fun.* Then I write my son's name and address on the envelope and I stamp it and drop it into the mailbox near the front door of the Island of Convenience. It isn't much, but this small monthly act feels to me like I'm laying one stone at a time across a dark, flowing stream back to my son.

Right now I just need to think of Drew, of celebrating twenty years of Drew Lowe.

10

TRINA MOVES DOWN THE HALLWAY AND LEANS AGAINST THE wall. Between her two fingers is an unlit cigarette, her Bic lighter in the fist of her other hand. Her pajama bottoms are low on her hips and there's a dark stain on her hoodie sweatshirt. She tucks a strand of hair behind her ear.

"You all right, Trina?"

"I kicked Brian out."

"Really?"

She nods at his empty coffee cup. "Your pain distracter?"

"No, just good vodka. I'm celebrating."

"Can I have some?" Trina grabs my cup, then goes into my kitchen. I hear her rummaging in the cabinet for a clean glass. "Don't you have anything I can mix this with?"

"Nope."

Outside a car drives by loud and fast, a police cruiser maybe. I glance down at my plank table. Beside *The Gulag Archipelago* lies the young cop's fines and the crumpled card for Kelly's Towing and Storage. "I'm getting my car back, Trina. I can drive you to the plasma lab if you want."

No, after I cash that check I'll *give* her some of my money. Just a gift. When's the last time anyone did anything really good like that for Trina?

Jamey, Trina looking genuinely happy when she came back from the food pantry.

"And no *ice*?"

"'Fraid not."

"Fuckin' Tom."

How about a hundred? That'd be almost four trips to the lab and back.

She walks in from the kitchenette holding my cup and her glass.

She hands me mine. She's poured me twice as much as I did earlier and some of it sloshes onto my wrist. She lights her cigarette and sits on the plywood next to me and takes a deep drag. Inside her glass is a white liquid.

"I used some of your milk."

"I have milk?"

"I fuckin' brought you some. Didn't you see?"

I shake my head and sip my Belvedere and try to ignore that Trina mixed this good vodka with milk. But when did I become a snob?

Trina blows out smoke, then drinks down a third of her drink. "He fuckin' hit me."

"Brian?"

"Nobody fuckin' hits me."

"When, Trina?"

"Which time?"

"He's hit you more than once?"

"I told you, no one fuckin' hits me." Her voice breaks and she blows out smoke and looks off to the corner of the room. Her hair is still full from washing it earlier, her face soft with a resigned sadness, and I think how in another life she would've been beautiful.

"Why didn't you tell me, Trina? Or call the cops?"

"Oh *please*. I got rid of him myself. Three strikes and you're out, motherfucker." She looks down at me on the couch like I just appeared there from a dream she was having. "You got your car back?"

"I will soon. I sold my tools, hon. All of 'em. I'll be able to go see my son for his birthday."

"But where's your car?"

"I'm picking it up day after tomorrow. Fitz'll drive me over."

"Fitz moved, Tom."

"Moved? When?"

"Today. Didn't you see his U-Haul?"

"I don't think so." I drink from my vodka and feel slightly abandoned. Fitz posting pictures of my tools for me. I was looking forward to thanking him for helping to sell them.

"Somebody new's moving in tomorrow."

"Do we know who?"

"Just more losers like us." Trina blows smoke out the side of her mouth. "Tom?"

"Yeah, hon?"

"You think I'm pretty?"

"Yes." My face heats up and I drink again.

"No you don't."

"That's not true, Trina. You're a lovely young woman. I've told you that before."

"When?"

"I can't remember, but I have. Where did Fitz move to?"

"Brian called me a fat ugly bitch."

"He's a piece of shit, Trina."

"Jamey says I should get my GED and go to college."

"I agree."

"But I'm bad in school, Tom."

"Bad how?"

Trina sips from her vodka milk. Her face is pale and her silver cross and blue star earrings look outclassed by her clean hair. "I could never concentrate. I think I have ADHD, just like my—my *kids.*" She begins to cry and I set my glass down and stand, my hip screws shifting, and then I'm holding her to me for the second time today.

"What am I *doing*, Tom?" She leans her cheek against my chest and I stroke her hair and rub her rising and falling back.

"You need a plan, honey. You need a plan to get out of this place."

11

I'M IN MY OLD NEW HOUSE AND THERE'S A PARTY GOING ON OUT on the porch, but I'm inside with Trina and I'm leading her by the hand, both of us looking for a place to make love. Sometimes it's summer outside, the sun high over the marsh and water and pines, and sometimes it's winter, snow falling, but always there's that party out there, Ronnie holding forth with a glass of red wine in her hand, laughing or giving a toast, and then Trina's on top of me on my adjustable bed, her pajama bottoms off, my pants pulled to my ankles, and it feels wrong what we're doing. Trina's moving as slowly and carefully as Ronnie did our very last time, but instead of being afraid that we're going to get caught, I keep reaching for the ledge behind a riser where I keep my baggie of Os. Then Drew's clomping down those very stairs, only he's not a boy anymore, he's Drew as a young man, tanned from the beach, his lovely abundist girlfriend standing beside him and holding his hand as they both watch me and Trina do it on my adjustable bed, Trina crying, her hips bucking, her tears warm as blood on my face.

I open my eyes to bright sun across my ceiling. I'm cold and my mouth is a cave of dust and I hope that Trina and I didn't do anything. Pissing in my toilet, my right hip screw scraping into bone, I have a flash of seeing her walk down my dark hallway, her clean hair bouncing against her hoodie. I rinse my hands in cold water and drink four handfuls.

So long since I've been with a woman. Ronnie. My lovely broken Ronnie.

The afternoon she told me, my most recent trip down O River was coming to an end. Except for a bloat in my gut that I knew was chronic constipation brought on by the O, my head was fairly clear. I even just did four laps to the kitchen and back, pausing only twice to catch my breath and stare out at the snow on the marsh. We had five weeks left before our eviction, and I'd been asking Ronnie for weeks if she'd had any luck finding a first-floor apartment for us because I had not, the O and my hip fires keeping me from concentrating on my laptop or the newspaper for more than a few minutes at a time.

That was the plan. The day we got our letter of default Ronnie cried and dropped it on my chest like it was evidence of something very ugly about me and me only. "You *sabotaged* us, Tom." And she went on about my subconscious and my fear of success and "projection" this and "complex" that, and I couldn't disagree with anything she said.

Then she climbed the stairs and slammed the bedroom door and kept crying on the bed we hadn't yet paid for.

But she didn't cry for long. She dried her eyes and wiped her face, and then she began to sell whatever we *had* paid for: our living room set, our kitchen stools (a walnut and black iron set that we'd bought together at a shop in Maine). We would just start over, that's all. We would mourn what we'd lost—which was nearly unbearable to think too much about—but we'd move on. Ronnie was beginning to make a decent income, enough for an apartment anyway. And Wyn had offered me help to finish my degree. Maybe I could find a teaching job at some local high school or middle school, a helper of the scarcitists.

I was sweating from my laps and still standing with the help of the walker, thirsty and thinking of a visit to the toilet, when Ronnie came into the house and poured herself a glass of red wine, though there was no place for her to sit and enjoy it—the dining room table and chairs gone, the sofa set that used to face the wall of windows gone, even that oak bench in the foyer—gone.

"We need to talk." Ronnie was wearing a black turtleneck sweater that used to cling to her. Her hair had gotten longer too, held loosely in the back with a barrette, and she was looking directly at me, her chin up, which unnerved me because she looked so beautiful but also so very far away.

My face began to warm. I was sure that she'd found my stash wedged under a stair tread where I could reach it from my bed.

I wanted water and I wanted to lie down. But now Ronnie's eyes were filling and she wouldn't look away from me. Then she dabbed at her eyes with her fingertips and swallowed wine and looked out the windows at the white marsh, at its exposed reeds bent under some unseen weight. "I'm seeing someone."

Seeing someone. Funny how wrongly I first heard this. Over the months I had come to see my wife as what she'd become professionally, a therapist, a fixer of other people's problems. And *of course* she needed to see someone herself: we had problems of our own. Catastrophic ones at that. And I wasn't much help. I knew that. But I still saw all of this as a simple setback, a big and terrible one, yes, but I still believed that one day the pain was going to stop and I'd be my old hardworking self again. And no more lies. I'd come clean about the O because I wouldn't need it anymore. We'd find a small but livable apartment somewhere nearby so Drew wouldn't have to change schools, and maybe I'd design homes, too.

Ronnie had been talking. A few more sentences had come from her. Something about the father of one of her clients. Something about crossing the line.

"Line?"

She was nodding, her eyes filling and spilling. Her raised chin was quivering. Not one time in our years together had I ever seen that, and I couldn't stop staring at it because it was the clearest evidence I ever got at just how brutally and completely I'd broken down that lovely girl. She was telling me more things and there were the words *love* and *I'm sorry* and *But* and *I love him. I do.*

My legs started to go. There came a sticky sweat, and I said, "I need to lie down."

"Of course. Of course." Then she was helping me to my adjustable bed, her arm across my back, her fingers digging into my ribs. She was sniffling and I could feel her hair against my cheek, then I was stretching out on my mattress and she was handing me a glass of water, which I drank down, each swallow a tiny punch. She sat on the edge of the bed holding her wineglass with two hands and she told me everything.

What was so strange about that moment is that I lay there looking at her like she was a woman I just met. No, I just met *again.* As if the years we'd shared—the good and now the very bad—had formed layers of time over my wife that had altered her into someone else, into a frightened, vigilant, accomplished, exhausted, and utterly disillusioned person. But now, telling me about this man Ed Flynn, father of Heather Flynn—"And I shouldn't say this, but she suffers from extreme anxiety disorder"—it was like being with young Ronnie again, lying beside her in bed as she spoke so passionately about stars and black holes and later about Carl Jung and Freud and the mutable nature of human memory. The thing is, in those brief moments that afternoon before Drew got home from school, Ronnie's eyeliner running down both cheeks, her barrette hanging loosely against her back, she felt like a friend again, *my* friend, because we used to talk about everything together. She who was so curious about all things, who even wanted to hear the details of concrete foundation forms and pressure-treated sills, here she was restored to me once again. And how cruel that we'd lost this along the way, even when things were good, when I was flush and we were in the early days in this house, we'd already lost what had bloomed here in Ronnie's horrible confession. Instead of taking time for moments like this, we had turned ourselves to raising our son and to owning property and to paying for it monthly, and I must've just asked her the question whose answer I didn't want because Ronnie turned to me and said, "Yes, today." She swallowed and nodded and looked away. "We made love." Her words were a cold blade shoved through me, but even as she started to cry again, covering her face with one hand, I couldn't stop feeling a bitter gratitude for what was happening, for Ronnie the abundist to show herself again, my Ronnie who had found a way to return to herself with no help from me.

And gratitude begins to fill me now as I walk carefully down the stairs, both hands on the railings, thinking of my tools and the miracle of all that money coming.

And Drew. Taking him to a nice restaurant in the same college town where his parents met. Does my boy even know that we met there? I must've told him that, but maybe I didn't.

In the kitchenette I boil water for the instant coffee I've grown to almost enjoy. *Dad.* Trina looking up at me. *I wish you were my dad.* While the water begins to boil I glance around the corner to my plywood couch, to my closed laptop and *The Gulag Archipelago* on my plank table, to Trina's three cigarette butts stubbed out in the paper plate. Everything seems to be in order. Nothing to worry about. The poor girl is in need of a father, that's all. And it was going to be good handing her a hundred dollars in cash. Or maybe I'll even take her to the mall with me. Let her pick something out—just for her, something that isn't pajama bottoms and a hoodie sweatshirt.

Cesar Ramirez's sons will be here at six. I should organize my tools. Nothing too heavy, but I should make sure the drills are with the drills, the saws with the saws, the squares and levels and tape measures all together too. But with this thought of getting my tools ready for strangers, there come the echoes of a loss I'm not sure I'll ever get through, my ability to make an honest living.

With my hands anyway. With my legs and back and shoulders. With my calculating mind.

I spoon instant coffee into the same cup I drank the Belvedere from, and I picture myself handing Trina two hundred dollars instead of the hundred I'd planned. I blow on my coffee and decide to sip it in the basement as I get my tools ready for Cesar Ramirez. The stair treads are covered with commercial no-slip rubber, but I take them carefully, my forehead pulsing.

At the landing the air turns cold and I hear a car drive by, then another. The exterior door to the backyard is open an inch or two, dead leaves in a swirl at the threshold. Trina's always telling me that I'm "soft" for not locking my doors. Now I use my free hand to push the door shut and hot coffee spills onto my other wrist, but I ignore this because something in the air is shifting and there's the bone memory of reaching for the next shingle just before my body began its inexplicable plummet, because there, at the bottom of the stairs, instead of my corded power tools lying on the floor or stacked in plastic milk crates, there's nothing but the concrete slab of my basement.

My coffee cup clatters on the landing behind me and now I'm

standing on that concrete. What I see feels like *not* seeing. Like walking into a dark room after being in the bright sun—a couch maybe a table, a lamp a vase: The steel shelves that should be holding my chop saw and my planer, my table saw and circular saws, my nail guns and compressor hoses and electrical cords, are empty. The floor at my feet—bare. Even my heavy compressors and two drill presses—gone.

On the casement window's dusty sill lies an orange three-prong adapter, the only thing of mine left behind, and now an icy sweat beads on my forehead and the back of my neck and I have to lean over and prop my hands on my knees. *Who?* Who would *do* this to me?

Cesar Ramirez? This man sending his "sons" over? Because how fucking stupid was I to tell him that I'm disabled and then offer my address? I might as well be a lamb exposing my milky throat to a wolf.

But how would "Ramirez" know how to get in? And where? I *had* been locking my basement door, I know it.

Fitz. Fucking *Fitz* in his robe with his Black & Mild cigar.

That night he took pictures of my tools, it would've been easy for Fitz to unlock the basement door from the inside. It would've been easy to wait until dawn when he knew I finally slept and quietly carry out one hard-earned tool after another. He would've needed help for the compressors and drill press, but one other man would have been enough, and now I'm sitting on the bottom step, curling up as tightly as if I'm being kicked by many men, my car out of reach, my beautiful son too, my nearly twenty-year-old Drew. There'll be no restaurant steaks with him and his friends. There'll be no shared coffee on some B&B's porch. There'll be no joyful visit to the mall. There'll be no gift for loveless Trina. I'm screaming, my throat burning, but I don't care because I see myself reaching for my hammer that is now gone and sinking it into Fitz's shaved head.

Just another revenue stream, brother.

One more score and I'm gone.

PART II

12

I STAND BAREFOOT IN MY T-SHIRT AND KHAKIS RAPPING ON THE locked glass doors of Larry's Liquors. I peer inside, shivering, but the lights are off. What *time* is it? The sun is high over the units of the 8 and a stream of cars pass by in the street behind me. It has to be late morning and now I'm walking into Dawn's Hair & Nails.

Sitting in three of its beauty chairs are three women, two with their wet hair being cut by the women standing behind them, a third having hers blown dry by a man in a purple vest. His arms are covered with tattoos, and half his head is shaved and the other half is long bleached hair. He turns to me and gives me the slightly alarmed look I've grown used to, but not today. Not to-fucking-day. "I need your phone. I've been robbed, and I need to use your phone, please." The tone of my voice is the kind I'd use on my subs when they needed to work harder and faster because we had a deadline to hit and we *will* hit it.

"That sucks." The woman closest to me is young, her lipstick the same purple as the man's vest. She nods in the direction of a desk set into a corner away from the windows. "It's over there."

I thank her and walk barefoot and sweating to the telephone. My mouth and throat are dry as rubber bands.

"911, what is your emergency?"

My *emergency*?

I fell. I fell off a roof and—I'm out of breath. I stare out the window across the street at my vinyl-clad unit in the 8, at its cracked concrete stoop. At the dead leaves covering my spit of yard. "I've been robbed. Someone broke into my house and stole all my tools." I'm about to tell her that they're in very good condition, that they're worth more than what I was planning to sell them for, but she tells me to wait one moment please and now there's a cop on the line. He says something about this call being recorded and I say, "I think I know who did it."

"Did what, sir?"

"I told you, I've been robbed."

"Name and address?" The policeman sounds like he's just been woken from a nap and isn't happy about it. I give my name and tell him where I live. He's asking more questions.

"Excuse me."

"When did this happen?"

"I don't know. Yesterday, last night, these are very valuable tools, Officer."

The door to Dawn's Hair & Nails opens and an Asian woman in a parka walks in. She glances at me like she sees me standing there on the phone every day, then she moves to a set of drawers in the back where she lays bottles of nail polish on a side table made of glass. I'm aware of music playing. Heavy bass and electronic drums and a woman singing how she loves to love you, baby.

"You'll need to come down and fill out a police report."

"Isn't that what I'm doing?"

"We need a stolen property report, sir."

"Yes, I'm reporting that right now."

"We need an itemized list of your tools, sir."

I inhale deeply through my nose. "I'm sorry, Officer. Your name please?"

"Sergeant Dooling."

"Sergeant, I don't have a car."

"You'll still have to come down to the station, Mr. Lowell."

"It's Lowe. L-o-w-e, Lowe."

"That's what I said, sir."

"No, you said—"

"Come fill out a report, Mr. Lowe." The click of the phone taps a hole in my head. Over the thumping music a woman's talking. It's the one in the last chair, the man in the purple vest brushing her hair back from her forehead. The woman—forty-five? fifty?—is talking about her husband having painted their house himself.

"I told him, but he never listens to me. Now we have to pay someone to fix it."

"God, honey, I'd make him fix it."

"At least he tried," I say, hanging up the phone. "At least he fucking *tried*."

THE INTERIOR DOOR TO my basement is still open and I slam it closed, pull on my socks and work boots, and look around for my old sweater. No, not that one. I need to look more like a citizen. I'll get nothing from the cops if I look poor, disabled, and alone in the 8.

In my bedroom, most of it taken up by the double bed Wyn and Nancy gave me from their guest room, I rifle through my closet and pull out the same button-down shirt I wore to my loan meeting with Mike Andrews. It's blue and needs ironing. I put it on anyway. Buttoning it and tucking it in, I'm aware that it's loose in the shoulders and tight at the waist when the opposite used to be true.

In a stack of cardboard boxes near the door I reach past my divorce papers and a few paperbacks, past socks with no partner, past the paperweight of a lion Charlie sent me from Germany for my birthday because I'm a Leo, though I've never felt like a lion. For a short time there was the feeling that I'd become a reliable workhorse, but for years now I've been nothing but a broken-boned dog.

The sweater I pull down over my head in the bathroom has tiny decorated Christmas trees across its chest. I have no memory of how it came to be mine. Ronnie? My mother? Nancy? But it's thick and clean and feels like it's never been worn. The hip fires have long been raging, but as I shave my face and comb back my hair, their heat feels less severe today, or maybe I just don't give a shit, and the first thing I need is Fitz's full name. Trina might know it. And if she doesn't, I need to see her anyway. I need to look her in the eye when I tell her that I've been robbed. I need to know that this'll come as news to her.

I need a list of my tools. They're all on my laptop, but I won't be able to carry that all the way to the police station, which is a mile away, maybe more. I'll just have to direct Sergeant Dooling to my Craigslist page, that's all.

And can they really not send a fucking cruiser over?

Outside on my stoop I pat my front pants pocket for the moneyless wallet that holds my ID. The October sky is a deep blue, the air cold, a new white van pulling in front of Dawn's Hair & Nails. It's the same kind of van I used to own and on another day it would have reminded me of my losses, but now, seeing it only pisses me off, and then I'm knocking on Trina's dented front door, and how strange that I've never done this before. She pushes it open before my third knock. Her face is pale and encircled by the hood of her sweatshirt. "I'm mad at you. I've never had a hangover this bad."

"I got robbed, Trina. Somebody stole all my fucking tools."

"What? When?"

"Last night? The day before? I don't know, but they're gone and I'm pretty sure it was that piece of shit Fitz."

"I told you he was a snake. Didn't I tell you? He steals drugs from where he friggin' works."

"I need his last name. Do you know it?"

"No. He was just Fitz. Call the housing office, they'll have it."

Inside her unit Cody's yelling at MJ or MJ's yelling at Cody. Trina jerks around and shouts through the doorway, "You two shut the fuck up!"

She pulls her cigarettes and lighter from the middle pocket of her hoodie. "So you won't be able to get your car back?" Her tone is both caring and self-serving and I shake my head. My tongue feels swollen and I want more water or a cold Coke. I need to lie down. I need to start my long walk to the police.

"Was your door locked, Tom?"

"Yes, Trina. It was locked."

"Where'd you get the sweater?" She nods at the tiny Christmas trees across my chest, an unlit cigarette between her lips. She's just about to light up when she looks past me and her eyes darken and brighten at the same time. It's Brian. He's walking quickly across the road, his hands in the pocket of his own hoodie, black and too big for him. Pulled low over his ears is a gray wool cap, but I can still see the blue scrawl of tattoos along the kid's neck, and now Brian's in the narrow empty parking lot of the 8, his eyes on Trina.

"The hell are you doing here?" This string of words seems to rise from my broken hips, from my cleaned-out basement, from twice holding crying Trina to my softened chest.

"Tom."

"What's it to you?" Brian's already climbing the steps, and maybe if he wasn't doing that so quickly, if he wasn't doing that while saying to me what he just did, maybe I would not be swinging my elbow back into Brian's nose, a hot jolt through my arm, Trina rushing past me down to the concrete walk where Brian sits, his tattooed hands pressed to his face, blood spilling between his fingers and down his chin.

"What the *hell*, *Tom*." Trina helps Brian sit up and there comes his muffled voice. "I'll fuck you up, motherfucker."

"No," I say, walking down the steps. "Hit her again, Brian, and I'll fuck you up."

13

HAVEN'T WALKED LIKE THIS IN YEARS. FAST. BREATHING HARD. MY strides long, my heart beating in time to my swinging arms. My limp is a slight roll of hip and pelvis that makes me lean forward and to the right, and there's the backward-falling sense that I have to catch up to something—Fitz selling my tools. I've got to get Fitz's name and new address to the police as soon as I can or it'll be too late.

A cold breeze in my face. The smells of car exhaust and rotting leaves. Up ahead at the intersection Shannon steps out of the Island of Convenience carrying a paper bag. Milk probably. A carton of eggs. Trina last night talking about all the teenage mothers, herself included.

I head west. It's a street of two-story houses, most of them sided with vinyl. Their yards are small and raked clean, and hanging over the porch railing of one is a banner of a smiling orange pumpkin. In the front yard of another are three inflatable skeletons, a light wind whipping them back and forth.

I have to rest again. Across from the CVS store a hundred yards ahead is a small pond, and on the far bank a crew of three is scraping the last of a gabled roof's shingles down onto a blue tarp thirty feet below. The crew looks young, in their twenties still, and there's not a rope or harness in sight. I'm thirsty. I need a bottle of water and a handful of ibuprofen. But my premature Belvedere celebration has left me with nothing.

On the other side of the CVS is a long hill that I'm going to have to climb, and then it's another eight or ten blocks to the police station. There's the thudding echo of a hammer on wood.

Two of the roofers are out of sight, and the one left is driving all the old roofing nails back into the sheathing. The kid works fast, bracing himself against the roof with one hand while swinging his hammer with the other. His free and easy movements are those of a man who has never fallen or even come close, and I want to warn him about gravity and human bones, about insurance companies and banks, about pharmaceuticals and lonely wives, about trusting anyone on this unforgiving earth to actually *help* anyone else.

I want to yell a warning to that kid working on the roof, but I'm too far away and Fitz could be selling my tools right this minute and so I need to put my head down and climb that fucking hill.

THE POLICE DEPARTMENT IS in a one-story brick building attached to the fire station. Parked halfway out of its open bay is a ladder truck, and as I pass, a plastic taste in my mouth, my T-shirt wet under my Christmas sweater, there's the memory of being carried to the ambulance past the fire truck that had come for me, its lights flashing under that blue sky. It was one of the painters inside the house who called them, a gray-haired guy smoking a cigarette on the grass as they loaded me into the wagon and drove me away.

Two firefighters sit in folding chairs staring at their phones. I need to lie down. When I finally reach the door of the police station and step inside, I feel like I'm owed something. And not just by those who've stolen from me, but by these local cops who made me walk as far as I did.

The waiting area is three folding chairs set against the wall. Behind a thick pane of glass a young cop sits in front of two computer screens. He leans close to a microphone. "Can I help you?"

"Sergeant Dooling?"

"He's out."

"I've been robbed. He told me to come fill out some report." My hips are engulfed in flames. I wipe the sweat from my forehead and I'm already too warm in my sweater, but I begin to shiver. The young cop calls to someone I can't see and then a policewoman steps into the doorway to a short hall. Her hair's pulled back away from her face and she looks young. Trina's age. Maybe even younger.

"Come with me please."

I follow her to a small room and now I'm sitting on the other side of a desk and the woman's silver name tag says that her name is M. Flatley. She taps keys on a keyboard. Under the fluorescent light she looks a bit older, an engagement ring on her finger. "Your name and address, please."

"I gave that to a Sergeant Dooling over the phone."

She glances over at me. She takes in the sweat on my face, the tiny Christmas trees across my chest. "I don't see it in the system, sir." Her tone isn't cold, but it's not warm either and I want to tell her that I had to walk here, that I'm not an able-bodied man and her department made me walk here.

"Could I get a glass of water?"

"Of course." She seems to take in something about my face. She taps another key, turns the screen toward her, then stands. "I'll get you some." As she leaves the room I can smell her clean uniform, her newly oiled gun in its holster. Outside the window a bare branch moves in the wind and I picture Fitz unloading my tools from the back of his U-Haul truck, his smooth hands outstretched for cash, *my* cash.

The young policewoman is handing me a Styrofoam cup filled with water. I thank her and drink half of it. My hip screws feel like they've shifted sideways inside me and my stomach feels too empty, but I need to give her Fitz's name. "Can I use your phone? I need to get you the name of the man who did this."

She holds her hand up. "First things first." She asks me my name and address and I tell her. She asks me what was stolen.

"All my tools." The skin of my face feels loose, like I just told her that someone I love has died. I want to tell her how long it took me to acquire each of those tools, only buying one when I needed it, only replacing one when I had to. But always taking good care of them. I always took such good care of them.

"When were these stolen?"

"I don't know, yesterday or the day before, I think."

Officer Flatley types this into her computer. Without looking at me she says, "From your place of work?"

"No, my home. I can't work. I got hurt."

She glances at me and in her young face I see the brief light of compassion, or maybe it's just a voyeuristic curiosity, the kind people have as they drive by a bad accident on the highway. "Over on Hampton Terrace?" The way she says my street address, I know that she knows I live in the 8.

I drink more water. I try to sit straight in my chair, but the hip screws are burrowing hotly into my bones and I need to stretch out and lie down.

"Do you have receipts for these tools?"

"What do you mean? They're my tools."

"So, no receipts?"

"Look." I'm about to say that I've owned some of these tools longer than she's been alive. "I used to have my own business. Those tools have been mine for a long time, and I was just about to sell them online."

Officer Flatley nods, her eyes on the screen as she types. "And you think you know who did this?"

"Yes, his name's Fitz, but I need to call the Housing Authority office to get his full name."

"Did he have access to your tools?"

"Yes, he used to live there."

"With you?"

"No, in his own unit, but he took pictures of all my tools for Craigslist."

She turns to me. I can see that she plucks her eyebrows, and above both is a slight redness. Her uniform blouse is pressed, and even sitting in a chair her posture is erect but relaxed. She is clearly a young woman who feels good about herself. An abundist maybe.

"Why do you suspect this Fitz?"

"Because he makes pornography and sells drugs. It's the kind of thing he would do."

She nods, takes a pen and writes: *Fitz?* "His apartment number?"

"The Housing Authority would know. Can I use your phone to call them?"

"No, but we'll look into that, sir."

"But he might be selling my tools as we *sit* here."

Officer Flatley pulls out a desk drawer, then hands me a sheet of paper and her pen. "We'll need a list and description of all your tools."

"I can't. It's too many."

She glances at me, one eyebrow raised into her red skin.

"But they're all on Craigslist. I can show them to you." I lean forward, but I must've made a face of some kind because Officer Flatley is asking me if I'm all right.

"No, I'm not. I need to lie down a minute. Is there a place I can lie down?"

AT THE STATION OFFICER Flatley let me lie on a steel bench in a holding cell, but just as my hip screws were cooling, she came back in to tell me that she was going to drive me home. Before leaving I showed her my Craigslist account and she printed out Fitz's photos of my tools, and now she pulls in front of my stoop and is out from behind the wheel and opening my locked door.

Brian and Trina are sitting on her top step sharing a can of beer. They're sitting hip to hip, both in their hoodie sweatshirts, and even from here, I can see that Brian's nose is red and swollen. Trina's smoking a cigarette. She looks away and stashes the beer can behind her.

Officer Flatley is saying something about my case and follow-up calls, but my eyes are still on Brian and I want to say: *He hits her. That punk on that porch hits that girl.* But what if the kid reports me? What if the kid walks over and accuses me of assault and battery?

I rise slowly out of the cruiser. My back and legs clench tighter than after a shift at the Island of Convenience, and I have to pull on the top of the doorframe to steady myself. Officer Flatley rests one hand on my upper back. She asks me if I need help getting to my unit, but it is so lovely to have her hand there that I can only shake my head. Under the midafternoon sun her slightly round face looks older, her plucked eyebrows too narrow. This makes her look almost comically sincere, but I can feel that sincerity and

I want to thank her for her kindness, but I've come back to the 8 without the promise of my tools, Fitz what's-his-name out there somewhere selling them for cash. A bolt of heat shoots down my legs and I need to get to my plywood couch.

She hands me her card. "Your case number is on the back, Mr. Lowe. Call me in a few days."

"It'll be too late by then."

"We'll do everything we can, sir." She steps back to give me room. Over her shoulder I see Brian follow Trina inside her unit, his eyes on me like the kid knows he's going to do something but not now, Trina's door shutting closed behind him.

14

IN MY DREAM RONNIE'S CRYING IN THE KITCHEN. HER EYES ARE ON mine, and she seems to be unhappy because I'm dead, but how can I be dead when I'm standing in this pond, my hands cupped around my mouth as I yell to the young roofer to be careful? The kid stops hammering long enough to stare out at me in the water, but it's Drew in Shannon's red wool cap. He says, "It's okay, Dad. I want to be just like you."

"Hello?"

More rapping. The light from the kitchen stove lies across my small table, the rest of the room dark.

"Mr. *Lowe*? *Hello?*"

It's the voice of a young man. I sit up. I'm too warm in my Christmas sweater and my head aches and I need the bathroom. There are two voices now. Low and in Spanish. "We've come for the tools?"

Ramirez. Goddamnit, Cesar Ramirez's *sons*.

I make my way to my front door and flip on my stoop's overhead bulb. Under the light are two handsome boys in their twenties. The taller one is clean-shaven, the sides of his head shaved too, the top a nest of thick black hair. It's October, but he's wearing only a T-shirt, *Ramirez Construction* stenciled in gold across his chest. His shorter, broader brother is in a Carhartt jacket, and between the thumb and forefinger of his right hand is what looks like a folded cashier's check, the lip of the roof rising away above me, my arms reaching and my hands clutching air.

I'm shaking my head as I open my door.

"Mr. Lowe?" Across the taller one's shoulders is a fine layer of sheetrock dust. "Our father sent us for your tools?"

I can only shake my head. I want to swallow but can't. The shorter one says, "Cesar Ramirez?"

Shame heats the back of my neck. I'm looking down at the men's work boots, the leather worn to its steel toes. I can see that these are men who work, and it's their polite and expectant expressions turning to concern that leave me without words. Because how many times had Drew looked at me like that? His hopes about to be stepped on by his father who had nothing to give? And so I tell these two men what I should have told their dad yesterday.

"I'm sorry. I should have let you know. I don't know why I didn't *do* that."

The shorter Ramirez brother just shakes his head like he has no time for this shit, then he turns and walks down my steps with that cashier's check between his fingers. But the taller one with the fresh haircut stands there looking sorry for me and for himself. "Our dad's helping us set up our own business. Those tools were for our crew."

I can only nod my head. I want to tell this kid that I know all about running a crew, the responsibility of it a joy really. A gang of men building something together. Not stealing. Not hurting anyone.

"I'm sorry you got robbed, sir." Then young Ramirez is gone too, their battered F-250 pulling out onto the street, every single one of my three thousand two hundred dollars driving away with them.

I'M BEGINNING TO LIE back on my plywood couch when there comes machine-gun fire louder than it's ever been on the other side of that wall. It's a *poppoppoppoppop*, then a shuddering explosion, then another, the volume turned up as high as it can go.

"Turn that fucking thing *down*!" I hurl *The Gulag Archipelago* at the wall and three books fall from the top shelf. Not a sound is coming from the other side, and I feel on the edge of remorse because what if Cody or MJ were playing that game?

A banging on my door. Louder than the video game had been. "Fucking make me, old man! Come out here and fuckin' *make* me turn it down!"

Before this afternoon's elbow to that kid's face, I was never in a fight except with Charlie, me and my brother swinging and swinging at each other.

The banging's louder now, hard enough to break plexiglass, and I glance around the room for some kind of weapon. I'm still hot in my Christmas sweater. I'd pulled off my work boots and now I wish I had time to pull them back on, but the banging won't stop and now I'm standing in front of my storm door, Brian's yelling face and swollen nose on the other side, me pushing open my door just to have a word with this boy, but the aluminum edge hits Brian in the shoulder and now he's rushing inside, his first punch a white flame that knocks me back down the hallway, the second a purple flower, the third a brown stone that's now being driven somewhere dark and wet, and I'm sinking with it, my arms and legs pinned under a furious weight, my face and head exposed to some terrible storm whose arrival shouldn't be such a surprise to me, but it is. It really is.

"TOM?" A DAMP NUDGING against my cheek, another on my forehead. "Tommy?" Funny how one eye doesn't open. Trina's hair hangs in front of her face, but she's a cat. Her nose is painted white and there are black whiskers across both cheeks, and she seems to be kneeling where my plank table used to be. She's also in a flat light and appears flat herself. There's the soft splash of something being dipped into water, then that nudging again, a nudging that burns.

"Cody, pick that up."

The crinkling of paper. Something sweet in the air. Licorice. Red licorice. I lift my head to see two rubber boots sticking out from the edge of my plywood couch.

"Tom, what the *fuck*. You should go to the hospital." Trina sits back and takes a short drag off her cigarette. She blows smoke out one side of her mouth. Even though she has the face of a cat, her eyes are free of makeup, the skin under them puffy.

"Why'd you hit him, Tommy? Why'd you fuckin' *do* that?"

There's a hot coal in my left eye. I try to open it, but both lids seem to be stuck together. That red licorice smells good. There's the flash of Brian rushing at me, just an angry face in a black hoodie, but he looked like a young boy and why didn't Drew ever get mad like that? He had every right to. Especially when his father asked him to do the things I asked him to do. *Don't tell Mom, okay buddy? We don't want her to worry.*

"You gonna call the cops?"

"No."

"Why not?" Her tone is relieved, this cat in this flat light who tucks a strand of hair behind her ear. She flicks ash from her cigarette into a cup on the floor. "He's on probation, you know."

"For what?"

"He's afraid he'll go back to jail."

"Trina?"

"Yeah?"

"Why'd you invite him back?"

"What? I didn't do shit."

"But you welcomed him back. Why?"

"*Cody.* I fuckin' told you. Put your trash back into your bucket."

"No you didn't."

Cody's mouth is full and Trina's movement is automatic, but my arm jerks from my side, my fingers grasping her wrist.

"No, hon."

"Don't you talk back to me, Cody. *Ever.* You *hear* me? Now fuckin' go home."

Trina pulls her arm free, then stands with the bowl, and what I can see are wet and wadded paper towels. Cody slides off the couch, one of his boots knocking against my shin.

He's wearing a cape made from a torn black sheet, a white plastic breastplate held to his shirt with duct tape, his face painted as green as the old wise one from those movies. The boy seems to be three characters in one, and now he steps over my legs with his light saber and orange pumpkin bucket. "What happened to your eye?"

"Cody, do you have more of that licorice?"

Cody looks toward the kitchen. There's the running of water from the faucet. "Black or red?"

"Red."

"But that's my favorite."

"Mine too."

"Cody." Trina's voice sounds farther away than it should. "Get home *now*."

The boy reaches into his bucket and pulls out a length of red licorice. He holds it up and stares at it, weighing just how much it's worth to him. He looks back down at this grown man lying on the floor between his turned-over plank table and his plywood couch. He tosses it onto my chest and is gone.

"I don't appreciate you telling me how to raise my own kid." Trina's somehow standing over me, one foot on either side of my hips. I take two bites of the licorice. It's waxy and sweet and tastes like some kind of hollow promise fulfilled. She holds her hand out for me to grab onto, which I do, though when she pulls, my hip screws heat up and the room darkens and I have to lie back down.

"I'm going to Larry's to call a fucking ambulance, Tom."

"Nope." I bite into the licorice. "No more hospitals for me."

Trina the cat sits on my plywood couch where her son Cody had just been. She lights another cigarette. From the other side of the wall comes the distant thud of an electronic bomb going off. "You have any of that good vodka left?"

I shake my head, though she doesn't seem to be looking in my direction. She blows out smoke. She crosses her legs and starts tapping her foot. "Brian went nuts cuz Jamey drove me to the fuckin' food pantry."

My head pulses. My eye burns. I'm still too hot in this sweater, but this red licorice seems to be going down well and all I want now is a cool glass of water, though I need the toilet, too.

My early hatred of Edward Joseph Flynn. For a few months I wanted to kill him.

"Jealousy's bad, Trina. You need to get rid of him."

"Your face looks like shit, Tommy."

I reach up and touch my cheek, but my own fingertips feel cruel against my skin. "I need the bathroom, hon. Try again?"

She stands over me, pulling on my outstretched arm until I can lean on one elbow and push myself up onto one knee, then the other, then she's squatting with both her arms around my back and there are the smells of cigarette smoke and soap and burned leaves and Trina is Ronnie again, our physical intimacies confined to all the daily help she had to give me. She even wiped me and changed my bedpan the first weeks, and she did this with tenderness and no complaints. Ronnie deserved better than what she got. She really did.

"I'm not gonna hold it for you, Tommy."

I tell Trina that I can take it from here, and then I'm upstairs pissing in my toilet, my head and face feeling hot and puffy while my hip screws feel oddly stable.

I flush, avoid the mirror, pull over my bruised head the Christmas sweater, and drop it to the floor. On the way out I can feel that photo of me and Drew on the wall to my left. My son is turning twenty. He's walking out of the woods of childhood and into the open field at the base of the mountain that will be his manhood, one he's going to have to climb himself, but not without a helping word or two from his dad.

Trina looks up at me as I come into the room. She's just finished stacking the books that are the legs of my plank table, but when she sets the board across both stacks, it's out of level. "You should at least put some ice on that eye, Tom. *Jesus.*"

Then she's gone and my head's a bag of wet air. What I should do is walk across the street to Larry's and call Officer Flatley, if she's still on her shift. Ask if she's at least gotten Fitz's full name.

Laughter on the other side of the wall. A high, breathless squealing. It sounds like one of the boys is being tickled, but by whom? *Brian?* Is he still *over* there? Maybe I *should* report him. Get him out of Trina's life that way.

My storm door slams and Trina walks in. Her face is scrubbed clean and she's carrying a plastic baggie filled with ice and water. "Sit and push the ice against this." I lower myself to my plywood couch and she touches a folded wad of toilet paper to my eye and I press the pack to a tender puffiness. I keep both eyes closed. She's applying something from a tube to my cheeks and forehead and lower lip. It smells like Vaseline.

"Trina, is he still over there?"

"No."

"Where'd he go?"

"Probably his fucking mother's."

"Look, I want you to know something."

"Here we go."

"If that kid comes back to your place, I'm going to report him for assault and battery. On both of us. He needs to know that, all right?"

Trina takes in a chest full of air. I get myself ready for her to start yelling, but there's just a slow hissing from between her lips. "This is my last friggin' cigarette."

"You out?"

"I'm quitting. They keep making me late with the rent."

"That's good, Trina. Quitting bad things is good."

She sits back, the plywood under me dipping with her weight. My bad eye aches from the cold. I open my good eye. Trina's feet are propped on my plank table, and in the flat light I can see that she's wearing blue anklet socks, the kind that emergency rooms give out with white sticky circles on the soles to keep you from slipping. She got them at the Goodwill up the river last year, a whole bag of them, and she gave me some, but they were too small for my feet.

"Maybe you could try one of those nicotine patches."

"With what money, Tommy? Cody turned six last week, so there goes my WIC for him now."

My bad eye aches. I lower the ice pack and set it on the plywood. Trina's feet drop off my plank table and I close my eyes and feel her tapping one foot on the floor. "Fitz wanted me to fuck him on the internet, you know. He said I could make a lot of money."

"And?"

"I told him to get outta my face, I'm not a fucking whore."

"Good for you. I think I could probably kill that man, Trina."

"Tom?"

"Yeah, hon."

"Me and Jamey are gonna steal more trash."

"Trina."

"He almost shit when I told him how many times I go to the lab, Tommy. He thinks it's really bad for me. Then, you know, we had a long talk."

"About?"

"Credit card companies. He friggin' hates 'em. He says they screwed his mother over so bad they were almost homeless. And then I told him about when I was homeless."

"You were homeless?"

"I told you that. The other night, when we were drinkin'."

"You did?"

She nods her head and blows out smoke. My hip flames are flaring up. Hovering inside me somewhere is an image of Shannon, MJ, and pregnant Trina sleeping in a rusted-out car in a field of weeds behind an empty mill building. Something about her mother's new boyfriend having kicked them out and *Ma didn't do shit*.

Then we were talking about kids having kids. We were talking about my fifteen-year-old mother.

In the one-dimensional air Trina's looking at me like she's just asked me a question and is waiting for my answer. With no makeup on, her lips parted, her hoodie bunched up around her neck, she looks to me like a young woman from a time gone by, a peasant girl who wants to be a queen.

"Don't look at me like that, Tommy."

"Like what?"

"Like you're fucking better than me."

"I'm not, I—don't think that." But I do. I judge her for living here. For not using her health and youth to work, work, work the way I did. I judge her for letting herself get pregnant by two or three boys. For yelling and swearing at her kids the way she does. For spending some of her plasma money on cigarettes so that she has to rely on lowlifes like Brian to help her.

"I fucking knew it." She bolts to her feet and steps over my plank table and runs the fingers of both hands through her hair. "You tell me I need a plan to get out of this place, well that's my fuckin' plan, Tommy. What am I, gonna win the *lottery*? That kid Jamey tells me to go back to school, but I can't even tell him I'm *learning* disabled. Words and numbers get all fucked up in my head, Tom. And I can't *work*. Who's gonna watch my *kids*?"

"Shannon?"

"*Shannon?* I don't even know where she is right now. I—" Trina shakes her head like a thousand bees are in her hair. "I'm not gonna cry. You can't make me fucking cry all the time, Tommy. *Shannon?* She wouldn't go trick-or-treatin' with us, so I told her she could stay in her room all night—do you even know she *has* her own room? *My* room? I sleep on the couch now, which Brian also don't appreciate, but she left, Tommy. No note. Nothing. And she's still not back and you know what I'm afraid of? That she'll get hurt? No, I'm afraid she's fucking some kid right now and then she's gonna be me. That she's—*fuck*." Trina turns, her clean hair whipping across her hoodie, her small back disappearing down the hallway, the door left wide open.

15

THE SNOW STARTED JUST AFTER DAWN. NOW, A FEW HOURS later, a light blanket covers the leaves in my small backyard, the overflowing trash barrel, the upside-down wagon Trina gave me. The wooden fence separating the 8 from the sidewalk is wet, its boards gray and untreated. A few are missing here and there, and it has always looked to me like a mouth with some teeth knocked out.

I stand at the window, a cup of black instant coffee in my hand. My lower lip burns when I try to sip it, though, and with each flake falling into my subsidized yard, it's like a button inside me is being pressed, and who knows what it'll do once it gets locked into place.

I need aspirin for my head. It's the first of the month. That means my disability check will come tomorrow, Drew's birthday two days after that. Instead of sending him a hundred dollars, I could use it for a bus ticket to go see him. There have to be buses.

No, god*damn*it, I need to get my car back and I need to gas it up and I need to drive the two hours west like the man I still am. But first I need to call the police, and if they haven't found Fitz yet, then I will.

I set down the coffee. I pull on my work boots and my old Carhartt jacket, stuff Officer Flatley's card into my front pocket, and now I'm standing on the edge of the street waiting for an opening in the cars being driven to work by people who work. With my one good eye the SUVs and small sedans seem to be moving by on a movie screen. The snow feels good on my face. But when I finally get across the street, breathing harder than I think I should be, the glass door to Larry's Liquors is still closed. Then I see the white index card taped to the glass. *Death in the Family. CLOSED till further notice.*

Death?

Larry's face just a day or two ago when I bought that Belvedere. He didn't look good and I hope that it was his piece-of-shit son-in-law who died and not kind and affable Larry. But then the door to Dawn's Hair & Nails opens and a young woman steps out and starts to shovel away the snow on their sidewalk. She's the same girl from yesterday who wore purple lipstick and let me use the phone. It's cold, the snow still coming down, but she's in a white sleeveless blouse, her spiked hair white, her lipstick white too.

I say good morning.

She barely glances in my direction. The light from the salon is on her gelled hair and long arms. I point my thumb at the liquor store. "Who died?"

The girl says something I can't hear over the scraping of her plastic shovel along concrete.

"'Scuse me?"

"The owner. Larry." She turns and carries the shovel back inside the salon. There's already a woman sitting in one of the salon chairs, her torso is covered by blue fabric.

Larry's sagging skin and cloudy eyes. His Beethoven. *Never better, Tom. Never better.*

I stand there, the snow melting on my swollen face, a hole in the fence of my life where there was a sincere smile and a warm greeting. What a relief that would be, to just drop to the floor and die: No more flaming hips. No more long days and nights of uselessness and self-loathing. But let me die another time. Not today. Not anytime soon, because I'm still here, goddamnit. I am still *here.*

I walk into Dawn's Hair & Nails. There are the smells of shampoo and electric heat, techno club music thumping softly. The girl with the naked arms and white lipstick looks over at me from where she stands behind the seated woman in the blue sheet. Wet strands of the woman's hair are in one hand, scissors in the other, but now the girl looks nervous and I remember how I left this place last time, saying, *At least he fucking **tried**.* But no, it has to be my closed eye, my fat lip and bruised cheek. I lift one hand and say, "I had a bad fall. Can I use your phone again?"

I don't know why I lied about my face. Maybe because I don't want her to associate me in any way with violence.

"This isn't a public pay phone, sir." It's the sitting woman with the wet hair. She's got to be my age for even knowing what a pay phone is and I want to ask her how this has anything to do with her, but now the young woman says, "I let him use it yesterday to call the cops. He got robbed."

"That's my business line, honey. What the hell." The woman's looking at my reflection in the mirror. "What really happened to your face?"

"Are you Dawn?"

"Maybe."

Both women are looking at me, and through my one good eye they seem to float in the flat air. "I hit a man who hit a woman friend of mine and then he hit me back."

"Across the street?"

I nod. My head throbs. My hip screws feel like shafts of rust.

"I've seen you around. Why do you need my phone?"

"To call the cops."

Now the woman turns in her chair and looks directly at me. From here, even in the bright flatness of things, I can see that she's an older woman, her face without makeup. "You don't have a phone?"

"Used to. I used to own a business too. Like you."

The woman looks past me out the plate glass to the snow falling on the 8. "You gonna report what happened to you?"

"No, something else."

She glances at me one more time, then raises her hand free of the blue sheet. "Go 'head."

As I pick up the receiver, I want to lean on the small desk the phone sits on but don't. I wish there was no music playing. When I speak to Officer Flatley I don't want to sound like I'm at some early morning party. I reach into my jacket pocket for her card. Next to it are two or three sheetrock screws. Touching them with my fingertips feels like touching my own face in a picture from when I was young and strong and worked for hours without a break.

But I left my reading glasses back in my unit, and even holding the card close and squinting my eyes, I can't make out the phone number. I look over at the two women who've been talking. "Pardon me?"

The girl's holding up strands of the owner's hair. The women don't seem to hear me, and I know this is because I used the too-quiet voice of the shamed.

I make myself stand as straight as I can. "I'm sorry, Dawn? Do you have some reading glasses I can borrow?"

The woman looks at me in the mirror with a knowing expression. Like she's had experience with men like me, but she says to the girl cutting her hair, "Go read it for him, hon."

The girl walks over with her comb in one hand and her shears in another. I hand her the card and she reads me the number and is back behind the chair before Officer Flatley's voice comes on the line.

"Detective Flatley."

Detective? I give her my name. "The man you drove back to Hampton Terrace?"

"You have anything new to tell me?"

"That's why I'm calling *you*."

The music has changed to an instrumental, though it seems to be nothing but synthesizer with a lot of electronic bass, and I can see now that the two women are quiet, listening to whatever they can of my conversation. Detective Flatley lets out a half-breath. "Yes and no. I talked to the Housing Authority, and I was able to interview your former neighbor."

"*Fitz?* You talked to him?"

"I did, yes."

"And?"

"He denies having anything to do with it, sir."

"No shit."

"He did say that he took pictures of your tools and helped you post them on Craigslist."

"Where's he live? I want to talk to him."

"Not a good idea."

"But he's the only one who could've done it."

"In my experience, Mr. Lowe, there's no 'only' anybody or anything."

There's more to this conversation, though none of it goes anywhere but to another kind of locked door. Just one more bolted in my face. The good detective talks about pawnshops and keeping an eye on them, but her voice begins to sound like it's coming from behind some iron vault. "Do you have insurance?"

"No."

"I'm sorry, Mr. Lowe, but we're doing all we can."

I see again her narrow plucked eyebrows, feel her hand resting lightly on my upper back.

"These things can take some time."

I wait for her to say more, but she's hung up and I place the receiver back into its cradle and shove both hands into my coat pockets. I just stand there. Dawn's staring at my reflection in the mirror, the girl in the white lipstick snipping, snipping, snipping, and the older woman who owns this well-lighted business on this cold and snowy morning seems to be watching me to see what I'll do next, not in her shop, but in my miserable life. She says, "You all set?"

I nod and thank her. I ask her if she knows the funeral arrangements for Larry, and she tells me and then I'm outside again, wet flakes on my swollen face.

I'm breathing hard, walking up the concrete steps of Trina's unit. Cody's Big Wheels is surrounded by dead leaves up against the vinyl siding, and to the left of Trina's dented front door is a Folgers can filled with cigarette butts. There are the sounds of happy kids. I turn and watch Amber load them into her Geo with no hubcaps. All three kids are dressed in new-looking winter coats, their backpacks looking new too, and I think of Cal working two jobs to get them all to a better place, Amber doing the rest, which is clearly a lot. If I were stronger, I'd offer to watch Trina's kids while she worked somewhere. But I'm not, and before getting behind the wheel Amber glances up at me and her face seems to harden and then I remember my own face and I knock on Trina's door.

Cars pass wetly in the street. I wonder if there'll be a service for Larry. The blinds to Mrs. Bongiovanni's unit are pulled closed like always, her porch steps coated with snow. Her nurse will be there soon. Her nurse who looked at me like I was a dog somebody forgot to put down. I raise my hand to knock again when the door opens and it's MJ.

He's barefoot and shirtless in a pair of hand-me-down corduroy pants, the cuffs rolled up past his bony ankles. His hair's short but sticking up in places, his gray eyes narrow and deep. He's seven or eight years old, but he's looking up at my bruised face and half-closed eye like he sees this kind of thing every day, and I can see him twenty years from now: tattooed and broken-handsome, living off some poor woman a lot like his mother.

"Morning, MJ."

The boy keeps looking at me.

"Your mom home?"

MJ turns and walks back into the unit, leaving the door wide open. I step into the smells of oatmeal and coffee. "Trina?"

I've never been inside Trina's unit. Unlike mine and Fitz's, there's no short hallway leading to a boxlike living room. Trina's door opens right into hers, which is clean, the linoleum floor looking mopped. The couch sits on a rug facing the TV that's turned down low and which MJ is already sitting back in front of, working the controls in his lap so that the soldier he is on the screen fires his automatic weapon at three other soldiers, each one exploding into blood splatter against a gray landscape.

The window blinds are slit open. Daylight comes into the room in horizontal bars over the small table where three mismatched bowls sit, spoon or fork handles sticking out of two of them. On the wall to my left is the wrinkled printout of an old woman smiling in front of a birthday cake covered with burning candles, a much younger Trina—thirteen or fourteen years old—kneeling beside her, both of them smiling up into someone's phone.

A toilet flushes upstairs, water runs in the pipes, then there are footsteps on the stair treads and Trina steps out of the narrow stairwell into the slatted light. She scoops up the three bowls on the table, me still standing there in the doorway.

"What the fuck, you scared me."

"Sorry. Your son let me in." I point to the image of her and the old woman. "Who's that?"

"My nana." Trina picks up the other spoon and a dirty napkin in a chair seat and walks through the doorway into her kitchen. I follow her. It's smaller than mine, barely enough room for one adult between the stove and the fridge across from it. Trina's hair is pulled back and she's still in her hoodie sweatshirt and pajama bottoms and blue hospital socks. She's running the water hot and fast, steam rising up from the bowls she scrubs with a worn sponge. Unlike my own countertops, hers are wiped clean, and her floor's swept too, her stovetop shining under the vent light.

"What do you want, Tommy? You never come over here."

"Larry died."

She looks at me over her shoulder. She shuts the water off. "*Larry* Larry?"

I nod.

"But he was so nice."

"Yeah, he was."

She turns the water back on, softer this time, and slowly washes and rinses the last bowl.

"Where's Shannon and Cody?"

"School."

Her tone is mildly defensive and I remember seeing Shannon a year or so ago walking Cody up the street to where the buses came. I only saw that because I had a good night and had been able to sleep and get up early, the way I had for years, or it had been a bad night and the hip fires kept me from sleeping at all, and there was Shannon in a man's fake leather jacket holding Cody's hand as they walked up to the corner across from the Island of Convenience.

"Your face looks a little better." Trina shuts off the water and squeezes the sponge, then drops it into its container near the liquid soap. It's a big bottle that she can't buy with her EBT card. I think of Brian and the money he steals from his mother.

"Trina?"

"I need a cigarette so fuckin' bad I could kill somebody." She rips a sheet from a roll of paper towels, squeezes past me, and wipes down the small table under the open blinds. It's still snowing out, and I think of the dead leaves on my patch of ground getting covered by it, something I never would've allowed when I wasn't much older than MJ, sitting shirtless in front of the battle he seems to live in.

I want to ask why *he* isn't in school, but then I remember Trina talking once or many times about MJ's learning disabilities, ones he got from his "stupid mother." She said this in a cloud of cigarette smoke in my car on the way to or from the lab, and now she's talking about needing to go to the lab again today, and as I watch this young woman scraping with her fingernail something sticky on her family's table, just a foldable one for playing cards, I know that I've misjudged this girl.

"Jamey's gonna bring me."

"To the lab?"

Trina nods. "But only if it's my last time." Her face is full of some kind of feeling I can't place. She moves past me back into her kitchenette and shoves the wadded paper towel into a trash bucket beneath the sink. "Want a coffee?"

"No, thanks." I watch Trina pour herself a cup from a coffee-maker that looks new. But then I see the Scotch tape holding the lid on top, a chip in the glass carafe.

"You here to lecture me?" She reaches into a bowl for packets of sugar and rips open two, which she dumps into her coffee. They're the packets from the coffee station up at the Island of Convenience, and I picture Trina stuffing them into the center pocket of her hoodie.

I shake my head. My back and hips ache. I want to lie down. She's leaning against her stovetop cradling her cup of coffee between two hands the way some women do, the way Ronnie used to.

"I just don't want you to get into trouble."

"Why'd you change your mind anyways?"

Kerry's shredded trash from the other night, her wine-stained ream of paper, her pills for anxiety and depression. I shrug. "I don't know, I guess I've just always tried to be responsible."

"So I'm *not*? What the fuck, Tom." She sips from her coffee, her eyes on the narrow shelves across from her. On them are canned goods from the food pantry, a half-eaten bag of potato chips held together with a hair elastic. *Responsible.* How many times since I fell off that roof have I thought of that word? The ability to *respond.* To the tasks and duties expected of you. To the hunger your wife has for a home in which to raise this baby you both made from love. To respond to those monthly bills that your daily work will pay. To respond to your hopes. To your *child's* hopes. To the cumulative hopes of a nation. That we're all promised the pursuit of our own piece of ground and whatever happiness we can find there.

MJ has turned the TV up. There're the sounds of revving engines and a sweeping laser beam.

"I need to lie down, hon."

I pass the couch. MJ's narrow back is to me as the boy stares at the TV, a whole universe opening up on the screen, the boy piloting some ship that's speeding through black space toward burning stars.

NIGHT IS HERE AND I lie on my plywood couch holding Trina's bag of ice to my swollen eye and lip. Through the wall comes the high joyous cackle she lets out when one of her kids actually delights her somehow, a sound I never hear when one boyfriend or another is with her.

A pounding on my door, an open hand doing it, and if that little shit Brian thinks he's getting the best of me again, he's tragically mistaken. My laptop and empty cup fall to the floor and I'm rushing down my short hallway in my socks.

"Tom? It's me, man. It's Fitz."

Fitz?

On the other side of the storm door under the overhead light stands Fitz in a maroon leather jacket. A scarf covers his throat, and his perfect bald head is hatless. "I didn't steal your fuckin' tools, Tom."

For a heartbeat or two I just stand there.

"I can see you there. You gonna let me in? It's fuckin' cold out."

Fitz possibly innocent, and now I'm opening the door. "Who did then?"

"Not me, brother. Let me in. I'm freezing my balls off."

In Fitz's gloved right hand is the neck of a bottle. It looks like vodka and it looks expensive, but I stay where I am, the icy air seeping in like evidence of something irrefutable. Fitz's teeth are beginning to chatter, his eyes watering, and I want to feel the hot animosity I had for him just yesterday, but opening up inside me is the terrifyingly soft void that comes with losing the object of one's hatred.

I push open the door and walk back into my unit, this too-warm and forsaken place I'm starting to feel I'll never leave. I step over the plank table and set my laptop onto the pine board.

Fitz stands in the doorway. "What happened to your face?"

"You didn't steal my tools?"

"You're hurting my feelings, man." Fitz holds up a bottle of Finlandia. "I shouldn't've even brought you this."

"Those tools were all I had, Fitz."

"You know how uncool it looks to have the po-po come to my house? The head of the condo association lives right next to me, man." Fitz wedges the vodka bottle under one arm, pulls off his gloves, shoves them into his leather jacket pockets, then twists open the bottle and walks into the kitchen. My cupboard doors swing open and shut. "How can you live like this?"

I can't. I don't.

The faucet turns on and off. There's the promising sound of liquid pouring into cups or glasses, and now Fitz emerges from the kitchen holding my only water glass in one hand and Drew's old sippy cup in the other. It's yellow and in the shape of SpongeBob

SquarePants, and Fitz is shaking his head as he hands it to me, then pulls out a chair and sits.

"You think I'd come here if I stole your shit?"

"It'd be a good strategy."

Fitz stares at me. He shakes his head, then reaches into his inside pocket for his box of Black & Milds.

"You bought a condo, Fitz?"

"Cool if I light up?"

"How'd you afford a fucking condominium?"

"I've been saving ever since I got here, you knew that."

"One last score?"

Fitz strikes a match and presses the flame to the tip of his cigar. There are the intruding smells of leather and sulfur and burning tobacco. He blows out smoke and watches it rise into the air. "I don't steal from friends, man. I tried to help you."

"So who did you steal from, Fitz?"

He shrugs. "The hospital. They're really fuckin' stupid over there."

"Stupid how?" It is as if Fitz has just called *me* stupid. And weak. And worthless. And even though my hip screws flame up whenever I sit on the edge of my plywood couch, I do it now, my rising anger keeping me from lying back.

"Put it this way." Fitz looks around for somewhere to flick his ash. "They don't lock up shit like they should."

"Like I didn't lock up shit?"

"I'm telling you, man. I tried to fuckin' help you."

"What about right and wrong, Fitz?"

"What about it?"

"They trust you over there."

"Hey, I'm not the only one who does it. I know a *doctor* who's lifting shit. So he can get off on it. Least I never do any myself."

"No, you just sell it to losers who do." I look down at Drew's sippy cup filled to the brim with this drug thief's vodka, and I'm seeing Drew when he was two or three years old, sitting in his booster seat with his curly hair and trusting smile, sipping his apple juice from this very cup, and I picture me handing my toddler son a hundred-dollar bill to carry outside to Fitz, waiting for him with a baggie of stolen Os. "Fitz, you ever think about what that shit does to the people you sell it to? To their *families*?"

Fitz shakes his head. He blows out a smoke ring, his eyes on it like he's just given it life itself, and Drew's sippy cup is flying through that ring, its contents splattering the wall and the kitchen's linoleum floor, Fitz jerking to the side as the cup bounces off his shoulder.

"Get the fuck outta my house." I'm up and there's a clattering sound and then I've got Fitz up against my bookshelves, his leather lapels in my hands, Fitz's face so close to mine that I can smell his cologne and skin, his warm breath and spittle in my face. Fitz is shouting something, or maybe these are just the grunts of a man being lifted off his feet and dragged and pushed down a dark hallway, then up against a storm door whose handle I fumble with, my other hand still gripping Fitz's leather lapel, Fitz twisting away as the door springs open and he has to slap the railing to keep from falling over it. "What the fuck, man."

"You know how hard it was to *quit* that shit? Is that how you're going to pay your fucking mortgage? With death money? You peddle *death*, you piece of shit."

Fitz straightens up and walks slowly down my steps. At the sidewalk he turns around and spreads his scarf across his chest, buttons up his jacket, and reaches into the pockets for his gloves. He looks up at me, breathing hard and feeling like I might throw up in my own doorway. "Do that again, motherfucker, and I'll blow your face off."

16

THE FUNERAL HOME IS ON A HILL STREET OVERLOOKING THE river, the afternoon sun glinting off its swirling surface. On the other side is a factory of some kind and its smokestack is seventy or eighty feet high, wisps of dark exhaust drifting from its top. From behind the front window of the parlor I watch an old couple in overcoats making their way slowly up the steps. Their arms are linked and their breaths leave them in small white clouds that vanish as quickly as they come.

Larry's casket lies at the front of the room framed by floral displays of all kinds. Ronnie would know the names of most of those flowers, but I don't. What I do know is that in the hour I've been standing or sitting in this room full of men and women, many of them talking loudly and laughing, only a few of the men in coats and ties so that I feel better about wearing my collared shirt under my Christmas sweater, a strange sense of peace has wrapped itself around me.

I took a taxi here, and as I paid the driver I wished him an excellent day with the kind of good cheer that comes from a heavy burden lifted. Though what that burden is I can't fully say. Only that as I and my hip fires made our way this morning to the bank across from the Island of Convenience, my disability check deposited there by federal computers the night before, I felt a certain clarity about things: (1) I'll probably never get my car back, and (2) I'll probably never get my car back because I'm not willing to be the kind of man that Fitz is, a man who knowingly hurts others to help himself.

In the bank's lobby, I then took thirty dollars from Drew's hundred, bought my son's money order for the remaining balance, and on the inside flap of the stamped envelope I keep a supply of in my kitchen drawer, I wrote: *I promise to send more soon.*

Love—Dad. Though how I'll do this is a mystery. And as I stepped outside into the cold, I could see the shabby buildings of the 8. My and Trina's and Jamey's escapade. It all seemed so foolish now. These graspings at dollars and coins when one day our hearts will stop as finally as Larry's has.

And so what's left that I can put my hands to?

Larry's widow is standing at the head of the receiving line. She's let her hair grow gray and keeps it short, a style that can be washed and then forgotten about so that all the tasks of the day can be confronted. The made-up skin of her face looks loose on its bones, and she's wearing a black pantsuit, a broach pinned to her left lapel. As I move slowly toward Larry's casket, I picture him buying that broach at some jewelry store just days before Christmas decades ago.

I kneel on the cushioned pad alongside Larry's casket and I can only hope that I don't appear to be the interloper from the 8 that I am, because I genuinely cared for Larry. How could I *not* care for a man who treated me like I was still the Tom Lowe Jr. I used to be? But what did I ever do to show Larry that I was grateful?

Nothing. And so let this gesture, as late as it is, be something.

Larry's body is in a gray suit and a black tie, his hands folded over his abdomen. On the ring finger of his left is his wedding band.

I avoid looking at his face. I lower my head and close my eyes and pray.

God, I don't believe in you, but I believe in Larry. Please take care of this good man's soul. Please take care of his wife, whom I will try to comfort now. Give me the right words, Lord. And thank you.

I can count on half of one hand how many times I've been inside a church. But I make the sign of the cross anyway and start to stand, flames licking down both femurs until I straighten and turn to Larry's widow.

The room's still loud with a sound I've somehow not been hearing for a while, men and women talking, a phone buzzing, a man laughing. I'm so much taller than Larry's widow. Her face is level with my chest, but she's not looking at my premature Christmas trees as I take her small hands in mine, she's looking up at me, her eyes lit with fatigue and curiosity and a tired gratitude.

"I'm Tom Lowe. Your husband was my friend. My dear friend."

"Did we know you?"

"Your husband did." To the right of Larry's widow stands Paul. He's dressed in a tieless white shirt and a suit jacket too small for his shoulders, and he's eyeing me the way he always does. I can feel Larry's widow's heartbeat pulsing in her wrists and hands I still hold in my own. I say, "Can I tell you something? I've been going through a hard patch, a real hard patch. And maybe you've noticed that people turn their backs on you when you're down, but"—a thickening in my throat, a welling in my eyes that I regret—"your husband didn't. He treated me with—he treated me with respect."

"Yes, yes. That was Larry's way." She smiles and almost laughs. "He was a softy for people. A real softy."

I don't know if she means this as a compliment or if she's pointing out an endearing flaw in the man she learned to live with in all the years they shared. Paul clears his throat and I let go of Larry's widow's hands, then lean down and kiss her cheek. There are the smells of age and medicated shampoo and a brand of makeup that maybe only older women wear. "I wish you peace."

"Thank you, Tom." Again, she's smiling up at me, and I feel buoyed that she has my name there on her tongue, that maybe what I said to her actually helped in some way.

Then I'm shaking Paul's hand. It's smaller than mine but stronger, squeezing once before letting go, Paul's eyes already moving on to the next person in the receiving line though there is no one else.

A woman who must be Larry's daughter stands in front of me. She's dressed in blue and gray and her hair is pinned back, and she smiles up at me though it's clear that she left this place hours ago, her body going through the niceties she can no longer bear. I rest my hand on her shoulder. "Your dad will watch over you always."

At first she doesn't seem to hear what I say. But then her eyes blink and fill and for a second I'm afraid I've said the exact wrong

thing, but she wraps her arms around me and cries into my Christmas sweater and I stroke her hair and think of Trina, of her pale
face looking up into mine. *I wish you were my* **dad**.

The young woman pulls away. She dabs at her eyes with a balled
tissue in her hand. "Thank you."

I smile and nod. What's left of the receiving line has broken off,
men and women talking to each other throughout the room. What
I've just told Larry's daughter surprises me, so does my prayer at
Larry's casket. I've never been a believer in souls or spirits. But the
endless love one has for one's child, how can that not live on after
our bodies end?

And as I make my way to the coffee table, I'm also all too aware
that I haven't watched over my own son, sure as hell not through
Drew's teens, which end at midnight tonight. But why ruin the
uplifting sense of virtue that I feel right now? The feeling that I've,
in some small way, been of service to Larry's widow and daughter.

How *else* can I be of service? What else can I do?

The fires inside my hips burn, but this pain feels somehow
diminished, and now a rising confidence propels me to the entryway of the funeral parlor, where a man in a black overcoat stands.

"Sir, I'm afraid I left my cell phone at home. Can I use yours to
call a taxi?"

"You bet. Follow me."

Just like that.

The man didn't even begin to look me over like I was unworthy of following him into the inner sanctum of this place. It's a
carpeted office with wainscoting along the walls and a big cherry
desk, the exact kind that Mike Andrews' has, and as the man in
the black overcoat presses a button on the phone and hands me the
receiver, it's hard not to feel that I'm in the heart of some kind of
higher lesson I should've learned a long time ago.

There's the humming of the dial tone, the smells of cashmere
and the man's cologne as he actually leaves the office to give me
privacy. At first I can't remember the number of the taxi company,
but then comes the memory of the girl at Dawn's Hair & Nails late
this morning, how she turned to me from her customer as I walked

into her shop. Her hair was still dyed white, but her lipstick was blue, her eyelashes thick and black. She looked like a cartoon character from a movie Drew used to want to watch over and over again, and she just shook her head and cracked a half-smile and pointed her scissors over her shoulder toward the phone. "My boss likes you. That's the only reason I can say yes."

This was a surprise to hear because the owner Dawn didn't look at me yesterday as if she liked me. But this small unexpected gift gave me the confidence to call Information on her phone, and now, leaning against the edge of the funeral home's cherry desk, that number comes back to me and I dial it and order a taxi to drive me back to the 8.

17

MY CABDRIVER'S NAME IS RAKSMEI AND HE'S HALF CAMBODIAN, half Vietnamese. He's also forty-three years old and wears wireless sunglasses and has a kind face I can see in profile from where I sit in the back.

Over the seven-mile ride from the funeral home, I learn that his mother was the Vietnamese half and that's what got her sent to one of Pol Pot's labor camps, where she was starved to death. I also learn that the man's father was Cambodian and a journalist, one of the "city people" and therefore a collaborator, which got him sent to a separate camp where he disappeared forever.

The cabbie drove slowly and he told this story with the detached tone of someone describing the plays of a very old chess match between two long-gone opponents. I thought of my own father driving off one day to the warehouse where his heart simply stopped, and sitting there in the backseat of that cab, I began to feel the darkly benign presence of something larger than myself. "How old were you, my friend?"

The cabbie shrugged. "I was a baby."

"How'd you survive?"

"My uncle."

"Any brothers? Sisters?"

Raksmei nodded. We were driving through a neighborhood of two-story houses, all the leaves raked and gotten rid of, the driveways swept clean. "Nobody knows what happened to her. My oldest daughter has her name."

"What's that?"

"Chenda." The driver smiled at me in the rearview mirror. "It means thinker."

"And your name?"

"Raksmei."

"Yeah, but what does that mean?"

The cabbie laughed. "Ray of light. My ex-wife thought that was a funny one. She called me 'ray of darkness.' I guess I'm depressed, I don't know."

I looked out the window. The late afternoon sun slanted through a stand of pine trees, and I could see Drew as a five-year-old running through them with one of his light sabers, me chasing after him with my own.

I said, "Can I ask you a personal question?"

"Another one?" But the man was smiling at me in the rearview mirror and I remembered those long nights driving my car for money when hardly any of my customers ever talked to me at all. This Raksmei looked almost grateful so I asked, "Was the divorce your wife's idea?"

"Oh yes. Who wants to live with a downer like me?"

"But you had a rough start."

"No, my childhood was a happy one. It really was. I'm just a downer." Ray laughed again, then shook his head and accelerated onto the highway for the last mile to the 8.

"My wife left me too, brother."

"Why?"

I shrugged. "I used to think it was because I fell off a roof and got hooked on painkillers, but maybe not."

The cabbie glanced at me in the rearview mirror. He looked like he had questions about my injury and affliction, but he just said, "Why then?"

"I don't know. I was drowning in a way. But was she supposed to drown with me?"

The cabbie nodded and kept nodding until he took the exit onto the ramp. Its curbstones were cracked, the brown grass matted all the way to a chain-link fence lined with paper trash and dented cans. Raksmei said, "My wife—"

"Yeah?"

"She used to scream at me that she didn't sign up for this shit. But I used to tell her, 'You did, and I did too. We sign up for each other's *shit*.'"

"But she didn't."

"No."

I wanted to ask the cabbie if he was sure that *he*, too, had signed up for it because I was beginning to think something I never had before: What if it had been *Ronnie* who was laid up for months in that rented bed in front of our wall of windows? What if Ronnie was sneaking trips down O River from a stash she hid? What if it was Ronnie lying to me and making Drew go buy her some more from some kid in a van out in the woods? What would *I* do? Would I love her anyway? *Would* I?

The taxi's engine is still running in front of the 8 and Raksmei prints out my receipt. Shannon steps out the front door of her unit. She's dressed in that big fake leather jacket, her red wool cap pulled over her ears. She rushes off the stoop and into the roadway, passing the taxi without even looking at it, and I lean forward and hand over the last of my money. I'm hungry. My hips and legs feel dipped in scalding water, but I feel like I've just made a friend in this Raksmei, who turns around and holds out my change, close to eight bucks.

"Keep it."

"You sure?"

"Maybe you and me, maybe we should cut our exes some slack."

Raksmei just looks at me. His skin is darker than it looked in the mirror and I think of his young mother and father butchered by madness. "It was good to meet you, Raksmei."

"You too, sir."

"Tom. Tom Lowe." I hold out my hand and the cabbie squeezes it, his own hand small, warm, and soft.

Then I'm standing in front of my stoop in the cold watching the yellow taxi drive away. Those eight dollars I gave him, it was so easy to do that. I don't feel one bit of regret for doing that, though if I'm not careful I won't be able to pay my internet bill, my one extravagance.

I'm shivering under my Christmas sweater, but the late day sun is on Dawn's Hair & Nails across the street, on two small sedans parked in front of it, on Larry's Liquors and a minivan at its door, on Jamey's shitbox facing Trina's unit, Cody's Big Wheels up against the wall in a bed of dead leaves, on Cal and Amber's raked lawn and swept stoop, on Mrs. Bongiovanni's mailbox and storm door and curtained windows, on the full dumpsters across from Fitz's former unit, which now holds new residents of this 8 I have yet to meet, and as I fold my arms across my chest and wedge my bare hands under my armpits, my teeth chattering like Fitz's last night, I remember his eyes as he watched his own smoke ring drift through the air: he knew not one thing about right and wrong.

But I do. I don't know why or how I do, but I sure as hell do. And I will not let this place make me a bad man. I will not be a man who takes from others. I will *not*.

Shivering and hungry and knowing that I should lie down, I move past Jamey's car and knock on Trina's front door. I'm breathing hard from the short climb up the steps. My eyes are watering and my ears and the tip of my nose burn. I knock again.

Cody answers the door. "What?"

"Cody, I said I'd get it!" Trina steps in front of the boy and pulls the door closed until it touches her hip. She's in a dark T-shirt and her pajama bottoms and she's looking up at me in a way she never has before, like I've come to collect the rent and she doesn't have it. "Yeah?"

"Can I come in?"

"Why?"

I'm not sure, only that my small acts of kindness back at Larry's wake, my pulling my cabdriver into a conversation we both seemed to need, it makes me want more of this possibly new kind of work that I can put my hands to.

From behind Trina come the sounds of MJ's screen carnage, its constant machine-gun fire and exploding rocket-propelled grenades. "You don't have to hide things from me, Trina. You know that."

Trina's eyes soften into some sort of confusion, one that she's somehow never been able to leave behind. Her bare arms break out into goose bumps. "Okay, but no fucking lectures, Tommy. I mean it." She pulls open the door and I step into warm noise that smells like cigarette smoke and coffee. MJ's a skinny shadow in front of the TV, his fingers tapping away at the controller on his lap I can't see. But what I can see is Jamey kneeling in a wide pile of trash spread around Trina's once-spotless floor. Up against the chairs of her card table are six or seven full garbage bags, some white, some dark green. On the couch squats Cody, his eyes on all the TV men that his big brother murders so fast one at a time.

"Hey, Tom." Jamey glances up as casually as if he were reading the paper. He rips open an envelope, pulls out what's inside, then holds it up to Trina. "Got another one." She takes it from him and steps barefoot past two empty ketchup bottles and opened soup cans, over a small mound of shredded paper and an empty bag of French Roast coffee beans, past eggshells and onion skins that are laid out on a towel to protect Trina's floor. She sets the folded papers on the table on a short stack of others like it. Then she turns to me, still standing near the front door feeling like the man who taught his eleven-year-old son how to lie to his own mother.

"Don't worry, we went somewhere else. That whole town's full of rich people, Tommy."

"Hey look, this one's got those checks with it, too."

"Let me see." Trina hops over the trash and takes it from him. She holds it close to her face, her eyes passing quickly over whatever's in that credit card company's letter sent to someone who's not her. I think of the learning disability she's convinced she has, though she seems to be understanding everything she's reading because she holds the letter over Jamey and says, "This is the best one so far, honey."

Honey.

She steps back over the trash and rests the letter on the table. "You want a coffee, Tom?" Trina's voice is careful, almost shy.

"Yes. Thank you." I follow her into the narrow kitchen. In a square of tinfoil on the counter lies a smoking cigarette. Trina picks it up and takes a deep drag and blows smoke out the corner of her lips as she pours me coffee into a white cup.

She turns to me, hands me the coffee. "It's not that old lady's, Tom. Why do you look so upset?"

"Maybe I'm worried about you."

"Me? It was your fucking idea." A strand of hair falls in front of her face and she tucks it behind her ear, her eyes on mine. From the living room Jamey calls out: "One more, Trina. We got another one."

"I'll be right out."

I think of how she called him honey earlier, Brian still her boyfriend only days ago. Jealous, no-count Brian. But this kid Jamey's going to school. And she should be doing that too, or at least thinking about some vocational training. Some kind of trade she can learn and then use in an honest way.

"Don't fuckin' look at me like that, Tommy. I'm only doing it to get outta this place." She exhales smoke, stubs her cigarette in the foil, then folds it up neatly and drops it into the trash.

"What if you get caught, hon? You could lose your kids."

"I'm losing 'em already, Tommy. *Jesus.*" She brushes past me and back out into the stolen trash.

I sip my coffee. It's too hot and burns my lip. I set it on the counter and walk over to the boy kneeling in the stolen trash. "This isn't cool, Jamey. You guys shouldn't do this."

"Why'd you change your mind?" Jamey looks up at me, and it's clear that he's stoned.

"I said no fucking lectures, Tommy." Trina sits at her table studying the papers. She looks like she's trying to decide which bill she's going to pay first, and a sadness drops over me like a black net and I carry it with me back out into the cold.

PART III

18

THROUGH THE WINDOW BLINDS ABOVE MY PLYWOOD COUCH comes the slow lightening of the sky, a gray that even this early looks heavy with more snow. Outside on the road something heavy drives by. Twenty years ago this morning Ronnie's water broke while she was making coffee, and then I was driving her too fast to the hospital in my work van. When she started to moan I reached over and kept my hand on her knee. "I'm here, honey. I'm right here."

Only three hours later Drew came out without a cry and he took right to her breast. She and I were both crying softly and Ronnie's sweat-dampened hair was stuck to her cheek and I brushed it back from her face and we both stared down at this unspeakable gift that had come to us, through us.

I've been awake a long time, my laptop open on my belly, my fines still on my plank table. But because I know that I'll never get my car back, it's like seeing photos of some old enemy I'm not afraid of anymore, and now I start deleting all three of my revenge folders.

The first one that I slide over to the trash icon is *Banks*, then the one on *Insurance*, and last is the one I started with, *Big Pharma*. Doing this feels like cutting out a vestigial organ, one I thought I needed when I got stranded here over six years ago, but now, the dawn of my son's twentieth birthday, it's hard to feel the feelings that created those folders.

I need the toilet. My lip feels like it might be able to tolerate some instant coffee, but I can't let another minute pass without sending something to Drew.

I don't remember my son's email address so type in *Drew* and here comes the most recent exchange between us. Four weeks ago? Has it really been a *month*?

How's school, son?

Fine.

Did you get my money order?

Two days later came Drew's answer. *Thanks.*

In the subject line I type: *Happy Big Two O! (from your dad)* The phrase looks forced to me and doesn't even begin to capture what I hope to say. I delete it and write: *A note from your dad on your birthday.*

That small blank page appears, but in the upper right corner of the screen is a color not usually there—red—the battery very low. The cord's on one of my bookshelves, but I feel in the presence of that same impulse that took Larry's widow's hands in mine, that made me ask my cabbie's name, that pulled me yesterday up the concrete steps of Trina's unit. And so I don't hesitate.

Dear Drew,

*It is your 20th birthday, and—*my face tingles with shame—*I have let you down in so many ways, my son. So many.*

*My hope was to be there with you today. You have every right not to believe me when I say that. **Every** right. But my car got towed and I just didn't have the means to get it back. I'm not proud to tell you that this broke me in a way. I'm not proud to tell you that I was already going to do something bad. But I didn't. Instead I was finally going to sell my tools, but they got stolen and*

Drew's young hopeful face, flushed from the cold as he handed his father a baggie of Os from Teddy in the van I used to own. What is it that I need to *say* to him now? What? I close my eyes, take a breath, and wait.

*The only reason I got clean, Drew, was so that I could be a father to you again. But how would you know that? You hardly ever hear from me. But all this time in this shithole, I've been working my way back to you. I have, son. But I guess it's taken everything I have just to learn to live with my pain that never goes away. To do this without drugs. And all along I've held out hope that I'll still be able to work someday. Remember when you and your girlfriend Hanna came to see me? As I've told you before, I was in a bad place because I was starting to see then that I'm not fit for work anymore. **Any** kind of work. But I've been* *fighting seeing that, which has put me in some kind of in-between place. And so I haven't reached out to you much. But all of this, my dear dear son, is only part of it.*

The truth is I have not been able to bear this thought of myself as useless. As some bum subsidized by those who can work. This self-hatred nearly killed my love—not for you—but for being a father. Because what kind of father am I if I can't help take care of my own son?

This man your mother's with now, he's been good to you two, and he can take care of you when I can't. This thought has been in my head for a while, but I didn't know how deep it was in me till I almost committed a crime. Less than a week ago. I'd had it, and if I'm being completely honest—and that's all I want to be with you today, Drew— I'd had it with my life.

But you know what? I'm starting to see things differently now. My car getting towed and my tools getting stolen, this may have been the best thing that's happened to me in a long time, because it's waking me up. It's

The screen goes dark and my breath goes still in my throat. I poke at buttons on the keypad, but the screen stays dark. For two or three beats of my heart I feel that old rage begin to rise again, that bitter echo of *why does this shit keep happening to* ***me?*** But it's an echo that immediately dies in some ancient canyon I seem to be moving through now. Its walls are sunlit and there's the sound of fresh water running somewhere up ahead, the feeling that I'm surrounded not by the ghosts of the dead along the banks of O River, but by the spirits that made the men who became those ghosts.

I put a pan of water on the stove, turn the burner under it up to high, then make my way slowly up the stairs. Standing at my toilet, it hurts me that what I just wrote's been taken from me. I know that I can plug in my machine and write it again, but then I'll be missing this new lesson I've maybe just been sent: my son doesn't need to hear my words, he needs to see my *actions*.

I dry my hands off on a towel I haven't washed in weeks and avoid looking at the framed photo of me and Drew on the wall. There's been enough staring at that and doing nothing.

A faint thumping. It's coming from outside and at first I think it's the wind. But no, it's the thumping of bass notes from some kind of music. Fitz?

Then I'm moving down the short hallway alongside the bedroom I hardly ever sleep in. It's begun to snow. Flakes of it stick to the window, and there, parked on the other side of the roadway, is Brian sitting behind the wheel of his mother's Pontiac.

Exhaust sputters out the tailpipe and his headlights are off. So's Brian's hoodie, his bald head nodding in time to the beat of this music turned up all the way. He takes a drag off a cigarette. Its tip glows bright and he looks out the window toward Trina's unit. He exhales smoke and slaps the wheel with his palm, and it can't be much later than six in the morning and this kid looks like he's been up all night. Up to no good.

I move quickly down the stairs and pull on my work boots and my jacket and step out onto the stoop. The air's a shock of cold, flakes of snow lighting on my face. As I walk slowly down my steps, Brian keeps looking over at Jamey's sedan in front of Trina's unit, and now Brian's looking straight at me stepping into the roadway and lifting my hand because all I want to do is talk to the kid.

He stops moving his head. He turns to jab at something and the music switches off. Then he stares back at me halfway across the road. There's only quiet. I think of what I told Trina to tell this Brian, that if he comes around here again I'll report him for assault and battery. But she doesn't have a phone, so Brian probably never got the message and I have no desire to bring it up.

Brian's nose is still a bit swollen, and for reasons I cannot begin to understand, the boy looks so young to me sitting there behind the glass of his mother's car. His bald head could be a baby's, and his eyes, usually lit with a lazy defiance, now look dark with pain and I know why too.

It's that car in front of Trina's stoop. The one owned by the same boy who drove her to the food pantry when Brian couldn't.

The sky seems lighter now. I stop a few feet away and motion for the kid to roll down his window. The glass lowers and, again, I feel in the presence of something that used to be invisible to me but isn't anymore.

"What?" Brian says. "You want another beatin'?"

"No thanks." I put my hands in my jacket pockets. Brian's eyes follow them so I pull them back out and let them hang at my sides. Wind peppers snow against my face. "I have a son about your age. It's his birthday today."

"Who gives a shit?"

"His mother left me for another guy. That hurt like hell."

The kid just looks at me. He takes a drag off his cigarette and blows smoke out through his nostrils. He shakes his head once and glances back at Trina's.

"The older I get, Brian, I think maybe we all hurt the same."

Cars pass by. Brian looks at me like I'm offering him something he maybe wanted years ago but now it's too late. It's just too late. "What's your fuckin' problem?" He jerks the Pontiac into gear and shoots out into the road, and there's the shrieking of brakes and a minivan swerving into the opposing lane, then bumping over the curb into the lot of the strip plaza, horns blowing as the Pontiac cuts left past the Island of Convenience and is gone.

I wait for an empty school bus to pass, then I walk across the street in a calm I seem to be hovering in as I get close to the minivan and wait outside the driver's window for the crying woman there to see me.

She's young, her hair curly and dark under a white wool cap. She keeps turning to look back at the rear seat, and she's talking and crying and through the rear passenger window I can see two bundled little kids strapped into their booster seats. One of them is looking straight at me, and the other's starting to cry with his mother. I tap the window and the woman jerks back and covers her mouth with a gloved hand. I smile at her, her window going down like a door that's been locked for so long but now I've found the key.

"You're okay, you're all right. You guys were lucky. Very lucky."

"Oh my God, my kids, my *kids*." She covers her face with both gloved hands, then twists around to speak to them in warm reassuring tones that sound desperate to me.

I say, "They're okay, hon." I step back and wave at them both through the window. "Right? Everybody's fine."

A loud hissing, more cars passing by. Snow on my head and in my face. In the strip of ground between the street and the lot is a dislodged section of curbstone and a deep tire track, and now the hissing stops and I can see that her front tire is flat, busted open on the curb the way this young mother's morning ride was busted open too. I can feel the lip of the roof leave me, the soffit rising above me so fast, the blue sky beyond like some witness to all things.

The woman's thanking me. She pulls out a tissue and blows her nose.

"I'm afraid you have a flat."

"What?"

Under falling snow, I walk around to the front of the minivan and inspect the other tire, then both rear tires. When I get back to the woman's window, she's already on her phone, punching in the numbers of her AAA card. I used to have one of those. I used to have a wallet full of plastic cards like that.

Now both kids are crying and it seems the woman can't hear the AAA dispatcher and she unbuckles her seat belt and opens her door and steps past me to finish her call. Before my accident I would've told her not to bother, I'd have this tire changed before their truck gets here.

She thanks someone on the phone, then pushes it into her coat pocket. Her eyeliner's begun to run and I can see that she's in a new-looking parka that reaches the hem of her skirt, that she's wearing nylons and rubber boots that match her coat. She's probably on her way to work, her kids to child care or preschool. She blows her nose on another tissue. "They said they're right nearby."

"I'd change it for you, but I got hurt a few years ago."

"Oh no, I pay for that membership. I may as well use it."

Both kids are crying louder now and she rushes past me and opens the rear passenger door, leaning into her minivan as the door keeps sliding backwards. I know the AAA driver won't want anyone in the van when he changes the tire, and now I'm telling this young mother that. "But I live across the street. You can wait there till he's done."

Both kids seem to be the exact same age, two or three, and they're bundled in little parkas of their own, boots on their feet, mittens on their hands, wool caps pulled down over their ears.

"We'll be fine. Thank you, though."

I can't tell if her reticence is because she doesn't want to impose or if it's that thing I've gotten used to, people taking in my mussed hair and unshaven face and untied work boots. The exile in my eyes. But within minutes the AAA van pulls into the lot and the driver asks for everyone to "wait outside the vehicle." His breath is white in the air and the woman asks him if her kids can wait inside his van.

"Can't do it, sorry. Against policy."

The calm I've been hovering in feels punctured. This man's words are the exact line shoved into me from so many since my fall, from my bank and insurance company, from my doctors and endless creditors, from the young officer who had my car towed. Even from my one and only Ronnie. *Can't do it, sorry.*

The man has an old burn along his throat, and he's already pulling the woman's spare tire from the back of her van. I'm about to say something, but the woman says, "Can you carry her across the street for me?" She's holding one of the bundled kids in her arms and she has the other by the hand and the snow's falling in big heavy flakes and the woman has to blink and turn her head to the side.

"Of course." I squat to take her child under the arms, this little girl who can't weigh more than twenty-five pounds. When I straighten up, my hip screws flare and I get my arm under her rear and steady the back of her tiny neck like she's an infant. Twenty years fall away and I'm holding Drew again. Except this little one's pushing away from me, her cap-enclosed face looking scared, and I have to strain to hold her close.

The young mother next to me waits for a car to pass, and then she looks both ways and runs across the street with her tiny son held to her chest, his small head bobbing. I follow as fast as I can though the girl is crying again and it's like my femur bones are being drilled with dozens of holes that ooze marrow and whatever blood I have left. But I don't care because I'm carrying a small child I don't even know to a warm place, my place, and when I get to my concrete steps they already have half an inch of snow on them and I'm breathing too hard but say to the young mother, "Careful. Careful now."

My unit smells like dirty dishes and dried vodka across my kitchen floor. But the pan of water I put on the stove is at a full boil, its steam rising into the air. I set the little girl down and offer the young mother a cup of coffee.

"Yes, *please*."

The girl has stopped crying. The woman's on her knees in front of both her kids, pulling off their wool caps, mittens, and coats. From where I stand at the stove, spooning instant coffee into two cups, I can see the woman taking in my plank table and the worn sheet of plywood across the cushions of my couch.

"I wish I had something for your kids."

"Oh no, they're fine. Thank you."

"I have ice cream."

One of the kids says, "Cream?"

"No, honey."

The boy climbs onto my plywood couch and stands on it and starts to laugh.

"No, Kyle, sit down, please." The woman has taken off her own cap, and when she turns to look at me over her shoulder I can see how young she is, barely thirty. And lovely. "I'm sorry."

"No, it's a piece of plywood. Don't worry about it." I stir the steaming water into both cups, my legs and hips on fire. I've come to look forward to this cheap coffee that's so easy to make, but now, its burnt-brown smell rising up into my face, it's the scent of poverty and I don't want to offer it to her anymore. But she's on her feet and walking over to me and so I hand it to her. "I have milk, if you'd like it."

"Black is perfect. Thank you."

I forgot about the milk Trina put in my fridge. "Would your kids like that? Some milk?"

"No, they just ate. Thank you, though."

The girl has now climbed up onto my plywood couch with her brother. She's dressed in a corduroy jumper and the boy's in a wool plaid shirt, its tails hanging out. "Twins?"

"Yes, but my daughter's older by seven minutes and, believe me, she acts like a big sister." The woman takes one sip of her coffee, and pulls out her phone. "I'm sorry, I have to call my work."

I sip my own coffee. The boy jumps and the plywood rises up under his sister and she falls onto her bottom and laughs, then scrambles back up for him to do it again. Their young mother's describing her accident to someone on her phone. She's saying that she'll be late for the first meeting but that Phil should start the presentation, she'll be there as soon as she can, and now her voice breaks, "Oh Mary, it was so *awful*. I had Kyle and Alicia in the car with me. I'm just such a mess right now."

I can hear this woman Mary's voice. She sounds older, my age maybe, and her tone's sweet and consoling. "Go home, Caitlin. Take a sick day. Phil can handle it."

Caitlin. A lovely name for a lovely young woman with two sweet kids jumping on my plywood couch.

"No, I'm fine. I am." She turns and smiles over at me. "A nice man is helping us. I'll be in as soon as I can."

A nice man. This stagnant hole of mine, it suddenly feels like it just got a fresh coat of paint.

Caitlin says, "No jumping, you guys."

The kids are laughing and they don't stop and now it's the boy's turn to fall and hop back up fast.

"*Kyle.*"

"It's fine. Really, it's no problem."

She smiles at me. She picks up her coffee and takes a big swallow. "I should check on that jerk's progress. Can you watch them for me for a sec?"

"Of course." I set my cup down and the kids keep jumping, but the girl's watching her mother disappear down the hallway and she looks like she's about to open her mouth just as her brother lands on his end of the plywood, and the girl springs forward and so do I, my hip fires sucking me backwards, but I lunge anyway and in my arms is the little girl and who cares if I'm on my back, my plank table and laptop on the floor too?

The boy's still laughing and lovely Caitlin rushes around the corner. "Oh my God, are you all *right*?"

"Yeah, she just went flying is all." I lift the little girl away from my chest. She's looking at me like she did when I stood outside their minivan, like she knows something about me.

"Kyle! Get down right this instant." Caitlin steps over my turned-over books and upside-down plank table and lifts her son down onto the floor. But unlike Trina, she doesn't swear at him. She doesn't call him a name. She doesn't slap him. This woman's clearly an abundist, and the thing is I, too, feel in the presence of an abundance. A kind I've never considered before. One I can't see or touch, but here it is anyway.

The boy's gone quiet and the little girl starts to whimper. Then she's rising in the air away from me and this Caitlin's kissing her cheek and brushing her hair back off her forehead. "You're okay, honey. Was that fun? Was it?" She looks down at me on my back on the floor. "Do you need some help getting up?"

"You have a nice name. Mine's Tom Lowe."

"Oh my God, see how rude I am? I'm Caitlin, and this one is Alicia." She sets her daughter down. "And that's Kyle. Now you two help Tom clean this up, okay? I'm so sorry, but the Triple A man seems almost done. Can I leave them with you for two more minutes? I'll be right back."

Then she's gone and both kids stand there quiet. One of the books I use for my table legs is lying on the floor next to me, a collection of black-and-white photographs by Dorothea Lange. I don't remember how the book came to be mine, but I pull it over and prop myself up on one elbow and open it.

The first picture's of a man in a black hat pulling a wagon down a dirt road under the sun. In the wagon are what look like folded clothes and blankets, a young girl in a white bonnet sitting on top. Twenty or thirty feet behind her walk two women. One's in a worn cotton skirt, the other in overalls, and the one in the skirt's holding the hand of a child the size of these twins, Alicia and Kyle, and that child's holding onto the hand of her older brother, a skinny boy in cutoff shorts. I turn the book toward the twins. "See? Kids. Like you."

Kyle steps closer and Alicia follows him. My legs lie across my overturned plank, and now I pat the floor and the boy sits while his big sister stays standing. I point to the man pulling the wagon on that road in Oklahoma almost a hundred years ago. It probably holds all they own, maybe some folded canvas in there to string up and sleep under at night. "That's the daddy." I move my finger to the woman in the skirt. "And that's the mommy. And this other lady? That's the auntie."

Kyle presses his finger to the image of the man. "Daddy?"

"Yes. Daddy." My eyes fill. I blink fast and shake my head.

Alicia sits on the stack of books. She looks down the hallway where her mother disappeared, then back at me turning the page to the next photograph. This one's of a haggard woman in the shade of a lean-to breastfeeding her baby. The woman can't be any older than these kids' mother, but she has deep worry lines in her forehead and around her mouth, and her open blouse and skirt look like they're made from burlap.

The boy points to the baby and says the word and I'm almost twenty years younger, Drew sitting on my lap naming all the household objects in the picture book I held open across my knees. This was before I bought land and built our house. We were still in our apartment in Salem, a two-room place not much bigger than this unit of mine in the 8. But its windows let in the sun from the east and it was a three-block walk to the water, where there were restaurants and moored boats and an ice cream stand, and Ronnie and I pushed Drew there in his stroller. We ordered cones and

Drew loved watching the gulls come flying down to the ground to pick at the last bits I always threw down there for them.

It was a two-room life then, but it was a good life and I never should've reached for more. Why did I do that? Ronnie and I had *everything*: our baby son, our health, enough to eat and drink, shelter, a cozy one at that. As Drew got older he'd need his own room, but why did his father have to reach for so much more than he could possibly deliver? And I know that these photos in front of me were of farmers whose livelihood had been decimated by drought, whose property went to the banks, that a handful of rich men continue to do wrong in insurance and drug company board-rooms, I know all this and something has to be done, but mean-while these two miracles in their corduroys are looking from me to the image of the young mother, then back at me.

Their faces are so soft, their hair and lips so new, and their eyes hold a bottomless trust in whatever I'll tell them. Lying there beside them feels like kneeling next to Larry's casket talking to a god I don't believe in, though now these two small children seem to have come from the same place I prayed to.

"She loves her baby, see? She loves her so very, very much." My voice breaks and I don't know why.

"Mommy." The boy points to the woman's face.

"Mommy?" Alicia says. She looks down the hallway, then back at me.

"She's coming. She'll be back soon."

"Soon?"

"Yes, she will." And that's why my voice broke: this Caitlin has left her precious kids in my care because she trusts me not to harm them in any way. She's spent so little time in my company yet she can see that I'm only trying to help.

The boy Kyle's turning the page of the picture book when the storm door swings open and cold blows down the hall. Lovely Caitlin calls out, "All fixed. You guys, we need to fix Tom's table."

"No, please, it's not a problem. Really." I want to say that she has that meeting to get to, but she's already squatting in her parka dusted with snow, helping both kids into their coats and mittens and hats. "I really can't thank you enough. You've been a lifesaver."

A saver of lives. I think of Ronnie helping people with their problems five days a week. I think of Wyn and Nancy teaching kids for decades. "I wish I could do more."

"Oh don't be silly, you've been wonderful."

Then I'm standing again, my hip flames shooting up into my ribs. I follow this Caitlin and her twins down my dark hallway. "I'll help you cross the street."

"Nope, we're right out front." She pushes open my door for her kids and turns to me. "Sometimes I lose faith in people. But meeting you helped me today." She smiles and reaches for my hand and squeezes it. I nod and have a hard time swallowing and now I hold the door open for her as she picks up her daughter and grabs her son's mittened hand.

I step out onto my stoop. The snow's coming down faster and I watch her hurry them into her minivan, where she buckles them into their seats. Before she gets behind the wheel she waves and smiles at me, her face filled with a kind of joyful relief.

And as she pulls into the road and drives away, I think how much Drew loves snow. He always did. And so what a nice gift for him today. All these heavy flakes of snow.

19

MY LAPTOP SEEMS TO BE DEAD. IT'S BEEN PLUGGED IN FOR OVER an hour and it still doesn't turn on. That fall it took when I caught the little girl. That harder fall it took when I threw Fitz out of my unit. The much harder fall it probably took when Brian beat me up. And it's old. A gift from Ronnie twelve or fifteen years ago. She bought it for me for my business, for QuickBooks and to type up my contracts, and so I wouldn't have to keep borrowing hers, which she needed then for graduate school. And is it any accident that the machine that's fueled my bitterness has now been taken from me?

But what I wrote to Drew, I need to remember that. I need to remember just how I put it, that my uselessness nearly killed my love for being his father.

After Caitlin and her twins left, I stood on my stoop thinking of all the snow forts that Drew and I would build between our house and the marsh, of our snowball fights, of the snowman Ronnie helped us build one afternoon. It had its own wool sweater and a cucumber nose and Oreo cookie eyes, and I felt only grateful that this had ever happened at all.

Then a blue SUV pulled into the lot across the street. I watched Dawn climb out of it and unlock her doors and flick on the interior lights. The uprooted curbstone was now covered with snow.

Hard flakes gusted against the side of my face, and I was turning to go back inside when Jamey's rusted sedan started up and the boy backed away without letting the engine get warm. Was he late for class? Would there even be a class in this snow? Or was he heading off to get cleaned up and change his clothes before walking into a bank with one of Trina's stolen checks?

I'm hungry. My next EBT card won't come in for another two weeks, and with piece-of-shit Fitz gone I need to find someone else I can sell it to for my pain distracter. I might still have a can of lima beans or creamed corn, but the thought of opening one of those dies in my head. I take young Caitlin's cup and drink the last of her cold coffee. If I had my car, Trina and I'd be driving to the food pantry right now or to the plasma lab, though when I think about those smoke-filled rides, Trina's knees against my glove box, there's the barbed feeling that for each trip there and back I failed to really be with another human being.

I drove her because her plasma kept gas in my car. I drove her because I told myself she needed my help to feed her kids. But I really drove her because doing that kept me feeling better off than she'd ever be, because I, Tom Lowe Jr., am a man with education and skills and a son. I am just a visitor to the 8. I don't belong here.

I check my computer plug and try it again, but the screen stays dark. Part of me feels strangely free, but the other part is in danger of falling into a black chasm because I can't see that screensaver image of Ronnie breastfeeding newborn Drew. That dark love in her eyes. The fiercely protective way that she held our son to her breast. The gray morning light over all of it.

I need to talk to her. There's so much I'm learning and I just want to share that with her. Because we were friends once. We were two people deeply interested in each other, and twenty years ago today we brought Drew into this plane of being.

I pull on my jacket. I stare at the tiny boot prints that Caitlin's twins left on the worn wood over flattened cushions where I've lain alone too long. I don't want to ask Dawn if I can use her phone again, but maybe she's a parent herself.

It's midmorning, but in the hurtling snow the lights of Dawn's Hair & Nails glow across the street like it's already close to night. In front of Larry's is a pickup, a length of pipe sticking out of the snowy bed like a grave marker. The only car in front of Dawn's is hers, and on its roof is a soft-looking layer of white six to eight inches high, and the wind is colder now, icy flakes blowing like shrapnel against the side of my face. Back when I was in the world I would've known a storm was coming. And as I wait for a city truck to pass, its light bar on the cab swirling bright yellow, I wonder if Drew knew that this was coming today. Still weeks away from winter and here it is, one of his favorite things.

I cross the street and think how living with pain like mine can't be much different from living in a bad marriage. You poke and jab at each other all day, and the poking and jabbing become the texture of your life.

Though I can only guess about bad marriages because before our catastrophe Ronnie and I had a good one, didn't we?

I tried, Tom. I did try.

To keep loving me, she meant. And she said this to me during one of those long quiet afternoons in our furniture-stripped house as I lay on my adjustable bed. But did *I*? Did I try to keep loving *her* after her betrayal?

When I step into the salon, Dawn's sitting in the farthest chair from the door staring at the phone in her lap. She's in black jeans and a blue sweater, the collar of a white turtleneck under her chin. Her hair's cut short with gelled spikes on top, her face round, and now she raises it with the kind of automatic smile that ensures a steady stream of business. But her smile falls away as soon as she sees me. "Oh, you again."

"Tom. Tom Lowe."

"You here to mooch off me?"

"I hope not." I stomp the snow off my boots and run my fingers back through my wet hair. Heat passes through my face and I still need to lie down. But even though Dawn isn't smiling, there's a growing curiosity in her eyes. *My boss likes you.* She's looking from my sweater behind my unzipped jacket to my face, which I wished I'd shaved.

"Your eye looks better."

I don't know what to say to this.

"Are those Christmas trees on your sweater?"

"I'm afraid so."

She stands and walks closer, squinting to better see the decorated trees across my chest. She looks like she's about to say something but shakes her head instead.

"Where's the girl who works for you?"

"Weren't you out in that storm? I'm about to close."

The place is quiet. No music, which somehow makes the overhead light seem too flat. Standing only a few feet away, Dawn is clearly my age. There are lines between her eyes and at the corners of her lips, the flesh under her chin loose and touching the top of her turtleneck.

"Who do you want to call this time?"

"My son. It's his birthday today."

"How old is he?"

"Twenty." I want to say more, but my throat has closed up on me. I look over at the phone on the corner desk to make sure it's still there.

This woman takes this in. She's looking at me like I may be a decent man just because I have a son. She reaches into her back pocket for her cell phone. "Here, my landline's for business only." She taps her phone screen a few times and hands it to me. She turns and walks to the back of her shop where there's a shelf of beauty products and a table underneath it.

"I've got a Keurig. You want a cup?"

"I don't want to trouble you."

"I'm having one anyways."

"I'm afraid I don't know how to use this kind of phone."

"You live under a rock? Bring it here." She's working the lever of her coffee machine, sliding a mug into it and pushing a button. As I walk past the empty barber chairs I can see myself in the mirror, this big slow-moving man in an outdoor work jacket I can't use anymore for work, but instead of the self-hatred that normally opens up inside me, I feel a certain resignation, maybe the start of some kind of peace.

She takes her phone from me, pulls her reading glasses off the beauty products shelf, and slips them on. "What's his number?"

"I used to know, but I don't anymore."

"You don't know your own son's phone number?"

I want to tell her that it's been years since I've owned a phone. "I usually email him."

"Where's he live?"

"Western Mass. He's going to school out there. I was going to call his mother first, if that's all right."

"What's her number?"

"I'm afraid I don't know that either."

"You say you're afraid a lot. Did you know that?" Her tone is hard but almost playful, and she reminds me of someone. I don't know who, only that I liked whoever that person was. And I like the directness of this Dawn, though her coffee machine's humming, her mug filling with a hiss, and she looks close to losing her patience.

"Her new husband's name is Edward Flynn. They live in Salem."

"Mass or New Hampshire?"

"Mass."

Dawn punches in 411, holds the phone to her ear, and pulls her mug of coffee from the machine. "Salem, Massachusetts." She pops open the machine and pulls out the old coffee pod, dropping it in a trash pail under the table, then pushes a new pod into the machine. "Edward Flynn."

Hearing this woman say the name of Ronnie's second husband is like finding out I have a friend I didn't know I had, or that I have a bank account with money in it I never bothered to check. She turns to me, her phone still pressed to her ear, and points to the full mug of coffee, then at a bowl of creamers and packets of sugar.

Such *kindness*.

My hip fires go still and I'm about to reach past her for the mug when she hands me her phone. Its flat surface is warm against my cheek and the phone ringing on the other end is Ronnie's phone, Ronnie's and Edward Joseph Flynn's. I've never spoken to Flynn, though once I came close when I dropped Drew off at the ship captain's house, my social worker idling in her car behind me, and Flynn stepped out the front door of his historically restored home, lifting his hand in a wave.

He was dressed in a yellow cashmere sweater and faded jeans and loafers. His thick gray hair looked a bit tousled in the back, like he'd been lying on his couch reading the paper or watching TV, and the thing is he had a tentative smile on his face that looked warm and slightly embarrassed, and then he was walking across his front lawn toward my car as Drew was climbing out and I said, "I'll see you later, buddy." And then I pulled away from the curb before Edward Joseph Flynn could get to the sidewalk.

If he answers the phone, what will I say to him now? How will I introduce myself after all these years?

But it's Ronnie who picks up, and hearing her voice is like stepping into a room that time let slip through its bony fingers. It's unchanged and comes from the center of her chest, but it's also coolly professional and it's not her at all but a recording of her telling me that I've reached the Finch-Flynn residence, that we're unable to come to the phone so please leave a message and we will be sure to call you back. There's a loud beep in my ear, and I watch Dawn take her coffee back to her chair. She sits and sets her cup on the counter in front of the mirror, and something about this makes me feel just a little better about the silence in my ex-wife's answering machine I now have to speak into.

"Ronnie?" I think how Flynn calls her Veronica. It feels like a slip to have called her that, a misstep that could make it harder to get Drew's phone number. "It's Tom. I was hoping to get Drew's number from you, so I—"

"Hello? *Tom?*" It's Ronnie and she sounds sleepy, or like she's been reading for hours and I'm the first person she's talked to all day.

"Yes, I—" My eyes burn. I turn away from Dawn sipping her coffee. I stare across her shop out at the gray storm blowing over the lot and the street and the huddled units of the 8. I want to tell Ronnie how good it is to hear her voice after so long, but again, my throat has closed up. I need to lie down and there comes the flesh memory of how gently she used to wipe me as I lay on my side on my adjustable bed.

"Is everything all right, Tom? Where are you calling from?"

"Can you believe he's *twenty*, Ronnie? I can't believe he's twenty."

She doesn't say anything. There's the running of a faucet, the clank of a dish. "Mostly. Other times his birth feels like a hundred years ago." It's the same sweetly reflective tone she'd use after making love, the two of us lying in each other's warmth, our skin damp. How wonderful and terrible to hear her talk this way now.

"Who's Dawn Porter? That's why I didn't answer our phone."

Our phone. It doesn't hurt me to hear this. It doesn't feel good either. I turn back to Dawn, her eyes on me over the rim of her cup. "I'm using a friend's."

"Have you got something to write with?"

I smile over at Dawn and motion that I need a pen or pencil. She shakes her head, then stands and rifles through a drawer in the coffee table for a Sharpie she pushes into my hand. Ronnie's already telling me our son's number and I'm not going to ask Dawn for one more thing, so I wedge her phone between my ear and shoulder and write Drew's number on the palm of my left hand. Funny how I still wear my wedding ring on that hand.

"I'm worried about him, Tom."

"Why?"

"He drinks too much."

"Didn't we then too?"

"No, it's not just that. He's suffering from anxiety and depression."

"He tell you this?"

"He didn't have to, I can see it. But yes, he did."

Dawn's business phone rings and she walks with her cup of coffee over to the corner desk to answer it. A snow gust swirls against the plate-glass window and it buckles slightly in its frame, and hearing this about Drew feels like I left my son out in that storm, then walked away. I wish Ronnie would just drive over here, even in this weather, and then the two of us could ride slowly and carefully west to see Drew, to help our son in any way we possibly can.

"What did he say, Ronnie?"

"That's not important. And I don't go by that name anymore."

"I forgot."

Ronnie lets out a breath. Another dish clinks in the sink. "He's afraid he's going to be like you."

"Like me?"

"You know, depressed."

The hip fires howl, their glowing coals sinking deeper than ever. Dawn hangs up her phone and writes something down in a notebook on her desk.

"I'm sorry."

"He thinks I'm depressed?"

"He knows you're depressed, Tom. C'mon."

She sounds like the old Ronnie now, the one who got so good at pointing out to me the obvious.

"Ronnie?" *Veronica*. But what her husband calls her won't leave my mouth.

"I have to go soon, Tom. I have a phone session with a client."

There's so much I want to ask her and to tell her. Dawn's walking back to her barber chair with her coffee. She glances at my face, then looks straight ahead with the expression of someone who's lived life and knows it's not easy for anyone, but here we are.

"Call him, Tom. That will be a good thing."

"Ronnie?"

She lets out a half-breath. "Yes?"

"Are you—"

"I really need to get going, Tom."

Happy?

I'm about to tell her that I want to have coffee with her sometime, or lunch. That I'll cook for her. But the image of Ronnie the abundist stepping inside my cramped unit in the 8 is quickly burned. I want to tell her that I wanted to visit Drew today, that that's been my plan for a while now, but I've had car trouble. And I've had other trouble. "Thank you for the number."

"Take care of yourself, Tom."

"You too."

And I mean it. For I sure as hell didn't take care of her. But is that even what she wanted?

"Did you hang up?"

I squint at the phone's screen. "I don't know."

"Give it to me." Dawn takes it and taps the screen, then hands it back to me. "You get his number?"

"Yes, thank you."

"Don't let your coffee get cold."

"You've been very kind." I'm staring at her, at her spiked hair and slightly made-up face that was young when I was young. "You have kids?"

"Two. One's married and one's a fuckup. Birthday boy your only one?"

"Yes." My hips and pelvis are a mosaic of dusty bones. I pick up my coffee, which I take my time sipping because now I'm afraid to call Drew. I'm afraid to call my twenty-year-old son who's afraid to be just like me.

"Well, make that call. I need to get home while I still can."

"You married?"

"Twice, you?"

"Nope."

She glances at the wedding ring on my finger. "It's none of your business, but my second husband slapped me around a bit. I guess I respect what you did to get that black eye and fat lip."

"I'm sorry to hear that, Dawn." Saying her name feels like I've crossed the line. My legs feel weak and I set my coffee on the table and I really need to lie down. "Do you mind if I stretch out for just a sec? I had an accident a few years ago and I can't stand for too long."

"You need help?"

I always need help. I rest her phone on the coffee table, press both hands on the corner as I kneel, then lie back on the floor.

"How long have you been like this?"

"Years."

"Car accident?"

"Fell off a roof." The floor's cold and hard under me and it feels wonderful. The light above is a bright LED in a hung ceiling of fire-proof tiles, and there comes the memory of a job I did in Salem on the first floor of our apartment building for our land-lord's office. I did it under budget and on time and it paid my and Ronnie's rent for months. "I was a builder."

"You on meds?"

"Not anymore." I turn my head in her direction. "My ex just told me my son's drinking too much."

"He's twenty."

"She says he's got anxiety and depression."

"Who doesn't? Here—" There's the squeak of her barber chair and then Dawn's standing over me with her phone. "Read me the number."

From here I'm looking at Dawn's upper legs and crotch and the hem of her sweater. I block this view with my hand and read her Drew's number written on my palm that's so soft when once it was nothing but calluses, years of them.

Dawn puts the phone in that hand and walks away. The ceiling's light above is pointing directly at my face. My son's phone is ringing in my ear, and each ring is like a long heartbeat rippling into blackness. When was the last time we actually *talked*? This past summer? Drew standing tanned and lean and handsome with his girlfriend in front of my stoop? Or was that a different summer?

"Hello?" A young woman's voice. From behind her comes rap music and laughter and then somebody shouts and there's more laughter.

"Hanna?"

"'Scuse me?"

"Is this Hanna?"

"No, who's this?"

"Tom Lowe. I'm looking for my son Drew?"

"Oh, hi. I'm Jess. I'm one of your son's friends."

"But isn't this his phone?"

"Yeah." A muffled sound, then quiet. I turn my face away from the light and can feel the floor against my cheek. I study the recessed screwhead in the metal base of the closest barber chair, think of the hammer drill I used to own that could sink those screws into this concrete floor. And I remember Drew when he was eight or nine on a Sunday afternoon helping his father organize all my tools into the shelves of my work van, how I told him what each tool did and when it should be used and when it shouldn't, Drew taking all this in like he was memorizing it for some test. Now it's not even ten in the morning and wherever he is, there's a party going on.

The young woman Jess is back. "Drew can't come to the phone right now. He says he'll email you."

There's no more music behind her, only muffled laughter, then something loud, like a handclap or a can thrown at a wall. I'm about to say that my computer's broken, but first I say, "Can you tell him I just called to wish him a happy birthday?"

In my ear is a vacuum of quiet. "Hello?" I squint at the screen of Dawn's phone. On it is a keypad of numbers. Did the girl hang up? Did she even hear what I said?

"No luck, huh?" Dawn walks over and takes her phone.

"It sounded like they were having a pretty good time."

"They call it day drinking. Can you get up by yourself?"

My eyes are back on the overhead light. *Day drinking.* I've done a lot of that myself these past few years, though it was just to tamp down my fires below, and I'm hurt Drew didn't want to talk to me. There's the sound of water running, a door closing, Dawn resting both coffee mugs back on the table. *He's afraid he's going to be like you.*

"You look like shit now."

"My son didn't want to talk to me."

She doesn't say anything to this. There are her footsteps across the floor, then the flick of a switch and the overhead lights shutting off. I turn onto my side and push myself up into the gray light of this place.

"Were you a good dad to him?" Dawn's pulling on her coat. She's looking right at me. Behind her, blowing snow buffets the glass.

"I was before I got hurt." I get on my hands and knees, then slowly stand. Something falls from my hip screws into ashes, and now the fires are raging again and all the good invisible feeling I've felt this past day and a half is as gone as a mirage you've gotten too close to.

"What happened?"

"I disappeared on him." I walk over to her at the front door. She looks like she wants to say something but doesn't. "Thank you for your help."

"Was it the accident?"

I smile. "And the foreclosure and the divorce and—" I look down at my untied work shoes, at Dawn's rubber boots lined with gray fur made in some factory. I'm standing close enough that I can smell the gel in her spiked hair, and I make myself look into her face, into her street-savvy but kind face.

"And the painkillers. I got hooked on those."

"Hey listen, that happens to a lot of people."

I nod and say nothing. I want to tell her that I made my young son my personal drug runner, that I charmed him into lying to his mother and grandparents and his friends.

Dawn pulls the door open for me and I step out into the blowing cold, the snow ripping wetly into my face. She takes out her jangling keys and locks up, and I clean off her windshield with one arm, then do the same to the back window, wiping down the side windows just as she climbs into her SUV and starts it up. Now I'm standing at her rolled-down glass as she flicks on her headlights and looks out at me. The wind is at the backs of my legs. I hold my coat closed and lean close to the glass. She's smiling but is clearly ready to leave.

"I just want you to know it's been six years. I haven't taken a thing in six years."

"Good for you, hon. Gotta go."

Hon. The word hangs in my head like a votive candle, its flame burning steadily as she pulls out into the soft road and is gone.

20

THE SNOW IN THE LOT IS SIX OR SEVEN INCHES DEEP, DAWN'S tire tracks already filling as I move through it. The wind is blowing my eyes almost shut, but that good feeling's coming back again and maybe I'm not standing in a mirage after all because this woman who at first was hard to me just heard some of my story because she asked to hear it and then she smiled at me and called me hon.

Across the street, the units of the 8 look like covered boats tied off in an icy cove. I wait for a pickup with a plow to go by. I'm beginning to shiver, but there's also the warmth of gratitude starting to open up inside me for how truly lucky I am to have this shelter. How very lucky that my ex-brother-in-law was able to get it for me. Did I even *thank* Gerard for that? Did I ever thank Wyn and Nancy for all of their generosity and hospitality? For putting up with my drug-addled bullshit?

On my stoop is Kerry Andrews' bag of trash, and it's high time I got rid of it.

The snow's coming down hard, swirling and whipping into my face. I clutch Kerry's trash to my chest, a hot ache spreading through my hips and legs. I walk by Amber and Cal's unit and then Mrs. Bongiovanni's and then what used to be Fitz's. On the other side of the lot the dumpsters are up against a thin stand of pines, beyond them a weed field blanketed with white, and beyond them the cinder-block buildings of the industrial park, the sky gray and pressing down on everything.

I squint into the whipping snow. I pull my coat closed and wish I was wearing a hat and socks, my feet knocking cold and loose in my work boots as I make my way past Fitz's old place. I can't say that I regret tossing Fitz out, but I keep hearing him say, *You're hurting my feelings, man.* He said this so sincerely. So believably really.

Mrs. Bongiovanni's nurse won't get here till late morning, but already the old woman's steps and stoop are under a layer of snow her nurse shouldn't have to deal with, and as I walk up onto Mrs. Bongiovanni's concrete stoop, there comes the face that nurse gave me the one time I tried to make conversation with her. Like she feared me, and she feared me because I was beneath her.

There's a broom handle against the wall and I use it to sweep the snow under the railing out into whiteness. But my hips have to pivot and a hundred flames flare along the screw shafts, reminding me that even this simple task, which I used to do after eight hours of skilled work with my many tools and instruments, even this is too much for me.

But it's only too much if I pay attention to it being too much. And I can only pay it attention in this way if I'm still hoping for the day when my hip fires have gone out. But that day will never come, I've known this for a long time, and so I—with no job and no car, with no telephone and now no computer—I have to do whatever I can.

What a surprise to see ancient Mrs. Bongiovanni standing on the other side of her storm door. To the right of her dried flowers lifting in the wind, her small pale face is staring at me. She nods and motions for me to come to her.

I climb the steps and set the broom against the wall. Through the storm door the old woman's smiling at me, nodding her head like she's answering a question I've just asked her. My hand sticks to the galvanized metal of the handle, and I turn it and pull Mrs. Bongiovanni's door open a few inches. She's speaking to me, but I can't hear her. "Pardon me?"

"Did Tony send you? My Tony?"

I've never seen Mrs. Bongiovanni this close before. Her white hair's pinned back and her eyes—blue—are set deeply above high cheekbones, slight jowls around her lips, which she's brushed unevenly with lipstick. She's wearing a black cardigan over a blouse and a black skirt, and around her lower legs are blood pressure socks, her tiny feet in black sneakers. At one time she was clearly a beauty and I'm struck that she's wearing lipstick. How long's it been since I've seen my mother? A year? Though she wasn't wearing any lipstick and kept talking to me like I was her husband, and then later, after spilling the hot chocolate I'd brought her, she thought I was Frank the insurance salesman though she kept calling me Charlie.

"No, ma'am. I'm your neighbor. Tom Lowe."

"My neighbor?" She looks like she's just been told that I'm from Saturn or Jupiter.

"Yes, the unit at the corner."

"I don't have any money to pay you."

"Course not. I wouldn't hear of it."

The old woman just stares at me. She looks down at my untied work boots, at my wrinkled khakis and unzipped jacket, at my big hatless head and unshaven face. "Well aren't you good to do this for me." Mrs. Bongiovanni's voice is not an old woman's. It seems to come from someplace inside her that's stayed unchanged while her body's gone on to age without her. She's looking up into my eyes, her narrow shoulders hunched, the wind blowing hard against the side of my face. "Come in, I made sweet bread."

Just like that. Again, a door opening for me, the feeling that I'm in the midst of discovering something timeless or else that discovery's finally turning itself toward me, and now I'm inside and the old woman is gesturing for me to sit as she moves slowly into her own narrow kitchenette.

Her unit has the same layout as Trina's, though instead of a long sofa facing a TV, there are two wingback chairs against the wall, a lamp table between them. On a woven rug are two hassocks, one of them worn and sunken in the middle. The one in front of the chair she pointed me to looks new, and if I were wearing socks I'd pull my boots off out of respect.

A radio's playing. It's coming from the kitchenette and it's an oldies station, Dean Martin or Perry Como singing a love song. Up against the wall is a boxy TV on a steamer trunk, a basket of magazines and stacked newspapers on the floor beside it. On the wall above are framed black-and-white portraits of men and women from long ago, and I pull off my Carhartt and lay it on the new-looking hassock and sit.

There are the smells of baking and coffee. Mrs. Bongiovanni's saying something to me from her kitchenette. No, she's humming and taking short steps toward me with a cane, holding a plate with a coffee cup on it and a creamer and what looks like a small bowl of sugar. I stand and my hips burn, and the old woman smiles up at me as I take the plate from her, which I can see now is actually a round metal tray, the cup spilling some of its coffee onto it, Mrs. Bongiovanni disappearing back into her kitchenette. Her narrow back is hunched. Her cane taps the linoleum floor as steadily as the ticking of a clock.

In front of both hassocks is a low glass table, and I set my coffee tray on it next to a dozen prescription bottles and one of those plastic pill containers with boxes for each day of the week. All seven compartments are open and I can see that Mrs. Bongiovanni was only on Tuesday when she must've seen me out on her stoop.

"Please, drink your coffee. Drink." She sets down napkins and a plate of sliced golden bread, dusted white. "Please."

The sweet bread is warm between my fingers, and I hold a napkin under my slice and bite into it. It's been so long since I ate something this wonderful. There are the nourishing tastes of grains and yeast, but also the luxury of butter and the sweetness of sugar. When did I eat anything for pure pleasure? When was the last time anyone encouraged me to?

Trina. Bringing me ice cream from the food pantry. Trina giving me half her jelly donut once on the way back from the lab, too sick to eat it but *you should have it, Tommy. Don't waste it.*

And this sickening feeling rising up from the floor as I sit on my jacket on the hassock, that I've been wasting my time. So much of it.

"This is delicious, Mrs. Bongiovanni."

"How do you know my name?" She's smiling at me. "Tom, is it?"

"Your son's car. His shoe business."

She nods and lowers herself to the other hassock, using her cane to steady herself. She pushes aside her pill organizer and takes her own napkin and a slice of sweet bread. "Tony's a good boy. I used to live with them, but hey—" She bats her hand at the air. "I don't think about that." She takes a small bite of the bread, then sets it down like that's it. No more for her.

"Did you make this from scratch?"

The old woman puts on reading glasses and pulls the organizer back to her. She studies the open compartment for Sunday, then Monday and Tuesday. She reaches for one of her prescription bottles and shakes out a pill into her palm, then drops it into Tuesday. "You have to excuse me, I get confused if I don't finish. You like pandoro?"

"I do. I've never had it before."

"You don't know any Italians? My mother only made it at Christmas, but I make it whenever."

Sitting this close to her, my big knee just inches from hers, I can smell the wool of her cardigan, some kind of medicinal cream on her old skin. I swallow my sweet bread and want more. "I've been a bad neighbor. I should've come over and introduced myself a long time ago."

"I've seen you. It took me a minute, but I've seen you." Mrs. Bongiovanni shakes another pill into her hand. I notice that the top of each prescription bottle is loosened, and I wonder if the nurse does that for her.

"I guess I've been depressed, I don't know."

She turns to me. Her blue eyes are magnified behind the lenses of her glasses. She says, "You have to fight that. Me, I listen to music. And I read. It gets your mind off things."

"What do you like to read?"

"The newspapers. Magazines. The people in them have it much worse than I do. Believe me."

I nod and sip my coffee. It's hot but weak and I think how I'm weak. Or have been. How much time have I wasted wallowing here in the 8? But sitting like this isn't good. Flames lick up around my screws and soon enough the ends are white hot. I need to go home and lie down. Out in Mrs. Bongiovanni's kitchenette, the radio DJ's reading about getting rid of water damage and draftiness and high heating bills. There's the sound of the old woman dropping a hard pill into its empty plastic box and I want to tell her everything about my own pills, about my fall, about Ronnie and Drew, about it being my son's twentieth birthday today and I don't have a car to go see him. I want to tell old Mrs. Bongiovanni that my own mother, much younger than her, has lost her mind and I hate that I haven't gone to visit her in so long, even though she doesn't recognize me anymore. I want to tell the old woman that I was getting ready to sell all my tools but they were stolen. I want to tell her that I feel like I'm learning something important, though I don't know what that is.

But I don't say anything because she's not saying anything, the two of us sitting side by side like we've known each another for a very long time.

Frank Sinatra begins to sing out in the kitchenette, and Mrs. Bongiovanni is counting quietly to herself, dropping a yellow pill into each day of the week.

"Do you get lonely here?"

She holds up her hand. It's small and covered with liver spots. "I'm almost finished. Eat."

I lean forward for another slice of sweet bread, melted steel pooling at my hips, but I take my time and chew slowly, gratefully.

"My youngest son was depressed, too." Mrs. Bongiovanni closes Saturday's box, then sets her glasses down and grabs her cane and uses it and the table edge to stand. I do the same. It feels good to be on my feet and it's time to get back to my plywood couch, but the old woman sits in her wingback chair and so I sit in the other. A few crumbs of sweet bread fall from my napkin and second slice. I pick the crumbs off my pants and put them into my mouth. "You have another boy?"

"We did, yes."

Winds gusts against the window and there's the scattering tick of snow. "I'm sorry."

"That was years ago."

"How old was he?"

"Young. Like you." She glances over at me and I can see that she means to use the word she's just used.

"I don't feel so young."

"Do you have a wife?"

"I did." I finish my sweet bread, swallowing it all down and wanting one more slice.

"She pass away?"

"Divorce."

Mrs. Bongiovanni nods. "People today give up too easy."

"I agree with you."

"My husband wanted to leave me many times, and I wanted to leave him, too."

"Why didn't you?"

She looks over at me again. The light in the room is dim and her face looks younger, though her shoulders are hunched and her hands are gnarled. "We have to play the hand God gives us."

I've heard this before, of course. These are not new words to me, but I've never quite thought about them, or if I have, I've only thought about the hand getting dealt part, I've thought about that a lot—Mike Andrews' smile across his cherry desk, that last roofing shingle I reached for before there wasn't a roof under me anymore, the fires burning in my hips as I came to in a hospital room, the plywood couch in my unit here in the 8 that has become my home—but I've never given real thought to the word *play*, that we're supposed to somehow stay at the table and *play* our hand.

A woman's singing on Mrs. Bongiovanni's radio now. Doris Day, someone who sang when my mother and father met so young and had me and Charlie, who would grow into having our own hands dealt. But Ronnie, she walked away from the table. She requested a new hand and she got it, and isn't she better off?

"I think my wife's happier without me."

"That's what you people think, you have to be happy."

"Is it wrong to be happy?"

"No, but people shouldn't want it every single day. My father died fighting Mussolini. I was ten years old. My mother wore black the rest of her life. That's just what we did."

I look at the framed photographs above the TV. One is of a man in a suit staring at the camera like he knows this image will be one of the few ever captured of him. The other seems to be of the same man standing beside a woman in a hat garlanded with flowers. He looks resolute and she looks hopeful, and I want to ask Mrs. Bongiovanni about her husband and her lost son, but she's pushing on both chair arms to stand. She reaches for her cane and turns toward me. "I have to see you out now. My shot takes me a while. Please, take the pandoro. If Joanie sees it, she'll kill me."

"She your nurse?"

"And my ex-daughter-in-law." She lifts her cane. "Let me wrap that for you."

At the door, my jacket back on, Mrs. Bongiovanni leans on her cane and hands me the pandoro wrapped in foil. She's smiling up at me. "Thank you for being a good neighbor to me, young man."

Like it's something I do often, like I haven't ignored this old woman for years because she's old and because she's in the 8. Like I deserve this precious homemade treat I thank her for. And as I step back out into the whipping cold, I know that I have not been playing my hand at all, I've been rejecting it.

Mrs. Bongiovanni's steps are again coated with snow, almost as much as what I'd just whisked away. I squint into the wind, set the wrapped sweet bread on the concrete, and grab the broom. My bladder's full, but I'm afraid that if I go back to my unit to use the bathroom, then I'll end up on my plywood couch, where I'll finish Mrs. Bongiovanni's pandoro, this whisper inside me that I've refused to play my hand, that I've been staring at those cards on my table and I've refused to even pick them up. If Trina had never walked into my unlocked front door six years ago to say hello, would I have ever talked to her? That twenty-one-year-old with her crying newborn and two other small kids?

These good things that have been happening, they've come because my recent misfortunes have forced me to pick up my hand and actually look at it.

And when's the last time Trina ate any home-baked treat? When she was a little girl?

21

TRINA'S BATHROOM IS AS CLEAN AND ORGANIZED AS HER KITCHEN. On the back of her sink are two plastic cups that hold her kids' toothbrushes and hers, the faucet wiped free of spots, the mirror too. The soap I use now is the liquid kind you pump into your hand, a luxury for people like us, and Trina has placed it on a folded washcloth to catch any drippings. Behind me against the wall is a chrome rack for her towels, which she'll have to haul in a garbage bag to the Laundromat, and they're folded into the rack Trina saw beside a dumpster one afternoon on our ride back from the lab. She asked me to stop and help her put it in my open trunk, and the lid knocked against it all the way back to the 8.

I wipe my wet hands off on my pants, then make my way down Trina's stairs. The walls are papered with crayon drawings and a few watercolors, and there's a Magic Marker sketch of a cannon shooting fire into a car with a man in it. Brian in his mother's Pontiac so early this morning, the way he gunned that sedan out into the road without even looking. I'm going to need to keep an eye out for him, and this is what I'm thinking about as I step into Trina's living room.

All the stolen bags of trash are gone and her place is quiet for once. Shannon's in her room and the boys are playing outside in the storm, the TV off, no virtual men getting machine-gunned or blown up. In the kitchenette Trina's pouring herself more coffee. She asked me if I wanted some, but I feel like I've already got some kind of current flowing through me, one that has nothing to do with the coffee I drank with the young mother Caitlin, the few sips I had of Mrs. Bongiovanni's and Dawn's. No, as I sit down at Trina's card table against the window, the wind whistling through the panes, it's like my blood has thinned out and is moving smoothly and efficiently through me, calling to my whole being to wake up. *Wake up.*

Trina has set what's left of the sweet bread on a paper plate, and she folded the foil into an ashtray her smoking cigarette lies in now.

"You sure you don't want any?" She walks out of the kitchenette holding a mug of coffee. I smile and shake my head. Trina's hair is wet from the shower, her ears sticking out a bit, and instead of her hoodie sweatshirt and pajama bottoms, she's in jeans and a tight sweater with a hole in one elbow. She sets a paper towel down, then sits across from me, reaching for her cigarette and a slice of sweet bread. "I can't believe she gave you this, Tommy. It's so fucking good." She takes a drag, blows out smoke, then bites into Mrs. Bongiovanni's pandoro, closing her eyes and swallowing it down.

"She's a nice lady, Trina. You should go say hi to her sometime."

"Nope, I don't like how she looks at me and my kids."

"How's that?"

"Like we're trash."

My face warms. "Why're you all dressed up?"

"Jamey's taking us to the mall. I mean, that's if, you know. And this snow now too." She runs her fingers back through her long wet hair, and she has the deeply hopeful expression of a kid looking forward to something good, something very good.

She takes another bite of sweet bread and peers through her dented blinds. She parts them and knocks on the glass and waves out at MJ and Cody in the wind. "I'm gonna buy 'em winter clothes, Tommy. And no fucking Goodwill this time. Brand *new.*" She lets go of the blinds and flicks ash into the foil. She sips her coffee, her eyes on the slices of sugar-dusted pandoro like they're just the start of things changing for the better. "My nana used to bake all the time."

"She live with you?"

Trina blows out smoke. "The apartment right next to us. So my fucking mother had to behave herself."

"How'd she not behave, Trina?"

"I've told you this like a hundred times, Tom. You don't listen."

I nod and it's like hearing Mrs. Bongiovanni tell me that her youngest son had what I have, Ronnie telling me that Drew's afraid to be like me. Hard truths. But I can still hear my ex-wife's voice and its long-familiar timbre is like a balm over an old wound.

"You're right, Trina. I haven't been a very good listener. Was it drugs?"

"Jesus, Tommy." She stubs out her cigarette and breaks a slice of sweet bread in half and pushes it into her mouth. Outside and close to the wall MJ is laughing and Cody screams something at him, his voice carried off in the wind. Trina wipes her mouth with her paper towel. "My mother was a drunk friggin' whore, and when one of her boyfriends tried to fuck her own daughter, she kicked *me* out, not him. I was twelve, Tommy. I lived with my nana for three months and then she died on me and it's like ever since then I've been trying to get those three months back—" She shakes her head. She stares out between her blinds, her sons' voices far off now. "This kid Jamey loves me, Tommy. I can feel it. No one's ever wanted to help me before like he does."

I'm nodding and my hips burn and I need to lie down again. I think how stoned the kid seems to be more than half the time, of how he called private property theft, and I think how wrong it is that I've been living next door to this young woman for this long, but she rightly never felt that *I* really wanted to help her.

I'm about to tell her that I'm worried about her. I'm about to offer my services watching her kids so she can do something positive and legal and right, but the front door swings open and cold rushes in like a wave and Jamey's standing in the doorway smiling. There's snow along the shoulders of his denim jacket and in his dark tangled beard. He's holding out what looks like his driver's license.

"You got it?" Trina is up and across the room. She snatches the license out of Jamey's hand, but Jamey's looking over at me sitting at the table like I'm the school principal and the kid just walked through the wrong door, which he closes now behind him.

"This looks so *good*, honey."

"Told you, my uncle's a pro." He nods in my direction. "Hey, man." Jamey runs his fingers back through his damp hair. He looks around the living room. "It's so quiet."

The door opens behind him and Cody runs in wearing a long-sleeved shirt too big for him, Shannon's red wool cap falling off his head. He rushes past Jamey and buries his face in Trina's sweater. "MJ's *mean*, Ma!"

"Where is he?"

"He kept pushing me into the *snow*." Cody's crying now. On one hand is a black mitten and on the other a drooping sock, and as Trina hugs him back Jamey takes the ID from between her fingers.

MJ walks in. He's in two T-shirts and loose corduroys, his face flushed.

"Close the fucking door, MJ, and apologize to your brother right this minute."

"Why?"

"Because I *said* to."

"He's a big baby." MJ slams the door and kicks off his wet sneakers, then hops over the couch onto a cushion. He picks up the remote just as Trina jerks away from Cody and slaps MJ hard on the side of the head.

"I said *apologize*."

"No."

"Then go to your fucking room."

"No." MJ flicks on the TV and Trina snatches the remote out of his hand and whips it at the screen. There's a popping sound. It's coming from the center of the TV where broken glass spiders out into lines of red, purple, and blue, one of them shifting into a green shard. I think of a modern art museum Ronnie and I strolled through in Cologne, or was it Berlin?

"Ma! Look at what you *did*." MJ's up, his voice rising with real terror, like he's just witnessed the accidental shooting of a child. "You *broke* it! How am I gonna *play* now? *Mom?!*" He rushes past me and up the stairs and then objects are hitting a wall and Trina's running up there too, a door slamming, her screams so ugly and so familiar, and I haven't allowed myself to really listen to them at all these past few years. But now I put my head down and I do listen: there are hurling words about respect and MJ being ungrateful and a bully and lazy and *it's your fucking fault!*

I force myself to stand. Cody and Jamey are looking at me like somebody should do something, but maybe not me. "Well, there are better things to do than play video games all day, right?" I turn and walk up the stairs past the drawings on the wall. My feet feel numb and I don't know what I'll say or do once I get to where I'm going, only that Trina's yelling has never sounded this shrill, her rare and blooming happiness just stepped on. And I have to stop it, that's all. I just have to get to that room and stop it.

"What do *you* want?"

It's Shannon standing at the top of the stairs. She's wearing her own pajama bottoms and a button-down work shirt. Her hair looks freshly brushed, and her left eye has eyeliner on it.

"I just want to help, Shannon."

"We don't want your help. Get out of here."

Trina's shouting behind the wall is just like another kind of storm, but in it the boy's crying and I just need to step into that storm. "Shannon." I want to keep climbing and slip past her, but in Shannon's hand is an eyeliner brush she's gripping like a knife and I can see now that she's *afraid* of me.

I hold up both hands and I'm about to tell this girl that she should never fear me, ever, but the door behind her yanks open and slams back against the wall and Trina pushes past her daughter and me, her voice already downstairs before I can turn around.

"Let's go, Jamey. I've had it. I've fucking *had* it!"

There's a muffled rustling, a low voice, then the front door slamming shut, two doors outside doing the same, Jamey's engine revving and then the almost helpless sound of wheels spinning in snow, then quiet.

Shannon's standing still at the top of the stairs. Her face is pale, her lips parted, and she looks like the kid in the schoolyard who said the wrong thing to the wrong kid at the exact wrong time.

"Shannon."

"I said *leave*."

I head back down the stairs, and I think of Trina's mother kicking her out of the house after one of her own boyfriends tried to do what he did, and I wish Shannon could trust me as much as her mother clearly does, leaving me here with her kids like this.

MJ's still crying upstairs, and Cody's sitting cross-legged on the couch eating a slice of sweet bread and staring at the broken TV screen. Its shattered lines seem to have multiplied and Cody's studying them like something special is in there, some kind of mystery that he alone needs to solve.

22

HOW MANY DISCUSSIONS—ARGUMENTS? FIGHTS?—OVER THE years had Ronnie and I had about love? *You're like a machine, Tom. You're just a fucking **machine**.*

The truth is part of me took this as a compliment because what does a machine do but perform tasks. It *works*. All I ever did was work. Many nights, even knowing Drew was pitching in a Little League game or Ronnie had a class to get to or she'd planned an intricate meal for me—like her coq au vin with pancetta and carrots—I worked late just because I couldn't stop, and I couldn't stop because I didn't really want to stop trimming out windows in a new addition or building hardwood shelves into a wall over a fireplace or laying out a tile floor that would make a kitchen more than just a kitchen. I did what I wanted to do because few things felt better than working. And then, late at night, drifting off next to Ronnie, whose back would be to me and who'd often still be mad at me or too tired to keep caring and so would be a hundred yards away just inches away, I'd kiss her shoulder and say, "Love you."

And I did love her. I loved our son. And I consistently told myself that all the hard work I did, week in and week out, was in service *to them*. But was it? Wouldn't I have worked just as hard and long even if I lived alone?

He's afraid he's going to be like you.

Is Drew drinking too much because he's worried about what's in his own blood?

Who doesn't? It was comforting to hear Dawn say that. It was comforting just being in the presence of a woman who knew something about things falling apart. But she was still soldiering on with her own business and spiked hair and warm eyes, and I want to know more about her. I do.

A rapping at my door. It's not Trina because she never knocks, and as I get up from my plywood couch as quickly as I can, I think: *Brian.* I think: *Fitz.* I think: *Trouble.* But as I move barefoot across the cold linoleum floor of my unit's hallway, the word *love* is in my head. *Love.*

Outside is darkness and I have to switch on the exterior light over my stoop. On the other side of the plexiglass is a UPS man in brown. He's middle-aged, a pink mole in the center of his chin, and he says hello and holds out a device for me to sign with my fingertip. Out in the street a plow scrapes by and I'm thanking the man, who bends down for the cellophane-wrapped basket he pushes into my hands.

I set the basket on my table. The top of the cellophane is tied off with a long red ribbon and I pull it, the wrapping falling away, and there, nestled in a bed of straw, is a bottle of red wine and sausage and three kinds of cheese—Swiss, Gouda, and Brie—and there's a box of wheat crackers and a card:

Thank you for being so good to us today!—Caitlin Murphy

She must have memorized my address on her way back into my unit, read the corner sign announcing Hampton Terrace, seen the peeling numbers *21* on my mailbox screwed into the wall at the top of my stoop. The care that took. The *thoughtfulness.*

I want to write her a thank-you note for her thank-you gesture. But there's no return address on that card or anywhere else. I pick up the sausage sealed in plastic and smell it. Even with its packaging there's the greased pork scent of pepperoni and my mouth floods with saliva and I head into my kitchenette for something sharp to cut into this sausage. But the overhead light brings me back to this morning. When I walked from the dumpsters, I saw through the window of Fitz's old bedroom a woman in her nightgown gently patting her husband's or boyfriend's chest. When Trina first walked into my unit six years ago, I'd been lying on my couch for days, staring at the wall she lived and yelled behind. Then she just walks in in her pajama bottoms and a tank top, smoking a cigarette, and she didn't bring me any food or welcoming gift of any kind, and in fact was asking me for a ride to the food pantry. But as much as I wasn't happy about her unannounced presence in my place, I'd been floating in cold dark space and now a fellow human being had floated over to me to ask for something, yes, but just having her there felt like she was leading me to a rope I could hold onto so I wouldn't drift off into nothingness.

I want to eat everything in this basket and wash it down with the wine straight from its bottle, but no, I won't be taking this gift basket for myself, because what is true giving if there's no sacrifice? An old word. In one of my classes at one of my schools the professor would constantly interrupt his lectures to take apart any common word he happened to just use, breaking it down to its Latin or Greek roots. Few of these words have stayed with me, but the word *compassion* has because it means *to suffer **with***, and is this not what I'm called to do now? Not to dull my own suffering but to move through it, despite it, toward another's? And sacrifice, somewhere in that is the word *holy*, I remember that much. Fucking *holy*.

I push the sausage back into the straw of the basket, wrap and tie it up, then pull on my work boots and jacket and head outside.

The snow's deep and soft and everywhere. It clings to the branches of the thin oak between my stoop and the street, it's thickened the phone lines from pole to pole, it's covered the narrow lot where under the streetlamps the drifts glitter. Does Drew still love snow as much as he used to? Will he take all this whiteness on his birthday as maybe a sign of better times to come? I need to let him know that my computer's broken. And why didn't I tell that girl Jess that right off? It's one thing not to have sent Drew something or visited him, but to not respond to whatever my son will write to me today or tonight, I can't have that.

There's the scrape of metal on asphalt, Amber shoveling out her Geo. I want to help her do this, but just carrying this basket down my steps that need to be shoveled has raised a conflagration down below.

Amber coughs and flips a shovel full of snow into the yard of her unit. Behind the gauzy curtains of her windows there's lamplight, and I glance up at Trina's. The bulb over her stoop is off, but every light inside is on, and Jamey's sedan accelerates past me from the street and swings into the snowy lot. Music's thumping inside and the headlights switch off and I can see Trina laughing in the passenger seat. Jamey's trunk is open, its lid tied down over a large rectangular box, and from where I stand, the cheese and wine basket clutched to my chest, I can see *Samsung* stamped on the cardboard. Trina's door opens and in her hand is the small glowing screen of a cell phone.

"We got Chinese, Tommy, you want some?" Her voice is as excited as a child's, and already Jamey is at the rear of his car untying the rope, his back to Amber, who coughs louder and stops to lean on her shovel. I *would* like some Chinese food, but how can I say yes to this?

Trina's walking over to me through the snow. She's in the man's leather jacket Shannon wears, and she's holding the bag of takeout to her chest the same way I hold the gift basket to mine. "What's that?"

"I'm bringing it to our new neighbors."

"Where'd you get it?"

"It was a gift." I nod in the direction of Jamey, who pulls from his trunk the new TV in its box, resting it on top of his head and walking carefully up the snow-covered steps of Trina's unit. "Please tell me he bought that with his own money, Trina." I can smell egg rolls and fried rice and chicken wings and again my mouth fills with saliva, but I also feel weak in the legs. Trina steps closer and says, "We got five *thousand*, Tommy. And it was so fucking easy."

"Trina."

"Nope. I don't wanna hear it."

Up on her darkened stoop Jamey sets the box against the wall. On its face is the picture of a widescreen TV, and under that, in black print: *60.*

"Trina, honey."

"Don't 'honey' me, Tommy. It was your idea, don't forget that."

I watch Trina walk into her unit with that warm Chinese food, and her new phone in one of her pockets. Then the exterior light comes on and one of her kids screams and MJ bursts out onto the stoop, jumping up and down like the little kid he is, Jamey lifting the TV box and carrying it inside.

Amber shakes her head and keeps shoveling. On my way past her I think of her husband Cal, whom I haven't seen in months. I think of the sixteen hours a day he works and of the rides he must get from coworkers, Amber left with their one car she's cleaning off now with a long scraper, its brush end half-gone. On her head is a kid's wool cap, half a dozen pink ponies knitted into it.

"What, they hit on a scratch ticket?"

If Amber's ever said three words to me, I don't know when or why. I stop. I pull the basket in closer to my chest. My fingertips have gone numb, my ears too. "Inheritance, I think. Her grandmother."

"They better keep that to themselves."

"You're right. How's Cal?"

She looks at me over the roof of her Geo. Her face seems so far away and again I sense that I'm stepping with both feet into some-one else's private room, the way I did calling Dawn by her name, the way I did taking Larry's widow's hands in mine, but I can also sense a growing welcome for the question and Amber lowers her scraper to her side, her breath in the air. "Who knows? All he does is work."

"He's a good man."

Amber nods. She brushes snow onto the ground, but she does it halfheartedly and it seems she wants to say more but doesn't.

"I admire how hard you both work. It'll pay off in the end."

"You think so?" Her nose sounds stopped up.

"I do, yeah." I think how Cal's probably hiding his second job from the Housing Authority, that he's squirreling away money the way Fitz did so they can get out of here. A cold breeze blows over sparkling snow in the lot that still hasn't been plowed, and I'm sure that Mike Andrews' street has been cleaned two or three times already.

Amber's saying something. She's brushing snow off the trunk of her Geo and saying something, but I'm thinking of Mike Andrews. No, I'm seeing him standing under the recessed lights of his big kitchen, horsing around with his daughter, this happy, lucky man, and I know that I have to forgive him. I have to go to Mike Andrews and *forgive* him.

Amber sounds like she's talking to herself. Her back's to me as she keeps brushing off the trunk and the side windows. From inside Trina's comes yelling and Shannon pushes open the storm door and rushes down the snow-drifted steps, ignoring me and my basket as she runs through the snow.

From her stoop Trina watches her. She's chewing on a chicken wing. She shakes her head once, then goes back inside.

My arms have begun to tremble. Amber's working steadily, her head down. I want to offer her something helpful about work and marriage and how balancing the demands of both takes people of unnatural clarity and resolve.

But she's tossing the scraper into the backseat and carrying her shovel to her unit, her front door closing behind her a warning to me to do better at listening next time, at concentrating, at not being so easily distracted, at being *now*, here.

ON FITZ'S FRONT DOOR the Smith & Wesson decal's been scraped off, but its shape is left behind. I knock directly on it and the man answers. He's just a shadow in the doorway, and even standing on the threshold step he's still shorter than I am. My new neighbor flicks on the exterior light and I smile at someone maybe ten years younger than I am, a man with the same gut and thinning hair, but also with broad shoulders under a dark T-shirt. "What can I do for you?"

"Not a thing. Here you go." I hand him the wine and cheese basket. A wave of heat rolls down my legs, and my arms feel light in the air. "A welcome gift. I'm in the unit at the corner."

The man peers into the cellophane at the wrapped sausage and crackers and bottle of wine. He looks back at me. "Well jeez, thanks."

"Tom. Tom Lowe." I offer my hand and the man shifts the basket so he can shake it, and coming up behind him is his wife or girlfriend. Her hair's still pinned up and she's in a robe. In the dark hallway her expression looks curious, and her man turns to her and raises his right hand so that she can see it. Then he does something fast with his fingers, raising his pointer and dropping it, his pinkie rising, then his thumb. He opens his palm against his chest and now the woman's nodding and smiling. She raises both hands, and as I watch her fingers lift and drop and point, one hand opening to receive the other, it's like watching an orchestra play on TV with the sound off, the violinists' furiously moving bows almost enough. The man turns to me. "She'd like you to come inside. Got a sec?"

This wasn't my intention, but to say no to this warm invitation would be turning my back on these gentle tugs I've been following ever since I knew I wasn't a thief. And now I'm stepping into Fitz's old living room, except instead of a widescreen TV against the far wall, there's a silk painting of a woman in a black dress on a trail in the jungle, across her shoulders a length of wood for carrying water.

"We were just sitting down to eat. Hungry?"

"I don't want to intrude." And I don't, but where Fitz had his leather sofa and lamps draped with red scarves, where he had his laptop set up for filming him and Lynn doing it for money, there's a dining room table that seats six and already the deaf woman is setting down a third place mat. She can't be older than forty, but her shoulders seem to slump with some private weight and there are already gray and white streaks in her pulled-back hair. She smiles at me and motions for me to sit.

The place smells like cooking beef and the cardboard boxes against the wall that they still haven't unpacked. The man has unwrapped the basket and pulls out the wine. "Let's open it. Doug, by the way. That's Minh."

Doug and Minh. From "new neighbors" to "Doug and Minh." As I pull off my jacket and drape it over the back of my chair, I again feel I'm learning something I should have long ago. Or maybe I did and just forgot it.

In the kitchenette behind me comes the pop of the cork, the light clatter of plates. Doug calls out, "How long you been here, Tom?"

"Six years."

The man sets down in front of me a water glass of red wine, then he takes his place at the head of the table with his own glass, the woman in the jungle hovering behind him. I think of that cabbie Raksmei, and I point to the painting. "Cambodian?"

"Vietnamese. Like Minh. She can't hear, you might've noticed." He raises his glass and taps it to mine and now his wife places in the center of the table a plate of sliced bread, then a bowl of thin noodles covered with shredded carrots and sliced cucumbers with sprigs of parsley on it. My mouth fills and I sip my wine. "You sure I'm not intruding?"

"No, please." Doug takes a gulp of his own wine. He has long fingers and big hands and there's a raised scar from his left wrist to his elbow. I want to ask him about it but don't.

"So, this Housing Authority, they all right? When do these inspections happen?"

"Now and then. Usually by a couple of kids who don't know their ass from their elbow. I don't think they've ever had real jobs before."

Doug nods. He looks down at the table and nods again. "I got laid off a year ago."

"Doing what?"

"Fabricator. Been doing it since I was in high school, for Christ's sake. Twenty-seven years and I only called in sick once. Just one day." Doug reaches for the plate of bread and holds it out for me to take a slice, which I do, Minh lowering a plate of shaved beef over rice on my place mat. There are the smells of steamed meat, basil, and mint, and I can't remember the last time I sat down to a meal made for me by somebody else. I shake my head and have a hard time swallowing.

"I don't know what to say."

"About what? *Eat.*"

The deaf woman is signing something to her husband. Doug gets up and follows her into the kitchen and carries out two plates of food, his and hers. He sets them on the table, taking his chair once again. "She'll be right back. Don't let it get cold."

My hip fires are raging again, but this warm meat and rice are wonderful, the tangy gristle and fat, the crunch of bean sprouts, and I wonder what my son's eating right now. Dinnertime on his twentieth birthday. Has he sobered up? Did somebody bake him a cake?

This Doug loads up his fork and pushes it all into his mouth. He swallows it down and drinks his wine. "You do this for all the new people?"

"No, but I should have."

In the corner on a small lamp table between boxes is a photograph of a teenage boy smiling into the camera. His cap is on backwards and he has one of those chin-strap beards framing his handsome half-Asian face. "That your son?"

Doug nods without looking over at the photo. He reaches for more bread just as his wife comes into the room, dressed now in a white sweater and jeans. She signs something to her husband, smiles at me, then sits and puts her napkin on her lap. It's something I didn't do and so I do it now. "Can you tell her for me that this is delicious?"

"You can tell her yourself. She reads lips."

She looks up at me and there's something fragile about her. Like she's been sick and is only now starting to find her way back.

"This is delicious. Thank you."

She nods and smiles and reaches for her own water glass, filled with the wine I brought them.

"Is your son here with you too?"

"No." The man says it quickly and the woman glances at the salad like she wished she hadn't just read my lips. The three of us chew quietly and I want to take back my question. I feel I should say something more but don't.

"Can I ask you something, Tom?"

"Please."

"How'd *you* get here?"

"Me? I got hurt." I set down my fork. The woman Minh is looking right at me, dabbing at her lips with her napkin, and it's clear that she's waiting for me to continue, but also in her attentive

face is a need for me to say something that might help her understand why she and her husband are in this place too. What I just
said about me getting hurt now feels like a lie, or like a mere sliver
of a sliver of the truth.

"What happened?"

"I fell on a roofing job."

"You a roofer?"

"Carpenter. I did it all, really. I—" My face has warmed and I
feel like I'm getting ready to tell an old story that's long since lost
its power. But why? Didn't I do it all? And wasn't everything going
along just fine until I walked into that bank?

"I made some stupid mistakes."

"Got it." The man bites into his bread. He glances over at his
wife, who's staring at me. She taps her husband's wrist and signs
something to him with both hands, her face coming alive with
such earnest expression that I'm moved by it. He sips his wine.

"She wants to know if you have a family."

"A son. Like you. Today's his twentieth birthday."

The man seems to be avoiding looking at his wife. He takes the
bottle of wine and refills my glass, then his. The woman smiles at
me and sets down her fork. She signs something with one hand to
her husband, then stands and leaves the room as quickly and quietly as some passing spirit.

Outside, the Housing Authority plow rattles by. Doug pushes
the rest of the bread into his mouth, then reaches for the salad
bowl and forks some of it onto his plate. I'm looking at the corner photograph of this couple's son. In that one grin, he has the
look that life is one big game and you better be a player or you're
out. I can feel the question rising in my throat, but rising with it
is the fear that I'm sticking my face where it doesn't belong, but I
hear the words come out of me anyway. "Is your boy all right?"

The man stops chewing. His eyes are on mine like I've said
something deeply insulting. I start to lift my hand in apology.

"He's a fuckin' druggie. We don't even know where he is."

"I'm sorry."

"It's killing his mother."

I nod. I lift my glass, then set it back down. "Can I ask what kind of drugs he's on, Doug?"

"Who knows? It started with pills one of his buddies stole."

"Painkillers?"

"That's right."

"I was on those. After my accident. They're bad."

"You get hooked?"

"I did, yes. But I've been clean for years."

"How'd you stop?" The man leans forward, his eyes passing over my unshaven face and premature Christmas sweater.

"A drug called Subaxone. Plus, I—"

"What?"

"I had my son to think of."

"Where's he?"

"College. Western Mass."

Doug stands and carries his plate into the kitchen and scrapes it clean into the trash. "Our son stole from us. From his own flesh and blood."

"That was the drugs."

"I swear I could kill him. I could."

The faucet's running and I'm done eating. I'm back in Wyn and Nancy's bedroom. Wyn made it clear that my staying with them would be "a temporary accommodation" only, until my unit in the 8 became available, though Wyn didn't call it that. I was down to my last few Os in a baggie I kept wedged behind one of Gerard's old high school textbooks. I was out of money and close to having to give up my cell phone and I had Teddy on speed dial, but I couldn't just have him pull up to Wyn's front door. Plus, how was I going to pay him?

It was a bright morning. Too bright. The old house was quiet and still smelled like the English tea Nancy had stewed before her class, like the cranberry muffins Wyn had baked just after dawn. He served me one on a heavy ceramic plate, and now here I was using my walker to get to the base of the staircase, then leaning all my weight on the creaking maple bannister as I and my glowing hip screws made our way upstairs to the open loft that belonged to my kind and future ex-in-laws.

Against the wall leaned a rod for opening the skylight, and I used that as a cane, and who was this man pulling open Nancy's underwear drawer? Who was this man fingering his way past all that folded cotton and silk for a jewelry box I never found? Who was this man going through Wyn's bureau and bedside table? This sweating, stinking, sickening piece of garbage who not so long ago had stood under the willow tree outside in a pinstriped tuxedo marrying their only daughter, who somehow saw in me the opposite of whoever I was now.

"You finished?"

I say that I am, though there's still plenty on my plate. It's time to leave, but not before I say to this man, to this father, to this laid-off husband living now here in the 8, "The drugs make you somebody you're not. Hate them, not your boy."

The man doesn't say anything, just stands at the entry to the hallway waiting for me.

I stand and pull on my old Carhartt. In the opposite corner of the room, where Fitz had his La-Z-Boy, there's a small sewing machine, a large bobbin of thread on the table next to a short stack of red fabric.

"She likes to sew. It gets her mind off shit."

"If she does it for money on the side, don't tell the inspectors that."

"Thanks for the heads-up."

At the door my new neighbor Doug thanks me again for the basket and offers his hand, which I take, squeezing once before stepping back out into the cold. At the steps that I only now notice Doug has already shoveled, I say, "Please thank your wife for me. I haven't had a meal that good in a very long time."

Not since Ronnie anyway. Not since my own wife whom I was somehow unable to hold on to through hardship, though this Doug has held on to his, a thought that fills me with respect.

"What was the name of that drug that helped you?"

I tell him. "And there are others. Let me know if I can help."

This man Doug nods, and I turn and walk down the steps, the stars high and bright over the snowy field on the other side of the dumpsters, the door closing behind me.

23

JAMEY'S WALKING OVER THE PLOWED ROAD UNDER THE STREET-light. He's balancing Trina's old widescreen on top of his head, and its dangling cord knocks against his side. "Hey, man."

"Can you swing by my place when you're done with that?"

"No problem." The boy's tone is as upbeat as Trina's had been when she stepped out of his car, and in it I can hear that he's in love. From the cracks on either side of Mrs. Bongiovanni's window shades comes the shifting light of her TV, and I think of her lovely old face turning to me to say that people give up too easily these days.

But did I? Didn't I fight for me and Ronnie?

No, I fought for our house. I spent hours and days and weeks on the phone on my adjustable bed trying to save it. But what did I do to save me and Ronnie?

The light over Trina's stoop is still on, and even from the road come the muffled explosions of MJ's habit returned to him. I wonder if Shannon's back now. I also wonder what could have gotten her so mad on the night that her mother brought home such a rare bounty.

I'm lying back on my plywood couch when Jamey knocks on the door and walks in. "Hey, Trina wanted me to bring you some food." The boy sets a plate of Chinese on the table, then sits in the same chair Fitz did the night I threw him out. Jamey's cap is pulled low over his ears and his curly beard looks wet. There are the smells of chicken fat and fried egg rolls and rice.

"I already ate."

"That's cool."

"I wish you guys hadn't done that today, Jamey."

The boy seems to go more still in his seat and for once his eyes look clear. "You're not gonna rat us out, are you?"

"No, but listen—"

"Why'd you change your mind anyways?"

My hip screws have cooled the way they do whenever I lie down in this useless position, but what do I say to this kid's question, because wouldn't five thousand dollars be a very good thing right now? I could have my car back in a day. In two days I could be sitting in a restaurant with my son a hundred miles away. "Jamey, how old are you?"

"Old enough."

"Nineteen? Twenty?"

"Twenty-two."

"When I was your age I was learning a trade and going to college at the same time."

"I'm in school."

"Can I ask you a question?"

"Maybe."

"Do you think you're in love with her?"

The boy's cheeks flush above his beard. "Man, I just want to help her. Like get to a better place. I offered her my student loan money, but she wouldn't take it."

I didn't expect to hear this, but of course this boy would do that. The kid's phone vibrates and he pulls it out of his back pocket and sets it on the table.

"You need to answer that?"

"It's just my mother." He sits forward in his chair and looks like he's ready to leave. Still written on the palm of my left hand is Drew's phone number, and I can feel it there on my skin as if those numbers are burning. I want to ask this kid if I can use his phone, but to ask for a favor from him now feels like the opposite of what I should be doing. I'm beginning to suspect that Jamey has had little adult guidance in his life. Probably far less than Drew, who at least has had loving Ronnie and steady Edward Joseph Flynn. Drew also had his real father for ten years, I shouldn't forget that. "I don't want to be the kind of man who steals, Jamey. That's why I changed my mind."

"Even from a credit card company? They're bloodsuckers.

When my mother needed money, they played her and played her. I mean they're *evil*."

"She raise you alone?"

"Yeah, me and my two sisters."

"So you see your mother in Trina." Again, this heavy-footed feeling that I've just crossed an invisible line where polite people do not go, but I also feel like I'm being propelled there by something inside me that comes from someplace very old and everywhere if you just let yourself know it somehow.

Jamey's staring at his fingertips resting on the table. "I don't think of it that way."

"How do you think of it?"

"Is this really your business?"

"No, it's not, but Jamey, one bad decision in this life can knock you off the rails for a long time. Believe me, I know."

The boy's phone buzzes again. He glances at the screen. "I gotta answer this. She doesn't like to text." He presses the phone to his ear and I glance at Drew's number on my palm and maybe I *will* ask if I can use that phone.

"You're welcome, Ma. Don't worry about it."

I can hear the woman's voice. It sounds jubilant but concerned, and I hear clearly, "But where you'd get it, honey?"

"I told you." Jamey turns sideways in his chair and lowers his voice. "It's a refund from my loan, don't worry about it."

There are more words from the boy's mother, but I can't make them out and I picture Trina waiting in the boy's car as he runs inside some rented box house to give his mother stolen money. The boy tells his mother that he loves her. He taps the screen of his phone and stands. "You should eat this. It's good."

"*You're* good, Jamey. That's what worries me."

"What do you mean?"

"Nobody ever gets away with anything, you do know that, right?" Except for bankers and Wall Street brokers and drug company executives and insurance men. "Tell me you know that."

"I used a fake ID, how are they gonna find me?"

"Banks have cameras. A shitload of 'em."

"We thought of that. I wore some really thick glasses and we parked like three blocks away. Both times."

"You went to two banks?"

"Yeah, twenty-five hundred each."

"How much did you give to your mother?"

"Trina did it. I mean like it was her idea. She's a really good person, Tom."

"Yeah? Trina takes care of Trina, buddy."

"Man, you don't even know her."

"Maybe, but I know she feels cared for by you, and that's good. But can't you find a better way to help her than commit a crime?"

"What if I don't think it's a crime?"

"It doesn't matter what *you* think."

Jamey stands, the chair legs scraping the floor. "Let me tell you something, man. My whole life I feel like I've watched bad things happen to my family and I couldn't do shit about it. I mean *nothin'*. Because I was a kid. Because I was too small. Because I was—whatever. But taking that money from those motherfuckers today? It's the first time I've ever felt like myself, like, I don't know, like the real me or the *better* me, and I'm gonna do it again, Tom. I'm gonna do it till me and Trina have a place of our own."

"What about her kids?"

"Yeah, of course, them too."

"What happens if you go to jail, Jamey? Have you thought about *that*?"

The boy pulls off his cap and runs the fingers of both hands back through his hair. "All I do is think. My whole life. And I'm fuckin' tired of it." The boy pulls his cap back on and is down the hall and out the door before I can say, *what* exactly? That I, too, am tired of thinking? That I'm tired of lying on this plywood couch feeling sorry for myself? That I'm tired of staring at the lives of others on my laptop and festering in the puss of old bitterness? That I too can understand the invigorating value of action?

More explosions through the wall, Trina laughing. I remember how soft her face looked this morning when she told me that no one's ever wanted to help her before the way Jamey does.

I need to call my son. Even if Drew's day drinking has turned to night drinking, he should hear his father's voice on his birthday. He should hear his father tell him that he loves him. That these twenty years of being his father have been the best years of my life. Despite everything. Drew just needs to hear me say that.

I'm tired. Deeply. Just carrying that heavy gift basket to my new neighbors, stopping along the way for Amber and Trina, my arms straining while my ashy bones turned into a new fire, and then that half-meal of beef and basil and rice, it's all fastened my legs and hips and back to my plywood couch, and now Drew and I are working together on a roof. My son's lean and tanned and handsome, but he's also small and chubby and young, both versions of him working alongside his father under a blue and hopeful sky.

I'm on my knees on the pitched roof showing my son how to reach for a roofing tack in my carpenter's belt while at the same time nailing the one before it, sinking it into the shingle with two swings of my hammer, and Drew's watching his father with the same expression he had on his face when he watched Shannon backhand her brother MJ into the street, MJ calling her a cunt, Trina running outside to yell at them all, Drew's face so darkly dumbfounded that this is his dad's home, and so I stop swinging my hammer and say, *They're people, too, son.* And I'm about to tell my son that I'm learning something about love, that maybe I've never been good at any of it, even loving him, and I want to apologize to Drew for not being the kind of father I should have been but now Drew's laughing at me like I've just told a funny story, only it's clear that Drew is drunk, his eyes glassy, his cheeks flushed as red as they got running back inside from the cold with a new bag of Os, and then I'm falling and there's a rapping sound and it hurts me that Drew's swinging a hammer up there when I'm about to hit the ground, and the rapping is what I open my eyes to, my unit flooded with sunlight, a woman's voice calling, "*Tom?* It's *Dawn*, from across the *street.*" She knocks again. "*Tom?*"

I clear my throat. I call out that I'll be right there. Something foul lies in my mouth and I'm sweating under my Christmas sweater and I want to clean up before I answer the door, but the rapping goes on.

I step over my plank table and run my hands over my face and then I'm pushing open my storm door to Dawn. She's in a wool sweater, her spiked hair gelled, and the snow on the ground behind her is too white under the sun, even though it feels very early.

"Your ex just called my phone. She wants you to call her right away."

Not one time in six years has Ronnie tried to reach me like this. My throat closes up and I'm just about to ask Dawn if I can use her phone, but she's already tapping a button on it and pushing it into my hand.

"Tom?" Ronnie sounds short of breath, like she's walking fast or running. "Drew's in the hospital."

"*Hospital?* When? *Why?*"

"Alcohol poisoning and, I don't know, hypothermia."

"Is he *all right?*"

"I don't know, I have to go, we're at the place on campus."

"*What* place, Ronnie?"

"The *hospital*, on, you know, *campus.*" Ronnie's tone is one I know so well it's like I'm still lying on my adjustable bed in front of the wall of windows, my wife scared and then mad for being scared, and somehow I'm standing at my table staring down at Trina's plate of cold Chinese food, Dawn taking in my plywood couch and shelves of books, my heart suspended in the air in front of my face. There's a man's voice. Flynn's. Low and muffled, then nothing, and I'm squinting at a screen of numbers shaking in my hand.

"Everything okay?"

"No, my boy's in the hospital. I have to go to him."

Dawn reaches for her phone and I look at her, at her aging face, her spiked hair a silhouette against the sunlight coming through the blinds behind her. "Can you drive me there? I don't have a car."

"Where's your car?"

"It's a long story."

"What happened to your son?"

I tell her the words Ronnie told me, but to take the time to even do this feels like I'm lying on some beach while Drew's drowning in the surf. "Can you drive me?"

"To western *Mass*?"

"Yes."

Dawn glances at the untouched Chinese food on one of Trina's chipped plates, at the plank of wood lying across two stacks of books, at the almost empty bottle of vodka on the floor up against my plywood couch. And this last detail seems to make up her mind for her. "Can't do it, sorry. I have a business to run, Tom."

Tom. Hearing her say my first name to my face in my cramped and overheated unit feels like a door she's opened just enough for me to see the lovely room beyond, even though she's now closing that door.

"I have to go." Then I'm thanking her and pulling on my old work boots and jacket, patting my front pocket for my wallet, which is there though it has no money in it, and I'm holding open the door for Dawn.

"I wish I could help."

"You have helped, Dawn. Thank you." And I mean that, the gratitude I feel to her for walking across the street with no coat on to knock on my door. Now I'm helping her down my snow-covered steps, taking her arm by the elbow, and I want to explain that cheap bottle of vodka she saw on my floor, that that's not why I live here in the 8 and don't have a phone or a car and can't go see my son in trouble without doing something I don't want to do, which is to go ask Jamey for his car. But what's this thought about *myself* at this horrible moment? What kind of man *am* I that I'm worried now about what this woman thinks of me?

There must've been parting words between me and Dawn, but I don't remember getting from my stoop to Trina's front door, which I'm knocking on now as hard as Brian had knocked on mine.

It's Trina who answers, Jamey right behind her. Both of them look like they were asleep and now they've just been caught and there's nowhere to run.

"My boy's in the hospital and I need to borrow your car, Jamey.

I'm sorry." Those last two words are stones in my throat. My eyes sting. Trina says, "Tommy, what happened?"

"I don't know, he drank too much, I don't know."

"I'll drive you, man."

"I want to come with you guys."

"It's two hours away, Trina. You can't."

Jamey's pulling on his sneakers and now he looks up at Trina, then me. "Where's the hospital?"

"Amherst. I'm sorry."

Jamey looks back at Trina, his eyes a dark question.

"We'll do it later, honey. Go."

It. Another *bank*? But there's such care and concern in Trina's voice, and only now do I notice that she's standing in the doorway in only a loose T-shirt and her underwear, that Jamey has pulled on his shoes but his jeans are still unzipped and he's shirtless, hurrying back to the sofa for the rest of his clothes.

"How'd you find out?"

"My wife. My ex. Trina?"

"Yeah?"

Up against the wall behind her is the big cardboard box for their new TV. A strand of hair has fallen across Trina's face and she tucks it behind her ear and crosses her arms, goose bumps blooming on her skin.

"I want to be a better friend to you. I haven't been a good friend."

"Oh, please." But she looks away, and while Jamey's pulling on his denim jacket and wool cap, I want to tell Trina that I know people—Gerard? Wyn?—people who've helped me and might be able to help her, and that I'm going to ask them to help her, I will. But Drew is falling and I have to catch him and then I'll come back and tend to Trina, this young woman hugging her new boyfriend like he's going off to war.

PART IV

24

JAMEY'S DRIVING FAST ALONG ROUTE 2 WEST, SUN-BRIGHT SNOW on the roofs of houses and strip malls and now a Wendy's, a hatless teenager in a parka shoveling the sidewalk near the back door. Lining a lumber store parking lot are dirty snow mounds eight feet high, the asphalt wet and glistening. Its surface is covered with a thin layer of sand and salt, and I think of the cinnamon toast I used to make for Drew in the toaster oven, that cheerful, hungry boy sitting at the granite island I built. Then I see other things, hospital hallways and nurses and empty gurneys, and I shake my head and make myself stop seeing.

A few miles earlier Jamey said he had to gas up. After filling his tank and paying inside, he climbed back into the car with two hot coffees and a bag of warm honey-dipped donuts. When he opened the bag and offered one to me, there came the sweet smells of working mornings from another lifetime ago, but I'd seen the wad of cash the boy pulled from his pocket walking into the station, and I just would not take any gifts bought with stolen money.

"No thanks."

Jamey bit into his donut, his mouth half full. "I don't know how you like your coffee, so I got black and you can add, you know, whatever." The boy pulled his own from the cardboard tray filled with sugar packets and creamers and my large Styrofoam cup of hot coffee I wanted so very badly, especially now as it sits warm and heavy on my lap. The phrase *alcohol poisoning* keeps tapping at the back of his heart like a malicious bird and the bird's voice is Ronnie's.

"You don't want your coffee?"

"I do want it. Very much."

Jamey glances over at me. He's been driving too closely behind a blue sedan, its rear bumper spotted with rust. The boy pulls his car into the passing lane and accelerates past what is a very old man driving that sedan, thick glasses slipped halfway down his nose.

"Were you guys planning on another bank today, Jamey?"

"I don't get why you won't drink your coffee. Or actually I think I do get it and I don't like it."

We're passing auto dealerships and auto supply stores, more fast-food drive-throughs, department stores and bank branches, their tinted plate-glass windows advertising *Low Interest Rates*. On one of those signs, in big blue letters, is *ARM*, Adjustable Rate Mortgage, and what a fool I was to think what I thought when Mike Andrews first presented that term to him, how much I liked the word *arm*, the limb that works the hand that performs the work, the limb that holds my baby son close, a word that also means to protect oneself, and so isn't that what I was borrowing all that money for? To build a refuge for Ronnie and Drew. To build a rain-proof, snow-proof, wind-proof nest. To arm my family against whatever may come.

The sun is shining in my eyes from the side view mirror. I lean away from it.

The boy is quiet for a mile or two. We're moving away from towns now and getting deeper into wooded country, snow weighing down pine branches, the trunks dark against all those deep drifts on the ground. Jamey taps his phone and adjusts his radio knob and a man is rapping softly about his mother.

Then Jamey glances over at my lap and says, "If you don't want your coffee, I'll drink it. I didn't get much sleep, you know."

"Why not?"

"Two people on one couch doesn't work so good."

I pull my lidded coffee from its tray and hand it to Jamey, who has already finished his own. He tosses the empty cup over his shoulder and sets mine into the console under the radio.

"I just hope you don't think you're better than us."

I'm looking at the small framed photograph of the golden retriever hanging from Jamey's rearview mirror. "I don't think I'm better than anyone, Jamey." Though since my fall, I've absolutely felt I'm better than the men whose way of life conspires against workers like me. For years I believed that I would never leave Ronnie the way she left me. And for years I believed I was better than anyone living in the 8.

"Good, because all money is dirty."

"Even the kind you earn?"

"Depends on how you earn it."

"Have you ever had a job, Jamey?"

"Ever since I was *thirteen*. I've washed dishes and mowed people's lawns. I've painted houses. I've even worked in one of the mills. I know how to work, dude." The boy's looking over at me, and when did he put on sunglasses? He looks older with them on, just a bearded face with my reflection in the lenses, a slumping man in the passenger seat who didn't even brush his teeth or take a piss after getting up to Dawn Porter's knocks on the door. "I'm afraid I need a bathroom."

The boy pulls onto the shoulder without putting on his indicator. Three cars pass one after the other. I swing open my door. It hits a plowed snowbank and I have to ram it a few times to climb out. As I stand in the snow and piss in the direction of the woods, snow gets into my right work boot and flames lick my hip screws and Jamey turns up the music, the rapper singing to his mother that he understands it wasn't easy trying to raise a man.

So long since I saw my own mother. In that sweet interval before her decline and when we still had our house, she loved being a grandmother to Drew. She'd stay overnight and one of those mornings I woke to Drew's laughter. He was only six or seven and his grandmother must've been tickling him because he was laughing so hard he had to catch his breath before laughing some more. There were the smells of pan-fried bread, of cinnamon and cooking eggs, and Ronnie opened her eyes next to me and said, "Don't you just love hearing that?" The sun shone through the muslin curtains across her bare shoulders and I said that I could listen to that sound forever, and then Ronnie and I were making love to it, to our son's happiness, to his grandmother's joy.

A semi rumbles past, its wind pushing against the back of my head. I zip up and pull off my right work boot and knock the snow onto the bank, then fall back into Jamey's warm car. The rapper's singing to his mother that he loves paying her rent when it's due, that he hopes she got the diamond necklace he sent her, and as I yank the door shut, I say, "I've lost so much, Jamey. I just don't want you and Trina to lose so much too."

Jamey accelerates back onto the sunlit road, his small engine straining. "Man, we have to get you some socks."

DRIVING THROUGH CAMPUS, the place where Ronnie and I found each other, this place I haven't been back to since, feels like stepping into a dream that's gone on long after I woke from it. There are still the many buildings crowding out a few bare maples, and dozens of bundled-up students are walking along shoveled sidewalks, the snow so white under the morning sun. There's the performance center and the student union and the long pond covered with ice, but seeing all this brings back no memories. I was an older student then and lived somewhere else, working all day and taking most of my courses at night when the campus was lit with streetlamps and students were in their dorm rooms studying or drinking or both.

Jamey's driving slowly and my heart's echoing off the back of my bad-tasting tongue. I need to at least rinse my mouth before seeing Drew and Ronnie. I wish I'd taken a shower and shaved and combed my hair. I wish I wasn't wearing this premature Christmas sweater I've slept in for days. I wish I wasn't showing up to see my son in the company of this young stoner and thief.

"Up ahead. On the right." I have no idea how we've stumbled on the Health Center, but there it is, a flat-roofed two-story building, a concrete ramp leading to its glass doors. My voice seems to come from the bottom of a deep, dry hole and I have no choice. "I need just one sip of that coffee, Jamey."

The boy nods and looks like he wants to say many things, but he just shrugs and parks his car in front of a bike rack. I take the plastic lid off the coffee and drink. It's warm and bitter and I swallow three times. Fastened to the brick wall of the building are aluminum letters spelling out *University Health Center*, and I feel queasy and shot through with a fearful sorrow.

Jamey shuts off his engine and reads something on his phone. He begins to tap out a return message with his thumbs.

"Is that Trina?"

"Yeah, she's worried. She wants us to call her when—you know."

I push the lid back onto the coffee cup and set it into its holder. "I need to go in alone, if you don't mind."

"That's cool, I'll go buy Shannon a phone."

I push open the door and climb slowly out, heat shooting across my lower spine. Jamey waves and drives out of the lot and I see again Trina standing at her door in her underwear, looking away when I told her that I want to be a better friend, and as I hurry up the ramp to the Health Center's glass doors, I feel moved that she cares enough about Drew to worry.

Just inside the doors is a men's room on the left and I step inside and wash my hands and face with hot water and soap. I wet down what's left of my hair and run my fingers back through it like a comb. I rinse my mouth out with cold water, then wipe off my face and hands with paper towels. The tails of the button-down shirt I wore to Larry's funeral are showing and I tuck them into my pants, and have I really not changed since Larry?

But I have changed—or am changing—I can feel it. This is something Drew should know, that his father is finally learning to play his hand. But I'm getting ahead of myself. Drew's glassy eyes and stewed grin on that roof in my dream. And alcohol poisoning can be bad. It's a thought that's been burrowing into me all morning and I'm beginning to feel like a coward for staying in the bathroom this long. My son needs me. He's needed me for a long time.

The young woman at the desk has an RN badge pinned to her sweater. She also has the superior air of someone who's recently acquired important skills. She smiles up at me and says, "May I help you?"

"I'm here to see my son, Drew Lowe?" My eyes begin to burn. I glance behind me at three empty chairs against the wall.

"Is he a student?"

"Yes, he was admitted here last night. Alcohol poisoning." My face heats up and I'm ashamed that I feel shame for my son as I say this. I cough into the sleeve of my old work jacket and wish it was clean.

"We don't keep patients overnight. He may have been transferred."

"Transferred?"

"Yes, we're not an infirmary. His name again, please?"

I tell her and she swivels in her chair to her computer monitor. *Infirmary.* The word makes me think of the Civil War and canvas tents and men's legs being sawed off as they scream and scream. Beads of sweat break out on my forehead and the back of my neck, and if Drew was transferred somewhere, how will I get to him?

"Yes, he's at Cooley Dickinson."

"Is that near campus?"

"Oh no, Northampton. You want the address for your phone?"

"I don't have a phone. Or a car. I got dropped off by a friend."

The young nurse is looking up at me like I just confessed something incomprehensible to her, though her reaction seems to be more about my not owning a phone than a car. She places her hand on her desk phone. "Do you want to call your friend to come pick you up?"

"I don't know his number." Flames are burrowing into my hip sockets, and another wave of heat passes through my face because I'm sick of giving answers like this to people who are only trying to help. The young woman's staring at the tiny Christmas trees sewn into my sweater across my chest. She takes in my whiskered face and unzipped work jacket, the way I have to shift my weight from one leg to another, and she starts to look a bit alarmed. I hold my left palm out to her. "Can you call this number for me? That's my son's. That's his phone."

"Sure."

Then I'm holding the Health Center's phone to my ear. I picture Drew in a hospital bed hooked into some IV, covered with a blanket for hypothermia. And why hypothermia? Did he go outside drunk and without a coat?

The joy I used to take in being able to buy my son new winter clothes, Trina saying that was the first thing she was going to get for her kids.

Drew's phone has been ringing, but if he's in a hospital bed, would he even have a phone near him?

"This is DL. Call back later."

DL? Do his friends call him *DL*?

"Drew, this is your dad. I came to the wrong hospital, but I'm on my way, buddy." That last word rings so false to me that I want to take it back. And I want to tell my son how very much I love him, but the young nurse is waiting to hang up the phone. "Would you mind calling the hospital for me?"

"No, that's fine." She seems less threatened by me now, maybe because of the message I just left for Drew, though if she sees me as a doting father, I feel like I've just lied to her in some way.

She hands me the receiver. I look out the glass doors at the bike rack, the snow melting under the sun. I hear a computerized voice and then I'm talking to an operator and finally a nurse on the floor where my son lies in some room. I tell her Drew's full name. "Is he all right?"

"Are you a relative?"

"I'm his father."

"But his parents just left, sir."

"They left? Is Drew still there? Is he *okay*?"

"Are you family?"

"I told you, I'm his father. That other man is his stepfather." The air seems to have stopped in my throat. The nurse covers the receiver and her muffled voice sounds like she's giving someone important instructions one more time.

"Your son is very lucky, sir."

My breath leaves me. The whole room shifts. "Can you tell me how he's doing?"

"I'm sorry, his nurse is busy with another patient. But call the main number and ask for room 214."

The nurse hangs up and the sunlight streaming in behind me is so very beautiful. An older woman is walking in from a rear hallway. She's in a pantsuit, a maroon silk scarf at her throat, and she's holding a teacup in one hand and reading glasses in another. The young nurse takes the receiver from me just as the woman smiles and says, "Is everything all right?"

"Yes, quite all right. Thank you." Then I say to the young nurse, "Can you tell me how to get to the hospital?"

"Do you want me to print out directions?"

"Yes, thank you."

Drew is "very lucky" and this young nurse is so helpful, and the older woman smiles at me as she sits at a larger desk in the corner, placing her teacup near a family portrait. I'm hungry and feel a little weak. I need to lie down. But there's such a quiet, attentive kindness in this room, a place where problems are solved calmly and efficiently, and I need to carry this with me somehow.

The printer pushes out a sheet of paper the young nurse hands to me.

"You've been so good to me. Thank you."

"Of course." She smiles and sits back in her chair with the satisfied air of one who's doing her job well. How fortunate people are to have *jobs*.

"When my friend comes back, can you tell him where I went?"

"Certainly." But she seems confused about how I'm going to get to the hospital without my friend.

"He's your age, with a beard."

"I'll tell him, sir." She looks like she wants to say more, but the phone rings and she smiles one last time at me before going back to her work.

25

EVEN WALKING OVER A MILE WITH NO SOCKS IN WORK BOOTS I should've thrown away years ago, my hip fires burning, I still feel in the presence of the good news, care, and warmth I was given back in that office. The sun is high and the temperature has risen to what early November should feel like. I'm almost too warm in my shirt and sweater and unzipped jacket, and if these folded directions in my pocket are right, the hospital's nine miles west. I know I can't make it there on foot. But I couldn't wait for Jamey to come back either. Who knows how long it's going to take to buy Shannon a phone. (And is that why she was pissed off last night? Because her mother came home with only one new phone?) No, I told my son I was on my way to see him and I *will* be on my way.

Cars pass wetly in the street. There's the steady dripping of melting snow off the tree branches and the stop signs, off the gutters of the clapboard houses I clomp by on mostly shoveled sidewalks, off the backstop of a baseball field covered with a sun-spangled whiteness.

In front of a shingled cottage with a mansard roof, a small child is rolling a ball of snow the size of his torso and his mother is filming him with her phone while calling out encouraging words I can't hear. But she smiles at me as I pass. She smiles at me like I know exactly what it's like to love a child the way she loves her own in her small yard of melting snow. And as I smile back, then step off the curb and cross a side street, my hip fires seem to burn brighter to show me that I'm broken and can do nothing, that my life is small and no longer useful to anyone, but what an illusion this has been. Because wasn't that smile passing between me and that woman something? In order for it to have happened, I had to be paying attention. I had to be awake enough to receive it. I had to be present. Not cooped up in my unit in the 8 on my plywood couch half-gone on pain distracter staring at my laptop.

Your son is very lucky, sir.

Thank God. These two words ring out in my own voice in my head, though I don't believe them. I don't believe that some all-knowing, all-loving entity is aware of my and Drew's existence. But there *is* benevolence out there, I can feel it. I think of how the deaf woman Minh's face became so animated and beautiful as she signed to her husband to ask if I had a family. Such hope in the question itself. A hope that seemed to come from her wish for my kids to be doing well, even if that meant better than her own. Because how could she ask it knowing her son was out there some-where afflicted if she wasn't also hoping to hear something good about someone she didn't even know?

My hip bones feel like they're being scoured by dull razors, shards of heat shooting down to my shins. But it's my feet that have more of my attention. The heels of both are being rubbed sore by the hardened leather of my work boots, and the tops of my toes have gone numb. Jamey's promise to get me some socks. What a good boy he is. Such a generous person. A giver and not a taker.

Ronnie's voice in my head. Her hair was wet from the shower and she stood in front of me in a cotton nightgown. I was in bed with a notebook and calculator on my lap, figuring the price of materials for a possible job. For weeks she asked me not to bring my work into our bedroom so late, and now her arms hung at her side as she stared at me, shaking her head. "Living with you is like living with a robot, you know that? You just keep doing the one thing you do, no matter what."

What followed this is lost to me, though it ended with her back to me as I shut out the light, her voice fluttering through the dark-ness. "You don't give, Tom. You're so afraid of the world, you can't let go and *give*."

I wanted to argue this point, but she said it with such finality, with such a resigned sadness, that I just lay there a long while thinking about it. She was wrong that I was not a giver, because look at what I gave her. All those months alone in those woods building her and our son a home. Even if I enjoyed doing it, that was still a giving act. Was an act of generosity true giving only if it took something from you? And how was I afraid of the world? Fearful people flee. Or freeze in some way so that their lives stay the same, and they never take any chances and so never change their lives. That wasn't me.

The first time my mother laid eyes on her son's home, she'd long since moved out of our rented house on that nameless dead-end street and into a two-room efficiency not far from where Carla's Copy Center used to be. When I drove her up to my brand-new house in the woods, Ronnie and little Drew coming out the front door to greet her, my mother had to cover her face with both hands, "Oh, Tommy, I can't *believe* it."

And I couldn't either. Not really. Not ever.

Not even after one of my ten-hour days of labor, Drew in his bedroom, Ronnie and I on the couch with glasses of wine in front of the wall of windows. While the last light of the sun sank into the marsh, I planned the next day's work, or thought ahead to the next job's proposal, and lovely radiant Ronnie, who was nearly always talking, would stop talking and ask if I was listening to what she was saying. I said yes, of course, but I wasn't, and even when we made love, Ronnie's arms and legs gripping me with an urgency I barely noticed, her yearning breath in my ear, I was uncoiling electrical cords and plugging in my compressor; I was reminding myself to oil my nail guns and check my saw blades; I was laying out walls and snapping chalk lines, on and on. I had climbed a steep mountain, after all, and now there was a wind up there and that wind was all the forces that could knock me off that mountain, and I had to be diligent. I had to hold on.

Under the blue awning of a bagel shop a man is begging. At his feet is a cardboard sign behind a coffee can, and as I get closer, the nearly cruel smell of sweet bagel dough in the air, I read the sign: *Will work for food or money*. The man's in a wool cap and overcoat tied off at the waist with a brown leather belt. He's also holding a cup of coffee or tea, and sticking an inch or two out of the side pocket of his coat is a cell phone, the kind Jamey owns and now Trina and soon Shannon.

One of my hip flames flares into my pelvis. I walk closer to this man who'll work for food or money though he can afford a cell phone, this clean-shaven man who's a good twenty years younger than I am and looks able-bodied and is staring at me like I might have something to offer him. But then the beggar looks across the street and doesn't seem to see the Starbucks there or the restaurant or the bank. I say, "What do you do for work?"

"'Scuse me?"

"You say you'll work for food. What do you do?"

"Whatever anyone needs me to do, sir." There's an edge to the man's voice, one that only a few weeks ago I'd hear as the defensiveness of the con man. But with this man in front of the bagel shop, I only hear the shame in his voice. And even though he has two things that I don't—a phone and a hot cup of coffee—if I had any money in my wallet, I'd give it to him. "I used to own a construction company. I'd hire you if I still had it."

"I appreciate that." The man sounds sincere, but he's also looking at me like he's hoping for a consolation prize.

"Sorry." I pat my pockets. "I'm broke." And as I step past the man and into the bagel shop, I think how, yes, I am indeed broke, but I don't feel quite so broken anymore. Even though my burning hips and legs tell me that they're done walking, even though my cold blistered feet are probably bleeding, even though the kid behind the glass counter's looking at me with the smile of one who believes he's about to do business.

"What can I get you, sir?"

There's music playing. A strumming guitar behind a woman's plaintive voice. Under a low ceiling there are small tables, each with what looks like a college student staring at a laptop or phone, and there are the pleasantly competing smells of onions and chocolate. The young man waiting for my order has his hair up in a bun. I say, "I'd love to order everything in this place, but I'm afraid I have no money to pay for any of it. I was hoping that I could use your bathroom, however."

It's the tone and choice of words I take on to show that I'm educated, that despite my present circumstances I've studied books
and learned things, but I need to stop doing this. I need to stop
apologizing for what's true about me, which is that I'm at the bottom of that mountain and will probably never get back up it again.

"Sure, man, go 'head."

I thank him, but the boy's eyes are already on the person behind
him, a woman in sunglasses I smile at before making my way
down a hallway to the men's room, where I piss and wash my
hands, then sit on the toilet lid and pull off my work boots. My
toes haven't started to bleed, but my heels have. I wet paper towels
down with hot water and soap and wash both feet as well as I can.
I drop pink paper towels into the bin as someone knocks loudly on
the door. I call out that I'm almost done, then pull dry paper towels from the dispenser and wrap both feet in white before wedging
them back into my work boots.

A knocking again. But instead of feeling hurried and irritated,
I make myself imagine the full bladder of whoever's on the other
side of that door. The discomfort of that. The need to be free of it.

I tie the laces of both work boots, but when I stand my feet feel
swollen. At the sink I avoid my reflection and run cold water into
my cupped hand and drink. I try to ignore how hungry I've gotten.

Back out in the hallway I see that the young man who's been
waiting is Drew's age and Drew's height and he even has Drew's
sullenness as he moves by me and locks the bathroom door behind
him. *Your son is very lucky, sir.* But not getting to the hospital
in a timely way feels like I'm somehow pushing that luck. I have
to hurry.

"Sir?" The boy behind the counter's holding out a small white
bag. "For you."

"Me?"

"Yeah, from the lady in line after you."

I look behind me, but there are only young people at work on
their screens. There are drums playing now, a man singing.

"She left. It's plain with cream cheese." The boy smiles at me
and I take the bag. I want to say thank you, but the words are

stuck in my throat so that I can only shake my head, my eyes sting-
ing as I and my hip fires leave the shop. Outside, a man in a tie
and cardigan has just dropped a five-dollar bill into the beggar's
coffee can.

I pull out the bagel, which is toasted and cut in half, and I hand
one of the halves to this almost young man who'll work for food.
At first he looks like some kind of trick is being played on him, but
I say, "Please, I can't eat the whole thing." Though I sure as hell
can. Then the beggar and I are eating side by side, chewing and
swallowing and not saying anything to each other. The bagel's soft
and warm and tastes like it's just come straight from the oven, the
cream cheese a silken loveliness.

"I hope you find work soon, my friend. Don't give up."

The man nods and swallows. "You too."

But the funny thing is that I *have* given up. And as I walk toward
the main intersection of downtown Amherst, warmly dressed men
and women strolling or driving by, the snow in the town green still
unsullied by footprints, I can feel that bag of Kerry Andrews' trash
I'd hugged tightly against my chest, I can see the floodlights snap
on hooded Trina in their backyard, I can hear Mike Andrews'
shout from the door that he's called the police, and my face is on
fire for how low I let myself slide.

At the corner next to a coin-operated newsstand is a garbage
barrel and I wipe my mouth with the empty bagel bag, then toss it
into the trash. I pull from my jacket pocket the printed-out directions, but my reading glasses are back in my unit and I have to hold
the folded sheet of paper inches from my face. Squinting with both
eyes, I can make out Northampton Road turning into 9 West, and
it looks like I'm going to have to travel through western Amherst,
then through Hadley before I have to cross the Connecticut River
into Northampton. I want to just lie down and rest a while, but my
own words burn through my head. *I'm on my way, buddy.*

I fold the directions and push them back into my jacket pocket.
A chill moves through me and I can feel the sweat drying on my
back and chest. How long's it been since I've *sweated*?

Three young women pass me, two of them in those tight black

pants they wear now. I'm about to ask where I can find Northampton Road when I read those very words on the corner sign. Then I'm walking away from the town center past two- and three-story houses, most of them with deep front porches and round wooden columns that don't need any paint. Hanging upside down from the tongue-and-groove ceiling of one of the porches is a bicycle, and I wonder if my hip fires would let me ride one like it? Why haven't I thought of this before? Maybe I could ride a *bike*?

But this walking can't go on for much longer. My heels have ripped through the paper towels and are rubbing against leather and I'm aware that I'm limping, that I have to swing my right arm to roll forward my left hip and then my right. I'm sweating again and breathing like I'm hauling a bucket of roofing tar up a forty-foot ladder. I stop and zip my jacket, my heart beating in my fingertips. The sun's directly over me but so far away, and if Trina were here with me, we'd probably get a ride just minutes after she stuck her thumb out into the air.

I'm starting to regret not waiting for Jamey to come back. Maybe I should head back to the Health Center. But what if that young nurse has already told Jamey where I went?

But at the entrance of the next side street, my body stops: *Primrose Drive*. How many early mornings had I turned onto this street in my work van? Eight weeks of them? Ten? And I can see it now from where I stand: the widow's house.

The fall I met Ronnie I was building a kitchen addition for a widow not far from campus. Her husband had been an anthropologist who'd published fourteen books, and the first editions were kept in a glass case that my partner Wally and I carried into the master bedroom for her. She was a soft-voiced, small-boned woman in her seventies, and she seemed to spend most of her days in her garden in faded jeans working on her hands and knees. She wanted a new kitchen for her grown son's family who'd be moving in soon, and as Wally and I laid out the footings, I'd glance over at this woman who had lost her husband only months before and see her sometimes looking off at nothing before wiping her face with the back of her arm.

Her name was Elizabeth and she'd been a concert pianist. She told us this over coffee one morning weeks into the job. *But once the kids came along, I gave that up. The travel was too much*, she said. *I lost something doing that, but you men are making me happy again. You do such good work, don't you?*

Yes, I believed. We did. It took years to be able to say that. Eight to ten before I could call myself a real carpenter. And even after I earned my builder's license I still considered it a means to some other end, one that would be more important than helping people improve their houses. But sipping coffee with this new widow in wrought-iron chairs in the middle of her garden, the leaves of her maples just starting to turn, I could see just how much she meant what she said; we *were* helping to make her happy again.

This sweetly pensive widow wasn't the first to tell me these things about my work, but it was the first time I started to see some value in what I did that wasn't simply material. And then I went to a weekend house party where I carried two bottles of beer to shimmering Veronica Finch standing in that doorway, and it was only days later, as we lay side by side in our own warmth under the sheets, that she asked me why I was a carpenter. I told her because I was good at it, and she seemed to accept this, especially after I told her that I liked creating things.

She had other questions for me, but I had already begun to love this Veronica Finch. Her first name was too hard-cornered for her, though, so I started calling her Ronnie. And as Wally and I spent the rest of that fall building the widow's new kitchen, my love for Ronnie only grew, and then that kitchen job was done and I was handing Elizabeth the keys to her new back door, tears in her eyes, and maybe if these two women hadn't come into my life at the same time, I thought for years, I might've gone on to do different work. But now I felt a new commitment to how I made a living, a trade, after all, that had always been in the service of higher things: like *home*, like *family*.

Four houses down on the left, just past the snow-dusted hedges of her neighbor, is the shingled two-story belonging to that kind, grieving woman who was in her seventies over twenty years ago.

She's most likely gone now, a thought that makes me sad, and, as if I'm walking into this sadness, I'm walking down the middle of Elizabeth's street.

The road's wet and bare, the sun glinting off pools of water near the plowed banks at the sidewalks. One of the pleasures of being a builder all those years was to drive by structures I'd built and see them standing years later. Those Saturday afternoons taking Drew with me on a run of errands, I took long detours while we ate fries off our laps just to point out to my boy a porch I'd built, or a roof, or a deck, or an entire house. Now I'm standing in front of the widow's house. The sidewalk's unshoveled, but there are boot prints in the snow, a newspaper wrapped in plastic hanging from the storm door's handle.

It feels right and wrong to be here. I should stay on the road to Drew. But doing this job for that woman had felt like an anointing of some kind, and all these years later I'm being anointed in a different way; I'm beginning to feel called to a new way of living, and so walking by this street feels like seeing an old teacher, one you have to stop to acknowledge.

I don't want to bother anyone, but I'm walking down her driveway. It's been cleared by a snowblower, a red one set against an empty one-car garage that wasn't there when I worked for the widow. Built into the back of it's an L-shaped cottage, its shingles matching the ones I'd nailed into the addition I stare at now.

The corner boards haven't curled. The shingles haven't either, and the soffit, fascia, and window casings look as straight and flush as when I first cut and fastened them. Somebody's kept the place up too. There's no peeling paint anywhere and under the windows are wooden flower boxes. I picture the widow in jeans seeding geraniums in potting soil, her son's family happily using the kitchen I designed and made for her.

"May I help you?"

There's a woman behind me. She has a dog on a leash and she's in a down coat and a wool cap with a white pom-pom on the top. The dog's staring at me, and the woman's not smiling though she doesn't seem unfriendly.

I feel once again like I've just stepped somewhere I shouldn't be. "No, I—" I nod at my addition. "I built your addition years ago and I just wanted to see it, I guess. I'm sorry."

"Oh."

The dog starts to pull forward on its leash.

"Did my mother-in-law hire you? Elizabeth Turner?"

"Yes, Elizabeth." Though I don't remember her last name, only her warm and sadly accepting face.

The woman seems to go still there in her snow boots. She looks at the cottage attached to the garage, then back at me. She takes a breath, but it seems to stop halfway and then her eyes are filling and she shakes her head. "I'm sorry. We just lost her." She covers her face with her mittened hand and I'm being pulled the way I've been pulled for days, stepping toward this woman to at least rest my hand on her heaving shoulder, to tell her that I was very fond of her mother-in-law Elizabeth Turner, very fond indeed, but there's a sound in the air I don't hear often and it matches a jerking heat in my lower leg, the sinking of the dog's teeth into my pants and shin. "No, Boyd! *No!*" The woman's yanking on the leash and I pull myself away and lower myself to one knee. I hold out my hand to this barking dog Boyd and say, "It's okay, boy. It's okay. I wasn't going to hurt her. I just want to help, that's all."

26

THE WOMAN'S KITCHEN SMELLS LIKE OATMEAL AND THE SOAPY
water she washes my leg in. I should've been humiliated when
she saw that I wasn't wearing any socks, only thin and ripped
paper towels, but she's being so apologetic about her dog that she
doesn't even seem to notice. My pants are rolled up, both feet in a
shallow rubber tub she's filled with hot water from the sink. She's
on her knees softly scrubbing the dog's bite with a soapy washcloth, and from where I sit on a kitchen stool at the granite island
that Wally and I installed when I wasn't yet a husband or a father,
I can see the crooked part in her hair, the gray roots of her scalp,
the rest of her hair dyed.

"I'm so sorry, he's never done that. I don't know why he did that."

"He was just looking out for you."

Before she'd grabbed the tub from a closet, she pulled the dog
into a back room and closed the door, and from behind it now
comes a whining that sounds to me oddly remorseful. This hot
water on my sore feet feels like a pleasure I haven't earned and
don't deserve, and once again I'm being given something.

Elizabeth Turner's daughter-in-law looks up at me. Her eyes are
olive, her skin pale and with no makeup. She has the tired, no-
nonsense look of someone who's done her duty for years, and now
her duty includes me.

"How long since you had a tetanus shot? Has it been over
ten years?"

"I'm afraid so."

"Can you drive?"

At first I think that Elizabeth's daughter-in-law is asking me to
drive *her* car, but no, she must think I'm a full citizen with a full
citizen's possessions. "I'm on foot."

"I can see that." She says this with a smile in her voice tinged with concern. Now she's running the washcloth lightly over the heels of both feet, and my face heats with shame for her doing that and for taking this detour that has slowed me getting to Drew.

I'm about to tell her where my son is and why, but she reaches for a towel and asks me to put both feet into it. Then she's standing with the tub of water.

"Do you need a ride?"

"I don't want you to have to do that."

"God, it's the least I can do."

The dog whines and paws the door and the woman carries the water to the sink and dumps it. The towel's thick and feels like love itself against the soles of my feet.

The woman is handing me a pair of gray wool socks. They look soft and clean. "My husband left them behind. My name's Mel, by the way. We should go." She seems to say this to shut down any argument about me taking her husband's socks, and so I thank her and pull on these warm gifts that let me slide my feet easily into my work boots, my hips lighting up as I tie my laces and stand, this woman Mel smiling at me like she's known me for a long time but doesn't quite remember whether that time was a good one or not.

MEL'S DRIVING JUST UNDER the speed limit on Route 9 West, her Subaru clean except for a fine layer of dust and dog hairs on the dash. Her heater's on too high, but I don't want to ask her to turn it down. My leg throbs from where the dog bit it, but it's just a lone instrument in the orchestra of pain I've endured daily and nightly for years, and maybe that's the first step I have to take down this new road I'm on. I've long accepted that my hip fires will never go out, but maybe I need to do more than that. Maybe I should give up *wanting* them to.

Mel's asking my name.

"Tom. Tom Lowe Jr."

"You always say Junior? Is there a senior?"

"There was. He died when I was a kid."

"I'm sorry."

"No need, that was another life ago."

Off to the right stretches the white fields of a golf course, its low club buildings made of brick and glass. There comes the foggy memory of hanging cabinets in the kitchen of one of those buildings, or was that a different club closer to the ocean? This woman Mel turns the heat down. "Does your leg hurt?"

"Oh no, I'm used to a lot worse."

"You are?" She's looking over at me in round sunglasses, her wool cap pushed back on her head. Its white pom-pom is a cheerful flourish that seems forced on her, and I can see that she wants me to elaborate, but I've gotten so tired of my own story and it occurs to me that its constant loop in my head over these years has kept me from writing a new story. "I appreciate this ride. I was going there anyway to visit my son."

"To the hospital?"

"Yes."

"You were *walking* there?"

"Trying to anyway."

She keeps her eyes on me, then looks back at the road. "Is he all right? Your son?"

"I think so." My face feels suddenly loose on its bones.

"What happened?"

We're passing the plowed parking lot of a Chili's. It's already half full of cars for the early lunch crowd, and I can feel how nervous I am to see Drew and Ronnie again. I try to swallow but can't.

"I'm sorry, it's none of my business."

"No, that's fine. He's there for alcohol poisoning and hypothermia."

"God, I hope he's all right. One of my daughter's friends almost died last summer. Xanax, Adderall, and vodka. We used to just get high, remember?"

"I do." Though I don't. Even in high school it was beer, beer,

beer. Sometimes a fifth of Southern Comfort. And in college I had to get up at dawn every morning and drive to a job site. No, I don't remember. "Where's your daughter?"

"UVM. My son's at Worcester Poly."

"And they're doing okay?"

She looks over at me again. Her sunglasses have slipped a bit down her nose, and I wonder how long she's been living alone.

"I worry about my daughter. My son's like his father. You know, a worker bee. But she's—"

"Anxious?"

"Yes, how'd you know that?"

"My boy's anxious. Depressed too."

"Do you have other kids?" I can feel her desire to give me something maybe more hopeful to talk about.

"Nope. Just the one I screwed up."

I've never said this quite so plainly before, even in my head. I feel suddenly naked, my ugliness exposed, though my words hang in the air between me and the woman like something that's not ugly because they're true.

"I feel that way a lot. About my daughter anyway. But maybe we're being too hard on ourselves." Mel's voice has gotten more reflective. I watch her watch the road ahead of us, but her attention's elsewhere, both of us suspended somewhere together in our separate pasts. And yes, I have been too hard on myself, but in only one way and that's my lack of ability to work and to be useful. But when I couldn't afford a phone anymore and didn't have to bear Ronnie calling me about our son, I was relieved. I don't let myself think about that. The deep worry in her voice. The perpetual optimism of the abundist gone. Our son was turning inward, but my hip pain was all I could handle while also trying to stay clean, or so I told myself, and I tried to be some kind of father to Drew with emails and my monthly money order. Wouldn't those gestures be enough for my boy to know that his old man had not forgotten him?

We're passing a Staples store and a Courtyard Marriott and then a Target, corporate franchises that remind me of some larger narrative of this life that I'll never be able to control, that this country of ours is a cold commercial machine, one that asks us to feed it and feed it, and whatever time we have left for our families we better use well, but it's hard to love when you're tired, it's hard to love when you're afraid you'll lose everything.

"I've been thinking for a long time that I feel so much for my boy that he must feel it too."

Mel nods and puts on her indicator. She turns in her seat and looks over her right shoulder, and as she does this I take in her slight double chin, the pensive purse of her lips. She seems to want to say so much and then we're in the right lane, guardrails half buried in snow whipping by. "My husband had the same problem. But he had it with me, too. No offense, but I think you men still believe that all you have to do is go out there and earn, and even if we women are earning as much as you are or more, we're still expected to do all the loving at home. A woman would never think that anyone could feel her love if she didn't *show* them every single day." She's leaning closer to the steering wheel and driving too fast. "I'm sorry. It's been a rough few months."

I want to tell her, no, please, I should be the one apologizing, because I feel like I'm standing on the edge of understanding something completely new about me and Ronnie, though I can't quite touch it yet. "I don't disagree with anything you just said."

"Thank you."

We're driving over a bridge, the Connecticut River far below. The snow on its muddy banks has melted into patches, and against a gray boulder lies a long tree branch the color of bones.

"I kicked him out, by the way. He didn't leave me."

Ronnie in her black turtleneck, her chin up as she held her untouched glass of wine and told me all about Edward Joseph Flynn. "Was there somebody else?"

"For him or for me?"

"For you."

"Please, when would I have had time for *that*?"

We've left the river behind and are driving by houses built in the last hundred years. Their big yards are planted with trees and their bare branches glisten under what has to be a noonday sun. "What about you? Still married, I take it." She's looking down at the ring on my cupped hand lying on my leg, the dog bite pulsing hotly upward.

"Not for a long time, no."

"She kick you out, too?"

"Nope, left me for a better man."

She turns into the hospital's entrance, glancing over at me with what seems to be a bitter satisfaction that softens into something else. *A better man.* For years I haven't been able to look at Ronnie's second husband in any other way. *Edward Joseph Flynn*, who finished college and law school. *Edward Flynn*, the working lawyer. *Ed Flynn*, who owns a ship captain's house on Salem Common and who can house and feed and clothe my son better than I ever could again. *Flynn*, who restored Ronnie to her abundant self.

But this new road I'm on, it feels like it might be able to lead me to parts of myself that may make me a better man too. Or at least better than I was.

Mel slows her Subaru and drives under a steel and glass canopy on brick columns. The sliding doors of the hospital are just a few feet away, and on the other side of those doors are well-lighted corridors, and I want to hurry inside to my son and I also want to stay right where I am with this nice woman with the sad, dutiful eyes who seems to see me for what I am and doesn't care either way. She reminds me of someone, but who?

Trina.

She takes off her sunglasses. "Do you need me to wait for you?"

"No, I have a friend coming. But thank you very much for your help." I hook my fingers inside the door handle. This woman Mel's looking at me like we were both in the middle of some story and now she won't know how it ends.

"I'm so sorry for your loss, Mel."

"Thank you, Tom."

I want to tell her how her mother-in-law's deep appreciation for my work made me value it for the first time. I want to tell her that I met Elizabeth when I also met my future wife. I want to tell her that I see Primrose Drive and my weeks there as a golden period that led to an even better one. But the throbbing in my leg is a chain of words being yanked through my veins. *I'm on my way, buddy. I'm on my way . . .*

Mel puts her sunglasses back on. "I'm going to kill that dog when I get home."

"No. Buy him a big steak instead."

THE DOCTOR'S SOMETHING CALLED a physician's assistant, a carefully attentive man with the narrow face of an endurance athlete. I'm sitting on the examination table with my right pants leg rolled up to my knee again, the wool sock on my foot making me feel both grateful and unworthy again, though as the assistant rubs ointment on my shin where the dog's teeth punctured my skin, I want him to just hurry up so I can go see Drew, who was "discharged" less than an hour ago.

"To *where?*" I'd asked the nurse on the second floor.

"His home, I suppose, sir."

It had to be the same woman I'd talked to earlier. She stayed in her seat in front of her computer and telephones, and she had the permanently weary features of someone who hasn't slept well in years.

"His home here at school, or—"

"You'll have to ask him. I'm sorry."

Two phones rang and she ignored them, then stood, grabbed a blood pressure cuff, and walked away from her station, a circular counter, and behind it was only one other person, a young guy typing something onto a keyboard while answering one of the phones. I wanted to ask if I could make a call with one of those, but I felt greedy and ungrateful that my son was well enough to leave this place and all his father could do was ask for yet one more favor from strangers.

Before I could see a doctor, I had to sit across a desk from a woman in white who asked me for my name and date of birth and address. As she typed my answers into her computer, its pale light reflecting off the lenses of her glasses, I told her I had no insurance and she stopped typing and gave me that look I've come to know so well, letting out a breath and opening a new screen reserved for people like me.

The physician's assistant finishes taping a pad of gauze to my skin. "You'll need to take off your sweater and shirt, please." He nods at the tiny Christmas trees across my chest. "Favorite holiday?"

"My only good sweater."

He smiles and opens a white cabinet where he finds what he's looking for, unwrapping a disposable syringe and sticking its needle into the bottom of a small gray vial. As I take off my sweater and shirt, I'm pretty sure that this young assistant thinks I'm joking about my sweater, and I'm aware that just a few weeks ago I would've made sure he knew that I wasn't joking. Or would I? This constant tension of wanting people—like Larry's son-in-law Paul—to know that Tom Lowe was once a full citizen but is still a man. And also wanting people like this physician's assistant who's clearly an abundist, who reminds me, in fact, of my former brother-in-law Gerard, that this land of ours is full of people who have little to nothing at all. But if someone's raised in abundance, then that person is raised with partial vision, and now the needle sticks into my shoulder like a sentence I don't feel the need to say anymore.

Instead, as I watch this young guy go about his work with the cordial intensity of a true professional, all I feel the urge to express is a deep gratitude bordering on wonder. "It must be very rewarding to help so many people."

"It sure is."

The man's voice sounds so sincere and I picture him competing in triathlons on his weekends off, swimming, biking, and running for miles before coming home to a lovely woman who also works in the medical field, or maybe law like Gerard, the two of them making love in a steaming shower before cooking a tofu dinner together. But where before I might feel the bitter envy of the permanently sidelined, I now feel only happiness for the bountiful existence of this skilled, disciplined, and immensely useful man in front of me.

The assistant wipes my bare shoulder with an alcohol swab, then presses a Band-Aid onto it. He pulls a pen from his coat pocket and writes something on a pad of paper. "I'm giving you a prescription for antibiotics. Be sure to take it all, even if you feel healed down below."

Healed down below. Something wells up inside me, though it seems to come from someplace dusty that used to be wet.

"The last time I was given a prescription, I got addicted to drugs." I'm smiling. The assistant stops writing and looks at me. I'm still shirtless and aware of the softness of my sedentary torso, but I feel no shame in this. My life has dealt me this hand, after all, and now I just want to give this young healer something too, though I'm not sure what that is, maybe just more of me before I go, a fuller picture of myself.

"Are you in recovery?"

"I don't take painkillers anymore, if that's what you mean."

"Yes." The assistant glances down at my chest and gut like he's looking for evidence of something I'm not telling him. I can see that his eyes are the same olive as Mel's, though they're less reflective, more scrutinizing. "Antibiotics aren't addictive. You'll be fine."

"I think you're right." And I do think this young physician's assistant is right, that I will be fine; this dog bite will heal.

"I broke my back and hips years ago, but the pain's never gone away." I'm still smiling and I'm not sure why I'm smiling, only I know that I'm not saying this because I want help from this medical man. I just want him to see who I am, that's all.

"It's chronic?"

"Permanent, I'd say." I pull on my button-down shirt, standing to button it. The cuff of my right pants leg falls to my ankle.

"There are excellent pain clinics out there."

"Not for the financially destitute." I shrug and can already feel this young healer drifting between wanting to help and needing to move on to his next patient. I need to move on too. I need to go see my discharged son. "I'm grateful to you, sir."

"Please, I'm happy to help." The assistant opens the door for me, and as I step through it I sense that this young man *is* happy to help, and why wouldn't he be? What can make anyone happier than being of *help*? I want to tell him how sorry I am that I won't be able to pay for what he's just done for me, that the state or the hospital will have to cover it. But instead of the self-loathing that would normally fill me so hotly at a time like this, there's just a curious letting-go.

27

JAMEY'S AT THE INFORMATION DESK JUST AS I COME FROM THE halls of the emergency room. Seeing the kid in his lined denim jacket and wool cap, his hair and beard looking so scraggly, is like seeing the shadow of my own son, both young men needing attention, because Jamey looks agitated. I call his name and the boy rushes over to me. "Why'd you *leave*?"

"My son was here. You all right?"

Jamey shakes his head and steps toward the glass doors of the entrance. "We gotta get back."

"Everything okay?"

"I don't know. We gotta go."

He's outside before I can fold the physician assistant's prescription. Jamey's rusted sedan is parked up against the brick columns of the canopy and he's already standing at the open door, exhaust sputtering from its tailpipe. He's looking across the roof of his car and waving at me to hurry.

I turn and wave at an old man in a sports jacket sitting at the information desk. "Thank you, sir."

The man nods and smiles, and now I'm climbing into Jamey's car, which smells like cannabis. On the backseat is a white box from Apple. "I see you got Shannon a new phone."

Jamey accelerates into the bright sun, dripping water from the canopy spattering across his windshield. The parking lot glistens black with all that melting snow, and I feel like a man who was luxuriating in a hot bath only to be yanked out into a cold room. "What's the matter, Jamey?"

"That kid Brian. That fucking *Brian*."

"What about him?"

"He hit her again. He fuckin' *hit* her."

"Where? When?"

"Just now, when I was at the *bank*."

"The bank?"

Jamey's driving too fast down the same street Mel used an hour earlier. A mailman's walking away from someone's porch, and as he reaches into his satchel for more mail, he glances up at Jamey's car zipping by loudly and shakes his head. I pull the seat belt over my chest. I haven't done this during my years in the 8, and the thought of driving back east before I've seen Drew feels like jumping off a roof.

"Jamey, pull over and tell me what's what."

"What's *what*?"

At a corner stop sign in front of a large Federalist, Jamey only slows before pulling out onto the main road for the highway. "He *hit* her is what. Don't you *care*? He hit Shannon too."

"Shannon?" Trina's daughter at the top of the stairs, the way she gripped that eyeliner brush in her right hand as I stood in the dark stairwell. "Is he still there, Jamey?"

"No, I don't know. She like hit him in the head with something."

"Trina?"

"No, Shannon." Jamey pulls his phone from the console and taps the screen three times. He seems to be driving even faster now, the engine of his small sedan making a clattering sound. The big yards with the old hardwoods in them are moving by much too quickly and I'm about to tell him to slow down, but Trina's voice is in the air and she's crying. "Jamey?"

"Trina," I say. "Honey, what happened?"

"Tommy?"

"Is he gone? Is your door locked?"

"Tommy, he hit Shannon in the *face*." Trina's crying and then the sound becomes muffled and she's calling out to MJ or Cody to wet another cloth. "Give it to her, please. Sweetie, just go give it to her."

"Treen?" Jamey's holding the phone close to his lips. We shoot past a convenience store, an old man stepping out of it with a loaf of bread.

"Did you call the cops? You should call the cops."

And it's like when I dream I'm working again, then wake up and see out the storm door of my unit a carpenter's pickup driving by, because there, coming at us from the opposite direction, is a police cruiser, its driver glancing out at us just as Jamey says for the second time the word *cops*.

Now Jamey does slow down and Trina's sniffling on the phone, saying she's afraid to, that that'll make him madder.

I want to say something to this, but my eyes are on the side-view mirror and it's a wonder how fast that cop does a U-turn, his cruiser lights flashing, his siren beeping loud as a nightmare. He's driving faster than Jamey and now is just a few yards behind him. For a half-breath or two Jamey seems to be deciding whether or not he's going to actually pull over, and Trina's speaking softly to one of her boys, "Tell her to come down. Please, honey, do that for Mommy."

Hearing this does something to Jamey. He hands me the phone, flicks on his indicator, and slows to a stop in front of a church. Behind a wrought-iron fence the church's snowed-in yard is small, the statue of some saint between it and the carved doors of the entrance. The sidewalk hasn't been shoveled, and of the four stained-glass windows, two are covered with sheets of weathered plywood.

"Jamey? Tommy?"

"Shit, does my car smell. Does it?"

I hold the phone close to my mouth the way Jamey did. "We'll call you right back, hon. It looks like we're getting a ticket."

"A ticket?"

I hand Jamey the phone and he drops it into his console just as the cop raps on his window. From where I sit I can see only the man's badge, his radio strapped to his shoulder. Jamey presses his window button and the cop asks for his license and registration, his voice flat, no sign of him having had to do a U-turn and step on his accelerator to pull this kid over.

Jamey doesn't say anything, just reaches over my knees and opens his glove box and fingers through it for his registration. There's a bottle of Advil in there and rolling papers and a pair of thick-framed glasses. Jamey finds what he's looking for and hands it to the cop. "Driver's license, please." The officer leans down and looks at me. He takes in my face and open Carhartt jacket. "I'll need an ID from you as well, sir."

"Of course." I lean back into the seat to pull my thin wallet from the front pocket of my pants and Jamey now seems alarmed. He leans forward and pats his rear pockets and then his front. He shoves his hands into his denim jacket, then pulls the empty coffee cup out of the console and lifts his phone and peers at the backseat and the floor.

"License?"

"My wallet. I just had it. I don't know where it *went*."

"Here you go, sir." I hold my driver's license in front of Jamey, who's going through his pockets again, the cop taking my ID. On one of the cop's fingers is a gold wedding band. He glances at my license, then slides it behind Jamey's registration.

"No license, Mr. Roche?"

"I just had it, Officer. I—"

"Sit tight." The cop walks back to his cruiser, its light bar flashing blue, and it's funny how I never thought to ask Jamey his last name. Roche. Jamey Roche.

"You leave it back at Trina's?"

"No, I just had it at the—you know, the bank."

"Jamey—"

"Yeah, so what. It was right next to the Apple Store and Treen and I were gonna do another one today anyways and—*fuck*." Jamey has spread his knees and is leaning forward and feeling around on the floor near his brake and gas pedals. A minivan passes slowly by. On the back bumper is the decal of a peace sign next to one of the planet Earth. It's faded into a light blue, like all seven continents have sunk into the seas. One of my hip flames has moved up to my chest. "Do you think you left your wallet at the bank, Jamey?"

"I don't know, Trina was crying and I just, like, booked it out of there. Wait, maybe—" The boy glances into his mirror, then pulls a white envelope from his side denim pocket. He parts it open and

thumbs through an inch-thick wad of twenty-dollar bills. *"Shit."*
He stuffs the envelope back into his pocket. An SUV passes from
the opposite direction, the sun a bright glare on its closed windows. "Did you have your real ID in that wallet too, Jamey?"

The boy looks over at me like I've just pushed a needle slowly
into his neck. *"Fuck."*

Of course he did. And I'm back on my adjustable bed, reaching
for the cash I kept tucked under a stair tread, my young son pulling on his winter coat with an expression of conspiratorial happiness on his round, soft face. It was my idea to steal convenience
checks. This kid never would've thought of such a thing.

"What am I gonna *do*?"

"Did you go to the phone store before or after the bank?"

"Before."

I want to tell him to stay calm, that maybe his wallet's lying in
the bank's parking lot and nobody's found it yet. I want to ask him
if his registration's current, and if it is, then he'll just be getting a
five-hundred-dollar fine, like I did, for driving without a license.
But Jamey's leaning over again and patting the floor at his feet,
and to tell this boy not to worry is to tell young Drew not to tell
his mother when what should be honored here is the *truth*.

"You do know it's a crime in the Commonwealth to drive without a license." The cop has one hand on the roof of Jamey's car
and is leaning halfway down into the window frame. The collar
of his uniform's unbuttoned. Sprouting from the top of his white
T-shirt are four or five gray hairs.

"I just had it, Officer. I think I lost my wallet."

"Any idea how fast you were driving? Know how many kids like
you I've had to scrape off the roads?"

"No, sir."

"Too many." The cop leans down farther and looks directly at
me. "Mr. Lowe? You're gonna drive. Your friend here's lucky I'm
not towing his vehicle." He hands me my license, the cop's hairy
arm inches from Jamey's face.

"Happy to, Officer. Thank you."

"And you, young man." The cop hands Jamey his registration

and five-hundred-dollar fine and what looks like another one for speeding. "Those funny papers in your glove box? You better not be smoking those behind the wheel."

"Course not. Never."

The cop straightens up, his hand back on the roof of Jamey's sedan. He seems to be looking off into the distance past the church and the houses on the other side like he's deciding if he's making the right judgment here. He has a flat waist and I picture him taking long walks at dusk with his long-married wife and maybe a dog. He seems to be a fair-minded man, and as Jamey pushes his registration into the glove box and slams it shut, I can see relief in the boy's eyes above his bushy beard.

The cop's face is back in the window frame. "You two switch seats now." He straightens, then waves at a passing Bronco, the driver rolling down his window and calling out, "Hey, Bobby. Looking good, Officer. Looking *good*."

28

I'M DRIVING JUST UNDER THE SPEED LIMIT ON ROUTE 9 EAST, AND even though I'm worrying about Trina and need to see my son, even though Jamey lost his wallet at a bank he stole from, the kid next to me on the phone with Trina now, I can't deny the joy I feel sitting behind the wheel again. I'm a man in charge of where he's going and why, which is to see my son in Amherst though I've never been to Drew's off-campus house, only have the address in my head from sending him monthly money orders: *116 Hatfield Street.*

At first Jamey wasn't happy about us having to delay getting back to Trina, but then he turned to me and said, "Can we go by that bank to at least, you know, check the lot?"

For a few blocks the cop who pulled us over followed in his cruiser, but when Jamey asked this, the cruiser turned left and disappeared down a street of apartment complexes and I took this as a sign that it might be all right to do what the boy wanted, that we might just find his wallet lying in some puddle near a curbstone he'd backed away from too fast while trying to calm Trina on his phone.

He's still trying to calm her, though Trina doesn't sound scared anymore. "I'm gonna kill him, Jamey. I swear to God I'm going to fucking *murder* him." Then she's talking about Shannon's lip, how it's twice its normal size. "And she's blaming *me.*"

"Trina?" I say. "Have you called the police?"

"No, I'm not calling them."

"Isn't he on probation? Didn't you tell me that?"

"If I put him back in jail, Tommy, he'll—" Her voice starts to break, but she puts a stop to it with a deep drag off her cigarette.

"Treen, we'll be gone by then. I got more money for us today. You won't even live there anymore."

"How much?"

"They could only give me five hundred on that one, but you know, I mean I have to pay this ticket, but—"

I say, "Trina?"

"Yeah?"

A black pickup accelerates past me on the left, the guardrails free of snow. There's a steep embankment and a thin stand of pines and then the massive parking lot of a Walmart Supercenter. I think of Cal, sixteen-hours-a-day-working Cal, and I think of my younger self, of years of getting up just before dawn, my knees, back, and shoulders sore, but there I was, standing in my darkened kitchen making coffee to get back out there again. Trina and Jamey wanting right away what should take years to earn, I feel sorry that they were never given a very important message about how to live.

"Tommy? You there?"

"You need to report Brian, hon. And you and Jamey need to stop doing what you're doing. We'll find a better way. We will."

From Jamey's upturned phone in his hand comes only machine-gun fire, MJ or Cody just feet away from their mother killing and killing, Trina crying again now, saying, "I can't take this shit anymore. I just can't."

THE BANK IS A one-story brick and glass structure under a high, impatient sun, its small lot half filled with the cars of its customers. On the drive here, it came to me that the first thing I have to convince Trina and Jamey to do is return the TV and the phones, and then to return the money. Not to the banks, who'd have them arrested, but to the man whose name Jamey's taken as his. I have no idea how I'm going to convince the boy and Trina to do this.

While I sit behind the wheel of Jamey's idling car, the kid's on his hands and knees peering under the chassis of a new sedan. Beyond him is a strip plaza, cars coming and going from its lot, the sun glinting off a jumble of shopping carts in their holding pen. Jamey stands, walks around the new sedan, then gets on his hands and knees and looks under it from the other side. At the plate-glass window of the bank a woman in a gray business suit is watching Jamey intently.

The passenger door jerks open and Jamey climbs in and slams it shut. "I'm such a fucking *idiot*."

Standing beside the woman is a man in a tie and he's watching us with his hands on his hips like a coach about to call a play out in the field. The woman's typing something into her phone, and I put the car in reverse and back out of the lot. "You shouldn't call yourself names, buddy." A horn honks a few feet behind us and I accelerate away from the bank and past the plaza, Jamey shaking his head. "I left it in the bank, Tom. I left my wallet in that fuck-ing *bank*."

What's there to say to this?

"I think, like, right on the *counter*."

At the corner I pull to a stop, squint up at the road sign, and see that Route 2 East is to the left. I wait for a Jeep to pass by, then turn toward Amherst, the dog bite a hot pulse in my lower leg.

116 HATFIELD IS A triple-decker, all three of its front porches sag-ging. From where I stand on the wet walk I can see how out of plumb one of the first-floor posts is and how that's forced the framing above to drop down, their damp joists hanging too low on one side. The windows are old too, their sills rotting and flak-ing paint. In the narrow driveway off to the left is a Vespa behind Drew's Honda, and as my flaming hips and I climb the spongy steps to the door, my heart's beating in the cheeks of my face. It's so wrong that I've never been here before. Can I really only stay for just a few minutes?

The porch is littered with empty beer cans, most of them bent in half. Up against the wall is the bench seat of some old Ford or Chevy, and in front of this, across two cinder blocks, is what looks like a kitchen shelf still wrapped in yellow contact paper. In the middle of this is a ski boot lying on its side.

There's no storm door, just a raised panel made of hardwood

many, many years ago. Its pitted surface is covered with years of paint, and as I knock on it, it's like I'm knocking on unrelenting time itself.

From inside the house come no sounds. I knock again, then turn and look back at Jamey's car, which I'd parked at the side of the street. Jamey's sitting low in the passenger seat, his attention on the phone in his lap, most likely talking to Trina again. I just promised them both that I'd help them find a better way than stealing, though I have no idea what that way is. Other than hard work and patience, and yeah, just a bit of luck. If they're ready for it, and the only way to be ready is to work. But I can't deny how fatherly I feel toward them both, which feels almost obscene as I stand here on the porch of my son's house, which I haven't once visited or even seen a photo of. I wonder if Hanna lives here too, lovely abundant Hanna, and I'm about to knock again when the door swings open and a kid stops short. "Oh, pardon me." He has a small head and the dark skin of someone from India or Pakistan. Dangling at his side is a shiny red helmet, and he's dressed in two thick sweaters, the straps of a backpack pressing into the wool. I'm about to introduce myself when the boy steps past me and heads down the stairs, pulling on his helmet as he goes.

From inside the open doorway of the house come the smells of damp clothing and cannabis, and I watch the kid start up his Vespa, back it down the driveway, then rev off out of sight.

Jamey opens the car door and shouts out, "We gotta go!"

I wave and step into my son's house uninvited and unannounced, which feels like one more unseen border I keep crossing. I'm standing in a darkened living room, every one of its windows but one covered with a sheet, its floor bare except for a throw rug in front of three couches, and they look like they were picked up off the street. In the center of the longest one is an upside-down laptop and a silver bowl, burnt popcorn seeds at the bottom. A large vodka bottle is lying on its side and I wonder if that's what my son drank.

I move through the room and down a narrow hall to a door I

knock on once. Sticking in the wood is a single dart, a long empty condom hanging from it, and I turn the knob. "Drew?"

On a mattress on the floor lies a young woman and a young man, both of them asleep. The blanket is pulled snugly over the woman's shoulders while half is off the kid, whose bare legs are thick and hairless. I pull the door closed, then move through a small kitchen that looks like it's just been half cleaned. Against the fridge is an overflowing trash barrel, three or four empty cardboard beer containers stacked beside it. In the sink drainer are nothing but washed glasses, not one the same size as the other, and under a *Star Wars* poster on the wall is a table and on it is an empty cereal bowl, a lone spoon lying in milk. There's an open bag of Doritos and three cans of Red Bull and an empty fifth of rum.

Tacked to the wall is a schedule board marked in Sharpie: CHORES—*There Is No I in Team, Motherfuckers!* I look for my son's name, but it isn't there. There's an Anna and a Vinod and a Mike and two or three others, but no Drew. Am I even in the right place? But just as I'm about to leave, I see next to *Yard and Trash—DL.*

Drew raking the leaves between the deck and the marsh, that look of concentration on his face as he worked. Drew loading our garbage barrels into the back of my work van every Saturday for our ride to the dump. If one of the barrels was too heavy, he refused his dad's offer to help. He squatted and hugged the barrel to his small chest and he grunted and lifted and pushed that barrel into his father's van.

Drew never liked getting help. He never liked asking for it.

Now I'm climbing a narrow stairwell, the creaking treads painted red. At the top of the stairs a bicycle leans against a radiator and there's the smell of puke. Smeared along an unpainted sheetrock wall is a streak of white frosting embedded with bits of chocolate.

I knock once on the first door I come to, then walk into what has to be Drew's room. On the wall over his unmade bed is a poster of that southern pitcher he loved as a kid, though in this one he's in the uniform of a different team, one leg raised high in his pitching windup. Next to this is a smaller image of a rapper in gold chains, and on a bedside table made from two stacked milk crates is a phone charger beside the lid of a jar of pot seeds and the nub of a joint. There's a small framed photo I pick up and have to squint at to see clearly. Drew and Hanna. Both tanned and smiling into the camera. I set it back down and glance over balled-up jeans on the floor, a sweatshirt turned inside out, a sneaker so big it's hard to believe it's Drew's. I step around it to the desk in the corner.

There are textbooks stacked beside an open laptop next to three empty beer cans and a hamburger wrapper streaked with ketchup, a coffee mug filled with pens. There's an open pocketknife, the blade broken in half, a few quarters and dimes, and in the back, in the shadow of a shelf holding a clip-on lamp, is an unframed photograph starting to curl at the edges. I can feel the slight pulsing of the dog bite below, and I'm in the sickening presence of a hope so sheer it can't be good for anyone.

It's not a photo of me, or of me and Drew, but of Ronnie and Edward Joseph Flynn. Both of them are standing side by side, their arms around each other, and they're smiling so happily into the camera. For half a heartbeat I'm floating once again in a black airless space, a nameless, useless man forgotten. But there's such love in this picture of my ex-wife and her new husband. For each other, yes, but also for the one capturing this moment in the life they've made—Drew.

I lean as close as I can to the photo without touching it. There are the hops and barley scent of drying beer, the tangy smell of old ketchup, but I'm studying Ronnie's smiling face. Her hair's longer than when I last saw her and she's gained a little weight, which looks good on her, natural. Abundance for the abundist. But I don't feel any bitterness seeing her smiling so joyfully in front of a Christmas tree. Last year maybe? Her husband's in a suit jacket and open-collared shirt, Ronnie's left hand pressing on the middle of this lucky man's chest. And that's how he's looking into the lens too, like he's fully aware of just how fortunate he is to have stumbled into such love.

Why does Drew keep this where he can see it on a daily basis?

Is it a totem of some kind? A reminder of something he needs to be reminded of? But he's got to have a picture of his old man somewhere. At least of the one I have tacked to my bathroom wall. There are drawers in this desk, but I won't open those. I'm already starting to feel like the man who limped through Wyn and Nancy's bedroom looking for anything I could sell, and I won't violate my son's privacy any more than I already have. Still, my finger taps one of the laptop's keys and the screen lights up and I pull a chair over. I need my reading glasses, but what's in front of me is an email and it looks like Drew either didn't send it or didn't log out after he sent it. The address is clear and in the subject line is written: *Thanks* . . . I lean forward and squint at the screen. A car horn honks outside:

. . . for the call, Dad, Father, whatever. I'm a drunk today. ALL day. Just shitfucked. Whatever, Mom just called. She's called like three times today. You never call and don't worry I don't give a shit. I used to think you were weak and then Hanna ghosted me and if I were you I would've offed myself. Seriously. Mom and her new boyfriend when you were so down and fucked? I'm not mad at her anymore but I think about your dad dying when you were a kid and it's like you died when I was a kid so I guess we're the same, old man.

Just drank another shot.

Going out again.

Thanks for calling —DL

Twenty? What do people do with THAT?

"Hello?" Standing in the doorway is a young woman in a white terry cloth robe, a hotel's insignia over the heart pocket. Her long wet hair is combed back from her wan but attentive face, and at the base of her throat, just above her bare clavicle, is the blue tattoo of a hummingbird. "Are you Drew's dad?"

. . . and it's like you died when I was a kid. I start to speak, but the words rise into a moist clump in my throat. It feels like a gift to me, though, that she knows who I am. How lovely that she knows this. I swallow. "Yes. I am."

"Cool. Drew's on his way back home. He wanted me to tell you."

"Home?"

"Yeah, his mom's. He said he got your message, but he's going back to Salem." In the young woman's right hand is a hairbrush and in her left is her phone. She doesn't seem in any hurry to leave. She's looking at me like she's heard about me for a long time and now she gets to make up her mind for herself.

"Can you tell me what happened?"

"Like, last night?"

"Yeah."

"He just drank too much. We all did." She pulls her lapels closer together. I hope it wasn't because I was staring at her bare clavicle.

"How'd he get hypothermia?"

"Yeah, that was bad. Nobody knew where he went."

"From here?"

"Yeah, after here. Like after we gave him a cake he kind of freaked out. He went looking for his ex-girlfriend."

"His *ex*-girlfriend?"

"Yeah, Hanna. You know her?"

"Did they break up?"

"I guess. I mean it's really none of my business, but yeah, she dumped him."

"I'm surprised."

"I'm not. She's a stuck-up bitch, 'scuse my language."

Hanna on my stoop, handing me the copy of the photo she made of me and Drew. The caring she showed for Drew doing that, the caring she showed *me*.

"I'm sorry to hear that."

"Well, don't be. She never let DL be DL. Not everybody wants to smile all day, you know."

"Where'd he go?"

"Her dorm. He was lying in the snow under her window. I guess he just passed out."

Drew alone. In the cold. "Did he have his coat?"

"I don't think so. Some drunk kid found him."

There are boot steps up the stairwell and she turns to someone coming down the hallway.

"I'm looking for Tom?"

She points her hairbrush at me just as Jamey steps into the doorway, both of these young people looking at me like two players in a game whose rules I'm only just beginning to learn. But now it's my move and what am I waiting for? "Sorry, man, but we gotta go."

29

AND IT'S LIKE YOU DIED WHEN I WAS A KID SO I GUESS WE'RE *the same, old man*. I'm driving north, the words of Drew's email sitting inside me like burning coals. My tiny money orders I sent every month to 116 Hatfield Street. My brief email exchanges with my own son because I hardly knew him anymore, and so what was there to say? I sure as hell had nothing to report on my end: *Drove Trina to sell her plasma today. Spent the rest of the afternoon on my plywood couch. Drank some pain distracter and read about rich thieves.*

But how could Drew, even drunk, write that it was like his dad had died?

Did he mean when his father fell off that roof? Or was it when I couldn't take care of them like I used to? Or was it when I handed Drew some cash, then told him to hurry down our driveway to the van that used to be ours? Or was it when Drew's mom got a new man and they moved in with him? Or was it losing our house? Or was it the whole fucking thing?

Jamey's using his thumbs to talk to Trina again and I need to borrow that phone. I need to hear my son's voice, or no, more than that, I need Drew to know that I went to two hospitals and then his house looking for him. I want to tell Drew how sorry I am to hear about him and Hanna, that hard things happen, son, and then you find out—you find out *what?* What you're made of? That old cliché?

Jamey reads the screen in his lap, then taps away at it with both thumbs. I pass a diner. There are patches of snow in its narrow yard filled with concrete statues of angels, and there's the flash of a memory of sitting inside that diner late at night years ago, drunk and eating eggs.

We're getting close to the snowy fields of the country club.

Already there are spots of ground showing, the snow around them pulling back like some sort of reprieve, but what really has my attention are the fast-approaching police cars behind me, three or four of them, each with their light bars swirling blue, and now sirens, many of them, and they may as well be a pack of coyotes closing in on me and Jamey, who has jerked around in his seat and begun to swear in one short burst after another, his face pale above his scraggly beard, but the thing is I feel as relaxed as if I've just lain back in a tub of hot water, the soapy baths Ronnie would help me into early after my injury, my hand in hers as I stepped in, then lay slowly back into the one sure thing that might help me today.

How easy to pull over and smile at Jamey and say, "It's better this way, Jamey. You'll see. You'll see."

I LIE STRETCHED OUT on the cot of my holding cell, my hip screws cool for the first time all day. The walls, floor, and ceiling are painted a deep gray, as is the steel frame of my cot and the iron mesh over the small window high up the rear wall, a lovely dappling of sunlight reflected off the locked door across from it. There must be a big hardwood out there, a maple or an oak, the shadow of its branches bobbing slightly in that sunlight against the door. Before I opened that door and before my interrogation, the young cop who led me here asked me to empty my pockets. All I had was my empty wallet, which he sealed into a Ziploc bag. He then asked for my belt, which I unbuckled, pulled free, and handed to him. He then asked me to untie my work boots and to "step out of them, please."

Behind the young officer stood two older ones who were in two of the cruisers that pulled me and Jamey over. There were commands over one of the car's loudspeakers, doors opening and cops standing next to those doors, their hands resting on holstered guns they looked ready to draw. There was Jamey starting to cry like the boy he is, and I patted him on the shoulder and then touched his cheek with the back of my hand. "It'll be all right. Just do everything they tell you to do, and all will be well."

How strange that this is what I feel now, that all *will* be well. That there's a certain rightness about what's happening to us both, one that has brought me a long-needed sense of peace. Because I was the one who gave Jamey and Trina the idea of stealing convenience checks from well-off people's trash. Never mind my change of heart. I was the one who lit the spark that turned into this fire. The truth may take its time, but it always has its way. Like me finally dropping all pretense and telling the young man behind the bagel counter that I wanted to buy everything in his place but didn't have any money to do it.

And while I'm not on this gray cot in this gray room expecting any reward for telling the cop who arrested me what I did, I do feel in the wonderfully eternal presence of another gift—I lie here feeling as naked as the day I was born to my lovely fifteen-year-old mother. Nothing to hide. No need to pretend I used to be anything other than what I am because I'm born anew. And it came when the officer was snapping handcuffs on my wrists behind my back, wrists I put there with no hesitation, the older cop smelling like chewing gum and sweat overcoming deodorant and something I couldn't name but that made me want to comfort this man, the older cop reciting my rights to me, words I'd only heard before in movies but were now as real as Jamey's stoic silence on the other side of his car as he was being handcuffed too, tears streaming into his young beard. I said, "It was all my idea, Officer. That boy had nothing to do with it."

Jamey looked over at me, his damp eyes dark with confusion. But the older officer just kept reciting to me my rights and then I was sitting in the back of a moving cruiser. My cuffs were tight and dug into my wrist bones and I had to lean forward to take the pressure off, but of course that poured gasoline onto my hip fires and then we were approaching Amherst Center and I turned to see Primrose Drive come and go, though I did get a glimpse of Elizabeth Turner's house under the sun, the sidewalk wet in front of it, and what came to me was the crooked part down the center of Mel's hair as she knelt and washed the wound from her dog Boyd, the gray hairs there, the softness of her voice and face, and where before there might've been shame at passing by in handcuffs in a cruiser, I just wanted to tell her why I was being whisked to the police station. Because there was the blooming hope that doing just that would help to make me a better man.

All that was happening to me might help to make me a better man.

You have the right to remain silent.

It was the first sentence the older officer recited to me. And when we got to this place and the young cop took my wallet, belt, and shoes, they then took off my handcuffs and two cops escorted me to a room with only a table and chairs in the middle of it. It was a table built of composite materials, an object not for meals and warm communion but for confessions, and the older officer pulled a laminated card from his wallet, put on reading glasses, and read me my rights again. "You have the right to remain silent. Anything you say can and will be used against you in a court of law. You have the right to an attorney. If you cannot afford an attorney, one will be provided for you. Do you understand the rights I have just read to you?"

"Yes."

"With these rights in mind, do you wish to speak to me?"

"Yes."

The older officer put away his laminated card. "You sure about that?"

"I am."

One of the policemen left the room and there were the sounds of cars passing steadily by outside. The officer across from me laid a pad of paper on the table and pulled a pen from his breast pocket. "Name?"

"Thomas Lowe Jr."

"Date of birth?"

"August ninth, 1966."

"Address?"

"21 Hampton Terrace, Amesbury, Massachusetts."

"Occupation?"

"I'm disabled."

The older cop wore a name tag I could just barely read: *Wilkinson*. He glanced up at me across the table and gave me the shadow of the look Larry's son-in-law Paul had always given me, that I was a bum. A freeloading degenerate who needed to use the phone and then buy the cheapest booze possible, and on another day in another month of my life I would've sat straighter in my chair, I would've felt the need to alter my language so that I sounded like anything but a bum, but I didn't feel any of this because this was the very first time that I'd said out loud, even to myself, that I'm "disabled." I called myself broken and an old workhorse who couldn't work anymore. I called myself unlucky and victimized. But I'd never sat across from a man my age and spoken the plain truth: *I am disabled.* As in no longer *able*, ever again.

This is the story I told Officer Wilkinson, a man who seemed to be both listening intently while not quite listening at all. There was that wonderful phrase about having the right to remain silent, but that is just what I've been these last few years. The dog hit by the car who crawls under the house to die.

No more silence! Because I have learned things, and this is what I tried to explain to Officer Wilkinson, whose lined face was so clean-shaven it had a sheen to it, though his color was bad, pasty, and while I left Trina out of the story completely, I described Jamey as a Good Samaritan, a boy who gave me a ride home in the rain one day and then became helpful in other ways because the boy's a giver, not a taker, and he only took from that bank because he was trying to help *me*, Tom Lowe.

At some point the younger cop brought me a cold bottle of water. I thanked him and drank deeply. Officer Wilkinson finished writing something, then looked up and told me I was being charged with larceny, forgery, and joint venture. "I won't know your bail till the magistrate tells me, Mr. Lowe. But it's Friday, so this could take a while."

"Of course."

"You get one call." Officer Wilkinson nodded at the younger cop, an almost handsome boy with a bald head as perfectly shaped as Fitz's. He left the room and I was about to tell Officer Wilkinson about all my tools being stolen, how that pushed me over the edge of a dark pit in my life, but then the young cop was handing me a cordless phone.

Officer Wilkinson pushed his chair back and stood.

"Can I ask where my friend is?"

"He's here."

Then there were just the surprising gifts of solitude and cold bottled water and a working telephone in my hand. There flew through me the thought of calling my former brother-in-law Gerard. He was a corporate lawyer, but still a lawyer. But if I were to call Gerard, it should be only to thank him, to belatedly thank him for making the calls that got me my unit in the 8. No, I wouldn't be calling any lawyers.

I held up the palm of my left hand, then punched into the phone Drew's number. There was Dawn handing me the Sharpie so that I could write down this number. There was her rushing across the street and knocking on my door. There was old Mrs. Bongiovanni and her hard wisdom and her sweet bread. There were my new neighbors Doug and Minh, the hot meal they laid before me. There was Trina sending over the plate of Chinese food I never touched. There was Mel on her knees washing my wound and feet.

Such unspeakable *gifts*.

And where before I was nervous about finally talking to my son, now, as I waited for Drew to answer his cell phone, I felt like I was still lying back in a hot soapy bath and I had only good news to share with my son, who often helped his mother lift me out of that bath, then held out a fresh towel in his two hands.

"Hello?" Drew sounded weak. There was a man's voice somewhere around him. Most likely Edward Flynn talking while driving them in his BMW sedan.

"It's your dad, buddy. It's your old man."

"Oh. How come it says Amherst Police on my phone?"

"How are you feeling? Are you *okay*?"

"I guess."

Ronnie's voice now. High and full of energy from what sounded like the front seat. It was the tone she would use after one storm or another had blown through, the upbeat resolve of the search party and the cleanup crew, though for me it seemed that very few storms had turned her way until I came along. Oh how I wanted to apologize to her.

"But you're feeling better?"

"Yeah, just, you know, overdid it."

Ronnie was asking a question. Her voice seemed closer than a few seconds before, and I imagined her turning around in the passenger seat, our son slumped in the back on his phone. "Who's that, honey?"

"Dad."

The way he said this! Like he said it every day. Like he called me by that name every day. But also in Drew's thin and exhausted voice, there was the nearly defiant but confessional tone of the boy who just got caught playing with a pistol and a box of bullets.

"Can I talk to him, please?"

There was soft static and then Ronnie was apologizing to *me*. "I'm sorry, Tom. Some kid told us that Drew was still on campus. Did you go to the hospital?"

A swath of sunlight lay across the floor and table. I looked out the police station window to see an old man walking his dog. There came the warming flesh memory of Mel's dog sinking his teeth into my shin, the fit and kind physician's assistant handing me a prescription for antibiotics that'll have to be paid for by the state. Ronnie was asking me if I was still there. "Tom, can you hear me?"

"I can now, Ronnie. I sure can."

"Tom?"

"I'm sorry, Ronnie." My eyes filled and it was as if that hot soapy bath had begun to flow over and I was floating along the top, my hip fires doused, my body light and lovely.

"Tom?" Ronnie seemed to be holding our son's phone closer to her lips. "Have you been drinking?"

"No, honey." An intrusion, that word. A transgression really, though it felt no more malicious than clean water running off my naked scar. "I'm just learning things, that's all. I've been so worried about Drew and I'm just so relieved to know he's okay, but Ronnie?"

"Yes?"

"All this time I've thought you should be apologizing to me, but I need to apologize to *you*, Ronnie, I—"

One morning in Germany, Ronnie brushing my hair back with her fingers, her skin smelling like the love we'd just made, yet I never believed it. I never believed what I was given. "You and Drew have been such *gifts* to me."

The door behind me opened and closed. It was Officer Wilkinson and the younger cop.

"Tom, you're scaring me."

"Oh no, I'm done with that. That's all I ever did was scare you. I just couldn't bear your abundance, Ronnie. That wasn't your problem."

"Mr. Lowe?" Officer Wilkinson was holding out his hand for the phone. Strapped to his belt was a black holstered pistol that seemed so unnecessary to all things, really. I smiled up at him and held up one finger. "Can I talk to Drew?"

"Where are you, Tom?"

"Mr. Lowe?"

"Just put him on real quick."

"Yeah?" Drew's voice was still weak but also carried a low note of hope that his father might just have something for him worth getting back on the phone for. I was about to tell him that I loved him, that's all, that I didn't have any profound answers to dark questions like why someone can just stop loving someone else, that Drew was going to hurt for a long time about Hanna, but getting drunk enough to pass out in the snow won't help anything. I was about to tell my son that I was finally letting go of being the kind of dad I was to him when he was a boy, a man with a new van and organized tools and steady work. I was about to tell him that I was going to be a different kind of father to him now, one who no longer lied to himself in any way about what he wasn't anymore or what he used to own or what he will be. I was about to say some or all of this, but just as I was about to say, *My son, man do I **love** *you*, Officer Wilkinson took the phone from my hand and pressed the button that would give Drew only nothingness on his end, his Hanna and now his father "ghosted."

"I was talking to my son." The words seemed to come from a fire flashing from my waist to my head, that old rage, the older cop explaining that this wasn't my living room and that I could make "personal calls later." And the officer's color was bad really, an unhealthy man, probably one with a bad heart that could just stop any day now. I thought of him being maybe a father, that terrible afternoon when Charlie and I and our mother were driven to the warehouse parking lot where Tom Lowe Sr.'s rusted station wagon was the last car left in the lot.

"Do you have kids, sir?" I could hear the gentleness in my own voice.

"Yep, grandkids too."

"What gifts, what blessings."

Then the younger cop with Fitz's perfectly shaped head was escorting me to this gray room, and while I lie on my cot, one arm propped behind my head so that I can watch the tree shadows bob against the gray door, I'm surprised and not surprised that I said the word *blessings*. Another holy word. Another word that I don't believe in but do.

I don't believe that the older cop's grandkids were given to him by any god, but the man was given the gift of them anyway. As I was given Drew, as I was given Ronnie and her unbearable love for me, one that I somehow found a way to kill.

You sabotaged us, Tom.

Oh how instantly I rejected that. How could I, a man who spent every waking moment building and then trying to keep what I'd built, be a saboteur of it too?

I think of the constant pain in my hips and pelvis that I see as fires burning inside me, a conflagration whose existence is dependent upon my continuing to have pain. But years before I ever reached for that final roofing shingle of my life, I felt similar seeds of dark symbiosis like this sprouting inside me. All those night classes where I sat in the back of the room, my limbs warm and heavy with fatigue from the nine to ten hours I worked that day, my hands swollen or freshly cut in places, my eyes on the professor and his or her notes on the board. But my eyes were also on the backs of my classmates, young people who seemed younger than I ever was, abundists stepping into waters that would carry them to future abundance. It was a destination so foreign to me that I was constantly tempted to just close my notebook and walk out of every classroom I ever entered, bits of sawdust still in my hair.

My mother's face as she stood in our small kitchen, her dumb-founded surprise that I wanted to go to college in the first place, that I wanted a completely different life from hers and my father's. But that wasn't really it. What I wanted more than that was what happened inside me when I read books like *Siddhartha*, the feeling that real life might just be inside us, not out there on our patchy lawns or in our cars or offices or job sites or malls or bars or dead-end streets or city sidewalks, but *inside* us, where the dreams of others merged with our own so that we were all bigger than before and no one was just one.

There was no other anywhere.

One night when I was still framing our house, Ronnie went out for a drink with her dance friends, and when she woke me lying next to sleeping Drew, she smelled like wine and dried sweat and she kissed me and led me to our bedroom. But instead of us making love, she told me in her excited way, her awed-by-everything-in-life way, a story one of the women had just told her.

It was about the woman's three-year-old daughter and what she said to her newborn little brother. The woman and her husband had put a monitor in the baby's room, and so when their daughter asked if she could say good night to the baby by herself, Ronnie's friend and her husband said yes but listened to the monitor just in case their daughter, who hadn't been happy about another child coming into the family, "acted out" in some way.

"But Tommy, do you know what they heard?"

I was stretched out on our bed in the dark, Ronnie on the edge of the mattress, the dim light from the bathroom on one side of her face.

"No, what?"

"They heard their little girl say, 'Quick, I'm starting to forget. What does God look like?' "

I might've said something about that being sweet or adorable, but I was drifting off, my mind already laying out the next day's bottom and top plates for the studs I had to cut, their lengths just out of my grasp because Ronnie's voice was so full of joyous wonder. Then she was warm and naked beside me, and I haven't thought of that little girl's story since, but it's here now, and I think of harried and grateful Caitlin Murphy's two young kids, how when I showed them photos of hardship from long ago, I felt in the presence of something infinitely open and accepting and maybe even suffused with a kind of ancient love. And it's this sense of people and places I want to be in the presence of all the time, starting right here in this gray room that smells like disinfectant and its own gray paint.

The clanking turn of the lock. The door opens and standing there is Officer Wilkinson with the bad heart.

"Clerk's letting you go on personal recognizance. You just have to pay his fee, which is forty bucks."

I sit up and lean on one elbow. "What about my friend?"

"Different story for him."

"But I don't have forty dollars, Officer."

"Can you borrow it from someone? A friend? Family member?"

Who? Ronnie, who's back in Salem by now? My sick son? Trina? Dawn? Elizabeth Turner's daughter-in-law Mel? "I don't want to trouble anyone."

Officer Wilkinson looks at me like I've just said something more important than I have. "You sure about that?"

"Yes."

"That means you stay here till you see the judge Monday morning. You want that?"

"I'm trying not to want anything. I'm beginning to think wanting is the problem."

Officer Wilkinson nods slowly. He glances up at the mesh over the high windows like I may have hidden something up there. The dappled light plays over the man's wide and pasty face. I say, "Do you take care of yourself? That's something I've never been very good at."

Officer Wilkinson's eyes pass over my rumpled khakis and Christmas sweater and unzipped work jacket. "You seem like a decent guy. Why don't you try acting your age?"

Then he pulls the steel door shut and locks it and I lie back on the cot. *Try acting your age.* At fifty-four I should be planning for my retirement. I should have my house paid off. I should be deep into my third decade of marriage with the same woman so that our daily lives together are as worn and comfortable as an old couch we sit in together every night watching TV or reading books side by side. I should be making regular visits to my doctor and eye doctor and dentist to maintain the body I want to live in healthfully until it one day stops, hopefully in the far future when my son's long established in work that sustains him and he has kids of his own, young miracles who call me Gramps or Pops or Pop-Pop or Pa.

But aren't these shoulds just the iron buttresses of false wants? Who's to say where any of us *should* be and what we *should* be doing at any one time?

Three feet across from my iron cot's another just like it, a stainless steel toilet at the head of it. I get up to use that toilet and I'm aware of my sore shin from the dog Boyd, of my sore shoulder from where I was given a shot, my first in many years. And as I piss into the dry steel bowl I think of how well my and Charlie's mother cared for us: taking us regularly to the doctor for our shots; to the dentist for our teeth; to the emergency room when Charlie hit a rock with his lawn mower and a chunk of blade flew into his shin.

How *awful* that I haven't taken better care of my mother these last few years. Yes, she's in a home, and yes, she hasn't recognized me for quite a while, but why not let this drifting take me to where I'm needed?

There's no sink, no faucet, no mirror. I wipe my hands off on my jacket and I wonder how Jamey's doing.

Different story for him.

He had that new bank cash in his jacket pocket. And that other, thicker wad of cash too. That wasn't good. But it was the truth and maybe this is just what the boy needs to set him straight. A correction of his course while he's still young, one that might correct Trina's too.

I can't take this shit anymore. I just can't.

I lie back on my cot. I need to do something about that Brian. He's on probation and so it's time to report him for assault and battery and breaking and entering or whatever the charges would be for just walking into my unit and punching me in the head till the lights went out.

Trina tending to me. Trina dabbing wet paper towels against my tender face, and now she and I and Drew are sitting in the back of Edward's BMW. Trina's in only a T-shirt and underwear and she's smoking a cigarette and blowing smoke to the front where Ronnie's laughing in the passenger seat. She turns and laughs at Trina's smoke like it's a funny story and Drew says, "See? Black fingers."

"Frostbite?"

"I told you, it's like you died."

"It's roofing tar, Tom." Edward Flynn from the front seat. "He's just like you, Tommy."

Flynn calling me *Tommy.* I want to say something to that except Drew opens his door and leans out into the snowbanks speeding by and Trina's hand is on my knee and she's saying something about Shannon's face, Drew's door clacking against one metal post after another.

"Dinner." A nudging of my foot. In Gerard's childhood bed I'd open my eyes to see sports-coat-wearing Wyn staring down at me like he still had faith not so much in me as in the world's ability to right itself.

It's the young cop with Fitz's bald head. He's holding a plastic tray and on it looks to be food of some kind, that, and a small milk carton I haven't seen since I was small myself.

"Thank you, Officer."

"Not a problem." He sets the tray on the opposite cot. The

food is a hamburger between two white buns, next to it a sliver of a pickle and a small bag of potato chips. I sit up. "You're very kind." I'm too warm in my jacket. I start to stand to pull it off, but the cop steps back quickly, his hand on the handle of the sliding steel door.

"Just too hot in this coat. Can I ask you something?"

"Make it quick."

"I was assaulted not long ago. Can I report it to you?"

"Where'd this happen?"

"Back in Amesbury."

"You need to call your local department."

I want to thank him for his help, but he pulls closed the door and locks it and I find myself staring at yet another gift given to me, a hot meal I didn't ask for but is just the thing I need at this moment. I stand to get it, and even my hip fires pause in their happy work.

30

The Day After Your Grandson's 20th Birthday
Dear Wyn and Nancy,
Please forgive this horribly late letter of thanks to you both.
You've been nothing but good to me, and I am deeply grateful
to you for this.

I read over what I've just written on blank stationery, the name
and address of the Amherst Police Department stamped into the
top center of the page. When the young officer, whose name is
O'Connor, came back for my empty paper plate and milk carton,
I asked if I could trouble him for paper and pen. Another crossing
of lines, because I enjoyed every bite of the meal he brought me, a
meal that only a week ago I would've seen as the dregs thrown to
forgotten men and women in the street.

An intermittent buzzing. In the ceiling above, recessed in the
concrete behind unbreakable glass, bright fluorescent tubes flicker
their synapses. I regret sleeping through the sun going down, the
colorful shadows that probably left on the door and wall. It seems
important now not to miss beauty.

The pencil Officer O'Connor gave me is the kind that mini golf
players use to keep score. For a few years, Drew had loved that
game. A cold fall afternoon and Ronnie in a wool sweater smiling
down at our son about to swing at the ball like the hippopotamus's
mouth was the right-field fence.

I am deeply grateful to you for this.
And how did I pay you back? I tried to steal from you.

Those creaking stairs to my ex-in-laws' open loft, their mullioned windows looking out over the fields of Trevors Academy.

Ripples of shame prick along my cheeks and forehead. Should
I really write this? Yes, because how can I fully play the hand I've

been given if I don't hold this card too, the one that made me do almost anything to keep my baggie of Os full.

I'm deeply ashamed to write you this, but I believe there is more shame in not coming clean. **Clean.** *These past few years I've been waiting for someone to give me a prize for getting off the drugs. I've been waiting for that and apologies and restitutions from everyone who had a hand in delivering me to what I thought was a useless life.*

But, Wyn and Nancy, I've had it backwards. I am the one who needs to apologize and make restitution. One afternoon when you were both teaching, I went up to your bedroom and looked through your property—

Too vague, not honest enough. I cross it out and write:

—I went up to your bedroom to rob you. I went through your bureau drawers and bedside table drawers and even your clothes closets, looking for money or anything of value I could trade for my painkillers that you, Wyn, asked me not to use in your home, but I did anyway, which you know already.

I never did steal anything from you that day, but I want you both to know that I tried. You deserved better. I hope somehow someday to make this up to you.

Sincerely Yours,

Tom Lowe Jr.

The clacking of the lock, the door swinging open and Officer O'Connor leading in a drunk boy. He's small, his long hair dyed purple. He's wearing loose corduroys and a sweatshirt. Coming off him is the smell of puke, Drew's second-floor hallway just this morning, or was that yesterday?

The boy seems not so much to see the opposite cot as sense that it's there, and Officer O'Connor guides him to it, one hand under the boy's arm as he collapses onto the thin foam mattress. The boy curls up against the wall and Officer O'Connor glances over at me. "There'll be more. You might have to share your bunk."

I nod. I'm about to say something to that, but the word *bunk* stops me. An army term. *Charlie.* What a terrible brother I've been to him. And I'm his older brother too, one Charlie should've been able to turn to over the years. Officer O'Connor pulls the door shut and locks it and I rip out my letter to Wyn and Nancy, fold it, and place it next to me on the cot. The boy against the wall makes a whimpering sound, then goes quiet.

Dear Charlie,

   I'm sitting in a jail cell.

Why should I tell him this? But why *not* tell him this?

   I suppose I'm telling you this because it's the truth and because for far too long I've been blaming everyone else for my troubles. Even you.

   No, I've never believed that you had a hand in my losing all that I have, but I have resented you for not losing <u>anything</u>. You with the secure job and a wife who loves you and two kids I barely know. You've sent me pictures of them on the internet, and I don't think I've ever written back to tell you how beautiful they are. And they are beautiful, brother.

How wrong it feels that I can't summon their little faces. Only their blond hair, Ulrika's pulled-back hair and slightly disapproving smile, Charlie's small handsome face though its lines are beginning to soften with age and whatever kind of work he does in that German factory.

   Brother, you and me, we've always been workers, haven't we? But not working for so long has made me a little crazy, which is why I'm in this cell tonight.

The boy across from me is snoring now, a light rattle.

But don't worry about me. I'm in a good place, and I promise to be a better brother to you from now on, a better uncle to your kids, a better brother-in-law to your wife.

   I wouldn't be surprised if you've reached out to Mom more than I have, even from Europe. I did call her once, just before I gave up my phone, and she sounded so happy to hear from me that I didn't call her again. I guess it hurt too much. I'm not sure she even knew who I was. I think she thought I was you, or Dad, who used to visit me when I was on painkillers. I think that's what I miss most about those pills. No more visits from our father.

You look just like him, you lucky dog.

I'll write again once I get out of this mess.

I love you, Charlie.

Your Brother,

Tom

A cough. Then another, deeper this time, the boy's narrow back curling forward just as a splatter hits the floor. It's yellow and liquid and I'm up and over there and I rest a knee on the boy's cot and lean down and get one hand under his arm, turning and pulling him so that his face is pointing to the floor, where he retches again, though not much comes out this time, and a familiar fire has fanned its flames in my back and hips and legs. I wish I had a towel or napkin to wipe the boy's pale face, which is covered with a light fuzz of day-old whiskers. The boy blinks and moans and his head falls to the side. I pull him all the way back onto the cot so that his cheek lies against it. Whenever Drew was sick, I slept on the floor of my son's room, sure that he'd suffocate on his own vomit or that his fever would get dangerously high without his father or mother even knowing about it because we were asleep in the next room.

I glance back down at the sleeping boy. His purple hair lies across one side of his face and it's clear that it's a good-looking face, his chin and cheekbones looking more feminine than masculine. For a second I think about staying at the end of the kid's cot in case he throws up again. But no, I'll be only a couple of feet away on my own cot, which I go back to now to write to Mrs. Bongiovanni, because she has no idea how much she has helped me.

I rip out the letter to Charlie, fold it on top of Wyn and Nancy's, and write *Dear Mrs.* when the lock clacks and the door opens. A man steps into the holding cell. He has a graying red beard and he's in a flannel shirt with the sleeves cut off at the shoulders. "This fuckin' place *stinks*."

"Watch your language, Clark.

"*Dr.* Clark to you."

Officer O'Connor has his hand on the door's steel handle. In the light of the hallway, his bald head glistens. He says to me, "That kid puke?"

"He did, yes."

O'Connor shakes his head, pulls the door closed and locks it. Mr. Clark or Dr. Clark looks from me to the kid's cot, then back at me.

"I can make room."

"Nope." The man takes three steps, then sits on the floor under the mesh-covered window, his back against the wall. He stretches out his legs and crosses one sock-covered ankle over the other, then folds his arms against his chest and stares straight at the door like he's waiting for bad news.

I look down at the letter I just started to write to Mrs. Bongiovanni. I want to keep writing it. But again, another want. I nod in the man's direction. "You a doctor?"

"That kid could fuckin' asphyxiate. You think they care?"

The boy's shoulders rise and fall and he's not snoring anymore. "I've been keeping an eye on him."

"*You* a doctor?"

"No, I'm nothing."

"Nothing? Nobody's nothing. Everybody's *something*."

"I used to be something, I guess. But I'm trying to let go of all that."

The man stares at me. His hair is thin but his eyebrows are thick, and there comes the flicker of a smile behind his whiskers. "You a fuckin' philosopher?"

"I don't know what I am anymore, tell you the truth."

The door clacks open and Officer O'Connor and a new cop, also bald but heavy, walk into the cell. "You two stay put." O'Connor pulls the boy up, twisting him so that his feet touch the floor, and then the other cop, who's chewing gum, pulls the boy to a standing position, his chin bouncing against his clavicle as they walk him out of the cell, the door's steel bolt sliding back into place.

"They did that just to cover their asses. You think they give two shits about that boy?" The man pushes himself up and steps over to the boy's cot and sits at the foot of it away from the puke and the toilet. The air smells like the other cop's spearmint gum and booze of some kind coming from this man Clark, both elbows on his knees, looking straight at me. "We've become a litigious people. Nobody wants to take responsibility anymore."

I look down at the letters I've written trying to do just that. I lay the pad over them and set the pencil stub next to it. From out in the hallway comes male laughter, then what sounds like metal wheels rolling over concrete.

"What're you writing?"

"Letters."

"Letters? How quaint. You expect to be here a long time?"

"Till Monday anyway, you?"

"Who fuckin' knows? This is my third violation, so I'm probably going straight to county."

"Violation?"

"Restraining order. Think about that a moment. They're *ordering* you to *restrain* yourself."

"Your wife?"

"And her fucking lawyers. And *these* pricks. But I never laid a pinkie on her. She just can't take my tirades. Her word, not mine." The man's looking at the Christmas trees sewn across my chest. He shakes his head and says something more to himself, then to me.

"I'm sorry."

"Why should you be sorry?"

I meant it as in, I didn't hear what the man said, but it also works the other way because I am sorry to see a man in such obvious disrepair. "It's good you never hit your wife."

"Is it? Why's that?"

Brian punching Shannon in the face. Trina's voice on Jamey's phone so angry but scared, and I can only hope that she'll change her mind and call the police. Or at least lock her door and windows.

"It reduces us, I think. Makes us small, if you know what I mean."

"I just wanted to talk to her. I didn't even go up on the fuckin' porch. I just stood on the sidewalk and gave my speech."

"You wrote a speech?"

"Twenty-six years at that university and I never wrote a lecture. Dr. Contempo-fucking-raneous. The kids loved me."

"You a professor?"

"Was. Forced retirement. So I drink, so what."

I've been sitting too long, the heat from my ashy fires deep in my legs now. I pick up my pencil stub and my writing pad and two folded letters, then lie back on my bunk. I wish I had a pillow so I wouldn't have to prop my head on my wrist to see the man across from me. But, no. No more wishes. No more wants. Maybe it's time for me to become a Buddhist. "I have to stretch out. Got hurt a while ago. I can't sit for long."

"How'd that happen?"

"Took a bad fall." My eyes are on the concrete ceiling high above. For a second I'm looking only at minute holes in it from the tiny bubbles when it was poured, but then I'm falling from that ceiling, falling and falling. "You addicted? Because I was. Pain pills. Took a long time to quit, too."

"You'd think they'd give us some fuckin' *water*."

I'm about to say something to this when there comes a loud pounding against the door, this Dr. Clark slapping his palm against it. "Hey! How 'bout some fuckin' *water*?! Aren't we entitled to that? Some *water*?!" Clark's pants are faded jeans hanging low on his hips. In the right rear pocket is the whitened silhouette of where he's been carrying his wallet for years.

"Hey!" He pounds the door with the meaty end of his fist, then stumbles back to his cot, breathing hard, his forehead shiny with sweat.

I wince and turn on my side, lean one cheek on my upper arm. From this angle the man looks sideways and completely different. Smaller, older, more vulnerable somehow. There's a lesson here, a lesson about looking at things from a completely different place, and even though I'm lying still, I can feel myself step yet again over some invisible border between us all. "You think you're addicted to the booze?"

"Oh yes."

"Ever try to quit?"

Half-drunk Dr. Clark is staring at me like he's forgotten why he's talking to me in the first place. He nods at my sweater. "We're about six weeks from Christmas, pal."

I don't say anything. This sideways Dr. Clark is sweating more, his face glistening under the fluorescent light. His beard is long and frizzy and looks like it needs a good wash. I picture him drinking alone in some small book-cluttered apartment no bigger than my place back in the 8, this man who stood in front of what probably used to be his home to give his ex-wife his speech.

"What'd you teach?"

"The disrespected discipline. Sociology. Put it this way, I'm used to not being taken seriously."

"I'm taking you seriously."

"Wonderful, my fuckin' cellmate takes me seriously. Why are *you* here?"

"I helped two kids steal money."

"From whom?"

"Banks. And, private citizens, I suppose."

"Impressive."

"I'm not proud of it."

"Well fuck banks anyway. I could deliver ten lectures on their helpful contributions over the years."

"I could too, but—"

"But what?"

Mike Andrews pulling into his garage while I stood beside his trash barrels, Mike's voice through the wall talking to the son he just picked up from school, Mike winking at me as he rounded up figures I knew damn well I'd never be able to live up to, but which I signed anyway. I signed my name and then I put my head down and I got to work.

I need to write Andrews a letter. I need to do it soon. I say, "You said it yourself. Nobody takes responsibility anymore."

"Which is why we have to fight the good fight."

"Against banks?"

"Banks, multinationals, corrupt fuckin' lobbyists, Wall Street motherfuckers."

The good fight. My revenge folders, my elbowing Brian in the face and all that did was open a hot spigot in him to come at me and then the woman who dumped him. Shannon this time too. That poor girl Shannon.

"I need a fucking drink."

"I always thought that once I got off the pills I'd be back to where I started. But that place was gone."

"Jesus Christ, you sound like my daughter."

"How old's your daughter?"

"Who knows? Thirty? Thirty-three? She's a fucking therapist. Are *you* a fucking therapist?"

"No, I'm just Tom. Tom Lowe."

This man Clark stares at me like stating my name is the most helpful thing I've said so far. He looks like he's about to say something but then lies down, his stocking feet where the boy's head had been. One of Clark's socks is dark blue, the other black, a hole in the big toe of the black one.

"I know I'm a drunk. Tell me something I don't know."

"I can't know what you don't know."

"Touché."

"I can say this."

"Yes?"

"It feels good to stop blaming other people for the shitty hand I got dealt."

"Does it? Well perhaps the deck is stacked and the dealer's crooked."

"They *are* crooked and the deck *is* stacked, but I still played."

"They got you brainwashed, pal. It's called blaming the victim. It's how predators predate. Don't be a sap."

This is called a sap. My father's voice, his three-fingered hand pushing a roll of nickels into a white sock, then tying it off with a double knot and holding it hanging from his hand. We were in my parents' small bedroom, the gray light from the window behind my father. Maybe it was raining. Maybe it was winter. My dad swung the weighted end of the sock into his palm, his hand closing around it like some unavoidable pact. *That kid comes at you again, son, swing this into his face.*

Dr. Clark's humming a tune. It sounds like an oldie about a love just out of reach. But then it sounds more like something Clark's making up as he goes and there's a reckless quality to it, a drink-up-boys-the-ship-is-going-down final shrug of the soul. I can feel my arms and legs sinking into the cot. I remember my work jacket. It must've fallen to the floor, and what a good pillow that would make. But no, I have to let go of all wants, and with my eyes closed now my young father is swinging that homemade sap into his three-fingered hand, the cot rising and drifting out the door as I worry that my father is trying to tell me something. He's trying to tell me not to be a sap.

31

M Y SKIN'S TOO SENSITIVE AGAINST MY CLOTHES AND THE OFFI-
cer driving me to court is a woman. From where I sit in the
backseat of the cruiser, my hands cuffed behind me, I stare at her
profile through the iron mesh. She can't be more than four or five
years older than my own son and she's lovely. Her hair's pulled
back and her neck is long, her jaw straight, her cheek taking on
the color of the outside world, which is gray this morning, though
over the weekend all the snow has melted.

We're heading west on Route 9, the same road Elizabeth Turner's daughter-in-law drove me down only three days ago, though
it feels like a lot longer than that. Passing by to my left again is the
country club, its putting greens sodden in places, the only snow in
thin rings at the base of a few bare maples. Earlier, when this cop
guided me into the back of her cruiser, she did it with a kind of
care that felt deeply respectful of me and my current situation, like
she's a doctor who knows that I'm very sick but hasn't given me
the full details. And I *am* sick.

Sometime early Saturday morning the door slid open and Officer O'Connor had Dr. Clark stand to be handcuffed. The professor had sobered up and looked small and pale, and just before he
was led out of our cell he half winked down at me.

Curled on the floor were two young guys, one black and the other
white, and just as soon as O'Connor locked the door, the white one
climbed onto Clark's cot and stretched out. From the floor the black
kid, who was wrapped in a raincoat, said, "You're such a douche,
Martin."

"Blow me."

I must've heard them come in the night, though their entrance
seemed part of my dreams, which I had no memory of when I
woke to see the black kid sitting on the cot and the white kid gone.

But something was off and it was me, because my hip fires had risen up to my face and head and my skin felt skittish. The black kid was talking.

"You think I'd still be here if I was *white*? Do you?"

The raincoat was a deep brown with big buttons and a sewn-in belt and I thought of the beggar in front of the bagel shop, how he used his belt to hold his coat closed, and then the cell's door slid open and I was staring at the empty cot and an older cop was handing me a bottle of water. "Sweat it out. Best thing for you."

There were more dreams, but the only one I remember now, sitting in the back of this cruiser heading to court, was of me standing in front of my homemade home giving a speech to Ronnie, and then a new man was on the cot across from me, a big man with bleeding knuckles, one of his eyes closing up, and I was talking to Brian, telling him that no man should ever hit a woman. Ever. But I only thought it and didn't say it. Then the big man turned into a smaller, older man with crooked eyeglasses and white whiskers, his hands shaking, his eyes not on me across from him but on the concrete floor where someone lay, a man I couldn't see, only the smell, and that smell was piss.

A man's voice comes over the radio. "That's a negative, Dennis."

The young officer stares at her console like more should be coming from it. She glances in the rearview mirror at me and I can see that her eyes are blue, though they're the fake blue of contact lenses.

"How're you feeling?"

"A bit warm."

"They should have transferred you. You get your flu shot?" Her eyes are back on the road. Ahead of us is a touring bus, its chrome bumper coated with water-streaked dust.

"Never have. You?"

"Every fall. You should, too. All people your age should." She accelerates into the left lane and passes the bus. Its side is fluted aluminum, its trim blue, and I think of men and women building that bus on some factory floor far away, a thought that moves me, for oh how hard and conscientiously most people work every day of their lives. And I wonder if I'll see Jamey where I'm going, this kid who says he knows how to work but steals.

"Do you know if the boy I came in with is going to be where we're going?" The words that just came out of me feel complicated and I'm tired from having said them. I want to sit back and rest, but my hands are cuffed behind me.

"I was told just to drive you, sir."

"My name's Tom. You can call me Tom." I'm about to ask her name, but there was Drew's friend pulling her robe closed, protecting her clavicle. I don't want this young and, yes, beautiful cop to misunderstand my interest in her and then become diminished by that. Because I'm grateful to her for her respectful professionalism and I'm thirsty and now a chill rolls through me and I shake my head to let it out.

She's studying me in her rearview mirror. "After court, you should go right to bed."

She must mean another bed in another cell somewhere, and it's strange how much like Trina she sounds. She might even be Trina's exact age, and I look through the iron mesh at her hands on the steering wheel, though I can only see her right and not her left. "Do you have kids, Officer?"

"That's kind of personal, sir."

"I'm sorry."

"Would you ask a male officer that?"

"I think so, yes."

She glances at me in the mirror again, her eyes too blue. "Not yet."

"So you'd like to have children?"

She doesn't answer me and now we're passing the Courtyard Marriott and the Target store, its round red-and-white logo looking like some lewd invitation to cause harm.

"Maybe."

"You'll be a good mother. You seem like a caring person to me. My ex-wife was a wonderful mother."

Off to the left, wedged between a Korean restaurant and a store called Kitchen Concepts, is a small liquor store. Larry and his consistent kindness. I should write a letter to Larry's widow too, a letter of thanks and remembrance. I pat my inside pocket and feel the two folded letters to Wyn and Nancy and my brother Charlie.

"Were you a good dad?"

"Yes and no, and I can't forgive myself for the no part." Is this true? *Should* I forgive myself? "Officer?"

"Yes?"

"Any idea what will happen to me this morning?"

"You mean legally?"

"Yeah."

"Have you got a lawyer?"

"No."

"Then the judge will assign you one. You're PR, right?"

"Pardon me?"

"Personal recognizance?"

"Yes."

"Then the judge will probably just set a hearing date and let you go."

"Let me go?"

"That's right." She's taken me off the highway and we're driving slowly down a street of clapboard houses, their lawns wet. In the middle of one's a massive beech tree, its smooth gray bark gnarled at the bottom like its roots are moving up to the trunk they feed. Being set free isn't something I've thought about. I haven't been thinking about my immediate future much at all.

Another gift. Another gift I haven't looked for and once again don't deserve. What is *happening* to me?

And now this caring young cop, who wants me to go straight to bed after my hearing, is turning in front of a brick courthouse. The entrance is two forty-foot white columns in front of tall double doors, and a man in a suit and tie stands in front of them smoking a cigarette and scrolling through his phone.

She pulls around to the side of the building and we go down a short concrete ramp and then we're in some kind of darkened garage, its overhead doors closing behind us and a dim light coming on over a doorway another cop steps through. He smiles and waves at my young officer, who's already out of the parked cruiser, the other cop saying, "Jenny, Jenny, you a lawyer yet?"

"I have to get in first, Bobby. Don't jinx me."

What comes after, I seem to be seeing from a softly burning place I float through: my young officer unsnapping her holster and placing her pistol in an iron box near the doorway where the other cop's talking to her. He's smiling and his teeth are big and white and she drops her keys in that box too, and then she's leaning into the backseat and touching my shoulder. I can smell the shampoo in her hair, her eyes so blue. I'm talking, saying that I need some aspirin, or maybe I only thought that because the court officer doesn't say anything to me as Officer Jenny's hand lets go of my arm, and then she's gone and I'm on another cot in another cell, though there's no window and the light above is so bright it hurts my eyes, which I close, my hands free again.

32

"**T**OM?" A PRESSURE ON MY SHOULDER. IT PULLS BACK, THEN TAPS again, a floating log pushing up against me where I lie in cold waters.

"Wake up, man, c'mon."

My teeth are chattering, and now Jamey's face is just inches from mine. It's a small face, like Charlie's and our father's, and the kid's eyes are bloodshot. He's sitting on the floor wearing his denim jacket, and his hair's pulled back into a ponytail and this makes his beard look more unruly.

"You sick?"

"How're you, Jamey?"

The boy's eyes fill and he shakes his head and collapses back against the opposite bunk. "I couldn't do it."

"What, buddy?"

"Call my mom." His voice breaks on that last word. He draws his knees up and pulls them in close and shakes his head again. My teeth have stopped chattering, though I'm cold in my work jacket, my exposed skin under some invisible sun.

"Jamey."

"So I called Trina, and she just sounded scared and like—I don't know—like she don't even *care*."

"She cares."

"She got mad at me. She told me I had to call my mother cuz we gave her that money and now I need it. But—" Jamey knocks his forehead against his raised knees. "I can't do that."

"You need to call her, Jamey. You don't want her to worry."

"It's already gone anyway. My mother got her car fixed, like, right away because she's been driving around for a year with her tailpipe wired to the bumper."

I think of that money being stolen, how this woman is now guilty of a crime herself.

"You don't understand. I'm the only one in my family who's not a fuckup. I'm like the only one in school."

A clanging of steel on steel, the fluttering of the fluorescent light far above us. I start to shiver under my coat and curl onto my side. From here the bearded boy looks like he's rooted in the concrete he sits on. But the boy wipes his eyes and is looking at me like he's waiting for something that can only come from me, and this brings me back to when the police closed in, me telling him it's better this way, he'll see.

"What do you think will happen to me?"

A man coughs. There's the jangle of keys, the cell door sliding open and the cop with the large white teeth gesturing to Jamey to stand and come with him. "Let's go, Roche."

Jamey stands. He's looking from me to the policeman, then back at me, and I remember him in his unit after our foolish escapade asking me if I was going to "rat" them out, so much unguarded feeling in his face then and now. I prop myself up on one elbow, my face and head in the hot thumping air. "This is how we learn things, Jamey. You'll get through this. You'll see."

"Hey, over here *now*."

"Tom?"

"Yeah, buddy."

"I still don't think I did anything wrong."

The cop steps into the cell, pulls Jamey's right arm behind his back and then his left, locking handcuffs onto soft-looking and narrow wrists. "Don't stop being a giver, Jamey. Whatever happens. Don't stop doing that."

But the boy's already outside the cell, the cop pulling the door shut, its iron lock clamping loudly and tightly into place.

33

IT'S BEEN YEARS SINCE I HAD A FEVER, AND AS I WALK ALONG THE dirt shoulder of Route 9 East, it's like I'm being pulled along on hot fragments of what's just happened and what has to happen next. The judge was a woman who looked like my ex-mother-in-law Nancy. Her hair was silver and she wore thin-rimmed glasses and had a kind face, though sitting up there behind her raised desk in her black robe, she had the relaxed posture of someone who had seen every sort of fallen human behavior pass before her and nothing she would hear today was going to be new to her.

My lawyer's suit seemed too tight for him. When he walked over to me standing there behind plexiglass, my hands bound in front of me with a new pair of handcuffs, the lawyer leaned in so close that I could see the pores in the skin of his nose. His breath was warm in my face and that sent a chill through me, my legs foldable sticks. I kept looking around the room for Jamey or for Officer Jenny, but there were only strangers. More men in suits and women and men in winter coats or heavy wool waiting for the judge to get to why they were here. Then my full name came from the judge's lips, but she glanced at me only once, then listened to my assigned counsel, a term the lawyer had used when introducing himself. Such a *phrase*. I could only see the beauty in it, the notion of each and every one of us being assigned someone to counsel us.

Then it was over and my hands weren't cuffed anymore and I was standing in the cold next to the tall white columns, my assigned counsel handing me his business card. His last words before going back inside were, "It'll be thirty days anyways."

Anyways. That final word sounded so uneducated and I tried not to judge him for it. It's the word my own mother would use, after all, and my brother Charlie, but its echo in the midmorning air left me feeling like everything that had just happened in that brick courthouse behind me had been a charade.

But Officer Jenny seemed to be long gone and those tall white double doors behind me were closed. I was actually being let go. What was there to do but start walking?

AND HERE I AM on the side of a road under a gray sky, sweating and shivering, cars passing by me so fast and loud that my shoulders hunch under my jacket. I seem to be burning one minute and freezing the next. I keep unzipping my old work coat and zipping it back up again, and my tongue feels thick and clammy. I want a glass of cool water or even a cup of hot tea, but I have to let every want fall from me like sawdust off my shoulders.

Many of the drivers look out at me with what looks like suspicion or mild fear or confusion or even disgust. They have jobs to do and bills to pay and families to take care of, and who's this grown man strolling down a state road like some kid with no responsibilities of any kind? How right they are to mistrust me really. How correct they are that I've been set free, and where's the justice in that?

THE HEARING THIRTY DAYS from now could lead to my imprisonment, though my assigned counsel—Frank? Fred?—told me "they have no case." He said other things to me, but I had trouble listening because the phrase *deep shit* was stuck in my chest like a fishbone, my assigned counsel having just used that phrase to describe Jamey's situation, that the boy had "the goods on his person" and couldn't post his bail, and remorse opens up inside me like a pocket of poison, followed by grief for what that kind boy may face, and here I am, free and wanting to turn to each passing car and yell to its drivers, *You have every right to condemn me. Every right!*

Now come the smells of hickory smoke and cooking meat. I'm not hungry, but hot meals being made nearby feels wonderfully hopeful, and there, off to my right, is a gravel lot leading to a low wooden structure. Its tin roof is held up by six-by-six posts, and under this is a porch without rails and a wooden bench up against a barn-board wall next to a plate-glass window. Painted across the glass in yellow letters is: *PJ's Barbecue North.*

My legs seem to have decided that this is where I have to go, and I find it interesting that when I think of my legs I'm not thinking of hip fires.

The air in front of my face is cold and hot, though the hot seems to be me and there's a hovering quality to my movements, the hard gravel under my work boots crunching softly from far away.

What I need to do is rest, and isn't it strange that the wooden bench against that barn-board wall summons Drew's bed back at 116 Hatfield Street? Because that's where I hope to go next. Back to my son's house, where I can rest until I'm strong enough to find my way back east to the 8 and Trina and all that I have to tell her.

Music is coming from inside this place. An old man's singing low over a loose-stringed guitar, his tone resigned yet resolute, and my footsteps up onto the porch are an intrusion to my own ears. I'm shivering again, and what a lovely dark hue to that bench, walnut or alder or even the same hickory this place's cook is using for the smoked brisket or ribs I smell gratefully as I sit on that bench, one that doesn't creak or shift under my weight, and as I zip my work jacket up to my throat and lie on my side, drawing my knees up and wedging my bare hands between them, there comes the reedy wail of a harmonica, then Drew's voice, *Dad.*

Such a recognition of his father! Such a warm hand reaching out to me. But when I open my eyes, it's a woman's hand just inches from my face. That and green corduroy and the hem of a down vest and then the tiny shoes of a toddler, Caitlin Murphy standing there in front of me holding her youngest.

"Sir? Are you all right?"

No, not Caitlin Murphy. Because this one has the ruddy face of a skier, her blond hair thick but short, and as I start to sit up I have the impression that she's a woman who not only isn't afraid of trouble of any kind, she welcomes it. And it's funny I didn't notice the man standing off to her left. He's a small man in a soiled apron and a flannel shirt, his face covered with a week's worth of young whiskers. One of his hands is covered with a dirty red oven mitt, and the music's louder now, but the wailing harmonica is a knife of sound pushing through my brain.

"Are you sick?" The voice is the man's, but it's the woman who leans forward with her child and rests the back of her hand against my forehead. Did she really just do that? This stranger?

"He's burning."

I sit as straight as I can, both my work boots on the porch floor. I'm having a hard time swallowing, but this young family is filling me with such a rising joy, the toddler staring at me like I'm a zoo animal he's never been told about before.

"Are you on foot?"

On foot. On leg. On wing. I shiver and cough into my shoulder. "Your son is perfect." Time must have passed because now the man in the apron's holding out to me a glass of water. My fingers are thick around it, the water flowing down my throat like a forgotten debt repaid with so much interest that I want to give it all back.

"You need to be in bed, sir." It's the woman. She says this as she's adjusting the wool cap on her little boy's head.

"I'm walking to my son's house."

"Is he nearby?"

"Yes, Hatfield Street. Amherst."

"You have no car?"

"I do, but I don't, no."

And that's all it took, another moment of speaking plainly, truly, and here I am being driven to Drew's house by the man in the apron, though he's taken it off and pulled on a down vest like the one worn by his wife, who, when I stood to leave, disappeared inside the restaurant and brought out a small paper bag. I took it and thanked her. I could feel under the paper a glass bottle and something soft.

"It's a root beer and cornbread. I just made it." She smiled then and those narrow green eyes became slits but her face opened into such warmth and goodwill toward me, this man she would never know, that I wanted to do so much more than simply thank her again as I climbed into the passenger side of her husband's small pickup truck.

To receive gifts of this magnitude is becoming almost unbearable, but what's there to do but try to ride the wave of them like the feather off the wing of some white bird flying toward the sun?

The young man's talking and I'm trying to listen. I can feel the movement of the truck and I want to close my eyes. My feet feel too warm in my new wool socks and my old work boots, and a light rain is falling, though this young cook, whose name is Peter, his wife Jill, *P* and *J* of *PJ's*, doesn't turn on the wipers. That's what this Peter's been telling me about, their business, so I must've asked him if they're the owners of that wonderful hardwood bench and porch and that smoking meat. And while the young entrepreneur talks, telling me how they also own another "store" south of here in Connecticut where they were both raised, my eyes are on the man's phone screen set in a case mounted on the dash. Its screen is a map showing just where we are and just where we're going and I want to tell him that I too used to have one of those. I had a phone and used its navigating system when I was a professional driver, though what I really am is a builder, a lover of wooden structures like this man's restaurant, and this is what I need to tell this kind young father and husband, that it's important to unapologetically love things and people, especially people.

"Hold on to that love."

"I'm sorry?" Peter is already taking us through Amherst Center. There's no more snow on the green, which is brown and wet, the tree trunks black, and I turn in my seat and look through the rain-streaked rear window to see the blue awning of the bagel shop passing by, that woman I never even met buying me a warm bagel with cream cheese.

"Do you mean love of food? Because that's really our mission. I think that's why we're having success."

Success. It's a word I haven't heard in a long time. Coming from the mouth of this ambitious and hardworking man next to me, it seems like such a dangerous word. I want to warn him how fragile that all is, how precarious it can be.

"Don't get distracted by that. Don't let it lead you astray."

"Success?"

My head is heavy and hot, and when I close my eyes I'm back on that bench on that porch, this Peter standing beside his wife holding their toddler son, mom and dad staring at me with compassionate scrutiny, yes, but also like I just might be a future they should probably avoid. My eyes burn and I blink and say, "You'll never have anything better than what you have now."

"But we want to grow the business—"

"I mean the three of you. Don't let anything take you away from that."

"Of course."

I want to tell Peter more than this. I want to tell him that for years I convinced myself that all the work I did was in service to my wife and son, but the truth is I couldn't bear the utter gift of them and so work became my home and then my home was gone and so was my work, but what I'm holding on to now without trying to hold on to *anything* is the tone of Drew's alcohol-poisoned, hypothermic voice when his mother asked who was on the line: Dad.

A green shoot in a pot of dead plantings.

"Is this it?"

Outside my window my son's Honda is still parked in that narrow driveway. There are the three out-of-level porches, the rotting windowsills and split clapboards I hadn't noticed before. At all of their butt joints the paint's flaking, and wouldn't it be something if I was still whole and could replace everything I'm seeing with something plumb and square and level and new. But no, I have to let that go. I have to let everything go. "You've been very kind. Thank you."

"You bet."

Then I'm back on my son's front porch, breathing hard from climbing those spongy stairs. I'm shivering again and that bench seat from some old sedan against the wall looks inviting, but I'm afraid if I lie down on it I won't be able to get up on my own.

The rain has picked up out in the yard and over the street, a cold November rain. I'm hot again and would like to open that root beer in the bag in my hand, but I have to get to my son's room first.

Once again the door isn't locked and the front room is still darkened with sheets over the windows. But there are new smells now—tomato soup and grilled cheese. Sitting on one of the couches is a young woman in a wool poncho, white buds in her ears, her glowing computer open on her lap. I've closed the door behind me and I'm about to explain myself with an introduction, but the woman only glances up at me before staring at her screen again. It's like this happens all the time, strangers walking into their home, and I want to thank her for letting me walk by her and down the narrow hall but I stay quiet, the heat of my head and face parting the air for me.

The bedroom door to my left still has the dart in it, but a condom isn't hanging from it anymore, and I step into the small kitchen, where at the stove is a big man. His head is shaved except for a tuft of hair at the very top that he's pulled into a short ponytail, his face wide and clean-shaven and confused-looking as he turns to me. A spatula is in his hand and two grilled cheese sandwiches are sizzling in a pan.

"I'm Drew's dad. Just need to rest a bit."

"Drew?"

"DL?"

"Cool." The big man turns his back to me, then flips the grilled cheese sandwiches, and it's hard to climb up the narrow stairwell of those creaking red stairs. I have to stop twice to get my breath, and my hips and back ache but I don't think *fires*.

At the top of the stairs the bike that had been in front of the radiator is gone and the wall's been scrubbed of my son's birthday cake. A woman's voice comes from behind a closed door. Then there's another voice, also a woman's but older, and it sounds like it's coming from the speaker of a phone or a computer, and as I walk through Drew's open doorway and shut the door behind me, I feel moved by these sounds—mother and daughter talking—the big man probably cooking for the girl in the poncho on the couch, Drew's bed still unmade, and how lovely to lie back on its sheets, to curl on my side and lay my head on the pillow where my one and only son breathes and sweats and dreams.

34

RAIN AGAINST THE WINDOW. A PELTING THAT CONTROLS MY chills. As the wind pulls back, so do the rolling shivers from my feet to my throat. But then I'm too warm and I have to sit up on the edge of Drew's bed and pull off my old work boots and jacket and then my sweater, dropping them to the floor next to my son's one big sneaker, but then I'm freezing again and I yank my son's covers over my shoulder and sink my face into his pillow, which smells like the cologne of a man I do not know.

The rain blows harder and then stops but then is back again. I believe I could happily die here.

Voices on the other side of the door. One's low but two are high and my father's leaning into the open hood of his station wagon, pointing to a clump of metal and saying to his two boys standing there in the driveway, "That's the alternator." Such a beautiful word, and Charlie's saying something about *alternatives*. It was an email he sent me. *There are alternatives, Tom. You have to make better choices.* But he's saying this out loud in a high voice, and now it's saying, "Mr. Lowe? You okay? Mr. *Lowe?*"

A small hand on my shoulder. It sends an icy ripple to my heart. Fingers touch my forehead and I open my eyes to a tiny blue hummingbird flying over a thin gold chain above pale skin, then the swoop of a black scarf.

"You okay?"

"Yes, you?" And I mean it. *Is* she okay? Because it's not easy being young. It's not easy going to school and hoping to find your way. The girl lets out a laugh and behind her stands the big man with the short ponytail coming out of the top of his bald head. Next to him is the girl in the poncho and she's looking at me.

I have to get back there. I have to tell Trina about Jamey and I have to call my own police department and tell them about Brian, and why does the girl in the poncho look so upset? I want to tell her that it's okay, that I'm Drew's dad and I'm just a little sick, that's all, but the blue hummingbird is handing me what looks like three little Os, round and small and nestled in the palm of this girl the big man calls Lauren. "He needs to sit up or he'll choke." There are the smells of aftershave and cotton and the big man's face is beside mine, his big hands under my arms, and I'm being pulled up with such ease that I feel deeply cared for but also like I'm being rushed to my final resting place without first being asked. My back's against the wall and this Lauren still holds out to me three little pills and a glass of water.

I take the water and sip it. The wall feels wonderfully reassuring against the back of my head. I roll my face toward Lauren, her expression bemused yet focused.

"I'm afraid of those pills."

"It's just aspirin."

"I got hooked on some that looked just like those."

"It's just Bayer, Mr. Lowe."

"Maybe Drew told you all that."

She doesn't say anything, but the light in her eyes seems to darken and she tilts her face slightly.

"It was a long time ago. I guess I've been trying to pick up the pieces ever since."

The girl in the poncho is standing so close to the big man that her cheek's touching his shoulder. She's looking at me like I'm telling her a story from her childhood, one that she forgot but would like to hear again.

"But some things you can't fix, right?" I smile at the blue hummingbird and hold out my hand for the aspirin and then I'm swallowing all three pills and I drain the glass, and there's Drew reaching into his coat pocket and handing his father a fresh baggie of Os, his face flushed with such an insistent love.

A burning wetness is on my face. "Is my son okay? You guys think he's all right?"

These three friends of Drew's have become blurry. The rain is whipping against the glass.

"DL?" the big man says. "DL's a poet."

"He writes poems?"

"No clue. I just mean the kid feels things. You should lie back down." He steps forward and helps me scoot back to where I was, then pulls the covers up under my chin. Lauren the hummingbird's saying something about depression and therapy and "Hanna didn't fucking help much." She stands. "He's coming home tonight. I guess his mother's driving him."

The door closes softly, respectfully. The rain blows steadily against the window. From out in the hallway comes a whispering, though that could be the rain, and I close my eyes and see Ronnie driving our son down a slick highway, this twenty-year-old "poet" I don't even begin to know, but I so *want* to know him and this wanting is a mad flapping of wings in the hot darkness my own voice slaps away. *Let go of those. You have to let go of those.* But wants are not needs and I *need* to know my son, though I'm shivering again, my teeth knocking against each other like some ancient chorus arguing the differences between wants and needs, and then a rising fire quiets them all and when I open my eyes again the rain has stopped and the light in the room has dimmed and what I need most is a toilet.

I make my way out to the hallway in my wool socks and rumpled khakis and dress shirt. I'm cold, but the shivering's stopped and my face doesn't feel on fire anymore. At the end of the hall a door opens to the sound of a flushing toilet and that Indian or Pakistani boy stands there smiling at me. "Hello. Do you need the restroom?"

"Yes, thank you."

"You're quite welcome." The young man smiles again and then disappears down the narrow stairwell of creaking red stairs. From down in that kitchen come the smells of onions being sautéed in olive oil, and I feel the need to eat and I must've slept the whole afternoon. I shouldn't be here when Ronnie and Drew come. Because who am I to have slept my sickness away all day in a room I don't even help to pay for? Who am I to turn to my son for help when I've done so very little for him?

Painted on the wall above the toilet is a black square with white lettering: *Resist*. Yes, I have to resist resisting what's true, which is that I needed my son's bed today. I didn't want it, but I needed it, and as I flush the toilet, then wash my hands with green soap that smells like roses, I picture myself living in a place like this, living with people again.

But I do live with people. Trina standing in the doorway in a loose T-shirt and her underwear, Trina days or weeks earlier pulling that underwear down to show me a heart broken in two.

"Is he still *here*?"

Ronnie.

In all these years her voice hasn't changed, and so it's like what's out in that hallway is the echo of a life I never lost, because in her question is that same curiosity she always had for the cosmos and then people and now me. Except in her voice is also a tone of worry and irritation, but also—I heard it—real concern, though I don't know if this is for me or our son or both.

There's a man in the mirror and I have no idea who he is.

There isn't any towel so I rub my hands across my face and through my hair, and then I'm gripping the doorknob. There was my mother hanging up the kitchen phone and turning to me and Charlie, her face so still, her voice just a thin ribbon of itself, "Your father—" and she couldn't finish and in that quiet, Charlie looking from her to his big brother, then back to her, a plunging terror opened up inside me that I haven't felt again till this moment, opening this bathroom door and moving through the smells of cashmere and perfume and those onions and now meat cooking in oil. The perfume is what Ronnie's worn since she was a young woman, the scent some night-blooming flower whose name is lost to me, and this leaves me dizzy in a far greater lostness, but the only way to get back at least some of it is to step through that doorway into the room that holds my wife and son.

Ronnie has her back to me. She's picking up off the floor my sweater and work jacket and Drew's balled-up jeans and sweatshirt and shoe. She's in a brown cashmere coat and black pants and expensive-looking boots, and Drew's sitting on the edge of his mattress staring at the photo of him and Hanna next to his bed. He's in a fleece jacket and jeans. His hair's so short it looks like he just shaved his head. His face seems thinner too, his eyes deeper set, his chin darkened with whiskers that are no longer a boy's. My heart beats in the air of the hallway behind me, and there's the withering sense that I'm dead and gone and only a spirit hovering in the doorway. But that spirit shimmers with so much love for these two that it's hard to believe it's not a sound in the room.

"Hi." Drew nods in my direction like he sees me. And now Ronnie turns to me. Her hair looks newly styled and she brushes it back away from her face, one that's softened with age into a loveliness that's deeply maternal but also somehow free of whatever constraints that's put on her. "What are you doing here?"

I look from her to Drew, then back at her again. My eyes fill and I have to shake my head and all I want to say is how very much I've missed them both, but I can't speak.

"Are you crying?" There's only a wisp of annoyance in what she asks. Her voice is like when she was young, lying in bed with me and asking why I drove a van and why I was a carpenter and why I was in college, just a pure and naked curiosity, and so it hurts that this is all she feels seeing me for the first time in so long, but who am I to ask for anything more?

And now my legs are moving again on their own, and while my hips and pelvis ache, how can I think of fires when I can sit next to my son and put my arm around his shoulders and pull him in close enough to kiss the top of his head? I can smell Drew's scalp and it's not a smell I even recognize, and oh how much work there is to do. "Are you okay, buddy? Are you?" My voice gets snared in my throat. My son nods and I can feel him lean away just a bit and so I let go.

"Drew just got his heart broken. He'll be fine." Ronnie lifts the photo of Drew and Hanna off the stacked crates.

"Mom."

"Don't perseverate, honey." She pushes the framed photo into a side pocket of her cashmere coat, then nods at the lid of pot seeds and the last bit of joint. "And no more of that, please. It's a depressant." Standing there in front of me, I see what looks like a wealthy woman, her inner abundance now matched by an outer one. It's what I was trying to do for her all along, though she never asked for it and she never seemed to need it and I can feel my son's leg touching my own, but what to do when the two people I love the most, my love for them the only anchors holding me to the earth, what to do when they feel like strangers?

"Lauren says you have a fever."

"I'm better now."

Drew stands and walks past his mother and sits at his desk. He looks like he's waiting for something to happen, though he doesn't know what that is. Sitting there with his back to his computer and empty beer cans, his head shorn, his fleece loose on his frame, he looks like some young artist exiled to a penal colony.

"Where's your car, Tom?"

"It got towed, Ronnie."

"From *here*?"

"No, back home."

Home. It's like I'm raising a subject I didn't mean to. I'm thirsty. At my feet's the brown paper bag that kind Jill handed me. I want that root beer. I reach down and open the bag and pull out the bottle and offer it to Drew. "Want it?"

"You don't want it?"

"No, I want you to have it."

"Yeah. Okay."

Drew starts to stand, but Ronnie takes the bottle from me and hands it to our son. I reach into the bag and pull out the square of cornbread. It crumbles in my palm and I hold it up to Ronnie. "Want some? This nice lady made it fresh."

"No. Thank you, though. How'd you get here with no car?"

Jamey with his bushy beard and tears as he was being hand-cuffed by a cop the age of the kid's father, whoever and wherever he was.

"A friend drove me."

"Is he here?"

I break the cornbread in half, push it into my mouth, then

stand, a jagged heat spreading from hip to hip. I step into the smell of night-blooming flowers and move by my one and only wife and hand the other half of the cornbread to Drew. My son stares at it a second, then looks up at me with a vague distrust, and why wouldn't he?

"It's good. You'll like it." As I say this, my voice shames me because it's the same tone I used on Drew to encourage him to take his dad's hidden money and hurry outside to the end of our pine-needle-covered road.

Drew nods and takes a small bite of his cornbread. He turns and places the rest of it on the ketchup-streaked hamburger wrapper on his desk.

"I've missed you, buddy. I—"

"Tom, who's your friend? Is he or she here?"

I turn to Ronnie. She's unbuttoned her cashmere coat and she's wearing a black sweater, maybe the one she wore when she drove back to our empty home and filled herself a glass of red wine and summoned whatever it took to tell me the truth about her and Edward Joseph Flynn. I want to look different to her than I do now, and I can feel myself falling back to where I hoped to keep rising away from, the unlucky man blaming everyone else.

"He's in jail."

"Jail?"

"Yes, and—" For a half-breath that sends a cold wave through my face I wish I'd left this place before they got here.

"I was in jail, too."

"Dad, what'd you *do*?"

"Something I'm not proud of."

"Jesus." Ronnie shrugs off her coat and drops it on the mattress and sits. "Are you in serious trouble?"

"I think so, yeah."

I look at Drew, who's looking up at me. He's such a handsome young man, though he doesn't look well, and while I had nothing to do with Drew's love life going bad or my son having drunk too much and passed out in the cold, it's hard not to feel that I had a hand in all of it.

"Tom? Are you going to tell us what you did?"

"I helped some people steal money."

Drew looks over at his mother, then back at me. "Did you steal it, too?"

"No. No, I didn't."

"Who are these people, Tom?"

"My neighbor and her boyfriend."

"Go on." Gone is Ronnie's tone of naked curiosity. It's the tone that came out of her the afternoon we got our very first adjusted rate mortgage bill. *But we can pay that, right?*

Ronnie glances at our son like she's having second thoughts about my continuing my story in front of him. A cool sweat beads on the back of my neck and I want to go to that bed and lie down again, but it's where Ronnie is, so I lean back against the wall, then lower myself to the floor, my legs splayed in front of me.

"I changed my mind. I was going to steal with them, but I changed my mind. I've been changing, Drew. That's what I want to say to you."

Drew's leaning both elbows on his knees, looking down at me. I look over at Ronnie.

"And you too, hon."

That last word is all wrong, I know this, and so here I am once again stepping over some invisible border in the air, but Ronnie's face doesn't change. She doesn't even blink and it's like that life I've been living back in the 8 is just some parallel story to this one, that a different Tom Lowe is back there living that life while this one has continued to be Drew's daily father and Ronnie's daily husband, but now this man sitting on the floor in front of them has to explain what he's learned or the two Toms will never meet and this wary boy looking down at me will never have a whole father. Ever. "I think I'm learning more about life."

"Don't change the subject, please."

"Yeah, who'd you rip off?"

In Drew's voice is—can it be?—*pride*? Some kind of dark pride that his pathetic old man actually got off his plywood couch and *did* something? I can't deny how good it feels to hear this. But how wrong it is to let myself feel good about it.

The light outside Drew's window's a darkening gray. Somehow this day that I started in two holding cells is coming to an end, but there's such a lovely sense of a new beginning here with Drew and Ronnie in this small warm room, and so I tell them about the thirty-two hundred dollars that was going to be mine when I sold my tools and how that would've given me my car back, and how all I wanted to do was to drive it here "to see you, buddy. And, I don't know, take you and your friends out someplace nice." But then they were stolen.

"I'm sorry about your tools, Tom." Ronnie's voice is sincere and now I'm talking about Trina, "this young kid raising her kids alone," and then I'm describing our Good Samaritan driving us to Mike Andrews' house.

"Mike Andrews? Do I know him?"

So odd that Ronnie doesn't recognize his name, and for just a second the old bitterness turns over inside me, the feeling that for years I had a pack of stones strapped to my back and every morning I stepped again into a swift river to swim alone across it. But I volunteered for those stones in my pack and I took pride in taking care of all the money details too, so why would Ronnie have Andrews' name lodged inside her the way it was lodged in me?

"He was our loan officer, remember? And I was still blaming him and his bank for talking me into that loan."

"Oh, Tom."

"So what'd you *do*?" Drew's interest seems to have deepened quite a bit. He also seems relieved to have his mother's scrutiny shifted to someone else.

"We stole his garbage."

"His garbage?"

"Yeah, for—credit card stuff." I shake my head. "But I just couldn't do it."

"Of course not, Tom. That's not *you*."

What a *gift* she's just given me. "Thank you. I'm glad you know that."

"Of course I know that. Drew does too, right, honey?"

"So why'd you get busted?"

I can't quite get the words to leave my mouth. *Joint venture.* I'm staring at Ronnie. Isn't that what this loving strong woman and I did together once too? Didn't we venture jointly into the unknown? And by stepping faithfully into it, we were given our son. We were given Drew.

"Why'd you get busted in Amherst?"

"My friend stole from a bank there."

"A bank? Like, he robbed a *bank*?"

"No, he cashed in on somebody else's credit account. A guy whose trash he stole."

"Identity theft." Ronnie's voice has the flat, instructive tone of a teacher, though she's looking from her son to me as if she wants Drew to sit farther away from his father. Like I've caught something Drew can't afford to get.

"So why'd *you* get busted?"

"I was driving his car."

"You were the *wheelman*?"

"Honey, this is not a funny story. Tom, do you need a lawyer?"

From downstairs comes music. It's from a piano, a real one, and rising from it are softly blended chords that sound to me like some kind of resigned acceptance though love remains. The phrase *identity theft* is pushing through my head on Ronnie's voice. That's what happened to me too, everything I once was taken away from me.

"Ed might be able to help."

"I can't afford him."

"He'd do it pro bono, wouldn't he, Mom?"

This Latin leaving Drew's mouth. I picture Edward Flynn sitting him down in his book-lined office in that ship captain's house on Salem Common, talking to Drew about the law and lawyers. But a guiding hand like this, I can only feel grateful for it.

"Do you have a hearing date?"

I nod. "There's this old woman back in the units. She's probably a hundred years old, and she made me this incredible sweet bread."

"You hungry?" Drew holds up the cornbread. "Want the rest of this?"

"I've been trying to stay the old me, son. But I'm not the old me."

"The old you?"

"Yeah. You know, a worker." I glance over at Ronnie. Her expression is encouraging, but she also has the thin-lipped look of someone who'd been hoping for this moment and others like it a long time ago. She checks her watch. It's on a thin sliver bracelet around her wrist, and it's a gesture that both hurts me and also lets me go.

"You guys want to eat?" Lauren stands in the doorway. I can only see her in profile. Her black scarf's gone and her thin chain lies across her hummingbird. "I made meat sauce and linguine."

"You're very sweet, Lauren. Thank you, but I have to get back." Ronnie looks over at Drew. "You must be hungry, honey."

"Nope."

"But you should eat. It smells wonderful."

Drew nods at Lauren, then smiles at her, and it's a smile I know so well because it's the smile of my little boy, the smile of my only son.

"Save some for me?"

"Yeah, sure. Mr. Lowe? You wanna eat?"

What I want is something cool to drink, another bed in this room so that I can rest next to my depleted son. But Drew's in a good place here. Living with good people. It's time to get back to the 8 and Trina and her punched-in-the-face child Shannon. And it's time to see what I can do for another depleted boy, one I helped to corrupt. "I have to get back, too. But thank you. Thank you for taking such good care of me today."

"No problem."

Then the girl's gone and Ronnie's pulling on her cashmere coat, her eyes on me like I'm a dog she doesn't have time to feed. "Do you need a ride?"

I don't want a ride, but I do need it. "Yeah. Sorry, Ronnie, but yes, I do." I glance up at my son, who now looks vaguely worried. "I might need some help getting up." I raise my hand and Drew grips it with both of his and then I'm being pulled to my feet by my son who's taller than I am. But I stand too fast, the top of my head a rising mist, and I have to rest my hand on Drew's desk and laptop to steady myself.

"You still have your mom's sweater, I see." Ronnie holds it out to me.

"My mother's?"

"You don't remember? She sent it to you for your birthday. That's when we knew something wasn't right."

"We should visit her again, Mom."

"You guys visited her?"

"Yeah, last summer. She thought I was you."

"Me?"

"Drew was great with her. He just sat there and acted like you."

I push my arm into the sleeve of my sweater and I'm about to ask Drew what that was like, but it seems so unfair for Drew to have to have done that that I can't talk. Downstairs the piano has stopped and someone laughs and Ronnie's reminding Drew about his two appointments this week with Dr. Salzman. It's so awful that I've never even heard of this doctor, and as I sit on Drew's bed to pull on my work boots, I feel my old self wanting to drive my son to those appointments and to pay for them, to then take my son out to dinner or the batting cages to either talk about those appointments or take a break from them. But that me is no more, and the one that's here, the one that's dependent on others for kindnesses that keep surprising and moving me, the one who's starting to sense a new way to be, he can help his boy in other ways.

"What if you have to go to jail?" Drew twists open the root beer.

"I've been in my own jail, son. I think I'm finally finding out how to be free."

Drew nods like his father's speaking a language he needs to learn himself.

"Well, it would be nice to be *free*, but I've got a conference I have to prepare for tomorrow. Tom?" Ronnie's looking at me the way she would whenever I rose from the banks of O River after drifting down it for hours. Like she's mildly afraid of me. Like she isn't sure she can handle whatever I might say or do next. Sticking out of the top of her coat pocket is the frame of the photo of Drew and his girl, and before I go I want to comfort my son. But what can I say about the death of love in front of Ronnie, her keys now hanging from one of her gloved hands?

I stand, my hips and pelvis hot embers crumbling to the floor. "This pain I've got?"

"Yeah?"

"In my head I think of it as fires burning inside me. But there are no fires, buddy. Not if you accept things." I want to rest my hand on Drew's shoulder, but it's too soon and I can't. "You have to accept things."

Drew nods and looks down at the floor. He sets his root beer on his desk so his mother can hug him, and as she does, telling him to answer her texts and to please eat something, I'm pulling on my work jacket, feeling again in the loving orbit of just the three of us, strangers no more, the three of us one family, and I don't want to leave this moment. But no, wanting and accepting cannot live in the same breath.

"I remember that jacket." Drew's staring at my old Carhartt. "You used to hang it on a hook in the van."

"I did?"

"Yeah, you did."

Then I'm hugging my son, though it feels more like my son is hugging me, the old me, the man who's not here anymore. It'll take a while to show him a new man. A useless but useful man.

Ronnie's already halfway down the hall, and I stand in the doorway. How to tell my son that I didn't die when he was a kid? How to tell him that?

"Come visit me sometime?"

"In jail?" Drew looks like he means this as a joke, though he's not smiling.

"No, back home." I smile at my son and lift my arm in a wave.

And all the way down the hall and those creaking red stairs, through the empty kitchen and its smells of cooked onions and meat and tomatoes, past the bedroom door with the dart in it and into the front room where Drew's friends are eating dinner off plates on their laps, a show on a TV in the corner, Ronnie smiling and blowing a kiss to Lauren before stepping through the front door, I can feel the words *back home* sitting between my lips like some undeniable secret finally revealed. Yes, back *home*.

At the door I wave at Drew's friends. "Thank you."

"No problemo," Lauren says. On the couch the big man is sucking noodles into his mouth, and he nods at me like whatever he did for me was what anyone should do for anyone else at all times, right? Beside him is the girl in the poncho. She bites into a piece of French bread and keeps her eyes on the TV, but just before I step out into the cold and the dark, she glances over at me and smiles and I can only feel grateful that Drew lives in such a place with such warm people.

35

RONNIE'S SUV SMELLS LIKE HER PERFUME AND ITS HEATED LEATHER seats. As she drives, her face softly lit by the dash controls, she's talking about Drew and his "challenges," but even though she's talking about our son, it's clear that she's nervous, that maybe the last thing she wants to be doing is going on a long drive with her ex-husband, Tom Lowe.

I think of that Christmas photo of her and her new husband back in Drew's room. Ronnie's hand on Flynn's chest in front of their lighted tree, her smile so deep and genuine, and isn't it remarkable how love can be found again? That new lives can come together and start something that might be even better than what was lost? It's like love is always with us, like it's simply floating in the atmosphere and we just have to walk through it and breathe it in again.

"I think she was abused, Tom."

"Who?"

"Hanna. All that sleeping around? That's such a red flag."

"Sleeping around?"

"God, you never change, do you? Have you not been listening to anything I've been telling you?" There's a smile in her voice, though she doesn't seem to be smiling.

"I'm sorry. I was never much of a listener, was I?"

"No, you weren't, but we don't need to get into any of that."

We're driving through woods down a long hill, Ronnie's head-lights sweeping past pines and bare hardwoods and a pickup truck parked on the dirt shoulder. As we pass I can see a man's face lit up dimly blue by the screen of his phone, and then Ronnie slows for a winding curve and I want to reach over and touch her cashmere-covered arm, but I leave my hand in my lap. "I could never stop worrying, Ronnie. Even when we were flush, I just couldn't let my guard down."

"Seriously, Tom, we don't have to talk about it."

"You told me once I was scared of the world."

"Did I?"

"Yes. And you said living with me was like living with a machine or a robot or something."

"Tom? I'd rather talk about our son, if you don't mind."

"I'm sorry."

"You apologize a lot."

"Do I?" That's a surprise. Since my fall I've been waiting for everyone else to apologize to *me*. "I think I'm learning things."

"Like how to be *free*? How nice for you."

We've left the woods and the road has flattened out and up ahead on opposite sides of the asphalt are the lighted canopies of competing gas stations. "You mad at me?"

"I used to be."

I could tell her that she was the one who left me. She was the one who strayed. She was the one who jumped ship and left me to swim away from the wreckage alone. Except I don't see it that way anymore. "I wasn't much of a lover, was I, Ronnie?"

"Oh for Christ's sake."

"I mean the loving part, not the other."

Ronnie slows at the gas stations, then takes the turn for the ramp onto Route 2 East, stepping on the gas, my head being pulled back against the seat. As the ramp levels off she passes a sedan and then we're moving steadily down the narrow two-lane that Jamey drove me down days and weeks ago, it seems.

"You should probably get some therapy, Tom. But not with me and not tonight, okay?"

"You sound mad."

"Well maybe I am, Tom. *Free?* What does that even mean? Free not to get a job? Free to ignore your son?"

"I tried to work, Ronnie. I think you know that."

"I really don't want to talk about this." She reaches into her console and sips from a driving cup. It's stainless steel and looks expensive, and when she sets it back down I eye the bottle of water behind it. There are wants and there are needs and my body, still weak from fever, needs liquids.

"Mind if I have some of that water?"

"I'm drinking cold coffee, Tom. I've got work to do when I get home, because not all of us are free."

"I mean that bottle of water."

She glances down and waves her hand in the air. "Go ahead, Drew didn't even open it."

I take the plastic bottle and drink from what was meant for my son. "That was good of you to visit my mother."

Ronnie takes a deep breath and lets it out. We're on a one-lane road lined on both sides with orange cones, Ronnie's headlights lighting them up as we pass by so fast it's like a gauntlet we have to get through in order to go on somehow. "I hate that Drew had to pretend to be me, though."

"Why?"

"Because—" My breath catches in my chest. Ronnie looks over at me. "You're right. I haven't been there for him."

The underside of her face is lit in that soft green light, her lips parted, her eyes shadows, and I want to tell her how truly lovely she is, and I also want to tell her that I still love her. I do.

But do I? Have I ever? I never really understood her or accepted her.

"I wasn't there for you either, Ronnie. I thought I was, but I wasn't."

Her eyes are back on the road. She takes another sip of cold coffee. "We weren't a good match, Tom. It's that simple."

"Really?"

"I was foolish. I thought I could change you."

"From what to what?"

"From unloved to loved."

"Was I unloved?"

"No, you were under-loved, how's that? Nothing against your mother, but I see it all the time in my practice."

"What?"

"When people are just trying to survive, they don't thrive, Tom."

Trina. Overwhelmed Trina and her Shannon and MJ and Cody. "We thrived for a while."

"Did we?" The gauntlet of orange cones ends and opens out onto two lanes, and Ronnie accelerates and flicks on her high beams. They light up the empty road ahead of us, and I'm back in our small apartment in Salem, the windows open in the summer, the laughter of men and women leaving the corner bar, the smell of the ocean, Ronnie's hair up in a bun as she sliced tomatoes at the counter and I lay on my back on the floor holding laughing Drew above my chest and face.

"I always felt like a burden to you, Tom. I don't know, like I was some heavy object you thought you were supposed to carry around all the time."

"I'm sorry."

"I do wish you'd stop apologizing."

"Remember Germany?"

"Yes."

"I think about that trip a lot."

"Do you?" She seems mildly distracted and glances down at her phone. She taps a few buttons and now the screen on her console lights up and she says, "Eddie, you're on speakerphone. I have Tom with me."

"Tom?"

"Drew's dad Tom."

"Oh, hey Tom, how are you?" Edward Flynn's voice is relaxed and in it is the magnanimity of the winner talking to the loser, though I don't feel like a loser anymore. How strange that this is my first conversation with this man. How odd that I feel so warmly toward him.

"I'm well. Thank you."

"How's Drew?"

"He's fine, I think, I hope." Ronnie's looking over at me and mouthing words that in the darkness I can't quite make out. Ed Flynn's talking about how that's good to hear and that he's "a strong kid" and Ronnie whispers, "Can I tell him about your situation?"

The old me would've said no. The old me would've needed to look like I had my house in order, but I have no house and there is no order, this life of ours is like flowing water and we're all floating in the grip of something bigger that we can't really control anyway. I nod and smile and here it is again, another gift I did not seek, Ronnie caring for me in some way.

"Honey, Tom needs a lawyer."

"Oh?"

And as Ronnie explains to her husband what I'm being charged with and how this came to be, I'm moved by how deeply she'd listened to me tell my story back there in our son's bedroom, how much of it—all of it—she's retained. But she was always this way. At least until my fall and our eviction, when she had to turn her attention to surviving instead of thriving. But here she is thriving once again, maybe more than ever in her life, a *caring* and constructive human being. The way she used to look at me whenever I spoke, her eyes on my eyes, or the way I was standing or how I raised a coffee cup to my lips or held a pencil between three fingers while I answered whatever sincere question she'd just asked me—about my day, about what I was thinking, about what I was feeling, about what I wanted from the week laid out in front me. Her chin would be slightly raised like she was trying to catch whatever I was *not* saying, though I never felt she thought I wasn't being honest. Instead, she wanted to understand all of me so that she could love all that had to be loved. Oh that unnerved me. I was just a man, a carpenter and a husband, a father and a son and a brother, and then this beautifully abundant woman had flown into my life from somewhere better than I ever knew, and she would fly away too. To a man who could hold all that she gave, to a man who somehow felt he deserved it.

"Tom, were you with this kid when he cashed in at the bank?"

"No. No, I was at the hospital."

"Then I'm not sure why you're being charged with joint venture."

We're driving on an overpass. Down below are the lighted signs and windows of fast-food restaurants, a shopping plaza, and a closed bank, its empty parking lot under the halogen glare of security lamps.

"I gave my friend the idea."

"The idea?"

"About stealing credit checks from people's trash. I told the men who arrested us that it was my idea."

"But he didn't do it himself, honey."

Ronnie's *tone*. It was the same one she used when I first met Wyn and Nancy at their house on the campus of Trevors Academy. It was a cold Sunday afternoon and the four of us were sitting with cups of English tea on the deep sofas of that low-ceilinged house built before the War Between the States. Ronnie sat next to me, smiling brightly over at her mother and father. "Tom's a builder. He *creates* things."

And now that same quiet pride. Her belief in me after all these years.

"Tom, did you help this kid steal those courtesy checks?"

"No."

"Then I don't really see a case here."

"Mr. Flynn?"

Ronnie looks over at me, then back at the road.

"Please, call me Ed."

"I'm more worried about my young friend. Do you think you might be able to help him?"

Flynn doesn't say anything, but then I hear the ruffling of papers, the click of a pen, and Edward Joseph Flynn is asking for Jamey's full name, which I give him. Flynn asks other questions about Jamey's age and address and job or schooling, and while I give answers to whatever I can, which isn't much, Ronnie sipping again from her cold coffee, I have the strange sensation that I'm making a new friend. It's how I felt with Dawn Porter too and the young mother Caitlin Murphy and streetwise old Mrs. Bongiovanni and my new neighbors Doug and mournfully attentive Minh. It's how I felt with Elizabeth Turner's daughter-in-law Mel, the way she washed my wound and my feet, the part in her hair that showed her age, like she wanted me to see that. Even drunk and bitter Dr. Clark and his rants, his warning me not to be a sap. Dutifully helpful Peter and Jill of PJ's Barbecue North. Lauren and the big boy and the girl in the poncho. Everyone—*everyone*—was just a breath and a beat away from becoming a friend.

"Ed?"

"Yeah, Tom."

"I was going to write you a letter. You and Ronnie."

"Okay."

Ronnie's looking over at me, a sudden stillness in the air. Up ahead's a minivan from Vermont. Stuck to its rear window are the stick figures of a family of five, and Ronnie flicks on her indicator and passes it. In the driver's seat of that van is a woman. "I—"

"Tom?" Ronnie's tone isn't proud anymore, it's on the verge of being scared, and oh how terrible it is that I ever scared her, that part of me—a small part, but there it was anyway— was happy to see her abundist illusions shattered in every way. It was the one thing about losing everything that finally felt equal; Ronnie was down with me now. "We don't know each other, Ed, but I want you to know that the way I grew up, I guess I was wired to live small, if that makes any sense. See, I came from people with low expectations. All my life I haven't been able to get past that."

"Tom, Eddie doesn't need to hear this."

"It's okay, Veronica," Ed says from the glowing console. "Let him talk."

"Thank you, Ed. I appreciate that. And I appreciate how you've stepped up for my son." A hot shiver ripples across my face and I can feel Drew's two hands around mine as my boy pulled me back to my feet.

"I hear what you're saying. Tom. It hasn't been easy for you, I'm sure."

"No, it hasn't, Ed. Thank you for saying that."

"You're welcome."

I want to tell him more. I want to tell him that I hated him for a long time. Not just because he stole my wife and son, but because Flynn was happy to live large when I could never bear it. And that his happy ability to live so large sent Ronnie right into his largeness, which was clearly her true home. "I think I'm changing, though, Ed." I don't know what I mean by this, except I meant what I told my son, that I do feel free of something. The desire to go back to whatever I was and whatever I had and whatever I won't have again. "I don't think I'll ever be able to leave subsidized housing."

"Would you like help getting out of there?" Ed's tone is sincere, but in his voice is the certainty of the upper classes that of course I want to get out of there.

"Some people will always need help, Ed. I don't think I'll ever not be one of those people. Not anymore."

"I see."

Does he? What a strange thing to say. For a second, this feeling of détente, of our shared experience as men, of our shared wife and son, is fractured and a cold wind seeps in with a whistle.

"Eddie, did you eat?"

"I did, I saved some for you. Tom?"

"Yes?"

"Can you call me tomorrow? To talk more about you and your friend?"

"I don't own a phone, but maybe I can use my neighbor's." I'm thinking of Trina and her new phone bought with stolen money. I'm thinking of the brand-new phone in its box on the backseat of Jamey's impounded car. And I'm thinking of Dawn Porter across the street, of her spiked hair and softened street-toughness. Her shop dedicated to beauty.

"Terrific."

Ronnie's telling her husband when she'll be home, and as she ends the call I notice she avoids calling him honey again or signing off with any affirmations of love. I can't help but feel that she's doing this out of respect for me, but I wish she wouldn't.

For a few miles we're both quiet. We've gotten onto another highway, heading due north, and Ronnie has her SUV on cruise control, moving along at 75 miles an hour, the red taillights of cars ahead like markers for something I should've paid attention to long ago. But maybe there's still time. I'm actually looking forward to getting back to the 8, to sitting down with Trina to try to help her, starting with talking her into reporting her ex-boyfriend. But as Ronnie moves into the fast lane and passes one car after another, the lights of a shopping plaza over her shoulder through a thin stand of trees, I want to slow time.

And here it is again, more wants.

"It sure is good to see you again, Ronnie."

"You too."

"I'm glad you're happy." That last word trips on the way out of my mouth and I wipe at my eyes with the back of my hand. Ronnie's looking over at me.

"You still drinking?"

"Drinking?"

"Do you even remember writing all those hateful emails to me?"

"No." And I don't. But there was coming to and getting off the couch and shuffling to the toilet, then later staring at my open laptop. Missives sent to my ex clearly typed by my drunk fingers.

"Addictions go hand in hand, you know."

As I sit here in Ronnie's heated seat, the pain in my hips is almost dulled, though I know it'll be back just as soon as I have to swing my legs out of her SUV. But I refuse to see my condition as raging fires. I just won't do that anymore. "I drink to help with the pain, but I think I'm just going to learn to live with it."

"The pain or the drinking?"

Live with it. That's what Mrs. Bongiovanni was talking about. I never learned to live with Ronnie and all that she gave me, but there's still time to learn to live with other things.

"You're not going to answer my question?"

"Ronnie?"

"Yes?"

"You're the best thing that ever happened to me."

"You trying to make me feel guilty?"

"Not anymore."

"Good."

I feel such tenderness for her now, such a deep gratitude, and then I'm back on my adjustable bed pulling Ronnie's black sweater over her head, our son at school for another hour, and taking off each other's clothes felt like stripping away the lies we'd been telling each other and ourselves, and when she lowered herself onto me she wept softly and I held her face in both my hands and then she kissed me with a whimper, and even though her face smelled freshly washed from what I knew was some sink in this other man's house, her body his only an hour or so earlier, I felt little anger or even hurt, because look how generously she was saying goodbye.

"I've got to make a call, Tom. Do you mind?"

"No, please." I drink from my son's cool water, then lie back in my warm seat. There's the ringing of a phone over the glowing console and then Ronnie's talking to a woman whose voice fills the SUV. Outside my window, across three empty lanes, are the lights of a car dealership, its latest models parked diagonally toward the highway. There are dark woods and an open plain, a farmhouse with a single light glowing on the second floor, and as Ronnie and her friend talk about mission statements and funding and the "keynote" Ronnie wants this woman to "proof" as soon as she can, it's clear that Ronnie's going to give a big speech in the morning to many, many people. I close my eyes and stone wings open inside me and then I'm being carried through that house party to that young woman in the doorway with that antique hat cocked on her head, that open smile she turns toward me as I stand there with a bottle of beer in each hand, this fifty-four-year-old man who couldn't be more proud of her, my chest filling with it, this man who just wants to tell her that. But time hasn't yet opened its own wings and so I have to be patient.

"TOM? TOM?"

Ronnie's hand is on my shoulder. On the other side of the windshield, all of Trina's lights are on, upstairs and down, though her blinds are pulled, almost every other slat missing.

"You feel all right?"

"I think so." I'm about to apologize for falling asleep but stop myself.

"You should go right to bed."

I look over at Ronnie. She's left the engine running, her hand resting on the gearshift, but in the few seconds we have she seems to be giving me her full attention. The light from Trina's casts itself across Ronnie's face and I picture her as a very old woman and then a young girl, the young girl she once was, playing on the grounds of Trevors Academy.

"Who are you giving that speech to tomorrow?"

"Oh, just a bunch of people-workers."

I take in that wonderful term and let it dissolve behind my rib cage. I want to sit here in this warm seat with Ronnie for a long time and I want to tell her about my pride for her, my respect, but now she's looking out the windshield at the lights of Trina's and it's time to go. I open my door and cold moves in like the present slapping the past. "Thank you, Ronnie."

"You're welcome, Tom. Don't forget to call Eddie."

"You bet." I reach over and touch her sleeve, then I'm outside on the buckled asphalt of the 8, closing the door as softly as if I've just left our sleeping son's room.

As I watch Ronnie's SUV take the turn cast, then accelerate past the strip plaza, the neon sign of Larry's Liquors looks too bright and too red. The windows of Dawn's shop are dark.

"Tommy?"

Trina's standing barefoot on her stoop in her hoodie and pajama bottoms. Her hair's pulled back and her arms are folded tightly across her chest, an unlit cigarette between two fingers. "Is your son okay?"

"I think so, yes."

"Shannon left me, Tommy. She fucking moved *out*."

36

I SIT AT TRINA'S CARD TABLE UP AGAINST THE COLD GLASS OF THE window, the TV on but quiet. Over MJ's and Cody's ears are headphones and they're tapping at controls on their laps, the image on the screen of city streets at night they're both zipping through. Across the table from me, Trina has stopped crying and she's telling me how Shannon used the new phone to call her grandmother and ask if she could come live with her.

"Your mother?"

"No, my ex-boyfriend's. She's doing what *I* did, Tom." Trina's voice breaks and she shakes her head and under this dull overhead light the bruise on her left cheek looks like a smear of ash. She lights her cigarette. She looks off at nothing and everything, and now she's telling me about how her ex-boyfriend's mother showed up with her own boyfriend, a fat man in a white Suburban who looked up at Trina on her stoop like she was "some fucking whore."

"Shannon didn't even say goodbye, Tommy. She just grabbed her bag of clothes and *left*." She covers her face with both hands, then drops them just as fast. "She hardly even knows that bitch. Just has some memories from when she was little."

"Trina?"

"I tried to stop her, but—" She looks off in the direction of the TV but isn't seeing it. "I feel so bad about Jamey. I can't believe he's in jail."

"I'll help him, hon. I'm already talking to a lawyer."

"You should've heard his voice on the phone, Tommy. He sounded so *scared*." She glances over at her sons, then looks back at me and wipes at her eyes again and takes a deep drag off her cigarette. "He's just a kid really. I had to talk him into calling his mother. How long can they keep him if they don't have bail?"

"Till the hearing, I suppose. A few weeks or a month, I guess. Trina?" My eyes are on that bruise on her face and I picture that angry bald boy swinging around and punching young Shannon in the mouth too. "We need to report what Brian did, honey."

"No way." She sniffles and pulls her phone out of her hoodie pocket and turns the screen toward me.

You piece of shit. She's a kid!

Fuck u treen. She broke my fucken head open.

If u ever come here again Im calling the cops. I mean it.

Ill kill u first u fucken slut. And yur faggot boyfriend and Ill kill yur ugly fucken kids too.

"I'm scared, Tom. He's serious."

"*I'm* serious, Trina. We have to report him."

"I never should have texted him but I was so mad I went on his fucking Facebook page and got his number, and now he has the one to my new phone and I don't know what to *do*, Tommy."

"You report him. I'll go with you."

"And when he gets out he'll kill me. Thanks for that."

My hips and back feel stabbed, and I'm weak from this fading flu, but it's time to start being a better friend and neighbor to this young woman I've known for years and don't know at all.

"Want me to stay here tonight?"

Trina looks like she might cry again. "Would you?"

"Of course."

"You can sleep in Shannon's room."

"The couch or the floor is fine, hon."

There's a strange sound in the room, a quiet grunting and a clicking and more grunting. It's Cody, those big headphones over his ears, his eyes on the screen, his mouth half open as he works the controls on his lap. The image on the TV is split now. MJ's is of a desert racetrack he speeds through, but Cody's flying off into space, the stars so tiny it's a surprise when one looms up fast and Cody grunts and flicks his wrist and is flying into a black hole.

"I know it's wrong, but I'm so glad me and Jamey bought those headphones. I just want quiet, Tom. That's all I want these days. Just peace and quiet."

37

TRINA COOKS THE FOUR OF US SOME CREAMED CORN AND BOXED macaroni and cheese, a meal she lets the boys have in front of the TV while she and I eat quietly at the card table. Each spoonful tastes like mealy sugar and fat, but I'm grateful for it. Trina tells MJ and Cody that they can play one more game, and I stand and thank her for dinner. "I'm going home just to change and clean up."

She's looking up at me and I can see that she's scared. "Lock the door after I leave. I'll be right back."

My unit is dark and too warm and something's starting to rot. I flick on my overhead light and there's that plate of Chinese food Jamey set on my table. There's the almost empty bottle of vodka on the floor next to my plywood couch. There's my plank table on two stacks of books and my broken laptop and the fines and the card for Kelly's Towing and Storage.

I grab the plate of fetid wings and fried rice and egg rolls, and as I dump it into the trash bin in my narrow kitchenette, it's as if that food's not the only thing rotting in this place; it's the way I have been living in these very rooms.

I set Trina's plate on top of the others in my sink. I want to turn on the hot water and find some soap and start cleaning, but Brian's misspelled words are in my head. *Ill kill u first u fucken slut.* Before heading upstairs I walk back into my living room and grab the vodka bottle off the floor, then open it and pour it over my dirty dishes and drop the empty bottle into the trash.

In my bedroom I hardly ever enter so I don't have to use the stairs, I take off my clothes and I'm surprised in the bathroom mirror by the Band-Aid on my shoulder. I leave it on, and as I wait for the shower water to become hot, my lower back and hips feeling impaled, I can't deny that while my body's still broken, the rest of me feels almost whole.

In the shower I wash myself quickly though I want to linger under that hot spray, because I seem to be cleansing myself for where I'm going.

IT TAKES A WHILE for the boys to fall asleep. While Trina's up there with them I sit on the couch and keep dozing off. Through the ceiling comes Trina's muffled voice, rising and falling, and why should I be surprised that she's reading a story to her sons? But when she nudges me awake and I ask her what she read to them, she says, "Oh I make it up."

"Really?"

"Yeah." She sits next to me and tucks her hair behind her ears. "MJ pretends he's too old for it, but he's always asking for the same characters."

"What are their names?"

"Cody and MJ."

"Your characters?"

"Yeah, but they have superpowers and tons of money and shit."

The overhead light flickers and fades and Trina curls her feet up under her. She looks at the new TV, its widescreen dark. "I wish I could afford cable. We could watch something."

"Talking's good."

"I know I shouldn't say this, but I wish Jamey had given me our money before he left."

"But you're done with that, right?"

"I can't believe he left his fucking wallet in that bank."

"He was worried about you."

She looks at me, takes in my old work jeans that are now tight in the waist, my paint-splattered sweatshirt. "You shoulda seen Shannon, Tom. The boys were like frozen rabbits, but she just ran into the kitchen and then I hear this fucking *crack* and—" She stops as suddenly as if someone just pricked her with a pin. She shakes her head once and walks over to the card table, where there are folded sheets and blankets she snaps open and lays on the floor between the TV and couch. "Better for your back, right?"

I say yes and thank her and Trina wipes her eyes. She turns and begins stuffing two small pillows from the couch into a pillowcase.

"Can we go report him tomorrow, Trina?"

"He texted me while you were gone."

"He did?"

"He feels bad. He wants to—"

"What?"

She drops my pillow onto the floor and bends her fingers into quotation marks. " 'Make it right.' "

I think of regrets and I want to ask her if she knows that boys like Brian don't change so easily. I'm about to tell her that I'm starting to see how hard change is for people.

But Trina's finishing making my bed and then she's staring down at me, her face pale and drawn, that bruise a cruel shadow under her eye. "I'm so tired, Tommy. Mind if I take the couch?"

"Not Shannon's room?"

Trina shakes her head like I'm suggesting something terrible. I slowly stand and stretch out on the floor and Trina flicks off the lights and pulls a blanket up over herself on the couch. Out in the street something long and heavy rumbles by.

"Tom?"

"Yeah?"

"Why'd you tell me you want to be a better friend? You know, before you left."

"Because I do, Trina."

"But you're the only friend I've got, Tommy."

Lying there in the dark, the room too warm and smelling like the food pantry dinner we ate earlier, I shake my head and swallow and don't know what to say.

"What about Jamey?"

Trina takes a breath and now her voice is smaller, like she's already drifting off. "He's my boyfriend, I guess. Tom?"

"Yeah, hon."

"Thank you for never trying to fuck me."

I say nothing. There was the way she looked at me when she pulled down her pajama bottoms and underwear to show me her broken heart tattoo. Like she was both tempting me and testing me, or maybe she was just being reckless. But something stirred in me then and now I'm shamed by whatever that'd been, even if it was just an arousal back into life. I'm about to tell her that she doesn't have to thank me for that, but then comes the light rattle of her snoring and soon I'm drifting in Ronnie's kayak in the shallow waters of the salt marsh in front of our house, the bow bumping the reedy banks and Drew pulling me out of the boat and into his work van, where the young man with the ponytail sprouting from his bald head is sucking noodles into his mouth, but he's shaking his head at me like I'm in danger and I better look out his van window right this second, and I wake with my breath snagged in my throat.

IT'S SOMETIME BETWEEN MIDNIGHT and dawn, and I've been lying here awake on Trina's floor for a long time. Through the blinds comes the pale light of the streetlamp, its striped shadows over Trina sleeping on the couch an arm's length away. Her face is curled in toward her chest and her hand hangs off the edge of the cushion, her fingers in a loosely clenched fist.

I feel deeply relaxed but also on edge, my heart a torn drum skin vibrating in my chest. Trina isn't snoring anymore and she sleeps without a sound. I want to reach over and tuck her hand under her blanket. In the morning, after I convince her to walk to the police station with me to report Brian, I need to call Edward Flynn about Jamey, and then I need to turn my attention to Trina's boys, who miss way too much school and descend for far too many hours into that big screen against the wall I share with them.

When I walked into their unit earlier tonight, they never even glanced over at me, and even when they stopped long enough to get their plates of food and I said hello to them, Cody moved by me like I said nothing and was nothing and MJ only nodded at me, then looked over at his mother, his gray eyes asking, *So, **him** now?*

Such sincere gratitude in her voice, thanking me for never coming on to her. And as she said it, she sounded not like a woman but like a girl, and I think of her telling me about one of her mother's boyfriends and what he tried to do to her when she was younger than Shannon, and there was Ronnie talking about Drew's girl-friend "sleeping around," how that's such a red flag. Lovely Hanna had seemed like such a pampered abundist to me, but what do I know?

And lying here on my back on Trina's floor, I feel myself fall into a darkly opening tenderness for her as she sleeps so close to me in this room she keeps so clean in this unit I have to help her earn her way out of. And maybe because I'm thinking about all of this, I don't at first hear the sound coming from the lot of the 8.

It's the low hum of a car engine and I'm on my feet. It's the fast-est I've moved in years, and whatever pain trails me to Trina's win-dow's beside the point. I peer through the space of a missing slat in the blinds and there's Brian's mother's Pontiac parked next to Amber's Geo. The Pontiac's headlights are off and Brian must've shut them down just as he pulled into our road or I would've seen the sweep of headlights against Trina's wall. Through the wind-shield comes the brightening glow of a cigarette and the boy's probably drunk again and jealous and remorseful and pissed off or all of these, and I'm pulling on my work boots and jacket as quietly as I can.

On the wall, in the dimly shadowed light, is that printed-out photo of Trina's grandmother smiling in front of a birthday cake and its flaming candles, young Trina kneeling next to her and smil-ing so openly up into someone's camera. And as I slowly unlock the door and turn the knob, I glance back at the couch, and how famil-iar all of this feels, me leaving the house before dawn to do my *work*.

I step out onto Trina's stoop and the night air's so cold and the Pontiac's door swings open. "So you're fucking her now too?"

Brian stands there in his black hoodie and an orange wool cap pulled low over his ears. He's staring up at me like he'll never understand this world, not one thing about it, then he flicks his cigarette and it bounces off the Geo.

"No, I am not. But you need to leave, Brian."

"I need to talk to her. And you don't fuckin' tell me what to do."

"It's late. Go home."

"Not till I talk to Trina."

"She doesn't want to talk to you, Brian. She made that clear."

"You her daddy now? She fucking *daddy* now?"

My hands are in my jacket pockets. Touching my fingers in the right are three sheetrock screws from another life. The boy also has his hands in his center hoodie pocket and he just stands there next to his open car door, the engine running.

"Go get her."

"Brian?"

"I'm not fuckin' around."

"Is this really the kind of guy you want to be?"

"Man, don't piss me off."

"I've seen your work." Trina's broken heart tattoo, the scrawl of flames and dragons up and down Brian's arms. "You're talented. You could make a good life for yourself. Don't you want a good life?"

"What're you even *talking* about?"

"Work. Doing good work and being a good man. Don't you want that?"

Brian's shaking his head. He pulls his hands from his center pocket and shakes his head some more. "I came to say I'm sorry, all right?"

"Good, I'll tell her that."

"No, I'm telling her that." Brian moves quickly and is already at the steps of Trina's stoop before I can pull my hands from my pockets. One of the sheetrock screws falls to the concrete and the sound it makes is so out of proportion I jump back, the storm door swinging, Trina rushing past me with a broom she lunges toward Brian's face. "My *kid*?! My fucking *kid*?!" But Brian dodges it and yanks on the handle and Trina falls forward down the steps, Brian slapping the back of her head just before she hits the ground, and now he's kicking her in the side over and over again. "You're fucking *him* now, you fuckin' whore?! You *whore*!"

I leap and then I'm falling, falling toward the boy in the orange wool cap who doesn't even turn to what's coming, me landing on him with what later I could only call an embrace, a hug that slapped the boy's head against Cal and Amber's Geo, something cracking, something else breaking apart.

Epilogue

IT WAS THE TIME OF TWO CRUTCHES, THE KIND WITH HANDLES JUT-
ting out that I gripped before fitting my elbows into the plastic
cuffs behind. After the operation I couldn't get on or off my plywood couch anymore, so Ronnie and Ed rented me an adjustable
bed just like the one I knew so well so long ago. They had it set up
in the middle of my unit where my plank table used to be, my wall
of books at my back.

The pain of those first weeks in rehab made all that I was living
through a simple prelude to the real symphony, the instruments
unrelentingly loud and out of tune, the string section cutting into
me again and again, the drums banging. But I only took the aspirin that the nurses gave me. Two were women and one was a man
and they seemed to float in and out of my room like attentive spirits and I loved them.

The day Drew came to see me in the facility, it was clear that my
son had gained some weight. His hair was growing back too, and
sitting next to my bed in the fleece jacket he never took off, Drew
seemed slightly medicated but vaguely hopeful. He also seemed
shy and kept leaving the room to bring his father a cup of water
or a bag of chips from the vending machine. He ripped open the
Fritos and tapped them into my hand and I asked him how his
therapy was going.

"How's *your* therapy going?"

"Mine's physical. How you doing, son?"

Drew shrugged. "I'm not so worried all the time."

"What were you worried about?"

"You know, the whole shit show." Drew popped a handful of
Fritos into his mouth. "Everything going to pieces."

I reached over and touched my son's knee. There was so much
to tell him, that even after everything goes to pieces there's always

a new thing, and whether we want it or not is beside the point. But all I said was, "I'm sorry I made you buy my drugs, Drew. That was just—*wrong*." I squeezed my son's knee and Drew nodded and crumpled up the Fritos bag and just sat there a while.

There were long afternoons of lying in a bath of pain. There were visits from my new friend with the gelled spiked hair. One of the nurses kept referring to her as my wife, though I don't think I'll ever feel that way about a woman again. Still, I looked forward to Dawn coming and I could never stop looking at her. Her aging face and short stiff hair, the way she held her shoulders back like she always had to be ready for some kind of crisis or fight. I found her beautiful. One late morning after therapy, my chest cool with my own sweat, I said to her, "The nurses here think you're my missus."

"Hey, don't get your hopes up. I'm just a fan."

And she made it clear what she was a fan of, me knocking out "that piece of shit" while driving my hip screws right where they didn't belong.

A few days before I was released, Dawn brought me the paper, envelope, and stamp I'd asked for. She stood beside my bed in her winter coat, her spiked hair starting to gray at the roots. In her earlobes, blushed from the cold, were gold studs that looked like tiny treasures, and she also brought me a cup of coffee that she set on my tray table.

"Love to stay, kid, but I got my class."

"Your class?" I took my coffee, this warm gift that wouldn't distract me from my pain but was still wonderful.

"At the Vo-Tech. I teach kids how to cut hair."

"You do?"

"Why do you look so surprised, Tom?"

"Can you teach my friend Trina to do that?" This stepping into the unknown, it had become my work.

"Maybe. Gotta go." She gave my shoulder a squeeze and was gone, though her smell lingered in the room—that hair gel and a deeper woman scent that I breathed in before swinging the tray table so that it was over my lap. I set the coffee on it and began to write:

Dear Mike,

I don't know what forgiveness is. I never have. But I'm trying to learn. I'm trying to learn whatever I can. The truth is that you have taught me things. By what I let you do to me and my family. Even though I know you're just a tiny cog in a massive and corrupt machine, I wouldn't have learned what I'm learning otherwise.

Which is that we are all cells in the same body. And that body is a miracle.

I wish you and your family health and happiness, Mike. I really do.

Yours Sincerely,
Tom Lowe Jr.

On Thanksgiving afternoon, Trina walked into my unit with a plate of donated sliced turkey and bread stuffing and cranberry sauce. She helped me out of my adjustable bed to my table, where she lit the scented candle Dawn had given me. "No offense," Dawn had said. "But this place *stinks*."

Not since that snowy afternoon waiting for Jamey to come back with his fake ID had I seen Trina so animated. She was wearing a sweater and jeans and Dawn had cut her hair even with her shoulders so that it looked thicker, which made Trina's face seem fuller somehow, less worried and bitter.

While I ate the gift of her meal, my crutches leaning against the table between us, Trina was talking all about shampoos and conditioners and hair follicles. She was talking about how there are different kinds of scissors and hair dryers and "*hair*."

"Did you know this dead shit is *alive*, Tom? Like it has a life of its *own*?"

And as Trina talked all about Dawn telling her this and Dawn telling her that, an unlit cigarette between Trina's fingers because she was trying to quit again, Trina's face was flushed with what I could only call a kind of love. The love one has for one's own mother.

Today my hearing came, but Ed Flynn said he got me a medical waiver so that I didn't have to be there. Late in the afternoon, the sky low and heavy with snow clouds through the blinds of my unit, Dawn taps on my door and walks in with her cell phone glowing. She has on a fleece vest over a wool sweater, her earrings two silver reindeer, and when she hands me the phone I put down my reading — one of the old textbooks on my shelf called *Social Problems*. It's dry and filled with statistics and talks about human hardship like it's some math equation to solve. I see it quite differently. Hardship has to be lived as fully as when times are good. I'm thinking about reading *Siddhartha* again.

Dawn nods at the phone in my hand. "Answer it, Tom. It's your lawyer."

Maybe to celebrate what Edward Joseph Flynn just told me, Dawn blows me a kiss and then she's out the door and I feel deeply unworthy of Ed's news: *Lack of probable cause. Dismissed.* "This one's on the house, Tom. It's the least I can do."

In Flynn's voice is gratitude, maybe for this opportunity for his own atonement, though I now see him as a real gift to my family, and the only way I can bear these gifts is to pass them on somehow, beginning with doing my rounds up and down the street.

It's what I do every morning and every afternoon. It isn't easy pulling on my old work jacket while leaning on one crutch, then the other. And it isn't easy making my way down the concrete steps of my stoop or over the buckled sidewalk, but once I get to the road I zip up my jacket and grip the handles of my crutches, the cuffs at my elbows fitting like I've never walked without them. I try to stand as straight as I can, but already the pain spreads throughout my hips and lower back and down my legs as naturally as the moon rising or rain coming or snow. There isn't anything malicious about it really. It just is.

These new screws in my hips and pelvis are larger and made of "better material," my doctor told me, "though why some people have pain and others don't is a mystery." But there are days when it's hard to take, and though I am in no hurry for it, I sometimes, without sadness, welcome thoughts of the inevitable, the one thing that will release me from all this.

The sky is wide and deep and gray, and as I start walking past

Cal and Amber's unit, pulling one crutch forward and leaning my weight on it before pulling the other up from behind, I take in the cold air that smells like woodsmoke and the dumpster ahead and I admire all the Christmas lights Amber has tacked up around their door, the inflatable Santa Claus on their strip of lawn spotted with snow.

At Mrs. Bongiovanni's, her ex-daughter-in-law's car parked there, I can see that she's shoveled the walk and steps, something I just can't do anymore, but I'll make up for that with a visit later. At least once a week, I do that now, sit with the old woman in her matching chairs, sipping weak coffee and talking about whatever comes up—the weather, the people in the news, lately the president who reminds her of Mussolini.

At the dumpsters and Fitz's old place I stop and rest, sweating under my clothes and staring at what's left of Fitz's Smith & Wesson decal. If I'm still mad at that kid, I can't feel it anymore, and I know that Fitz's "scores" will catch up to him one day as sure as gravity, and however hard he lands will be his teacher.

I picture Minh inside there sitting at her machine and sewing something useful and maybe even beautiful to help take her mind off her son. I'll visit them later too.

From where I stand I can see straight down the road of the 8 and across the street to the strip plaza, Dawn's shop lit brightly and all of her barber chairs taken. Standing behind them are Dawn's employees—the young woman who wore a different-colored lipstick every day; and the man with the tattoos and half a shaved head; a couple of others and Dawn herself, standing with Trina behind the chair closest to the windows, holding what looks like a comb and a pair of scissors over a seated woman with wet hair. Trina leans forward and carefully lifts a lock, Dawn nodding and talking, Trina bringing the scissors to that lock of hair as tentatively as if what she is about to do will change everything, one way or the other.

One week into his sentence Brian called her cell phone from prison, but she didn't answer it and then she reported him without me asking her to. The boy was given eighteen months but could get out earlier than that, and when that happens I'll be here, though maybe Trina will have gotten away by then. Her boys too.

At Trina's stoop I rest again. I'm breathing harder than I should, but I can feel myself getting stronger. A pickup truck drives by, its rack loaded with fresh lumber, and I turn and make my way up Trina's concrete walk and the steps of her stoop. The boys will be home from school very soon and I want to be sitting on that couch when they come in.

It's what I did every afternoon while Trina was in training, and I promised her that I'd keep doing it once Dawn put her to work.

And that's what I want to teach these boys, the joys of work, of putting your head and heart and hands to making something that wasn't there before. But I take it slow. Let them first eat whatever they can find in Trina's narrow kitchen, usually potato chips and cups of milk. Then I let them play for one hour and one hour only on that TV bought with stolen money. I'd hoped Trina would bring it back to where she and Jamey had gotten it, but with what car? And when? And so it's still here, a reminder of the boy she'll visit very soon, on a bus that'll take her all the way to Jamey's jail in western Mass. She hopes to make his visiting hours at least twice a month for the full year Jamey will be there. "Though he feels like a little brother to me, Tommy. Is that bad?"

"Not if Jamey knows what's what."

She smiled and took a drag off her unlit cigarette. "Does *any-body* know what's what? About love, I mean?"

I don't. I know that much. But as I step into Trina's quiet and clean unit, the air too warm and smelling like dish soap, I look forward to MJ and Cody coming home. I look forward to the way they glance at me as I lift my hand to them from the couch, like they are both resentful of my presence but also maybe relieved. I look forward to waiting for them to finish jerking the controls in their laps while their screen selves race and kill and explode and race again. Because then it will be time for everything to slow down.

It will be time for MJ and Cody to sit with me at their card table, sometimes with their homework, other times with drawing paper and pencils and Magic Markers. Sometimes they elbow each other and swear and I do what I can to calm them, which isn't much but enough, and today I plan to take a sheet of paper for myself and then a pencil and draw for them a house in the woods on a marsh. I'll begin with its frame and take my time doing this, this searing heat in my hips or not, and I will tell these boys the names of every piece of wood. I will tell them what each one does and why. I will tell them how every single one has to support the other or the house will fall.

And boys, shouldn't we do everything we can to keep that from happening?

At Trina's couch, I set my crutches against it and pull one arm out of my old work jacket, then the other. I fold it and rest it on the cushion, pain shooting through my abdomen that goes away as soon as I lie down. I stretch out and close my eyes, and then I'm falling, though I'm not afraid because clouds are parting for me and below are sun-spangled waters and the air is warm and smells like sweet bread and pine and my son's hair, my son who wanted to drive his father to see his grandmother, who does not recognize us but loves us anyway, the door opening and MJ's voice ringing through the room, "Is he here? Is Tom here?"

Acknowledgments

I AM GRATEFUL HERE for the expertise of my friend and lawyer, Andy Caffrey, as well as John C. Fraser, Esquire. I am also indebted to my old friend, retired police sergeant Rick LeBel, for his hard-earned knowledge of small-town law enforcement. Once again, I must thank my wife Fontaine and most especially our son, Austin, for their profoundly helpful insights on earlier drafts of this novel. And I am eternally grateful to my longtime editor, Alane Salierno Mason, for her undying rigor and unwavering support. Lastly, I dedicate this book to my late literary agent, Philip G. Spitzer, who, since the mid-1980s, fought tirelessly for me and my work. But more than this, he was my dear friend and a member of my larger family, and we will never stop missing him and his steadfastly loving and bighearted joie de vivre.